Every Last Step

Brand of Justice
Book 15

Lisa Phillips

TWO DOGS PUBLISHING, LLC.

eBook ISBN: 979-8-88552-299-1

Paperback ISBN: 979-8-88552-300-4

Published by: Two Dogs Publishing, LLC. Idaho, USA

Cover Design by: Sasha Almazan and Gene Mollica, GS Cover Design Studio, LLC

Edited by: Lost Canyon Press Editing, Janice Boekhoff

Every Last Step

Chapter One

All eyes in the room were on her. Kenna Banbury, no, Kenna *Jaxton* sat in front of an expansive room packed with people. A camera flash erupted from one corner, and she blinked against the glow. Cameras rolling. Pens poised. A gallery full of reporters waiting for what she had to say.

Waiting for her to explain.

"Mrs. Jaxton?"

She smoothed her hands along the knees of her slacks and looked at the prosecutor, her comfy frame in a stylish suit. Hair curled, makeup perfect. She knew she would be on the news, or even in documentaries in years to come, and she'd prepped.

Meanwhile, Kenna was still trying to figure out why this court case was nothing like any case she'd testified in. Ever.

None of it made sense. But then, this wasn't a case like any other, was it?

Kenna scanned along the tables on either side of the aisle, all surrounded by teams of high-profile lawyers. Over her right shoulder, perched above her was an older Caribbean American man in judge's robes, wearing a scowl on his face. The jury sat to her left, people the government had handpicked as a cross section of the nation.

She closed her eyes, half expecting to feel the baby within her. But it had been months. Their daughter was safe with Jax right now—and would be forever. No matter what happened here, their child would be cared for. She would grow up never knowing the terror Kenna had lived through, or the fight their family had undertaken to free the world of a deadly force of puppet masters intent on changing history.

"Your Honor," the US attorney said.

Kenna heard the unspoken judgment in her words.

The judge said, "Mrs. Jaxton, would you like the prosecution to restate their question?"

She opened her eyes and looked at him, still wearing that scowl. "Sorry, Your Honor."

"This courtroom...this country...does not have the time or the inclination to sit here waiting for you to explain these events."

Was she supposed to say sorry again?

Kenna cleared her throat. "Can the prosecution please restate their question?"

US Attorney Rebecca Hasworth smoothed down the front of her suit jacket and shifted her weight from one heel to the other. Regretting wearing the shoes that made her seem taller than she was?

Someone in the jury coughed, breaking the quiet. It was strange that so many people could make so little noise.

The attorney took a couple of steps toward her. "Mrs. Jaxton, would you please enlighten this court as to your involvement in the events of January 30?"

Everyone knew what she was talking about, but Kenna wasn't going to answer a question she hadn't been asked. "Which events specifically are you referring to?"

Hasworth was a professional, and she'd earned her position here today. She didn't exactly bristle, but it was close.

"I was in Evanston, Wyoming, on January 30. What are you asking if I was involved in?"

"We've all seen the news reports. It's why we're here. The court of public opinion has deemed you guilty by association, or perhaps the source of the threat itself. But public opinion does not determine guilt or innocence here. That is something we ask the jury to decide. Therefore, as this is the matter that has brought all of us here, you are required by law to give this court an honest testimony. The massacre that took place in Chicago on January 30 is public record, and we are here to determine who the guilty party is. The people of the United States of America demand justice."

"Objection," the defense said. "Sounds like counsel is seeking to testify, not ask a question."

"Sustained."

Only someone who had never investigated a crime would think justice was something that could be demanded.

"The question is, what does justice demand of us?" Kenna stared at the prosecutor, resolute in her determination to honor the system. She'd worked to uphold it her entire life. But the cost? She'd paid a high price to see this through to the end, and a lot of that time hadn't been all in with the fight. It felt more like being dragged into something, kicking and screaming. Just at the point in her life when she wanted to live her happily ever after, she'd been sucked into the fight against *Dominatus*.

And for what? She and her family had barely survived.

They'd been sifted like wheat. What was that expression? Weighed, measured, and found wanting. *But God.* The only reason they'd made it out the other side was because He had brought them through it.

Most of them, anyway.

"Justice demands integrity," Hasworth said. "It demands that you give this court the truth."

If only Kenna could see things so simply. But with the birth of her daughter, things had changed. Not only had her priorities shifted, but it seemed as if the rest of the world had also. "I have no intention of providing this court with anything but the truth. However, as I was not present, all I have is my impression of the events occurring that day in Chicago."

"The court isn't interested in your interpretation. Just the facts."

What did the facts matter when the world had already decided the truth? That was what happened nowadays. The internet spread ideas, rumors, or straight-out lies. People believed what they heard, or what they wanted to believe. Unless a person was present and in possession of all the facts, how was the truth ascertained?

"I can only tell you what I know." Kenna cleared her throat, shifting in her seat, wishing she could rub some warmth into the long sleeves over her arms. "It started a long time before Chicago."

Hasworth waved a hand. "By all means, go back to the beginning and tell us what happened."

Kenna's mind drifted back to the days before her daughter. Before Jax. When her arms ached with a constant pain. When life seemed simpler, because she didn't know then what she knew now. "Her name was Ellayna Feathers, and she was kidnapped by the Seventh Day Killer. When no one else could find her, her mother called me, and I took the case. That's how I came to be in Salt Lake City that winter evening. Rescuing a terrified little girl from the basement of a theater."

Chapter Two

"The house is as it was when the police got here?" Maizie glanced over her shoulder, halfway down the hall, probably more excited than someone should be at a murder scene.

Kenna wasn't going to dampen the young woman's enthusiasm. She was simply going to walk slower due to the fact that she was just two or three weeks from her due date.

"That's right." Kenna followed her through the house with Jax and Zeyla behind them.

She could have had a local crime scene cleanup company come through but wanted Maizie to see the scene as it was after Shawn Terrance had been murdered. Unfortunately, that came with some unsavory smells.

Kenna tugged the small tin from her pocket and dabbed some menthol gel above her top lip, just enough to take the edge off the nausea. Thirty-six weeks of pregnancy meant she was long past the perpetually sick feeling of the first trimester. But who knew how her stomach would feel about the combination of the breakfast she'd had this morning and a murder scene.

Not her first. It probably wouldn't be her last.

However, Kenna wasn't here to work this scene. They'd taken the case so that Maizie could get some hours in undertaking an investigation that seemed to be in her wheelhouse.

She leaned against the open doorway into the living room, where Maizie stood by the TV, surveying the scene. Jax squeezed Kenna's arm and headed down the hall with Zeyla—who was, for all intents and purposes, Kenna's sister. The two of them went in and out of rooms off the hall, this time looking for evidence. They'd already been through the house to clear it once, before Kenna and Maizie had even stepped foot inside, but this time would be a lot more methodical. Maizie's job was to draw conclusions from the scene itself.

Kenna folded her arms. "Are you surprised the police ruled it a home invasion gone wrong?"

"Not really. But is that what the evidence led them to believe, or was it just the easiest explanation?"

Maizie was a college student, a tech genius, and Kenna and Jax's adopted daughter. She also had more tragic history than anyone Kenna had ever met. The young woman wanted to learn how to investigate crimes. Kenna would be proud no matter what kind of life she carved out for herself, whether that was following in Kenna's footsteps or not. Or maybe this was only about Maizie and Zeyla taking on most of the legwork of Banbury Investigations cases while Kenna was at the end of her pregnancy and, soon, when she went on maternity leave.

Things were changing.

Not only had their lives shifted over the past two years, but they would continue to shift in the months to come.

Her phone, tucked in her coat pocket, remained silent more than she wanted it to. Amara and Bruce were off doing who knew what. Literally and figuratively. Kenna was waiting for a callback, or some kind of update, but they were curiously silent. Ramon had gone to mutual associates, a group of former private security operatives on the front lines fighting their enemies. He was also supposed to report in but hadn't.

Kenna was out of the loop—and trying not to get frustrated at being the pregnant one everyone safeguarded and, as a result, no one talked to.

She focused on Maizie and the murder scene, which amounted to a cushion on the floor, instead of on the couch, and a wide bloodstain on the carpet. "What are you thinking?"

Maizie lifted out of her crouch and looked around. "The police probably made the most logical assumption they could. We know now it might be more, because the victim's sister asked us to look into it. If she hadn't provided us with those published web pages detailing his issues with the tech company he worked for, we would never have known Shawn was a whistleblower."

"Could just be a conspiracy with no basis in reality."

"You're the one who doesn't like conspiracies, and neither do I," Maizie said. "I get that from you."

Kenna smiled. "What else can we learn from the house?"

Maizie looked around. "We need one of those K-9s trained to sniff out electronics."

"If that would help, we could hire one."

"Aside from that, I guess we just look everywhere, and assume the forensic evidence collection the police did must have missed something, I suppose." She wandered a couple of steps to the fake fireplace and the empty mantel above. "He was forty-two and a software engineer. He lived here for just over a year before he was killed. Not new to the company, just new to the place."

"And?" Kenna could see the wheels turning behind her eyes.

"He started whistleblowing, or at least gathering information, around the time he moved. The two could be connected. Like he moved here because he was a whistle-blower, maybe?"

"I wondered the same thing. It could be this place is cheaper, or more convenient. Lots of reasons people move. But it could also be that there's something about this house he needed access to," Kenna said. "Especially when you consider the company might've been on to him. A lot of his actions were those of someone who believed they were being watched."

Maizie looked up at the sensor in the corner of the room. "Is it normal to have internal cameras or sensors in your house?"

"Define normal, because I have no idea what it is."

Maizie smiled at her, and they shared that moment. Neither of them were entirely used to what "normal" society, or the average person, did or experienced. They made their own way, sticking together as a family.

Kenna said, "If I had a house and a dog and a day job, I would put cameras in so I could check on my dog throughout the day."

Maizie nodded. "Me, too." She tipped her head to the side. "Are you and Jax going to get another house?"

Kenna wasn't sure she was ready to share the recurring dream she'd been having lately. "Maybe one day." That was saying too much when it felt like a secret for her to hold in her heart. Something she needed to set before the Lord, set it on the altar in prayer—as it were—and see what He might do with it.

She looked at the camera on the wall. "Can you hack his security system?"

Maizie lifted her chin. "Can you?"

"Fine." Kenna laughed. "In the spirit of role reversal, I will attempt to 'hack the system.'" She dug her cell phone out of her pocket. "Do I need a laptop? How will I get on the internet? Do you think his password will be hard to guess?"

Maizie bent double and started laughing. "You didn't watch those training videos I sent you?"

"They were confusing!"

Maizie laughed harder.

"Maybe you should solve this murder old-school style, with footwork and research." Kenna laced her fingers together and rested them on her baby bump. "Rather than relying on tech. It won't be around forever."

"Right now, an EMP sounds good. Throw society back into the nineteen hundreds, before technology ruined everything by connecting us all and making information accessible twenty-four seven."

"I'm not sure where to start," Kenna said. And she didn't mean the murder. *Nineteen hundreds?* Oh, boy.

Maizie put her hands on her hips. "There are no signs of a break-in. So, unless the attacker is the best burglar in the world or he can move through walls, we can surmise that Shawn Terrance let his killer in."

"If there's a doorbell camera, we might be able to see

who it is, but it's likely the police already looked through what footage there is." If they had and the killer was there for all the world to see, then the person would be in custody. "But like I said, survey the scene. Work through what we know. I'm more worried about his sister's safety because I think whoever killed him was hired to do it."

"An assassin?" Maizie's eyes lit up.

Kenna snorted. "With any luck, you'll see them skulking around, probably dressed in all black like a ninja."

"Spoilsport."

Kenna grinned. "Anything else to see in here?"

"Not unless he's got a secret room we don't know about."

Kenna waited.

Maizie eyed her. "You know something."

Kenna shrugged. She'd looked through the photos on that real estate website and seen the difference between the living room when the house was purchased eighteen months ago—before it was turned into a rental property— and the living room in its current state.

A low-slung, dark gray sectional hugged the wall. A TV unit was covered in cases for game console disks. No art on the walls, but for a single man, maybe that wasn't so surprising. He hadn't lived here long enough to make it his. Except for the changes that—she assumed—he would've run by his landlord.

"What?"

Kenna said, "I studied the interior photos we found online before we came. The detailing in the wood columns of the fireplace surround isn't the same."

Maizie dashed over just as Jax and Zeyla came back in. Zeyla glanced at Kenna, then at Jax and waved away whatever she saw. "It's been minutes. You guys don't need to make moony eyes at each other because it's been *so long* since you've seen each other." She stepped up behind Maizie. "What are we looking at?"

The young woman crouched, explaining about the detailing. "Maybe there's a hidden compartment, or something."

"Or he just liked this trim better than what was previously there." Zeyla went to the other column.

What did Zeyla mean about "moony eyes"? Jax was just looking at her. Then again, when he looked at her like *that*. She cleared her throat. "Find anything?"

He shook his head, about to say something when the doorbell rang.

Maizie spun around, almost falling out of her crouch. "What do we do?"

Jax said, "You rely on your team." He strode out of sight, down the hall.

Kenna pulled her gun because having it ready in her hand was always better than being caught off guard. She had no intention of getting into a gunfight, fistfight, or any other kind of fight.

She backed up to the wall and peered around the corner just as Jax opened the front door. He held his gun behind his leg, out of sight. He'd swapped his FBI suit for more casual clothes lately, and today he wore black boots, tactical black pants with plenty of pockets, and a long-sleeved Henley in light gray.

"Can I help you?"

A high-pitched squeal came from the doorstep, and Kenna spotted a flash of blonde hair beside his shoulder. "It is you! I thought I saw the *team*. Are you really all here in Pueblo? Are you investigating a murder?" The woman gasped. "Is it a *serial killer*?"

Jax stepped outside and pulled the door closed behind him.

Kenna turned back to the fireplace and the two women in the living room. "Nosy neighbor came over to fangirl."

Zeyla smirked. "You probably want to go out there and rescue your husband from an overzealous suburban housewife."

"He's a big, strong guy," Kenna said. "I'm sure he can handle one woman."

Maizie grasped the pillar on the left of the fireplace, wrapping her hands around it. She wiggled it away from the wall, and it popped free. "Here we go."

Kenna wanted to cross the room and see, but right here, she had a better vantage point of the back patio door and the hallway. "What is it?"

Maizie dug behind the wood in what looked like a recess. Maybe a cutout in the wood used as a secret hiding place. "Flash drive." She held it up. "I think this is what Shawn Terrance was killed for."

Chapter Three

Maizie swung her backpack from her shoulders and pulled out a tablet. She inserted the flash drive into a port on the side but quickly shook her head. "Nothing is coming up. Like I didn't plug anything into this port. It's not registering the flash drive." She paused for a second, chewing on her lip.

"What is it?" Now that they had what they were looking for, they needed to hit the road. Before whatever was causing this antsy feeling between her shoulder blades came into fruition.

Years of investigating murder had left Kenna with instincts that now yielded to the voice of the Holy Spirit. Either way, she figured that the impulse to pack up and leave because of safety would protect all of them. The adults in the room, and the unborn baby she was carrying.

"This kind of flash drive is something I've seen before," Maizie said. "I actually bought one online a couple of months ago. The drive pairs with a port that is effectively its twin. You can only access it by marrying the two together."

Zeyla shifted her weight from one foot to the other. "So

there's a port somewhere in this house? Or some kind of drive?" She turned around to the fireplace and tried to peel back the column on the opposite side. "This won't budge."

"Too easy to hide it there." Kenna looked around. "It will be somewhere out of sight."

"Or in a piece of tech that hides it in plain sight, like a modem or cable box." Maizie went over to the TV unit and crouched in front of the console. "Take a look at the symbol on the flash drive and then find something around here that's a USB port with the same symbol on it. That's the only way to figure out which one it is, other than trying every single USB port in this house."

"How many can there be?" Zelaya wandered out of the living room, into the kitchen. "There's a desktop in here on a little table, by the way."

"Look for the symbol." Maizie continued peering at ports on the gaming system and TV console.

Kenna moved to her and looked at the flash drive she had set on the TV stand now that she had taken it out of her tablet. A small swirl in the plastic looked like it might have been designed as some kind of flame. It was possible Shawn Terrance thought his evidence would burn down the company he worked for.

She headed down the hallway, wondering if he had even known all this would happen when he first decided to become a whistleblower. The tech company he developed software for had been in the business of building servers and programming them for particular uses. That was back nearly thirty years ago when they had first started.

Now the company was in four countries, and their products had spread to routers, artificial intelligence programs, and so many other cutting-edge technologies she couldn't even begin to understand the scope of what they did.

If there was a connection to *Dominatus*, Kenna didn't know what it was. Once again, she found herself trying to stay as far from any of them as possible. But when the president of the United States had her on speed dial and constantly sent her cases she was supposedly meant to investigate, it was difficult to lay low.

She'd had Maizie set up an auto-reply for anything that came in from the Oval Office, indicating she was already on maternity leave—and that she would be for the foreseeable future.

Not a foolproof way of convincing the president they were out of whatever game she was playing, but it could be enough for now.

Kenna snagged the TV box from the bedroom but didn't see any other tech with a USB drive in it. She unplugged it and took it to Maizie, who could use a power supply in the living room if needed. As she walked, she tried to see if the USB port had the same symbol on it, but it was buried inside the console.

She glanced at the front door as she passed it, but Jax hadn't come inside. Was he still talking to that neighbor?

Kenna found Maizie with a screwdriver and the open circuitry of a game console. "Here's one you can try. I didn't find any others."

"Zeyla tried the desktop tower, but it wasn't any of those."

Maizie hit the remote, and the TV flickered to life. She changed the input to one for the game console and plugged the flash drive into the port. "It doesn't have the symbol that I could see, but we have to try everything."

Nothing happened on the screen.

When she tried the console Kenna had brought in, the screen on the TV flickered to life. "Now we're talking." But the display required them to enter a password. "Any idea what it might be?"

Maizie shook her head. "It might take me some time to break into it. We could have that be your first lesson in password cracking."

"Sounds exciting." Kenna tried not to let the lack of excitement seep into her tone.

In exchange for teaching Maizie how to solve crimes, Kenna had agreed to some basic lessons in IT support—the kind Maizie gave to their team when they needed it. Definitely something Kenna could do at home with the baby, on an uncertain schedule. But that didn't mean she had an aptitude for it.

Maybe she just didn't want Maizie to be disappointed if Kenna turned out to be terrible at dealing with advanced computer systems.

"Let's bring it all with us and get out of here."

Zeyla strode into the room. "Good idea. Did you notice the camera up there?"

Kenna spun around and heard Maizie behind her disconnecting cables. Up on the wall, the camera in the corner now had a red light on it. "Someone is watching us?"

"Like you said." Zeyla shrugged. "Let's get out of here."

Kenna headed first to the door because Jax would be out there, and she wasn't going to let fear control her actions until there was a reason to be afraid. She knocked on the door first, though. Alerting him to the fact that they were coming out.

The door opened before she could reach for it.

On the doorstep, Jax lifted his chin. "Time to go?"

Before she could answer, someone else spoke. A slim

woman in athletic wear, her brown hair curled into waves that didn't move, with a smile that was far too excited. "It is you!"

At the end of the leash she had a hold of, a tiny Chihuahua trotted around, jingling a bell on its collar.

The woman's expression brightened even more. "I'm so glad I could meet you all." She leaned toward Kenna conspiratorially. "Your husband has been so polite. But I know what he isn't saying. After all, I've been following your team since that press conference with the president!"

Kenna frowned. "Following?"

The woman nodded. "Did you know there is a true crime podcast that's going through all your old cases? It's fascinating!"

From behind her, Zeyla said, "We are aware."

Yeah, that tone said enough. Kenna felt the same way about the guy who was recounting every single thing she'd ever investigated as if he was some kind of expert on her. As far as she knew, Kenna had never even met the guy.

"We should be going." She glanced at Jax. "We have what we came for, and we may have been exposed."

"What does that mean?" The woman glanced between them. "Are you investigating Shawn's death?"

"Ma'am, this is a case," Kenna said. "We aren't at liberty to give out the details of our investigation."

The woman frowned. "That's what your husband said. But if I could just get my phone and record a video, everyone on Instagram will—"

Kenna held up her hand. "I'm sorry, you aren't going to be recording us. A man is dead."

"I know that! I live on the street, don't I?"

Kenna wasn't sure how she was supposed to have known that.

The woman continued, "If you need to know anything about Shawn Terrance." She brushed her hair back from her face, and the Chihuahua strained the leash, sniffing at the edge of the grass. "You could interview me." She squared her shoulders.

Jax pulled a business card from his wallet. "I'm afraid we don't have time for that right now, but you can always shoot us an email if you think of anything."

The woman probably didn't notice that he hadn't offered for her to call. If she did, she could leave a voicemail and tell them what she knew.

"We really should be going." Kenna glanced down the street, looking both ways. Just in case someone showed up for the flash drive and its port. Maizie had both tucked away in her backpack, but if someone on the other end of that security camera was on their way here to retrieve it, she didn't want them to be found standing on the front doorstep.

Jax handed her the keys. "You and Maizie get to the car."

The woman looked disappointed.

Kenna said, "It was nice talking with you. You should return to your home now, just in case."

She brightened up a little. "Is something going to happen? Is there going to be danger?" Her smile faltered, and she looked down at Kenna's baby bump.

"I'll be in the car." Kenna set off down the front walk.

Maizie came with her, sticking close enough she could whisper, "Why does it seem like everyone is interested in us? Stuff like that happens every time we run into people."

Kenna smiled at her. "The president made us famous, whether we like it or not. People are interested in what seems exciting and different from their own lives. I just want to figure out who this true crime podcaster is so we can tell him to quit going over every detail of my life."

She hit the unlock button for the low-slung Mercedes at the curb, opened the front passenger's door, and slid in.

Maizie climbed in the back, shifting across to the left side so they could look at each other and so Zeyla could get in without going around. "Being famous is not so bad. At least I'm not famous for real things that have happened to me. It's all just the president's stuff."

"You're not worried about when the true crime podcaster gets to the case where I found you?" She shifted in the seat so she could look at Maizie and, thus, caught the look on her face. "Zeyla will take this case. You don't need to do anything to try and find Shawn Terrance's killer. If you want to just focus on finding the podcaster before he connects the dots on who you really are, we can do that. It's important."

Maizie shook her head, tears in her eyes. "I need to do normal things where I don't feel like I have to hide who I was. Where I can be who I am now."

Kenna understood that better than most. Her own life had a series of dividing lines between who she had been and who she became after a traumatic event, or a massive shift in her situation. But she had tried to feel normal weeks ago, on the East Coast, and they had still wound up tangled up with *Dominatus.*

When Shawn's sister called, Kenna had accepted the case because of the grief in the woman's voice. Because Kenna knew loss in a way a lot of people didn't. She wasn't going to be who the president seemed to need her to be. Probably for her own agenda. Kenna would rather do what she could to help people.

Like finding out who had killed a software developer.

Balancing her life, being who she was now, like Maizie had said. Doing what she could to help one person, or one family, at a time.

Watching out for the people she cared for in the same way that they watched out for her.

Having this baby.

Maizie shifted. At the same time, Kenna spotted something dark in the side mirror. She glanced at the back window and saw a trio of black SUVs turn onto the street.

Kenna leaned over and honked the horn, long and loud.

Chapter Four

Jax motioned with one hand in a throwing motion across the street, probably ordering the woman to get to her house as quickly as possible. The woman spun around, almost tangling herself in the dog leash, and hurried across the street. She started to fast walk much too early, drawing attention to herself. With the SUVs barreling down on her and them, there wasn't much time.

Kenna tapped her foot, jogging her knee up and down while she watched her husband sprint around the front of the car and duck his head, climbing inside.

The door behind Kenna slammed, and Zeyla patted the shoulder of his seat. "Hit it."

He slammed his foot down on the gas, and they set off. The car quickly gained traction.

Kenna looked in the side mirror to her right and saw the pursuing vehicles. "I'm guessing they're going to follow us and not head into the house."

"So far."

"With three vehicles, one could stay at the house. That means our fan is in danger."

Jax gripped the wheel with both hands. "You want me to hang back and she see if she's okay?"

"I don't know how we're going to make sure all three cars follow us." The wrong kind of person in those vehicles might stick around the neighborhood, track down the woman now hurrying into her house, and torture her until she told them everything. After which, her body would be disposed of.

Kenna said, "Keep driving. I'll call 911 and report this to the police."

When the dispatcher answered, she fumbled over what to say but, hopefully, got her point across. Just because they were famous didn't mean she could name-drop herself and get whatever she wanted. The police in Pueblo might be aware that her team was here, but she would rather as few people as possible realized it.

Maizie said, "I think she got into her house."

They were too far away to see now, and Jax swung the car around the corner. Kenna checked the mirror and watched the first SUV follow them. Seconds later, a second and third swung around the bend in the road. But that didn't mean no one had jumped out back there to cause trouble.

Maizie continued, "You think the software company was watching everything we were doing in the house and sent them to retrieve what Shawn stole?"

Zeyla answered first. "I would be. If you know a traitor stole from you, you're going to set up surveillance just in case someone else finds it."

Kenna glanced back at Maizie, one hand gripping the bar on the inside of her door. "We have it. So now all we need to do is get away from them."

The problem was that these people knew this town

much better than her team. They were from here. Lived here. Worked here. Whoever was driving might even live around here.

Jax said, "Once we get on the freeway, we can get some space between us and them."

She didn't look at Maizie. Kenna didn't want the young woman to see on her face that she wasn't sure Jax's plan would work. Three SUVs tailing them? It would be far too difficult to lose them, especially without having an elaborate plan set up.

"Any other ideas?" She glanced at Jax. "We could call Preston back at the house, but I don't think his helicopter is nearby."

"You want to stop long enough to climb into a helicopter?" He glanced at her for a second, then focused back on the road. Traffic was starting to build up, so he swung the car around the corner onto a side street leading away from the center of town. Keeping them in a more residential area.

Kenna tapped the dash screen and recalled the address for the ranch Preston had rented a month ago when the case started, purely so he could provide them with a place to stay. The guy was an ex-con who had been accused of the murder of his wife and served his sentence. He'd found Jesus through a prison ministry. Also a billionaire, he was a guy with the resources to help them—and a dog in this fight, for sure—but Kenna didn't like putting anyone else in danger unnecessarily.

Still, he'd insisted, and given how close she was to the birth of the baby, there wasn't much point in arguing. Especially not when she got this car out of the deal.

"Maizie, is there any way to tell this thing we need a route that gets us to the ranch while also losing this tail?"

Maizie leaned forward and pointed. "Tap evasion."

"Nice." Kenna hit the button and watched it calculate the route they should take. "Zeyla, call ahead and tell Preston we might be coming in with some company."

She didn't want to let all the bad guys in this part of Colorado know where they were staying, but the security at Preston's ranch was top-notch. And it was where she wanted to be right now rather than out here, exposed in the car.

Even with all its safeguards and security measures, she still felt vulnerable in a vehicle on the street traveling at high speed.

Jax turned the next corner sharply and hit the brakes. Two kids on bikes at a crosswalk wobbled and almost fell but made it across to the other side. He hit the gas and set off.

The first SUV rounded the corner behind them, and the front passenger's window eased down.

"Zeyla, do you see a gun out the window?" In Kenna's condition, she couldn't twist around far enough to look, and the angle at her side mirror was terrible.

"We might need to duck our heads in a second," Zeyla said. "Unless you guys want me to lean out the window and shoot him before he shoots us first."

Maizie shimmied down in her seat. Kenna couldn't get that low without sitting on the floor, and even that would be incredibly difficult if she didn't ease the chair all the way back.

Kenna said, "Isn't the police station up ahead?"

"The sheriff, yeah." Jax nodded, taking them around another corner.

All of them leaned to the side, swaying with the movement of the vehicle. A second later, a gunshot exploded from the car behind them. She heard it hit the back quarter panel of the car. A dull thud that meant the bullet embedded itself in the armor plating.

"If we make a lot of noise," Jax said, "maybe they'll come out and chase these guys down for us."

Maizie said, "Assuming they're not in on it." She looked scared, because who wouldn't be right now? But she also seemed to be keeping a lid on the abject terror that probably wanted to rise up in her and send her into a spiral.

Kenna wasn't doing as good of a job keeping a lid on the fear. She wanted to reach for Jax but dared not distract him while he was driving. So instead, she kept her grip on the door handle and closed her eyes for a second. Long enough to pray silently that God would protect them through this and keep the baby safe. That justice would be found for Shawn Terrance, and that the company that had destroyed his life—and the lives of many others—wouldn't be allowed to continue terrorizing people.

"Hang on." Jax hit the gas, and they sped up.

Kenna spotted a semitruck approaching the intersection in front of them from the left and guessed what her husband was about to do. But she didn't like the idea of it even one bit. She prayed again for their safety and hung on while Jax performed his maneuver.

He managed to get them past the front end of the semi, then he hit the brakes and pulled up the emergency brake, using the wheel to make a sharp turn to the left and get them on the far side of the semi as fast as possible. As the vehicle turned hard in that direction, the abrupt change shoved Kenna into the door.

The driver of the semi laid on the horn, but Jax put the emergency brake down and hit the gas.

From the back seat, Zeyla said, "Take another turn or two, and we can lose them."

Jax scanned the road in front of them, and she saw when he did the slow-down signal for the school zone. He took a right turn behind the row of stores on Main Street, taking them into a sort of alley.

"What about the dumpster?" Kenna suggested.

"Too big."

She assumed that meant the car was too big to be disguised by the huge trash can on the side of the building. They reached the gap between a chicken restaurant and a clothing store. A street led between the two into the neighborhood where the school was located.

Jax turned the corner again, just not as fast as before. Kenna took the opportunity to watch for the SUVs and saw one pass the end of the alley, while another pulled in. She wasn't sure if they saw her Mercedes disappear around the corner.

"I think we still have one behind us." She shifted in the seat, and the car speakers instructed them to continue straight for two hundred yards.

Jax complied, probably for lack of another idea of where to go in this open parking lot. The second the SUV behind them turned the corner, they would be able to see this vehicle. Their pursuers would alert the others, and in minutes, all three SUVs would be back behind them.

The voice from the speakers said, "Proceed into the car wash."

Jax bumped the curb into the car wash entry and sped around the corner. Within seconds, they were in the darkened interior of the car wash, staring at a very surprised employee. The pimply faced teen wearing a company ball cap and a polo shirt stared at them, then promptly waved at the selections beside him.

Jax shook his head, whipped the wheel to the right, and

bumped them out of the lane. He drove down the aisle through the car wash while the cleaner mops remained stationary. The side of the car brushed against one, and metal scraped metal.

Kenna winced. It didn't sound good, but this vehicle could withstand a whole lot more.

At the end, Jax eased them to a stop, where hot air pelted the car.

"How do we know when the coast is clear?" Maizie asked from the back seat.

Zeyla unclipped her seat belt. "I'll go check. And I'll tell that kid back there not to call the police on us."

She shoved open her door and climbed out, jogging back toward the employee.

Jax peered at the rearview mirror. "You okay back there, Maze?"

"Family outings with you guys are so fun."

Kenna looked at her, and they shared a smile. For a long time in her life, she probably would have forced a confrontation with those men purely to find out who they were and what they wanted. But those days hadn't lasted long, and in this season of her life, she had far too much to lose.

After years of solitary existence, she had invited these people and others into her life in a way that she would not be the same without them. As someone who knew exactly what it felt like to be destroyed by grief, she wanted to shy away from caring about them. But that wasn't what family meant.

Not anymore.

Chapter Five

San Jose, California

Ramon Santiago ducked behind the tree, hiding in the shadows where he could see the ten-story office building. A square structure on the corner between two usually busy streets. This time of night, there was only the occasional car and more vagrants on the street than vehicles.

He listened, watching the building and the area around it. An older man had hunkered down for the night in an alcove away from the front door, where the security guard wouldn't have seen him.

Ramon needed to avoid both of them—while attracting the notice of the private security team when they got here.

When he was satisfied no one would see him, Ramon moved silently along the tree line that ran perpendicular to the building, skirting a courtyard where office workers spent their lunch break.

He reached the exterior locked closet, where utilities

connected to the building, and then jimmied the lock open with two picks. Once he had found the right connection point, Ramon unplugged the building's internet connection for a second. Just long enough to add his own into the mix.

Maizie had explained the whole thing to him, but somewhere shortly after she'd started, his eyes had glazed over, and he realized he had no idea what she was talking about. But the bottom line was that he had to add his connector between the signal coming into the building and the building itself so that he could get through the building's firewall and be able to monitor the activity. Otherwise, he would never get in without the security guard seeing him on one of the monitors.

She had written a program that would spoof the surveillance cameras and allow him to move around inside undetected.

Ramon checked that app on his phone, confirmed that the whole thing was up and running, said a silent thank you to Maizie, and headed for the door on the side of the building that the employees used when they needed to duck outside without being noticed. Or so they thought, anyway. Security monitored the whole thing—just not right now.

The lock on the side door took a little longer, but he got inside. Once he connected to the network in the building, he would be able to download everything on it. Hopefully, with that, he could trade the information for what he wanted. But not if he didn't get there in time.

He crept along the hallway, found the stairs, and went up three floors to the level where the server room would be.

Sure, this whole thing would've been much easier with Maizie and the rest of the team here. But the point was that he had to fly solo in this. Whether or not he was more used to being part of a group on operations these days wasn't the point. Just because something was normal now didn't mean it was the best place to be.

Ramon had been on his own plenty of times in his life. Even when he was part of a group or supposed to feel as if he was.

The FBI. A cartel. Now Kenna and her team. He had landed in the best of those three, but given everything, it was time to solve this problem his way instead of watching them all face danger. Like seeing her standing in front of that table on a military base on the other side of the country. Facing off with dangerous men who thought they could do whatever they wanted. All Ramon had been able to do was sit on the floor against the wall, his hands tied behind his back. So helpless while he had to witness Kenna, an expectant mother, and her husband be the ones to take all the risk.

This was a gamble, sure. But everything in his life had been a game of chance for so long that he didn't know any other way to play the game.

He emerged onto the third floor and immediately heard a voice. Ramon stayed by the door to the stairs, listening intently. The voice grew louder. A janitor in overalls pushing a cart turned the corner at the end and headed toward him, earbuds in. Ramon ducked back into the stairwell and held the door cracked, listening to the janitor speak in rapid Spanish—presumably talking to whoever was on the other end of his call.

The janitor told the story of how his girlfriend was currently acting *loca*, and Ramon found himself smiling at the normalcy of the conversation.

As soon as the janitor passed him and moved far enough away that he wouldn't hear Ramon behind him, Ramon slipped out and held the door so that it didn't click shut or make a noise. He headed down the hallway, the rubber soles of his shoes silent on the floor, and found the server room.

The connection he'd added outside should have wormed its way into the system by now, and he'd be able to access the network without being noticed. He checked his phone and pulled the tablet and cable from his backpack.

Later, he was going to tease Maizie that her job wasn't so hard. But right now, he was grateful she knew what she did about tech because without her gear, he would never be able to pull this off.

Ramon watched the signal bar move from left to right, the percentage rising as his tablet downloaded the entire database this company had on their network. It got to 72% before he heard them coming.

"Fancy meeting you here."

Ramon looked at the open door and saw it was Bear staring back at him.

"Isn't that how the saying goes?"

The tablet in his hands vibrated to indicate the download was complete, and Ramon pulled out the cord. "Is it?"

Half of the team stared at him from the doorway, keeping him contained in the server room with nowhere to go. Ramon didn't mind facing off with them—in fact, it was the entire point of him being here.

Bear seemed confused, not that the guy let any emotion be obvious on his face. "Please tell me you didn't wipe the system."

"I only copied it. And I'm willing to share." Ramon motioned with a lift of his chin. "Did you guys see the janitor on your way in?"

"We took care of him." That was Hollace, looking over Bear's shoulder.

Ramon flinched. "Tell me you didn't kill him."

Bear shook his head. "We just knocked him out. You hacked the surveillance?"

"I'm guessing that's Maizie's handiwork?" Hollace asked.

"You're welcome."

Bear looked around, not that there was anything in this closet out of view. Or anyone. "Where is the rest of the team?"

"This isn't a Banbury Investigations operation. I'm doing this on my own," Ramon said. "Trying to find out more about *Dominatus* from this system."

They knew as well as he did that this company was connected to that group. After all, it was why they were here.

Hollace looked at Bear, but neither of them said anything. If they weren't going to be forthcoming, then Ramon was going to have a hard time convincing them to let him in on their plans.

"Kenna is busy with Jax, getting ready to have their baby. Zeyla and Maizie are working cases together. Who knows what Amara and Bruce are doing." Ramon shrugged.

He needed to convince them to let him be a part of their team. "That leaves me floating around, trying to figure out how to fix this. Because there's got to be a more decisive way to take care of the threat than waiting to see what *Domi-natus* is going to do next."

He waved the tablet a little bit so they would know he was the one who had the information. Hopefully, they would guess that he had only come here and retrieved it first to force them to accept the fact that he was capable of being an asset to their group.

That was true, even if the rest of what he said was somewhat more dubious.

Ramon said, "But maybe we could have this conversation somewhere other than in the closet?"

Hollace grinned. Bear backed up, his expression a little more inscrutable, given the beard that covered the lower half of his face. Most of his team was more clean-cut than he was, but he had that Special Forces air to him, where grooming standards were more relaxed.

Bear looked one way down the hall, then the other, and finally motioned for Ramon to exit the closet.

Was he supposed to call the guy *sir?*

Ramon walked out into the hall. "You guys were here for this, right?" He waved the tablet again.

Hollace reached for it, and Ramon turned, moving it out of the other man's reach. There was a third member of the team in this hallway as well. All of them bristled, apparently unaccustomed to Hollace not getting whatever he wanted.

"I'm willing to trade if you're open to coming to an agreement." Ramon looked around.

Bear was clearly in charge, no matter that all the guys on his team were alpha males. But Ramon still wanted to get a read on what they all thought.

What he needed was for them to invite him to be a part of their team.

Hollace glanced to the side. "Copy that." He looked at Bear. "Security is about to start their rounds."

"Let's go," the team leader ordered.

Ramon walked with the group to the same stairwell door he had used. He wanted to comment that it seemed like they had a lot of people to steal just one copy of the network but didn't think that would endear him to them.

On the ground floor, the team confirmed it was clear

before heading outside. Ramon said, "I need to get my connector from the exterior connection box."

"That's how you did it." Bear shot him a look. "Hazel was wondering how you managed to spoof their security system. She was hoping to see Maizie again."

Ramon shrugged. It would be easier if they believed there was a wedge between him and the rest of the Banbury Investigations team. "When did you guys figure out that this company was connected to *Dominatus?*"

Ramon crouched in front of the connection box and retrieved his tech, not wanting anything Maizie had come up with to be left behind. Traced back to her. Stolen by someone else who wanted to re-create the same technology.

Who knew what might happen these days, given all their enemies and the way the president had exposed the team.

All the while, these guys had been doing their own thing.

Former members of Miami Security International, Bear's team was something much different after their boss had been exposed as a *Dominatus* operative. They had gone underground, taking control of the research platform off the coast of Alaska.

Bear led them down the street to a van. "It isn't the whole company. Just one guy whose name is in those files you just copied. That's all we were after."

"One guy?"

Bear stopped by the van and nodded. "We only need his name. You can have everything else on the network."

"Listen." Ramon ducked his head, as if he didn't know how to broach the subject. Hearing that they were chasing one specific person was interesting. It seemed as if they might be a few steps ahead of Kenna—not that she was actively seeking out *Dominatus*. Who was the one person they wanted to dig up?

Ramon lifted his head. "You probably already guessed I didn't come here to get something for Kenna." He shook his head. "I came here to talk to you guys about joining the team."

"Things aren't going well at Banbury Investigations?" Bear studied him.

Ramon had worked undercover plenty of times in his life, and this would be no different. He shrugged. "It's time for me to move on and work with a team who knows how to get things done."

Bear slid open the door on the van.

The janitor lay on the floor inside, bound at the hands and feet and with a gag over his mouth.

"You want in?" Bear asked. "Then get in."

Chapter Six

Ramon climbed from the van and looked at the building, with its peaked roof and smashed windows. Red brick tiles. Overgrown trees stretched up on either side, reaching over it as if trying to cover the shame of the building from viewers.

"Nice place."

Bear shut the driver's door, and his boots crunched on the gravel as he made his way around the front end of the van. "It's just a pit stop. I'm not taking this guy anywhere we actually frequent."

That was fair enough, but while they hadn't been able to openly talk about what was going on in the van—where the tied-up janitor would've been able to hear them—they could now, right?

"Who is this guy?" Ramon motioned with his chin in the direction of the van.

"You tell me." Bear folded his arms, making his expansive chest look even bigger. But even if some might consider it to be an attempt to intimidate Ramon, he didn't see it that way. It was, however, a challenge.

"That's not how this works," Ramon challenged right back. "I don't have to prove myself to you. You all know who I am and what I've done. It's you guys who dropped off the map. I figured you had something going on I could sink my teeth into. Something other than getting ready for the birth of a baby."

He shifted, as if he was about to walk away.

Bear said, "Fine. You can stick around."

Ramon wanted to quip back, something sarcastic, but kept his thoughts to himself. One of the other guys came over, and they walked the janitor down an overgrown path and into the building. "What is this place?"

Inside didn't look much better than outside, not even after they hit the switches on a couple of floodlights that they'd set up. A massive, abandoned warehouse of some kind, with the moonlight coming in through the windows up high at the peak of the wall, where it met the roof.

Ramon was pretty sure he spotted bats hanging in the rafters above their heads.

Bear's guys walked the janitor across the leaf-strewn floor to one side, dragging his feet through the debris. His head hanging forward. Out cold still?

When they were out of earshot, Bear said, "I guess it used to be a milk bottling plant. Whoever owned it abandoned the place years ago." He motioned for Ramon to follow him and set off across the expansive room to a set of tables on the far side where Hollace and one of the other guys, who hadn't been at the office building, worked on laptops. "We needed somewhere to bring him, or whoever was waiting for us at the company, without them seeing our base of operations. Such as it is."

They'd get to that. But for now, Ramon said, "I don't get

why you grabbed that guy. Did he do something or say something that indicated he was an agent of *Dominatus*?"

Hollace sat back in his chair. "Let's just say, I'm surprised he didn't try to kill you." He turned his laptop so Ramon could see the screen. "We've come across this guy a number of times already. Spotted him tailing us in crowded places. Seen him show up where we are. He's tracking us. We just don't know what his endgame is."

"Was this even about the network, or some name you guys need?"

Hollace nodded. "We do need that name. But even I'm starting to wonder if it's just a wild goose chase."

Bear pulled out a chair of his own and sat. When Bear opened his computer, a video call connected, and Hazel, their technician—their equivalent of Maizie—flickered on the screen. "Hey, boss."

The full-figured woman had a dark pixie cut with three shaved slashes on either side of her head above her ears. "Hi, Ramon!"

He lifted his chin, then went to Hollace. "This guy shows up where you are, and he's following you. Why be a janitor? He wasn't lying in wait, ready to pounce. You guys caught him."

"We set a trap."

And Ramon was the one who'd fallen for it? At least, along with the janitor. "Who is he?"

"That's what we're going to find out," Hollace said, stretching his arms above his head. "Just as soon as you head in there and get his prints."

"First, tell me about this name."

Hollace smirked. "Figures."

"That I'm not going to walk into this blind? No one

knows what you guys are doing. It's been *months*. At least we managed to out that general." Ramon didn't want to talk about the particulars, especially considering he'd thought the guy had died. Then it turned out he hadn't; there was another one running around. Nope. Definitely didn't need to discuss that.

He asked, "What progress have you guys made?"

Whether Hollace thought that was amusing or not, Ramon couldn't tell. "You think I'll just run down everything we've been doing because you asked?" He dumped the two front legs of his chair back on the ground. "Nice try."

"Tit for tat."

"Ramon," Bear called over. "You have that hard drive?"

He handed it to the team leader. "Let me know if you find any suspicious names on that thing."

Bear looked at Hollace. "Tell him about the money."

When Bear went back to his call with Hazel, which involved him plugging the drive into his laptop, Hollace was frowning at his boss.

"Tough luck, buddy," Ramon said. "Tell me about the money." He lifted his brows.

Hollace looked like he wanted to punch Ramon, but Ramon didn't really care. He just needed information he could pass back to Kenna.

Yes, this was about him being a double agent for Banbury Investigations, but it also wasn't. They trusted Bear and his team. They just didn't know what on earth the guys here had been doing for the last few months. Kenna needed to know if they were going to do something that concerned her—or put anyone she cared about at risk.

However, Ramon wasn't acting when he told Bear and the

team that he wanted to be here, and if she didn't know that, he wasn't going to tell her. Truth was, Ramon had felt like he was on protection detail the past few weeks. He didn't mind caring for the people on their team, but with the whole of *Dominatus* to unearth and take down, he'd rather be on the front lines.

Kicking in doors.

Dragging out suspects.

Generally, getting business taken care of.

Much better than feeling like he was sitting around waiting for something to happen. He'd rather make it happen. Like these guys were, hopefully, doing.

Hollace typed on his laptop. "All of *Dominatus*, each 'splinter cell' as it were? Far as we have learned, they all pay a kind of dues to the organization. Each person who is in the group gives a tithe of their endeavors."

"Seriously?" That was the first Ramon had heard of anything like that.

Hollace nodded, showing Ramon a ledger. "This is a photograph that was taken and handed to us. But we have no idea who took it or where to find this ledger. Somewhere in the world, there's a paper book where *Dominatus* keeps a list of all its members. We're trying to find the ledger, which means we're trying to find the name of the person who keeps the ledger."

"Like an accountant, or some kind of business manager?"

"Right," Hollace said. "We think it's a chief financial officer or accountant."

Ramon whistled. "One person who can break the whole thing open."

Hollace nodded. "So, maybe go get a fingerprint from this janitor so that we can find some leverage to get him to tell us who ordered him to surveil us, or who the accountant is."

"Could be on that drive." Ramon motioned to the tech he'd given Bear. "Right?"

"We have to know it when we see it. Let Hazel do her job, and you do yours."

Ramon figured the tone in Hollace's words was about Bear ordering him around. "Fine. I'll play."

Hollace lifted a small device that looked like a GPS tracker or palm pilot. "Scan his fingerprint into this. It'll immediately upload the image to our system and start running his ID."

"Back in a sec." Ramon wandered across the empty warehouse, skirted around a couple of pallets, and headed along the trail left in the dirt from when they'd dragged the guy in. The guys here, formerly Miami Security International, might have actually hit on a way to uncover all of *Dominatus.*

What would the world think when the president was exposed as one of their assets? Or when nations fell because their leaders were embroiled in this scandal? The fallout of releasing all that information to the public would be desta-bilizing.

He'd hoped it would reach that scale when they'd dumped the general's entire research database onto the internet for all to see. Only the president had brought in the FBI to "investigate," and they'd kept the entire story focused on that one rogue US Army general as the figurehead. Not one word about an international conspiracy had been spoken.

Instead, it'd all been about what the general was doing. And how the president had supposedly hired Banbury Investigations months or years ago—he wasn't sure which it was meant to have been—to uncover it all and bring justice.

Now they were pawns in her game, and the team had the whole online world speculating on what they might be doing next. Picking apart what was known of their actions. Discussing it all to death. At least until another news story overtook people's attention.

Through the doorway, there was a long hall about as clean as the rest of the place. Two of the MSI guys flanked an opening to the right. Ramon showed them the fingerprint scanner as he approached, and the one closest to him nodded.

Both guards stayed where they were as Ramon went inside the room, a slim space about the size of a prison cell with a dirty white sink on the left side—just without the toilet. The detainee had been tied to a folding chair, hands behind his back and his ankles secured to the legs of the chair. He was facing the wall, away from Ramon, so that he could see the guy's hands but not his face.

His head was dipped forward like he had his chin on his chest. Sweat had dampened the back collar of his custodian overalls and under his arms.

Ramon only needed a fingerprint.

He palmed the scanner and grabbed the guy's index finger. It flexed in his grip.

He was awake.

Ramon took the print, holding the digit steady while the scanner did its thing. The guy convulsed in the chair, not quite pulling against Ramon's grasp of his hand, but it was close. A beep sounded from the scanner.

He looked at the screen.

Print not found.

So...not in the system? He looked at the image the

scanner had come up with, but it seemed more like a blob than an actual fingerprint. He looked at the end of the guy's finger and saw a patch of scar tissue. Ramon checked the others, then glanced at the doorway. "Go get Bear!"

"What is it?" The operator on guard peered into the room. "What's going on?"

"This guy has no prints. They've been burned off."

Chapter Seven

Kenna lifted her coffee cup from the saucer it sat in and leaned back in the wicker chair, shifting her weight against the pillow behind her back. She closed her eyes and inhaled, pretending the drink wasn't decaf.

A loud sigh from across the all-weather patio drew her attention. She opened her eyes and watched Maizie for a few moments. The young woman sat at a small round table in a wicker chair of her own, working on her laptop. She'd plugged the drive into a port on the side and had the flash drive plugged into that.

"Not making any progress?"

Maizie wore checkered pajama pants and an oversized gray sweater with no writing on it. She had secured her hair in a high bun with plenty of bumps and wisps of hair all over. "Not so far."

They had to raise their voices a little to hear each other

across the expanse of the patio, which was surrounded by a half wall. In summer, there were screens above the wall, but right now, given the winter temperatures outside, fitted clear plastic panels preserved the view but blocked the cold air from outside.

Kenna wouldn't have minded some cold air. It was pretty warm in here. "Aren't you worried they'll be able to trace you when you access the flash drive?" After all, it contained information from the company servers, but it might also access their network somehow. What if those people in the SUVs could trace them as soon as Maizie broke the security features on the flash drive?

Maizie shook her head. "This laptop is air-gapped. It isn't connected to the internet at all, it doesn't even have the ability to. So, no one can hack this computer."

"Maybe that's why you can't get into the drive?"

"It isn't."

The door behind Kenna opened, and Preston Light-wood stepped out, wearing athletic clothes, with sweat on his forehead. He carried a tall glass filled with a green smoothie.

"Hey." Kenna figured Maizie wouldn't mind if she was distracted—so that she quit distracting Maizie.

"Your husband is still going. I tapped out." Preston blew out a breath. "That kind of workout is not for an old man like me." He eased into a chair at the table with her.

Kenna chuckled. She wanted to commiserate with the guy that he felt old but was also secretly proud of Jax for pushing them both in a workout. "Any updates from Zeyla?"

Jax would have passed information to Preston for her if there was something she should know.

Preston said, "She hasn't called in yet this morning."

"It's still early. She spent hours following those SUVs after we parted ways, and she didn't get to sleep until after four this morning."

Preston sipped from his glass and managed to mostly hide the grimace at the taste of it. "You really hid from bad guys in a car wash?"

Kenna set her cup down and grabbed a hash brown from her plate. "Gotta give it to the car. It found us a decent place to hide." She took a bite of her potato.

"Of course, it did." What he didn't do was remind them all how much it cost him to supply them with that vehicle.

Kenna's first instinct had been to turn it down when he'd called a month or so back and insisted. But after talking to Jax about it, they both realized it was far safer for them to ride around in a vehicle with armor plating and defensive capabilities.

She wiped her greasy fingers on her napkin. "We stayed put in the car wash for a few minutes. The car told us to ease around the back of a dry cleaners and slip into the drive-thru for a Vietnamese restaurant. It actually seemed like it knew where the pursuing cars were—like it connected to the local traffic cameras to tell us how to avoid those specific vehicles."

She didn't really want to know if it did, because that would be illegal. But then again, the boundaries of justice, right living, and getting results often blurred in ways that could be conceived as her being an accessory to a crime. Denial, or avoidance, might not be enough to protect her from the law.

More than likely, one day, it would catch up with her.

Her phone screen flashed, but the cell made no noise and didn't vibrate. Kenna leaned over and looked at the screen, then rolled her eyes. "Another podcast episode just dropped." She lifted the phone and unlocked it, scrolling to the email she'd received alerting her to the latest episode of *True Crime Northwest*.

"Anything good?" Preston's tone was so neutral.

She wanted to throw her phone across the room.

Out of the corner of her eye, Preston glanced up behind Kenna. She heard the door, and Jax said, "Hey. Everything okay?"

She turned far enough to see him coming on her other side and showed him the screen. "New episode. Though, I'd rather talk about how we're going to take down this software company and finish what Shawn Terrance started."

She navigated to the text thread she had with Shawn's sister Gabby, but there were no new messages. She'd told Gabby Terrance that she would contact her as soon as she had news. Hopefully, they would soon, because possessing the drive and it being more than a tiny paperweight were two different things. They needed the information from the storage device. But pointing that out would just put undue pressure on Maizie, and it was clear from watching the girl that she was all in to solve this puzzle.

"Want me to skim it?" Jax held out his hand.

She slapped her phone into his palm. "I'd love that."

The low-grade irritation she'd been feeling upon hearing a true crime podcaster recount every case she'd ever worked over the past couple of years wasn't going to let up until they figured out who he was. Hopefully, that happened before this guy realized where Maizie had joined their group from, and how she'd been raised.

"He knows entirely too much about you." Jax thumbed the screen, still reading the transcript, and reached over with his other hand to squeeze her knee.

"Question is, how did he find out?" She glanced at

Preston, who was finishing his smoothie. Jax probably needed a plate of food after his grueling workout. She shifted in her seat, uncovered a couple of the platters the housekeeper had prepared, and dished food onto Jax's plate.

Preston set his empty glass on the table and reached for the carafe with regular coffee. "Maybe someone gave him all the information. I mean, it isn't readily available like in police reports. There's no log of all the cases you've ever worked."

She'd been wondering about that. "Unless someone tracked my movements for years, watched what I was doing and kept that log for me."

"You think it was *Dominatus?*" Preston stabbed a single sausage with his fork and ate just that to accompany his morning coffee.

Kenna shrugged. "Who else knows more about us than we do? The only other option that makes sense is that the president wants all the information out there for some reason. I don't know why she'd feel the need to undermine me by telling everyone everything about what I've done, unless it's to toot her own horn and take the credit..." She decided she wasn't making sense and just sighed.

Jax squeezed her knee again. "Okay, here's the highlights. You took a cold case, missing girl from Ogden. There was no reason to believe she was still alive. Pretty sure the police had given up hope, but the family still wanted answers. They gave your number a try, a referral from someone else you'd helped."

Kenna nodded. "That's how I found cases for a long time. Just word of mouth."

"You tracked the guy from Ogden, where he'd taken her, and managed to find him in Montana. You left him on a bench for the police to find, handcuffed with a box of all the evidence next to him."

She remembered that. "He wasn't happy. But neither was anyone else, considering the little girl he took was long dead and buried. I left the information in the box because he told me where he'd left her. The police dug her up so the family could bury her."

Kenna placed a protective hand over her pregnant belly. Everyone would know why, and they'd all be so sympathetic to the plight of motherhood. Wanting so badly to keep this new life safe, being responsible for a tiny thing. Protecting her every day of her life.

The dread was the worst part. And the dreams.

Every day was one day closer to the reality of being responsible for a baby. She wasn't so much worried about feeding, changing, and sleep schedules, though she'd been doing plenty of research into those things. Kenna was way more worried about their enemy finding her with the baby and using the child as a pawn.

They would know she'd do anything to protect her family.

Which made her love a weapon they could wield to get whatever they wanted.

Jax covered her hand with his. "He mentioned a witness you never managed to track down, who originally provided the police with testimony about a car used by the kidnapper."

She couldn't remember specifics but did recall visiting an older woman. "The cops had the make and model of the car and a partial license plate. It was a matter of legwork at that point, and unlike them, I had no other cases and as much time as it took."

She'd also had the freedom to go outside her jurisdiction, unlike the police, who had to coordinate with other law enforcement departments and agencies.

Kenna continued, "I remember talking to an older woman. She had sold her car to the killer, or at least she gave me a description of the guy who bought it. That part didn't ever totally make sense."

"Because she told you he had a scar above his eyebrow?" Jax asked.

Kenna nodded. "It was a private sale; he gave her cash. Years later, she got a ticket and realized the car was still registered to her. She was trying to get it out of her name."

Preston said, "You tracked the car? Is that how you caught him?"

"I found the vehicle in a junkyard just outside Bozeman. Not far from where he got the parking ticket, actually."

"And it led you to him?"

Kenna shrugged. "In a roundabout way, through a whole lot more legwork. Talking to the junkyard owner and his nephew, going person to person, trying to find out who they'd spoken to and where he went. Eventually, I found a cabin he'd been renting and staked out the place. I followed him for a few days and realized he was gearing up to take another girl."

Preston hissed out a breath.

"I hit the cabin in the middle of the night before he could," she said. "I wasn't about to let him anywhere near another little girl after what he did to the others."

"There were more?" Jax asked.

There was something in his expression she wanted to ask about. A lingering question—and she might not like the answer.

"Yes." She shifted in the chair and faced him a little

more. "You should eat. But also tell me what you're thinking."

He gave her a small smile and picked up his knife and fork. "The scar."

"It delayed me for a while. I'll admit that it didn't help to have contradicting descriptions of the guy."

He finished chewing, then asked, "Did you consider an accomplice or partner?"

"More likely just someone else he paid to buy the car. Other than that one occasion, he was never seen by anyone I spoke to." She frowned. "You think there were two of them?"

"It's not about what I think."

"Fine, then you don't want to dig up the case file and take another look through everything."

Jax started. "I didn't say that."

She smirked. "I'm not going to be offended if you figure out that I missed someone. I got a very bad guy off the streets."

"Sure?" Jax didn't seem convinced.

"I'll be annoyed and complain loudly if you want me to."

Jax leaned over and gave her a quick kiss that tasted like egg and ketchup. "Maybe I just need a puzzle to solve."

A puzzle that meant she'd missed something. "I got that little girl's killer."

"I know." He nodded. "I'm just going to confirm there isn't another bad guy out there, connected to him, who might also be worth finding."

She didn't like the idea of a loose end. "I'll help."

"It would be good for you to walk me through your steps."

"You already read it all in that blog transcript of the

podcast." She let a little of how she felt bleed through in her tone.

Jax smiled around his fork.

"Why isn't Zeyla awake yet?" she asked aloud, not to anyone in particular. "And we have Shawn's sister to consider. Should I update her? Maybe she's worrying about if we made any progress."

Jax glanced over. "Did you read your Bible yet today?"

Kenna let out a long sigh. "I should go for a walk or something."

The view through the windows stretched left to right in a panorama and out to the mountains. The world as far as she could see was nothing but landscape, wildlife, and peace. She could listen to the Bible on her phone and center her heart and mind in Christ. Hopefully, then, the residue of fear from her nightmare would dissipate.

She needed to cling to the Lord, or she wouldn't survive —if only mentally. Her peace of mind felt brittle and ready to shatter.

"I'll get you a radio." Preston started to shift his chair back from the table. "Do you want to take one of the dogs with you?"

He had three dogs on the property, two of which were trained protection dogs. The other followed suit and thought he was one of the team. Watching the Airedale bound after the two short-haired German shepherds was amusing, but she tried not to laugh at his eagerness coupled with their intensity.

"I'll go with you." Jax shoved another bite of food in his mouth, picking up the pace of his eating.

Kenna said, "Looks like we're on the move. You good here, Maze?"

"What?" The young woman looked over and saw them

all start to get up from the table. "Oh, I'm good. Whatever." She waved a hand, refocusing on her work.

Kenna pushed her chair in, and her phone, still on the table, flashed to life with a notification. A new message.

She unlocked the device with her thumb and tapped the notification. Her heart sank at the image on the screen. A terrified woman, bound and gagged. Hair in her eyes. Blood under her nose.

Gabby Terrance stared at the camera.

A message popped up.

> Give us the drive or she dies.

Chapter Eight

Kenna took a sip of her water and set the bottle back in the cupholder. Jax was in the driver's seat of their armored vehicle, and Maizie's voice came through the speakers.

They'd only been gone from the ranch for a couple of hours. Their current base of operations was far enough from Pueblo that no one could follow them without being noticed, but it meant that in order to look for Gabby or, as was the case right now, report her kidnapping to the police, they had to drive back to town.

Maizie said, "I have a program of mine working on the drive, trying to gain access. In the meantime, I've been checking on everything else."

"What'd you find?" Kenna asked.

"The neighbor from Shawn's street, the one who came over to talk to us? She's posting videos all over socials, all about how"—she used a higher pitched, valley-girl tone—"'Kenna and her team are investigating his death, so it's got to be murder, right?'" Maizie continued in a normal voice. "Now she's digging up Shawn's blog posts about the software company he worked for and how their AI system was being used to spy on people who had their tech at home."

Jax hissed out a breath. "She's going to get herself hurt."

"Or slapped with a lawsuit from this corporation."

Maizie said, "Or kidnapped like Gabby Terrance."

"Anything from the photo or the number it *didn't* come from?" Okay, so that was a roundabout way for Kenna to mention the "unregistered" number the message had originated from. It wasn't magic. It had come from *somewhere*.

"Nothing." Maizie sounded disgruntled. "I'm working on it, but given who they are and what they can do, I don't like my chances. They have a habit of getting away with murder."

Jax pulled the car into the police station parking lot. "We won't be able to pin it on one person in the company. They'll have created separation between whoever gave the order and the person who carried it out."

"So follow the money?" Maizie asked. "Because there's no way they weren't paid for murdering him."

Kenna nodded slowly. "That's one way to go about it. Have you heard from Zeyla yet? I'm hoping she is awake, and she can get out on the streets. Kick some doors in and get us closer to finding where they have Gabby."

Jax slid the car into an open space in the parking lot and glanced at her. "After we file this police report, we can swing by her hotel and wake her up."

Kenna wouldn't have minded being the one to kick in some doors herself, but it wasn't wise in her current situation. This wasn't a case of waiting for things to get back to normal. It was a new season in her life—one that would last for the rest of it. She wasn't ever going to *not* be a mother. Not anymore.

She had to accept the shift as permanent rather than

just a season. After she had the baby, she would be spending her days keeping the child safe. Life wasn't ever going to go back to what it had been.

Kenna would need to rely on her team to do the door-kicking instead.

She grabbed the door handle. "Let's get this report filed."

Jax met her at the front of the car. "Not our usual way of dealing with a kidnapping." He held out his hand, a slight smile on his face.

She clasped his fingers, trying not to waddle when she walked. "The police don't have a chance to find and rescue her or bring charges against the company if they know nothing about it."

He nodded, pulling the door open and holding it so she could enter the lobby where the temperature was considerably higher than outside. It had a distinct scent of burned coffee and humanity, and behind the desk was a mess of file cabinets, stacks of paper, and plaques on the wall.

Kenna peeled off her coat and hung it over her arm, tugging her hair from her collar so it could hang loose. The uniformed officer behind the desk had sergeant chevrons on the sleeves of his shirt. He typed on the computer beside him, the desk phone between his ear and shoulder.

"Got it." He paused. "Yeah, copy that. Thanks." He hung up the phone. "Can I help you folks?"

Kenna stepped to the side, turning slightly to face Jax.

Her husband stepped up to the counter and explained who they were. Kenna showed the sergeant the photo on her phone, and Jax told him about Shawn Terrance.

The sergeant, whose nameplate read *Baxter*, frowned. "Wasn't that ruled a home invasion?"

Kenna said, "His home was certainly invaded. But we

believe he was targeted specifically because he was a whistleblower."

Baxter stared at her. "You think it was an assassination?"

"I think Gabby Terrance is in mortal danger, and we would like to report this crime. Shawn is dead, so there isn't much any of us can do about that. She's alive." Kenna motioned with her phone. "At least, for now. Whether she stays that way or not is up to you and this department."

The skin around his eyes flexed. He snatched up his phone. "Get me the chief." Pause. "Just do it." He dropped the phone back in its cradle. "Can you email me that image and the information that came with it?"

She nodded, got the information, and sent it all. Not that there was much to send beyond the picture. "Gabby asked us to help figure out what really happened to her brother."

"That investigation was closed." A guarded look crossed Baxter's face.

"Did you find the person who broke into his house and shot him?" She wasn't going to get him to open up by asking this. It would sound more like an accusation.

If the question made him uncomfortable, Baxter didn't betray it in his demeanor. "The lack of evidence, coupled with the way the scene was left and the lack of witnesses, means we could've let it go cold, and it wouldn't have made a difference. Everything pointed to it being random."

Kenna bit the inside of her lip.

Jax shifted slightly, and she knew he wanted to argue with this guy. "Not everyone was satisfied with that answer. Like Gabby Terrance, for instance. And because we investigated further and discovered something more than what your department concluded, the perpetrators are attempting to silence Ms. Terrance."

Baxter glanced between them. "Is that your way of admitting fault?"

Kenna said, "You think this is our doing? We didn't kidnap her. We also didn't kill Shawn. But we can do something about finding justice for Shawn and locating Gabby. Rescuing her and saving her life."

A tendon in Baxter's jaw flexed.

Jax said, "We came here to report this crime. Just in case the Pueblo Police Department wants to *do their jobs*."

An older man stepped into view through the doorway behind the desk, wearing black slacks and a white uniform shirt. Given the emblems and badges, this was definitely the chief. "Sergeant?"

"Yeah, Chief. These people want to report a crime."

At least he didn't refer to it as a crime they'd committed. Kenna stepped back from the counter and shifted her coat to the side, so he'd see she was very pregnant. "I don't know about the rest of you, but my feet hurt."

Hopefully, he didn't offer her a chair in the waiting area. She'd rather be in the chief's office.

The sergeant continued, "They also want us to reopen the Shawn Terrance case as a homicide, as they believe we failed to find the assassin who killed him."

His chief raised two bushy eyebrows and rocked back and forth on his shoes. "Is that right?"

"A woman has been kidnapped," Jax said. "If that isn't something you're interested in, then I suppose Banbury Investigations will be taking the case and making contact with the kidnappers to try and secure her release."

Baxter looked at his computer screen and frowned. "Do you have this flash drive they're asking for?"

"We have the personnel to make an exchange." Jax had a flat tone.

Both she and Jax were trained in hostage recovery, but she was pregnant. Zeyla would help but had no law enforcement training. She was more of a mercenary. Preston could provide backup, although Kenna didn't especially want to lean on his skills.

Jax was a guy who knew the value of backup. If that backup was their team, or people with badges, either way he'd have someone there to keep him safe.

It just wouldn't be Kenna.

She didn't need to fear the unknowns of Jax going into a dangerous situation. He would do it if it meant getting Gabby back safe. They'd only met with Shawn's sister once, but that didn't matter. Everyone needed someone willing to fight for their rescue. The kind of person who knew the ninety-nine would be fine while they went and retrieved the one.

The chief scratched his jaw, his attention on the monitor. "I'm sure we can locate this woman. Make the exchange." He turned to them. "This department can take it from here. That is, if you're prepared to hand over this drive they're referencing."

Kenna could see that he thought they might argue with that idea, unwilling to give him what they had. She shrugged. "We can bring it to the meeting."

Jax said, "It's too valuable to be carrying around with us, don't you think?"

The chief stared at them. He couldn't possibly believe they would just hand over everything they had. After the way the police had bungled the investigation into Shawn Terrance's death, Kenna wasn't willing to leave Gabby's fate in their hands.

"I guess if she's paying you to find her brother's killer, you'll have to stick it out to the end," the sergeant said. "Otherwise, you might not get your money."

Kenna looked at him. "Who says we charge anything?"

His brow crinkled for a second, and he looked over her shoulder. She glanced back and saw two men and a woman enter, all of them in business suits. The man at the front spotted her, and his eyes flared. His gaze moved to Jax, and his demeanor tightened.

Uh-oh.

They looked like lawyers, though.

"Can we help you folks?" the chief asked.

"Yes." The tight man in front nodded. "We're here to report the theft of company property from NextGen Innovations."

The other two stopped behind him, flanking him like it was necessary for him to go everywhere with his entourage. NextGen had its team of high-priced lawyers.

"Where is Gabby Terrance?" Kenna folded her arms above her baby bump.

The man glanced at her. "Considering you're the one responsible for the theft of our property, I'm going to refrain from answering that."

The flash drive. That had to be what they were here for.

Kenna said, "I'd love to know what you think I did."

He huffed, moving around her so he could go stand by the chief. "Could we speak to you privately, Chief?"

"Even if you had nothing to do with Shawn Terrance's death," Jax said, "his sister has been kidnapped. Her life is in danger, and the person responsible wants your tech. You can't pretend you don't care what happens to that drive."

Kenna said, "Sounds to me like we're on the same team."

Assuming she and Jax weren't about to get arrested.

The lawyer guy looked at her like she was on the slide under his microscope. "I'm interested in you handing over our tech. But I have nothing to do with a private citizen and the trouble she seems to have gotten herself into."

Was he really going to pretend they weren't responsible? What if they weren't?

And if they really weren't, then who had kidnapped Gabby?

Chapter Nine

Oliver Jaxton pulled the car onto the bridge hours after night had fallen. He was alone in the car. Alone on the bridge...until he saw the other vehicle. People over by the railing. The bridge was the old trestle kind that rumbled under the tires.

For the last few hours, they'd gone over and over contingencies. He and Kenna and Zeyla—once they'd tracked her down and she'd shown up at the police station. The cops and their "team," who would be working this.

Seemed more like hanging Jax out to dry, but he wasn't going to argue. At least he could control the outcomes when it was him on point. To an extent, anyway. Operations like this never went the way they were planned. So when they finally got the time and location for the exchange—the flash drive for Gabby Terrance—he'd had them give him the particulars of the location but advised them to stick to "if A, then B" scenarios.

He stopped about twenty feet from the SUV parked in the middle of the bridge facing him. Headlights blinding.

Jax angled his car to the right so he could get a look at the people.

More than one man, dressed in dark clothing. Faces covered by masks.

Gabby was standing with bound hands and a gag over her mouth, far too close to the edge. She looked like she was freezing in jeans and a short-sleeved T-shirt. But the fear she felt right now was probably worse than the cold. Jax didn't know her, didn't care about her the way he cared about his family, but she also should never have been caught up in this situation.

Her brother had done the right thing and been killed for it.

She had tried to find out the truth of what happened to him, and now she was a pawn in someone's sick game to get something that didn't belong to them. Or did. He wasn't convinced the company was innocent, despite their protests.

Whoever this was, if they weren't part of the company, then they were a competitor, and the lawyers sent by the company's board knew who they might be. Right?

Either way, it was Jax putting his butt on the line.

And honestly, it felt more normal than a lot of what had been happening in his life lately.

He made sure the weapon he had stashed in the back of his belt wouldn't be visible and climbed out. Even if they spotted that one and had him throw away his weapon, he wouldn't be without protection. Thanks to Kenna's tactic of stashing weapons in all kinds of places.

He held his hands up. No one behind him on the bridge. Just his car, with the engine clicking as it cooled.

He hadn't worn a jacket, hoping the Henley he'd pushed up to his elbows made him look casual and nonthreatening to these guys. He walked forward in the glaring beam of the SUV headlights.

The man beside Gabby held her arm while she whimpered and cried.

Behind him, Jax could see another guy. There to cover his buddy. Probably more men were around, out of sight in the dark. But he could only see these two.

"Let her go," Jax called out, "and I'll give you what you want."

He stopped about ten feet away.

Neither man spoke.

Jax pointed at the railing beside Gabby. "Bring her back from that edge!"

Another man emerged from behind the SUV, over to Jax's left.

He had zero control in this situation. If he said the code phrase and the cavalry sped onto the bridge, Gabby would be dead, and most likely so would Jax. They'd kill him, take what they were here for, and then shoot their way out of the situation.

The man holding onto Gabby yelled, "Show us the flash drive!"

Jax lowered his left hand slowly, stuck two fingers in his left front pocket and raised it to show them the drive and the port that it went into, both in a plastic baggie. He had a vest on, sure, but didn't like feeling this vulnerable one bit.

If he had to guess, these were the same guys from the day before. They'd escaped into the car wash and evaded these men.

Guys who knew they'd been in the house. Probably watched them through a link to the internal cameras. Realized they had discovered the drive everyone was looking for. Came after them. Jax's family. His pregnant wife. His young adult daughter. His wife's cousin—sister—whatever.

No. Didn't matter what kind of guys these were. This would be over tonight.

Jax held the bag out. "The drive for her." He motioned with his chin like he hadn't even bothered to learn Gabby's name. "Everyone walks away."

"Okay, FBI," the guy holding Gabby said. "Hand it over."

The guy to the left started toward Jax. He came close enough to grab the bag out of Jax's hand. Jax took half a step back. "Let her go at the same time."

Despite the cool night temperature, sweat ran down his back.

The thug to his left produced a gun and pointed it at Jax's head. He lunged forward and grabbed the drive, then backed up.

At the same time, the guy holding Gabby shoved her.

Over the edge.

Gabby screamed. Jax ran to the spot where she'd been standing. Gunfire broke out from the rear of the SUV—the man who'd been covering his friends.

Splash.

Jax stumbled on instinct but kept himself from falling. He ended up in a crouch beside the railing.

For a split second, he waited for Gabby to surface and scream. But he didn't hear the sound in time. With his gun drawn and aimed at the men, he squeezed off three shots as the men jumped into their vehicle.

One fired back wildly.

Jax crouched in the dark, praying God would hide him in the shadows.

He fired back, shooting at the tires. FBI policy didn't

allow for shots to be fired at a fleeing vehicle, as there was often a high chance that a bystander could be hit. But he wasn't FBI anymore, and there were no innocents on this bridge.

The SUV reversed at high speed. Jax left the police to pursue the men and rose, grabbing the railing and looking over.

A boat motored into view, coming out from cover under the bridge. Someone switched on a light, shining the beam on the water. Jax spotted the figure in the murky depths and didn't want to know how cold that water would be.

When he was certain they were good to pull Gabby out of the water, he turned and ran back to his car. Jax waited while a stream of police cars with red-and-blue flashing lights sped over the bridge in pursuit of the SUV, and then he flipped around to head to the rendezvous point.

He grabbed his phone, found the walkie-talkie app, and hit the button. "I'm clear. Headed to the pier."

Zeyla responded a few seconds later. "We have Gabby on board. See you there."

Jax cut off the road, bumped across some grass, and drove onto the asphalt of a single-lane road that ran along the riverside. After a mile or so, the trees gave way to a wooden pier. He left his car on the street and jogged down the wooden boards to where the boat stopped.

Zeyla jumped off the deck onto the pier and caught the rope the boat's owner tossed to her. She tied it off like an expert.

Jax threw out, "Where'd you learn how to do that?" while passing by her and stepping onto the boat just as the pilot cut the engine.

Gabby lay at the front of the boat.

Jax crouched by her. "Ms. Terrance." He patted her cheek.

The pilot eased down to sit on a bench seat in the nose of the boat. "How is she?"

"Apart from soaking wet? She was standing on the bridge, and I didn't see any visible wounds, but who knows what they did to her."

Zeyla crouched by him. "Blanket." She laid it over Gabby.

"We need to get her to the hospital." He put one knee down and slid his arms under the unconscious woman. "It's probably faster to drive than to call an ambulance."

He'd suggested they have one on standby for the operation, but the chief had shaken his head. Apparently, the crew in this county were voluntary, and it took at least forty minutes to get them to a scene. Why that meant not having them on standby, the chief didn't answer.

But he'd given Jax the address for the closest hospital—which turned out to be more of a medical center. They didn't even have an emergency entrance. Just twenty-four-hour staff and a buzzer at the door to be let in.

Zeyla ran ahead of him. "This woman needs help!"

Jax carried Gabby inside, and when the nurse waved him over, he followed her. She frowned at them, holding a set of doors open. "What happened?"

"She fell off the bridge on Rowland Road. But that was after she was kidnapped and held at gunpoint." He laid her on the bed in the empty room, and the nurse grabbed a phone off the wall.

"Doctor Walsh to room four." The nurse's voice came through an intercom system, ringing down the hallway. "We'll take care of her. You need to fill out paperwork, and I'll be out in a moment to give it to you. *Don't* leave."

Jax nodded. "Got it. Just help her."

The nurse shifted the blanket open so she could assess Gabby. Far too pale, the woman hadn't woken up yet. Jax realized he didn't know if she had family other than Shawn, who'd been murdered. Did she have next of kin, or loved ones? Friends she considered as good as family.

He needed to find out.

The doctor rushed into the room, lifting a stethoscope from around his neck. Older man, graying hair. He'd probably served the people of this county for decades. Presiding over births, deaths, ailments, and emergencies.

"What on earth?"

The nurse shifted back the hem of Gabby's shirt, revealing a ragged wound that had been stitched.

"What is that?" It looked like she'd been seriously injured—or someone had hacked into her.

The nurse yelled at him, "Go wait in the waiting room!"

Before she'd even finished, the doctor started giving orders. Jax left them to it and headed back to the waiting area. He could write down some basic information on a paper and leave it, but they weren't hanging around for hours. Gabby was in good hands. They'd be able to contact her next of kin and probably the police, as soon as she woke up enough to speak to the staff here.

Zeyla hung back in the waiting area, texting on her phone. As he approached, she looked up. "Did she wake up?"

He shook his head. "Not yet. They found a nasty wound on her abdomen that was stitched up." He winced. "I almost don't want to ask what they did to her."

Zeyla lowered the phone to her side, staring at him. "How wide was it?"

Was he supposed to know that? "I don't know. Like all

the way across her belly. You think they took out organs or a baby or something? She wasn't pregnant when we talked to her."

His greatest fear was surfacing again. He wanted to pray the fear away and get to the place he could trust God in the moment, but Zeyla brushed past him.

"She wasn't pregnant." Zeyla headed across the lobby. "And they didn't take something out. They put something in." She started running toward the double doors.

A ricocheting boom thundered through the medical center, followed by a fireball from an explosion. It hit the double doors and flung them out.

Zeyla stumbled, half diving and half falling into a slide across the floor. The fireball blew over her head while she curled up. Arms over her face.

Jax felt the rush of heat and concussive force slam into him, shoving him back toward the front of the building.

His head hit something, and everything went black.

Chapter Ten

Kenna stood watching out the back window, tapping her foot. It had been hours since the hospital explosion. She still hadn't talked to Jax or Zeyla. "Come on, Preston."

What was taking them so long?

Kenna kept tapping her foot. "You're driving me crazy."

She glanced over at Maizie, back at her same workstation, working on the flash drive and the port it connected to. Hacking into the drive of whatever Shawn Terrance stole from his employer.

Jax would be back soon. *Continue to protect him, Lord.*

The danger wasn't over. She could argue that the danger would *never* be over. And soon enough, they'd be bringing a child into the world. Another innocent life at risk.

Maizie sat back in the chair, her body still. Hands poised over the keys. "I think... I'm in. I did it." A wide smile stretched across her face.

So wide it was infectious. "That's amazing!" She walked over and squeezed the young woman's shoulder.

"You always surprise me with what you can do, but I also don't know why I'm surprised."

Maizie glanced at her, and Kenna smiled. She was worried about Jax and Zeyla, but Preston was taking care of them and getting them back here.

"I won't ask yet what you have on there." Kenna motioned to the screen with her chin.

"By all means, keep pacing back and forth and tapping your foot."

Kenna chuckled. "Sorry." She put her arm around Maizie's shoulders.

"You love them. I'm worried, too." Maizie leaned her head toward Kenna, in line with the baby bump. She reached over and patted Kenna's stomach. "We'll be all right."

"Yes, we will." Because Jax was going to be here.

Maizie said, "In the meantime, it looks like I have all the files. Plenty of them."

"It'll take you some time to go through them all. Need some help?"

Elizabeth and Craig Stairns, a retired couple Maizie lived with—meaning her Airstream was on their back lawn—helped a whole lot with work like this. Reading through papers. Stairns was a retired FBI agent and Kenna's boss from years ago, and Elizabeth was a counselor who helped them all in more ways than they could count.

"You think Preston will care if we print hundreds of pages?"

Kenna chuckled. "Guess I need to remember how to speed-read."

"It isn't like you need to be doing anything else except putting your feet up and reading documents."

"Yeah, yeah." She wandered back to the window and watched the horizon, looking for Preston's helicopter.

She spotted a couple of his security team members patrolling the grounds. Jax had spoken to them all, but she and Maizie had stuck to the house for the most part. After the deal with MSI and how their boss turned out to be *Dominatus*, she wasn't eager to trust another private security team. If Preston and Jax were satisfied with their answers enough to trust them, she would as well, but that didn't mean she needed to make friends.

A black dot emerged over the mountain range in the distance.

"I see them." She hoped it was them, at least.

"Are you going to be like this every time he goes on an operation?"

"Probably." Kenna could admit that much. "I have no idea how women whose husbands are deployed in war zones or spouses whose other halves are a cop or firefighter handle it. I'm a mess."

"You'd probably be less of a mess if he hadn't been blown up last night."

Kenna didn't turn back from the window. "I was a mess as soon as he left."

Sure, hearing the hospital had exploded didn't help, but it wasn't worse than knowing her husband would be alone on that bridge, facing gunmen by himself. No matter what, all of them were in danger. Being here was more like allowing herself to be lulled into a false sense of security, versus being actually secure.

With their enemy and the reach *Dominatus* had, there was literally nowhere they could hide. Even the security and anonymity of this ranch was on a clock. And time was running out.

The black dot grew bigger until she could clearly make out the outline of Preston's helicopter.

"I was a mess as well. But it was more about whether the fake drive and fake port were going to hold up to scrutiny," Maizie said. "I figured as soon as they got it, they would test it and realize it was a fake."

They hadn't told anyone they were keeping the original and had no intention of handing it over. "Unfortunately, that might be what caused the explosion."

Kenna pushed open the French doors and stepped out onto the patio, a patchwork of red stones surrounded by planters with all manner of greenery in them. Ferns and cacti. Preston had told her he requested plants that didn't take much work for his landscaping staff and that would remain green even in winter.

He was probably only trying to distract her from worrying about Jax on his mission, even with Zeyla there to back him up. It had mostly worked, though she had no intention of ever taking up gardening.

Unless she should?

Maybe it would be a decent distraction for times when Jax was on a mission or stepped into a dangerous situation—or headed to the street to check the mail. At some point, she might venture out with him, but when there was a baby to protect, neither of them was going to jump at the chance to leave the baby and go out together. Not even if there was an army back home to protect their daughter.

The helicopter lowered slowly to the ground, and she walked across the lawn toward it. Two armed security guards flanked the aircraft, far enough back that they were keeping watch on the area around her and her family.

She needed to tell them thank you.

Kenna stood with her fingers laced over her baby bump

while the rotors created a wind that whipped her hair around.

The helicopter engine shut off, and the rear door opened. Preston stepped down, turning immediately to help Zeyla out. Zeyla had a white bandage on her left temple and one on her right wrist, and she walked with a limp.

Kenna came right over, and they hugged. "Are you okay?"

Zeyla nodded. "I'm good." She gave Kenna another squeeze and headed toward the house.

Preston helped Jax out of the chopper, and Kenna got a look at her husband. She tried not to wince. He'd been hit by a bullet while wearing a vest just a couple of months ago and had only recently fully healed from that. Now he had a new crop of bumps and bruises, or worse.

His left arm was in a sling, but she didn't see a bandage. It had to be his collarbone. He'd, of course, refused to run down all his injuries for her and simply stressed that he would be back soon.

Broken ribs. Sprains. Who knew what else.

He had a similar limp to Zeyla and walked with Preston holding his elbow. Jax shrugged him off.

Preston said, "I'll go get the golf cart, so you don't have to walk."

"I can make it. I don't need a ride." He looked grumpy.

Kenna wanted to roll her eyes, but that wouldn't go down well right now. She slid under his nonbandaged arm. "I'm glad you're fine. You look great."

He didn't laugh.

Another man climbed from the helicopter, carrying one of those old medical bags. Preston's private doctor? She'd heard that he had one before but didn't want to be paranoid right now that they needed someone on hand.

They set off, walking slowly toward the house while Preston watched them. She wanted to ask Preston what he knew of their injuries, but not with Jax here.

He and his doctor friend walked behind them, talking quietly.

"Are you really all right?" She spoke in a low voice so only Jax would hear her.

"Everything important is in one piece and functioning."

"That's the bar we're measuring things against?" Didn't seem like a super high bar to her, more like rock bottom, baseline health. Or aliveness. Not even health, because that required something to be optimal.

"The doctor gave me something, but it's wearing off, and I'm due for another dose in an hour. I just need to lay down so I can hold on until then." Jax blew out a slow breath as they stepped from the grass onto the stones and headed for the French doors where Maizie stood watching them.

Jax continued, "He has this experimental pain management stuff that isn't a narcotic. Seems like it works pretty well."

"That's great." She'd rather he didn't need it in the first place, but that wasn't the reality of the lives they led and their jobs. "Let's get you to the couch."

She and Maizie both helped him up the step into the back porch room, then over to a small couch. Zeyla had slumped into a chair over by Maizie's workstation, where she now had her head back against the wall and her eyes closed.

Jax lay back with a groan.

Kenna looked over at her sister. "You good, Zeyla?"

"Peachy." She didn't open her eyes.

"Maybe Preston can explain to me how a bomb packed

in Gabby's stomach exploded in the hospital, killing her, the doctor, the nurse, and the janitor on the floor above them." Kenna folded her arms above her baby bump and resisted the urge to tap her foot. "Because I'm having trouble assimilating how you were both almost killed."

Jax opened one eye. "Zeyla realized it. But we were too late." He paused to take a breath. "I'm surprised she didn't explode when she hit the water, to be honest."

If that had happened, and the device planted in Gabby's abdominal cavity blew at that point, she would have likely killed Zeyla and the owner of the boat. "I had the same thought."

Maizie said, "They probably realized the drive was fake and hit the button to blow the bomb."

Kenna glanced at her, then back at Jax. "But if they went to the trouble of packing it in her stomach, they planned to blow her up, regardless. It was just a question of when that happened."

The doctor wandered to Zeyla and pulled up a chair to sit in front of her, clicking on a tiny pen light.

Jax said, "They thought they got what they wanted. They were never going to let her go."

"Who were they?" She'd rather have said it more diplomatically than that, and with a whole lot more patience to find out if he saw their faces and could somehow describe them.

Jax shook his head, which looked like it hurt. "They were wearing masks." His voice had started to slur. "I didn't see them."

He was falling asleep or passing out. "Doctor?"

The older man had black slacks, shined shoes, and a white shirt with the sleeves rolled up to reveal tattoos covering his forearms. He pushed his chair back from Zeyla and came over. "Sleep is good, but I'll keep an eye on him. He has two broken ribs and a bruised collarbone, but no head injury and no internal bleeding."

Was that good? In the grand scheme of things, probably. But the next few weeks weren't going to be fun.

She turned to Preston, who looked up from his phone. "We have the information from Shawn Terrance's drive."

"That's good."

She nodded. "We still have what we need to prove Shawn was right to blow the whistle on the company he worked for, but with no idea who those guys that kidnapped Gabby were, we don't know if there's another group in play. A bigger threat than the company's team of uptight lawyers."

After how it went at the police station, talking their way out of theft charges and helping work on the operation... Of course, they were supposed to have done that as a favor and also given the drive back to the company—which they did not do. Kenna didn't figure they were super pleased with her team right now.

"We can give them the original, now that we can make copies of everything." She turned to Maizie and saw that Zeyla's eyes were open. "They won't be able to sweep this under the rug."

Her sister, usually ready to jump into a fight at any time, looked exhausted.

"We'll regroup and come up with a plan to hand over the drive, plus also blast the internet with the truth." She headed toward Maizie and pulled up a chair beside her. Not the most comfortable chair in the world, given that it was wicker with a thin cushion, but it was better than standing all day with swollen ankles. "What do you think, Maizie? It's your case."

The younger woman glanced over from her computer screen, and Kenna saw an odd look on her face.

"What is it?" Kenna asked.

Maizie hesitated. "Another episode of that podcast just dropped. It's about the Seventh Day Killer."

A host of memories, most of which had Jax in them. Some with her first love, Bradley, before he died. All of it was mixed together in her mind. Kenna forced them all back and focused on Maizie.

"He's getting closer to recounting crimes that we all investigated together." Maybe Maizie was worried about the truth of where she'd come from being discovered.

The younger woman shook her head. "He's got a special guest on the show. He's interviewing the Seventh Day Killer's final victim, the one you saved."

"Ellayna Feathers?"

Maizie nodded.

"She's a child!" Kenna nearly exploded out of her chair, remembering that night at the theater when she'd found Ellayna in the basement and had to fight off the killer to save her. They'd been through so much. Ellayna's mom emailed Kenna every few months to check in and let her know how the girl was doing. She'd just had her twelfth birthday.

Maizie pointed at the screen. "She's a guest on his show."

Kenna gripped the sides of the chair. "I want to listen to it."

Chapter Eleven

"The sheriff's office burned down, and he didn't make it. Because people like Sheriff Joe Don Hunter might not always do the right thing. But when it counts, they don't let others suffer. They stick their necks out for people because a life—any life—has value."

Hasworth, the US attorney prosecuting this case, stood up from her perch on the edge of the table. "Is that what your team does? You pick and choose who to save. Judge, jury, and executioner. Is that it?"

Kenna reached for the water glass on the little shelf in the witness stand with her. She didn't want to look at the defendant. The fact that she wasn't the one on trial was a minor miracle. But how could she thank God for small things like that when this was what her life had turned into?

Everything she'd thought she was about had been turned upside down. Kind of like this court case that made no sense. All the rules had gone out the window.

"No," Kenna said. "That isn't it."

Hasworth lifted a hand and held it out, as if motioning for Kenna to continue. "We're all here until your testimony is concluded. But I can't help thinking that you're stalling for time. That certainly seems like something you would do."

"I'm not dragging this story out. The case requires context, and I have to give that to the court, or the jury cannot possibly make an unbiased decision. None of us can until we see all the sides."

She would love for the door to open, and someone she considered family to bust in like Aragorn at Helm's Deep and rescue her. But that wasn't what was going to happen.

"Where were we?" Hasworth asked.

On the same side, or so I thought. "Bishopsville. It's a town in northern California."

"Right, of course."

"Joe Don Hunter was a family friend. I lost him like I've lost so many others to these people." She took a deep cleansing breath. "I didn't know then what I know now. That it was all connected to *Dominatus*. The town was in the grip of people who exploit others for money. I followed the trail and rescued who I could, but Sheriff Hunter paid the price. So, no, I don't save the people I deem worthy. I do what I can for everyone. Especially people I care about."

"But there was bad blood between him and your father, specifically over how your mother died. Isn't that correct?"

Kenna said, "I doubt you want to get into that. It's a sticky web that even I don't know how to untangle." She shook her head. "I found an autopsy in a safe in Joe Don's cabin. I still have no idea who that woman was or how she connected to anything. All I know is that my 'mother,' or the woman I consider to be my mother, isn't dead. She's been fighting against *Dominatus* for longer than anyone. Her name is Amara. And again, it's complicated." Kenna shrugged. "Go figure."

Someone in the jury snickered, but Kenna didn't look to see who it was.

Kenna glanced at the judge. "I'll do my best to stay on topic so as not to waste the court's time."

He nodded, and mostly, she figured none of them had the energy to argue. "You have some time, then we'll be recessing until tomorrow. You can continue your story then."

"Thank you, Your Honor."

The judge said, "After *that*, the defense will no doubt be ready to cross-examine you."

One of the men behind that table rose halfway, smoothing down his tie. "We will, Your Honor." Given the look in his eye, he'd already thought of an angle. It matched the smug look in the defendant's expression.

Great. She wasn't on trial, but her family wasn't innocent. Not by any stretch.

"Continue, please, Mrs. Jaxton." The judge leaned back in his chair, and it creaked. "But keep it to the relevant highlights. We don't want to be here until Christmas."

Kenna nodded. "We managed to tie the exploitation in Bishopsville to a group who had a stranglehold on the town of Hatchet, New Mexico."

"We?" Hasworth asked. "Please clarify for the court who you're referring to."

Could she say it? The wound was too raw.

"I didn't know it at the time, but Maizie was helping me."

"Your adopted daughter, Maizie Smith. Sometimes referred to as Maizie Jaxton or Maizie Morrow." Hasworth flipped over a page in a file on the prosecution table. "Is that correct?"

"That's correct." Kenna swallowed against the lump in her throat. "Even back then, she was feeding me information. Connecting the dots for me." She'd nearly said "us," but it was really only Kenna and Cabot, her dog, in those days. Then Jax had joined her, and they'd faced a dangerous killer together—the kind of person who had money behind them.

Enough to renovate an entire floor in a hotel.

She should've known then that it was all different factions within *Dominatus*. That everything she had faced back then was all about drawing her into their web and controlling what she learned. Where she went.

Testing her mettle.

"Maizie was helping me fight for the people destroyed in the wake of what *Dominatus* was doing."

Kenna had done what she'd done to keep her family safe in a way that was permanent. But they would never be able to walk away from this.

By the time they realized they were in too deep, it had been much too late to get out.

"People like the FBI director, is that right?" Hasworth asked the planned question. Because they knew it would come up, and the US attorney wanted to get ahead of it.

"That's right," Kenna said. "The FBI director attacked me, and I had no choice but to use lethal force to defend myself."

"And in doing so, you saved a young girl from the worst kind of situation."

The defense attorney shot up. "Objection. Relevance."

"Sustained," the judge ruled.

Chapter Twelve

Kenna pulled out a chair at the dining table and grabbed a slice of pizza from the box in the middle of the table, trying to get close enough to reach it without jamming the baby against the edge. She sat back, pizza in hand, and let out a breath.

Preston glanced over from the head of the table with a mouthful of pizza. He seemed to find her predicament amusing, but she was going to ignore that.

Maizie sat to her right, poring over a stack of pages, arranging them side by side and scouring for details.

Jax had taken one slice and then headed to their RV, eating as he went. The vehicle was parked in the barn. She figured he needed sleep, and since they had no answers as to what was going on, it was a good time for him to rest.

He'd kissed her before he went, attentive and making

sure she didn't need anything. She needed him, but it wasn't more important than his healing.

Kenna chewed, trying not to think about the podcast and the sound of Ellayna's voice on the line. She'd listened to it so many times she could practically recite the girl's words verbatim at this point.

She saved me.

Zeyla kicked out a chair and sat, a diet soda in one hand and a slice of pizza held aloft in the other. "Did you try to call Mom?"

Kenna nodded. "She didn't answer, so I left a message."

Zeyla swallowed her bite of pizza. "Why don't you explain this to me like I have no idea what you're talking about? Because I don't."

Kenna set the rest of her slice on the plate and wiped her fingers on a napkin. "Ellayna Feathers was the last victim of the Seventh Day Killer, Gerald Rickshire."

"And he's in prison now, right? 'Cause you caught him?" Maizie took a big bite of pizza, leaning forward with her mouth over her plate.

"He is." That was part of how she'd first met Jax. He'd been talking to Rickshire in the prison, and she'd listened to Jax essentially accuse her of colluding with the guy. After that chat, she and Jax had gone to the diner where she found Cabot had been abandoned. Now the dog was living her best life at the Stairns' house, getting spoiled and sleeping on the comfy furniture.

"Ellayna's mother hired me to find her when the police were facing roadblocks in the case. Given the seven-day timeline, it was clear that time was running out." Kenna took a sip of her caffeine-free soda. "She has a little brother who would be two or three now."

That was the same visit to Salt Lake City where she'd

helped Valentina and Javier Ryson, her dear friends, and their new baby. She'd also been shot in the chest in her Class C—which made her rub her sternum right over the massive scar she'd been left with, thanks to Bradley's mother.

Kenna shook her head. "A lot happened, but it didn't have to do with the Seventh Day Killer. He was already in prison."

"*Dominatus?*" Zeyla asked, as if that was a complete question.

"There was no indication more was going on then. I didn't learn anything about powerful families controlling society or international organizations until much later."

Maizie raised a hand. "I knew."

Preston said, "So did I." He winked at Maizie, and she grinned back at him.

Kenna said, "I worked it out eventually."

Preston smiled at her. She didn't want to get off topic and wind up recounting all their journeys to get here, but she found herself nostalgic for the way her life had been when she didn't know about *Dominatus*. Then again, given what she had now—the good and the bad—would she wish for it to be gone?

That would mean giving up this family. Losing Jax. The gift of motherhood that God had given her, this time in a way that He blessed—because she had chosen righteousness as a way to live to honor Him.

It had been a long road, but she was here now. "Presto chango, here I am."

Zeyla frowned. "Was that English?"

Kenna shrugged. "Long story short?"

"That one makes more sense. But we're talking about Ellayna." Zeyla leaned back in her chair. "He must have contacted her mom and requested that she come on the show."

"I'd presume so, but someone unscrupulous might have reached out to her. Maybe Ellayna has social media accounts, and he contacted her through those." Kenna didn't want to think that Ellayna might have reached out to him, asking to be on the podcast so she could talk about her experiences.

Who knew what was going through the preteen's head. After a trauma like the one she'd suffered, she might be a precocious girl acting out, trying to prove herself to the world. Ellayna could already be on a spiral of self-destruction, even as young as she was. Without more information, it was hard to tell.

"How old is she now?" Preston asked.

"Twelve or so." She glanced at Maizie. "Can you…" The girl was up to her eyeballs in work right now. Kenna didn't need to be piling more tasks on her plate. "I'll look for Ellayna on socials."

"Thanks." Maizie slid a paper over and scanned the text. "Huh."

"What do you have?"

Now that Kenna had thought about the Rysons, she wanted to call Javier, her police officer friend in Salt Lake City, and ask if he could check on Ellayna and her family. Get a sense of the situation and maybe find out why Ms. Feathers wasn't answering the phone.

But if Maizie had something from Shawn's stolen files, they all needed to know what it was. What both Shawn and Gabby had died for. What someone was willing to kill to get their hands on.

Maizie slid over a paper. "From what Shawn down-loaded, it seems as if the company's AI software was cataloging information about its users. Putting them in socio-economic groups, like what their interests are, their income, and how they use their finances. Based on decisions they made, how susceptible they were to the suggestions the algorithms made, and how it affected what they bought or chose to watch."

"So, a giant data collection operation?" Kenna scanned the page, but it looked like computer code, or some kind of foreign language. She would need a bachelor's in something she knew nothing about to decipher this stuff.

"Kind of. Only..." Maizie shifted a couple of papers. "That's a code I know."

Preston said, "You've seen it before?"

Maizie bit her lip and scrunched up her nose. "I know what this whole program does, but this line of code is like a signature that tells me who wrote it. Like recognizing someone's handwriting or their speech patterns."

"What is it?" Kenna asked.

"You didn't want to do anything connected to *Dominatus*."

"And I'll be so surprised to discover everything is connected to them anyway, no matter how hard I try to avoid them?" At least this wasn't a case they'd been sent by the president. But in trying to avoid what she wanted them to work on, Kenna had fallen into the same situation, regardless.

"The person who programmed this artificial intelligence works with or for *Dominatus*," Maizie said, her tone cautious as if she worried Kenna would be mad. "Because they programmed the system on that deep-sea platform where you were held."

"So, we're dealing with an enemy vicious enough to put a bomb in an innocent woman's abdominal cavity, and it turns out to be the people we know who are vicious enough kill a bunch of people," Zeyla said. "I'm shocked."

"And they have the resources to disappear." Preston tapped his index and middle fingers on the table. "I'm going to pay the Pueblo Police Department a visit. See what I can find out about their pursuit of the kidnappers."

Maizie sighed. "If they're collecting invasive data from people's lives, maybe it's about controlling them."

"Or it's market research," Kenna said. "Or they're using the information to steer votes their way. Or public perception. Or the people being spied on are all targets. Or assets."

Zeyla nodded. "That fits."

"What does?"

She bit into a piece of pizza. "Everything you just said."

Kenna would rather they narrow it down further than that. "Maybe see if you guys can figure out which it is." She stood, pushing off the table with one hand and grabbing her phone from the back pocket of her maternity jeans with the other. "I need to make a call. Get someone to visit the Feathers' house and find out what's going on."

Zeyla lifted her chin in a nod that told Kenna she was going to keep an eye on Maizie. The two of them were becoming good friends, kind of like Ramon and Maizie. Maybe Zeyla was taking the time to connect with the young woman he referred to as his little sister. The three of them might well end up being the boots on the ground division of Banbury Investigations, while Kenna and Jax stayed on the home front, so their learning how to work as a team who watched each other's backs was a good thing, as far as she was concerned.

She pulled up her message threads and asked Ramon to check in. However it was going with MSI and their operation attempting to take down *Dominatus* by force, she wanted to know.

Then she found a quiet spot with an armchair she could sink into and called Ryson.

"Kenna, hey." Affection softened his tone into a low rumble.

"Are you whispering, or did you lose your voice?" She tucked her legs up on the chair and settled in

"I'm hanging with Carlos, trying to get him to settle down."

Kenna smiled to herself. "How is he?"

"*Mi hijo* needs to learn how to settle, but babies are like that. Especially little boys who want to battle the world, take no prisoners, and never surrender."

Kenna chuckled. "He's six weeks old."

"I can tell already. My Luci is a sweetheart, as long as she gets what she wants. We are officially in the terrible threes."

"I thought it was the terrible twos?" Wasn't that what everyone said?

"Oh, girl, you have no idea." Ryson chuckled quietly. "I've dealt with criminals that weren't as stubborn as my girl. And the smart ones are half as clever as she is."

"Uh-oh."

"Don't worry, I'm sure your girl will be an angel. With any luck, she'll take after her father."

Kenna laughed aloud. "I'm planning to enjoy every moment, no matter what."

"Good." Ryson paused. "Did you call for baby tips? Is it time?"

"Couple of weeks yet," Kenna said. "We hope."

She explained about the podcast, then reminded him who Ellayna Feathers was. He'd been working that night, and they'd reconnected over a case. But underneath it all, they would always be friends first and investigators second.

"I tried to call her mom. I don't know if Ellayna has a phone," Kenna said. "If she does, I don't have the number."

"Send me what you have. I'll look her up on a precinct computer. See what I can find out." Ryson made a shushing noise. "*Mi hijo*, settle down. Do you want me to pay them a visit?"

That was exactly what she'd been planning to ask him. "If you could, I'd appreciate it."

"Do you know who this podcaster guy is? I could shake that tree as well. Have a word."

Kenna smiled. "I have a line of people ready to do that. But his name is an alias. The accounts online are all aliases, and when we dig, there's nothing to find." Nothing but a loose thread from an old case she wanted to tug on. But was it worth doing that so close to her due date? If Amara would answer the phone, Kenna could send her and Bruce to check it out.

"Someone is protecting him."

"We don't know. And I have no idea what their agenda would be."

"Distracting you. Tying you up in knots right when you need to be focusing."

Kenna said, "I'm not focused on taking them down. It's not like I'm a threat right now. I'm having a baby."

"As if that would stop you from being the biggest threat they have."

"That's the point! I'm not even trying." She sighed. "Every time I turn around, I stumble over a *Dominatus* operation."

"Would you have it any other way?"

"Yes, I would have tweaked the timing. I don't like being in danger and feeling vulnerable."

Ryson started to chuckle. "Does anyone?"

"I guess not."

"Leave it to me. I'll make sure they're okay."

"All right. Thanks, Ryson. I appreciate it." She was going to let Jax and Zeyla heal from their injuries, while she made a case. One that local law enforcement in Utah or Montana could use to bring charges against the accomplice to a child's death. Someone she'd missed during her investigation. "I've got plenty to do."

"Me, too. If I can get this baby to nap on his own," he said. "How is everything else?"

"I need Valentina to tell me how she deals with you being at work, potentially in dangerous situations, and worrying you might not come home."

"I don't walk a beat anymore, Kenna. Guess why."

"Because of her and the kids," she said. "That's why you took the lieutenant's exam?"

"Sure is."

"So that you could work a safer job."

"And come home at the end of my shift," he said. "The risk is still there. But I'm not on the streets. I work at a desk, for the most part. Sure, I used to do SWAT and patrol. Plenty of our officers in those roles have kids. But it's not for everyone, and Valentina needed the peace of mind that I was doing what I could to stay safe."

"So you shifted your duties."

"Comes with a bigger paycheck, which helps. But giving up patrol was a sacrifice. I loved the job."

"You're a good man, Javier Ryson. She's a blessed woman, and your kids have the best kind of father."

"Tell that to me in twenty years when I'm bailing this kid out of jail."

Kenna chuckled. "Maybe we'll have to introduce him to my daughter. See if we can give him a reason to settle down."

"Oh, boy. Now there's an idea." He chuckled softly. "Gotta go."

"Love you guys."

"Yeah, yeah." The call ended.

Chapter Thirteen

Kenna sat with her head back on the recliner, earbuds in. Not quite asleep but not all the way awake either. It was too early in the morning to be fully awake.

Ellayna's voice drifted through her earbuds. "I remember it was really cold."

She sounded young, but not like the child she'd been years ago when Kenna rescued her. This was a preteen who had seen far too much and understood the horror in the world better than most adults—because she'd stared it in the face.

"He told me to call him Ricky. He wasn't nice, and it was really cold."

The podcaster said, "And then Kenna Banbury came?"

Steven didn't cut her off before she began to describe what the Seventh Day Killer had done in the days before he planned to kill her. But it was close. Making Kenna wonder if they'd discussed what they'd be talking about, that Steven didn't want Ellayna to get too descriptive about her trauma.

At least he had that. This wasn't about gratuitous information for the sake of downloads and ratings. It seemed this really was about the case.

"I thought she was a ghost," Ellayna said. "Or an angel." There was a moment of quiet, then she continued, "First, I was alone, and then she was there. She told me that Mommy sent her, but I wasn't supposed to go with strangers." She exhaled across the line. "I told my therapist that because it doesn't make sense. I went with Ricky, but when Kenna showed up, I didn't think I could go with her."

"How did she convince you?"

"She said to me, 'Mommy said to tell you that Bubby loves you,'" Ellayna said. "That's how I knew she was telling the truth."

Kenna sniffed back the moisture gathering in her sinuses. She couldn't let Ellayna's story get to her, but becoming a mother had messed with her hormones and expanded the capacity of her heart in ways she hadn't expected. It seemed like she felt so much that the organ was about to burst out of her chest. Gross analogy, but fitting.

She didn't want to feel this much. But the alternative would be to live as a robot with no feelings whatsoever.

Still, it was far better right now to focus on working. She needed to find this Steven guy and shut him down before he did more damage to people she cared about. But given that they were drawing blanks trying to identify him, she might have to call the president. Surely, the government had secret spy technology that could find someone who didn't want to be found.

Especially when the president was an agent of *Dominatus*. They definitely crossed lines, undermining people's privacy, and they'd claim it was all for the greater good. Meanwhile, so many people who worked for the government in good faith didn't have a clue they were following a dangerous world power.

No, she would wait and not call in the big guns. Not yet.

Ellayna's voice cut across her thoughts. "Then he came. While she was standing there. He walked in."

Steven said, "The Seventh Day Killer—Ricky. He showed up?"

"He came into the room. She fought him like a superhero."

Kenna smiled to herself, thinking back through the tools she'd used that day. Ways she worked to account for the injuries she'd sustained to her forearms years ago. Surgery hadn't fixed it, but *Dominatus* did. She almost wanted that part of her life back. Without the constant ache, she almost didn't feel like...herself.

"She took him down?" Steven asked.

"Yeah. Then she carried me out. All the way to the ambulance."

Kenna remembered the slight weight of the girl and how her arms had ached afterward. But she'd done it. She'd carried Ellayna to safety because she had to. God had sent her to rescue Ellayna, the way He sent Jesus to rescue the world. *Thank You.* He had given her the ability to sweep that child out of a horrible situation and a hundred others besides that one. And yet, how much more had God stepped in to save people—whether they thanked Him in return, or not.

"She called my mom, and I went home."

"And Gerald Rickshire went to prison," Steven said. "It's a pretty amazing story. You were very brave."

"I didn't feel brave."

"Bravery might not have anything to do with how you feel. It's more about what you do."

"Like Kenna fighting him off?" Ellayna said.

"And you keeping your cool. Knowing you could trust her. And leaving with her. Letting her save you from that. You were very brave to take that chance and trust her, Ellayna. You should be proud of yourself."

Ellayna was quiet for a long moment. Then, she said, "Thanks."

"I'm sure it's been hard. But you have a therapist, right? You mentioned them."

"I'm supposed to talk about it." A smidge of teen attitude peeked through in her tone, making the corner of Kenna's mouth curl up.

Steven said, "We all need someone to talk to about things that have happened to us, so thank you for talking to me today."

"You're welcome." Ellayna sounded in that moment every bit like the little kid in that basement that Kenna had found.

But that wasn't what gave her pause.

It was what Steven had said—about things that happened. She'd heard it in his voice. Something had happened to him, and maybe this podcast was his way to talk about it.

The ending credits music began to play, but it cut off abruptly. Kenna opened her eyes and looked at her phone screen on the arm of the chair. *Amara calling.*

She slid a finger across the screen. "Morning."

"Are you even awake?" Her mother's smooth alto tone had some cracks in it, but it always made Kenna feel better. Of course, Amara wasn't her mother any more than Zeyla was really her sister. But she wanted to claim them as such anyway, because *Dominatus* had taken plenty from her. She was keeping this for herself and for her baby.

"Mostly." She explained about Ellayna on the podcast.

"A child? That's unconscionable."

"And we're surprised by that now?" Kenna figured they'd seen enough in this world that what should be unthinkable had happened right in front of their faces in a way they couldn't deny.

"Careful you don't hit a point where you aren't surprised by anything. It's a rough place to be."

Kenna asked, "Are you finally returning my calls?"

"I can dispense wisdom."

"You can also help us work cases. But you pretty much disappeared."

Amara didn't respond right away. When she did, she said, "I needed to figure something out with Bruce."

"And?"

"We're good. We got it settled."

Kenna asked, "Should I know what that means?"

She spotted movement out of the corner of her eye and saw Jax wander out from the hallway and go into the living room. Hair mussed all over the place, looking like he'd been asleep for days.

She smiled as he approached, pointing to her right earbud and mouthing *Amara*.

He braced his hands on the arms of the chair and leaned down to touch his lips to hers.

Amara said, "Bruce and I found a small chapel and got married."

"Congratulations!"

Jax glanced at her.

"But aren't you supposed to have witnesses at a wedding?"

"We found some locals. There wasn't time to call you all down to Mexico once we settled it and decided to find a preacher."

Kenna said, "Good, because I'm going to need some time before I go to Mexico."

"Plus, I don't think they let you fly as pregnant as you are."

"Hmm. True." Kenna sighed. "I appreciate the distraction from thinking about Ellayna and what possessed her mother to allow her to go on a podcast and talk about what happened to her—"

"Assuming she knew," Amara said.

"Or wondering when those guys in the SUV are going to show up looking for the flash drive."

"I thought you were safe there. Didn't the police follow them from the scene?"

"They couldn't catch them. The kidnappers got away." She should have called them killers. They'd murdered multiple people while trying to get what they wanted, with no regard for innocent lives. "Who knows what will happen next." She tried to sound nonchalant when she said, "What are you and Bruce working on now that you've gotten your deal resolved?"

"Nice try." Amara paused. "But...there is something I haven't been able to tell you. I wasn't sure if it would cause a problem. Bruce said I should've told you months ago, but I didn't want you to think I was a terrible person."

"You're a person who has lived their whole life in a war, and war makes you do things you never thought you'd have done." She wanted her mother to have lived a different life, not one fighting constantly against *Dominatus*. Playing both sides—sometimes simultaneously. "What did you do?"

Amara fell silent.

Kenna wondered if she even should've asked. There might be a better time to have this conversation or a better place both of them could be in. But the question was out now, and it was up to Amara whether she shared.

An alarm blared through the house, coming from speakers high on the wall that Kenna had noticed but didn't know what they were for.

"What is that?"

"I've got to go." She hung up on Amara and tugged out her earbuds as Jax raced back into the room. He caught her hand and helped her out of the chair quicker than she'd be able to manage. "What's going on?"

"Incoming. Two black SUVs coming down the lane." He was already walking toward the hall.

She rushed after him, heading to where they had stashed go bags for just in case. "Where's the third?"

"I don't plan to stay here long enough to find out."

Zeyla rushed in the front door. "Maizie!"

The young woman stumbled out of one of the bedroom doors a second before Preston emerged at the end of the hall, wiggling his feet into a pair of running shoes as he walked. He grabbed the strap of Maizie's backpack and righted it for her where she was struggling to get it on her shoulder.

Jax grabbed his duffel and Kenna's, and Preston tossed him the keys to their armored car.

Preston said, "Rendezvous point?"

Maizie, at the door with Zeyla now, glanced back. Fear on her face. Kenna said, "Go!" The two women would take the RV and use a fire road to escape the property. Kenna prayed the work Preston had done filling in potholes and smoothing out the rough dirt track had held.

"Yes." Jax grabbed Kenna's hand, and they headed for

the kitchen, out the side door to the covered car port that kept the car out of sight. It was far too heavily armored to be towed by the RV, so they had to drive separately, taking a different route Preston had mapped out.

But would they meet the third SUV on their way? Or would Maizie and Zeyla?

Preston ran out the door. "Get going! I'm going to check with the team, then I'll be gone, too."

Across the back lawn, the chopper engine whirred to life.

"Sure you don't want to fly?" Jax asked her over the roof of their car.

"No, I don't." She slid in the passenger's side. "Sure you feel okay to drive?"

"Adrenaline is a good pain reliever." He shoved the lever to drive and hit the gas.

"Until it dissipates, and you can't move because you hurt so bad."

"We'll burn that bridge when we come to it." He gripped the wheel with both hands, bumping over the grass toward a track that skirted the cornfield.

Kenna grabbed the door handle and held on.

Chapter Fourteen

J ax whipped the car around a tight corner.

Kenna held her breath, praying in her mind, which she hadn't stopped doing since they left the ranch.

He had his phone in the dash clip, the screen open to the walkie-talkie app. If Zeyla and Maizie or Preston hit the *talk* button on their devices, it would immediately play—about as live as it could get.

She scanned the terrain where the dirt track wound through tall pine trees that disguised them from anyone behind them for a few seconds after every bend. The sky had no clouds, just a mass of bright blue that looked more pleasant than this day was turning out to be.

No one was visible in the side mirror; the view of the road behind them was empty. But did that mean they were going to get out of here without running into anyone?

Kenna laid her free hand over the baby.

"You both okay?" Jax gripped the wheel, all his attention on the road. But not all his focus.

"We're fine," Kenna said. "Do you think whoever

planted these trees knew we'd be using them as cover for evasion?"

Jax hit the gas on a straight stretch of road. "Preston told me the house was owned by a guy from Chicago. It's the height of the Depression, and he leaves the city and settles in the middle of nowhere, Colorado? The house has a load of secret cupboards behind panels in the walls, and he told me there's a tunnel between the house and the barn. But it collapsed years ago, so it's unusable."

"A gangster from Chicago?" That sounded interesting. "He was probably fleeing the law or someone trying to kill him. Like a rival."

"Turns out he single-handedly revived the local economy. Hired residents to help out around the house. Threw parties and gave gifts to local food banks. The church. The medical center. He kept the people in this area from starving."

"Wow. A gangster Santa."

Jax chuckled. "Something like that."

"We should do that in Wyoming, where the cabin is. I mean, not the party stuff. The rest of it, though. Help people out if they need it. Give donations. That kind of thing."

He reached over and squeezed her knee. "It's a good idea, and a biblical concept. Providing for the poor, orphans, and widows."

"And such were some of you?" That was a biblical concept as well. No one could claim the higher ground. Everyone was an equal in the eyes of the Lord. No one was a worse sinner than anyone else, and no one could say they were better than another. Or more holy.

He gave her knee another squeeze. "Something like that." He flinched, his attention flicking to the rearview.

She looked at the side mirror. "I see them."

Jax hit the talk button on his phone screen. "We have company."

Kenna said, "One black SUV in pursuit," then she tapped the screen to turn off the talk function.

Maizie came back. "We haven't seen anyone yet. We're almost to the top of the ridge."

When she was done, Kenna responded, "Copy that. Stick to the plan." Then she said, "Preston? How do things look from the air?"

His connection was a whole lot louder than theirs. "Coming your way now, Kenna."

She held off replying and instead checked the progress of the SUV. "They're coming up behind us fast."

"We're faster."

"We're probably heavier, too. With all the armor plating."

"We're more maneuverable because we have so much more power."

She rolled her eyes. "Good, because they're going to kill us to get what they want."

Jax hit the gas, and they sped up. "I'm not going to let anything happen to you or Emma."

"That isn't her name."

"Charlotte."

"Nope."

"Madrid. No, Barcelona."

"Antigua is a cute name." Kenna bit her lips together to keep from laughing. "I'm still thinking about it."

"We should decide."

"What if we choose a name and, when she's born, she doesn't look like that's the right name for her?" Besides, it wasn't like this was the time to choose a name.

Even though she'd sort of already chosen one, it wasn't the time to tell him about that either.

Jax sighed loudly, but he seemed more amused than anything. "I hear the chopper."

Kenna tried to see it but didn't have much visibility out the windows, and there was no sunroof. "Probably above us."

"There." He pointed left, out the window beside him.

The chopper crested over the trees and passed above them, heading toward the SUV that was rapidly coming up behind them. She watched in the side mirror as whoever was on board opened fire at the SUV, spraying bullets at the hood, the windshield, and the roof of the vehicle.

After they'd gone overhead, someone leaned out the side window of the SUV with a rifle and opened fire on the helicopter. Return fire caught the guy, and he slumped down, still half out the window.

"That was close." Kenna gasped. "Helicopters just seem like spinning death traps."

Jax hurtled them around the corner in a spray of gravel that nearly sent them down an embankment. He corrected out of the skid. "Sorry."

"Don't be. You're doing better than I could."

"Wanna take an advanced driving course to refresh your skills?"

"Not really." She grinned. "Maybe it's super sexist or something, but I prefer it when you drive."

"Works for me." He pressed down on the gas, and they sped up again.

The SUV nearly went over the same edge they almost had, but the driver obviously had similar skills to Jax.

"Come on, Preston." She watched the rearview, giving her a limited scope of what was happening behind her.

There were more gunmen in that SUV, but they didn't fire. Maybe they knew her car had armor plating, so there was no point in firing at it and achieving nothing. Along with run-flat tires, the kind usually found in cars in war zones—the ones driven by the warlord. They weren't perfectly safe in this car, but it was as close as they could get.

The chopper swung into view in the air above the road, rapidly approaching the back of the SUV. They sprayed the vehicle with bullets again, security guys on either side of the helicopter's open doors—or windows. She couldn't see from this distance.

The rear window shattered, and the car swerved.

"Keep going," she urged Jax. "Don't slow down."

The SUV careened to the side and hit a tree.

One guy stumbled out, lifted his gun, and fired at the helicopter. It dipped in the air. Kenna gasped again. *Please don't let them shoot down the helicopter.* She watched it regain altitude, expecting a fireball but not seeing one before her eyes started to burn, and she had to blink.

"We're good," Preston said through the phone app.

Kenna started to let go of the tension she'd been holding.

"We aren't!" Maizie's voice came through loudly. "We have a vehicle behind us now!"

Preston said, "On our way."

The chopper banked and swung north, and she thanked God for paid security staff. And friends like Preston, who offered secret ranches. How these guys had found them, she didn't know. Probably some kind of tracker, or computer virus.

Jax eased off the gas pedal, turning the next corner much slower. Thanks to a satellite internet connection, she saw on the dash screen that they weren't far from the highway. Pretty soon, they'd be safe on the blacktop. Or as safe as they could be, she supposed.

For now.

The chopper flew over the treetops toward where the two women were in the RV, making their own way to the rendezvous. Kenna pressed her lips together and prayed for them in her mind, while Jax navigated to the highway.

About a quarter mile from the end of the dirt track, where it met the blacktop, her phone rang.

"It's Ryson." She put it on speaker. "You've got me and Jax."

"Hey, guys."

Jax said, "Everything okay?"

"I paid a visit to the Feathers family. Mom, name is Crystal, Ellayna, and her brother, Abe. They aren't at home."

Kenna frowned. "As in, she's at work, Ellayna is at school, and Abe is at daycare?" It was early in the day still, but it was possible they got where they were going for the day soon after they woke.

"No signs of a break-in. So, there's that." Ryson didn't sound happy with the lack of results on this search. "But I talked to the neighbor, and she said there was a van outside the house a few nights ago. She only saw that, though. Not that they got into it. But she hasn't seen them since. Doesn't know why they wouldn't be home lately."

"Maybe they went to stay with someone?" Crystal Feathers might have a boyfriend or someone she took the kids to see. Like her mother or the kids' other grandma.

"The neighbor told me about Abe's dad. I'm going to pay him a visit now. I just wanted to keep you updated."

"Thanks." Kenna didn't like this. "What about phones? Any way to get the numbers so we can trace them?"

"Not without probable cause for a warrant. I'll open a missing person case and see how far I get."

"We appreciate it," Jax said. "I'd hate to think that her going on that podcast put them in danger."

Kenna nodded. "Me, too."

"I'll keep you updated."

"Thanks." Kenna looked at the screen, but Ryson had already ended the call. "He sounded exhausted."

"Broken sleep and worry."

She smiled. "I guess we have all kinds of fun to look forward to."

"I can't wait." He reached over and held her hand, navigating the dirt road with one hand on the wheel.

"I want to go to Salt Lake City and help him look for them."

Jax's fingers flexed between hers. "They might not be missing, or unsafe. I'd rather chase down this podcaster."

There was also the accomplice she might have missed all those years ago, in the previous case the podcaster had revisited. And the SUV guys on this stretch of dirt, trying to get the flash drive and port. The device was currently in a box on the back seat of this car, so they could drop it off.

"After we give the software company their tech back, and halfheartedly try to convince them we didn't already release everything on the internet, we should go to Salt Lake City. We have a few days, so why not see if there's a way we can help?"

"I'm not going without the others, and we need to see if Zeyla and Maizie get through this unscathed first."

He was right. They didn't know what was happening with the RV and the chopper. *Lord, help them, please.* Just like they didn't know what was happening with Ramon and the guys from Miami Security International.

"We need to ID the podcaster and send the information for that case you worked to local law enforcement." He glanced at her for a second, then slowed for the blacktop. He pulled out onto the barren road and set off, going north toward the rendezvous where Maizie and Zeyla should meet them.

"True." She still wanted to know that Ellayna was all right—before she tried to talk some sense into the girl. "But if something happened to their family because of the podcast—"

"Not because of you. As long as you know that."

"I know." She nodded. "I still want to try and help." She reached over and hit the talk button. "How is it going, Maze?"

Kenna waited a few seconds, plenty long enough. Assuming they weren't otherwise indisposed.

She tapped the button again. "Preston, can we get an update?"

Nothing.

She twisted in her seat, scanning the sky in the direction they should be. "I don't see his helicopter."

"We shouldn't have split up. We should've stayed together."

She wanted to point out that what he was feeling happened to be exactly what she felt in hearing the hospital in Pueblo had exploded, but now might not be the time to commiserate about caring for someone who regularly put themselves in dangerous situations.

Instead, she said, "Zeyla won't let anything happen to Maizie."

"I'm more worried about her driving the RV." He tried to make light of it, but it didn't quite work.

Jax hit the gas pedal again, probably breaking the speed

limit. They sped around a bend in the highway and passed a parked cop car. The officer held a radar gun pointed at them.

"Uh-oh." Kenna watched in the side mirror as the officer pulled out, following them. Red-and-blue lights turned on, and the siren started. "We could tell him my water broke, and I'm in labor."

"He'll try to escort us to the hospital." Jax braked and eased to the side of the street.

"Good point. The truth?"

"Worth a try." He stopped the car partly on the shoulder.

The cop parked behind them and climbed out of his car. Jax had the registration in hand before the cop started toward them, leaving the glove box hanging open. She closed it so he wouldn't see the pistol tucked there. Jax slid the driver's license from his wallet and eased his window down.

"Of course, we're going to get a speeding ticket after fleeing armed gunmen." She didn't know whether to laugh or be annoyed.

The cop came into view by the back window.

She heard another vehicle, probably just someone driving on the highway. Or she thought so until the cop stopped by Jax's window.

A second later, a black SUV slammed into him with a sickening thud.

The SUV blurred past, going way too fast. No time for anyone to avoid the intentional hit-and-run.

The cop slammed to the ground in front of their car, a ragged mess.

Kenna screamed, covering her mouth with her hands.

The SUV driver hit the brakes and swerved the car

around in an arc, stopping with the driver's side visible. Two windows lowered, and automatic weapons were pointed out at them.

Jax raised his window.

Muzzle flashes. The relentless *pop-pop* of rounds slamming into the car, rocking the vehicle.

Kenna ducked her head, but the armor held. The window caught bullets but didn't shatter. The rounds barely made indents in the clear material, but the illusion of safety wouldn't last.

She slid her phone from the cupholder and called 911.

"If we go, they'll keep chasing us."

Kenna said, "We can't wait for Preston." The call connected. "We need help! We're being shot at, and one of your highway patrol officers is down! He was—" A lump clogged her throat, and she had to cough it out.

"Officers are en route."

"If you have a helicopter, send it! And SWAT." She had to breathe. *My baby.* "These people won't stop until we're dead."

The phone fell from her hands.

Jax grabbed the gun from the glove compartment.

She grasped his elbow. "Don't get out." She didn't want to be in the car all by herself. She also couldn't stand to sit here, doing nothing to help, while he faced down armed men to keep her and the baby safe, risking his life for them.

"I could climb in the back, use the car for cover, and shoot them over the roof."

"They should've installed turret guns with all the bells and whistles on this thing." She had to distract herself somehow from thinking about the three men now approaching them.

Each man fired round after round at the body of the car.

The windows. Any point of weakness they thought they could find, including the gas tank cover.

If one of them shot into the tank, would it ignite and explode?

Surely, there were safety measures in place.

Lord, help us. She needed the police to get here as quick as they could. *Please don't let us be too far out.* She'd never prayed for the police to show at a scene as hard as she did just then.

And yet, part of her still wanted to be with Maizie and Zeyla, helping them. Or asking Preston to come here. But they couldn't.

They would keep each other safe. She and Jax were on their own.

A man rounded the car to her side and tried the door. *Locked.* He jiggled the handle like he wanted to tear it off, and when it didn't open, he lifted his weapon and fired at the window. Shooting at her from point-blank range.

The bullets embedded themselves in the window, but it didn't break.

She wanted to curl forward and cover her head. That wouldn't help her if this guy got through the car's security measures.

One of the others hammered the butt of his gun on Jax's window. Another man climbed on the hood and kicked at the spot that had been shot already, trying to weaken that point and get through the window.

Jax put the car in drive and hit the gas, going forward a few feet and then stopping sharply. The man on the hood fell to the side.

Red-and-blue flashing lights and the sound of police sirens drew her attention and that of the men around the car.

The cavalry had arrived.

She watched out the windshield at a stream of police vehicles, three of them, speeding up the road toward their car. Jax grabbed the wheel and started the car moving so the police cars passed them, and he pulled over with the police and gunmen behind them now.

He twisted in his seat. "One just hit a guy. Payback."

She winced.

"They're taking care of it." He covered her shaky hand with his. "We're good. We're safe."

Kenna wasn't so sure about that.

Chapter Fifteen

The entire aircraft shuddered under him. Ramon grabbed the seat handles, while the rest of the guys held their drinks up so they wouldn't spill and continued their conversation like nothing had happened.

Bear, sitting opposite him, eyed Ramon. "Not a comfortable flier?"

"I'm fine." Ramon managed to bite out the words. Pretty sure he could keep from puking if he had to.

Bear said, "You square on what we're doing?"

Ramon understood well enough, he was just surprised no one cared he was coming with them. Or they didn't care that he was going to report back to Kenna what they were doing at some point. Probably once they'd actually achieved more than kidnapping a janitor. "I don't get how we went from a guy with no fingerprints to a town in Norway that's supposed to have the *Dominatus* accountant in it. The rest of it, I have it straight."

He needed Bear to explain it all over again, but only so that Ramon could listen and focus on not freaking out.

The plane shook again with the turbulence that came from traveling over mountain peaks, through changes in air temperature and pressure.

"The janitor has no name," Bear said. "Not even Hazel could find out who he is. With burned off fingerprints and no way to access any dental records, given those are private, we took blood samples and did some genetic testing."

"And it came back positive for Norway?"

Bear smiled slightly. "Kind of." He shrugged one shoulder. "The World Health Organization has been doing a study on herd immunity in Norway and discovered a group of people with a unique genetic code that protects them from getting things like chicken pox and measles. They all live in the town of Vinterdal, up in the mountains. The terrain is sufficient that it necessitates parachuting in."

"Great."

Bear seemed to find that amusing.

"But it's only interesting in the sense that *Dominatus* has likely been testing and doing research on these people for generations, and this is the result. But it doesn't mean this is where their accountant lives."

Bear nodded. "You're right that they are likely guinea pigs in a larger experiment. But the results drew some notice, and their genetic code ended up as a matter of public record. So, when we ran the janitor's DNA, we got a hit with the people in this town."

"It's a reach from there to the accountant."

"Not if they're brothers."

Ramon frowned. "You know that?"

"It's close enough with Vinterdal; they don't intermarry much with outsiders, so their genetics are much purer than the average person in the US—at least that's what they claim. The information you downloaded from that computer network in the office building yielded some encrypted communications between someone we believe is a Grand Master with *Dominatus* and the accountant."

Bear lifted the mug from the tiny airplane table beside his chair and took a sip. "The communication originated in this town. The IP address leads us to a guy called Lief Holmberg. Fifty-four years old. Excellent health. Several degrees in advanced math and accounting. He fought in the Norwegian army for a decade right out of school. This is a guy who can take care of himself, and he's incredibly smart."

"So we parachute in at night and hope we catch him off guard."

Bear tipped his head to the side. "Pretty much."

"He's who you've been looking for, this Lief Holmberg guy?" Ramon wanted to believe one man could make or break the fight against *Dominatus*, but given who those people were, it was highly unlikely this would succeed.

"He's their weakest link."

"Doesn't seem weak to me."

Bear said, "That's the point. If this guy is the weakest link in *Dominatus*, then we've got our work cut out for us. He won't go down without a fight. But it's the only thing that connects the entire organization. It's like a spider web, but each time we find a thread, it seems like it isn't connected to anything. Holmberg is the one weaving the threads together." Bear pushed out of the chair. "We're thirty minutes out. Everyone, gear up."

They'd given Ramon a pair of black cargo pants and a

fitted black shirt, under which he had base layers to keep the warmth close to his body. Each team member donned a protective vest and strapped on weapons and extra ammo. He was carrying his pistol and nothing else except a knife Hollace handed over.

Ramon pulled on a beanie and gloves. Hollace handed him wraparound safety glasses, and Ramon made a face.

"For the jump."

Right. "Thanks."

"Been a while."

"Since I went on an op?"

Hollace shook his head. "Since you parachuted."

Ramon said, "I've never parachuted."

"Bear!"

Ramon kept himself from flinching.

Hollace yelled over his shoulder, "Our man needs a tandem jump! It's his first time."

"Explain it," Ramon argued. "Give me the instructions, and I'll be fine."

Hollace looked at him like he'd grown a second head. "We train for stuff like this for years. You don't learn it in three minutes."

"Good thing we have ten."

"We don't." Bear eased between his guys. "The headwind picked up, and we caught a current."

"So talk fast."

Bear stopped in front of him. "This is a terrible idea."

"At least I'm not on your insurance plan."

"That just means you're a liability." Bear shook his head. "I'm gonna regret this."

"Just think." One of the other guys clapped Bear on the shoulder. "If he bites it, he can't report back to Kenna what we're doing."

Bear winced.

Ramon wasn't going to deny it. "I haven't contacted her yet, and I'm not going to."

Of course, he would eventually. He didn't work for them. His loyalty had Kenna as a filter. At least, until he trusted himself to see the truth in people.

He'd been wrong before—so wrong. But he didn't want to be wrong about these guys.

So he lied. "She and I have parted ways. I don't work for her anymore. Otherwise, I'd be wherever she is, pitching in with the case she's working."

Their boss had been revealed to be the one turncoat working for their enemy, so he figured he was good with the rest. They were most likely trustworthy.

But he was still going to watch his own back.

Ramon reached over and grabbed the parachute from Hollace's hands. "Now explain this."

Ten minutes later, he was sailing through the air because Hollace, laughing, pushed Ramon out of the plane.

Ice-cold wind whipped at his face and clothing. He tried to remember what Bear had said, but it really amounted to "Pull the cord."

That, and "It's not the fall that will kill you. It's the sudden stop."

Ramon counted in his head and, as they'd instructed, waited until the right moment to pull the chute free.

His entire body jerked back up in the air, the parachute caught the wind, and he descended much slower.

He held the toggles and looked around at the others, dropping silently in the night sky. "I hate all of you guys."

Of course, there was no way they would hear him. That wasn't the point.

He steered the chute in a straight line, and when he

neared the ground, he pulled both toggles down to flare the parachute. The action pulled the back of the chute down and allowed him to touch down.

Going too far too fast.

His knees came up quick, and he fell awkwardly to the side, mostly on purpose. All around him, the guys landed on both feet like freaking gymnasts.

Hollace bundled his chute up and stuffed it back in the pack so they wouldn't leave anything behind to let anyone know they had been here. He came over while Ramon was rolling his and helped him repack it. "Not bad for a first time."

Ramon matched the guy's volume when he replied, "I'm never doing that again."

Hollace's teeth flashed in the dark. Not quite a laugh, but Ramon got the idea. The other man slapped him on the arm with the back of his hand. "Come on."

Ramon jogged after them, and the group moved as a unit through the shadows off this ridge, which turned out to be a rolling green hill. Not that he could see the color in the gray night, but they were running on grass that muted their footsteps.

Bear wound up beside Ramon, probably so he could keep an eye on him. Or make sure Ramon didn't shoot any of these guys in the back.

The lead operator reached a barn that had been constructed with what looked like cobblestones. A huge wooden wheel leaned against the doors.

They all crept around the back, hopped a four-foot brick wall, and traversed two fields—one with sheep and the other with cows in it. Ramon tried not to think about what he was stepping in and kept up the punishing pace these guys set. He'd never been in the military. There wasn't much call for exercise while working for a Mexican cartel, at least not the traditional strength training and cardio most people did. He should probably start working out on a regular basis.

Ramon glanced at an oak tree they passed, craning his neck.

Bear grabbed his shoulder and dragged him into a crouch. He whistled at the same time. Everyone in the party crouched immediately, with nearly no sound.

Ramon whispered, "What is it?"

Bear flicked on a tiny light and shone it above them, in the tree. Hanging down from the branches under the canopy were strings of something that glinted in the light. It looked like decorations of some kind, crystals or glass.

Ramon stood slowly and reached for one. At the same time, the crystal burned and felt cold to the touch. He let go too quickly, the pads of his fingers sliding across the tacky surface. He hissed and dropped back into his crouch.

Bear shone his light on Ramon's fingers, now wet with blood and too many cuts. Pain echoed through Ramon's mind more than his fingers, which seemed almost numb. Or as if the nerve endings couldn't tell what had happened. His hand looked like he'd tried to catch a bunch of razor blades thrown at him.

He hissed through clenched teeth, and his head swam.

Bear slapped a bandage on his hand and wrapped the ends around his fingers, tying it off. "You good to go, or you wanna head back?"

"I'm good."

"Okay." He didn't sound convinced.

Ramon stood slowly, making sure he didn't accidentally touch the tree decorations again. It was crazy dangerous having something like that hanging from a tree. Whatever kind of people did that, they had no concern for animals or local kids who might get interested and wind up bleeding.

He shook his head as they walked, wondering if it was some odd kind of booby trap. Or a warning to strangers.

The hillside descended sharply, and they continued going down, exposed to the open between trees and the odd building. They passed a broken-down outbuilding, and as they neared a larger structure, he realized it was a farm with shattered windows and no one home.

Another half mile past that, they came to a squat building in the middle of nowhere.

"This is it," Bear said. "The IP address came from here." He peered at the screen of his phone, the brightness turned as low as it would go.

"It's a shed." Probably an abandoned one, at that.

"Let's knock and see who's home." One of the guys approached the door.

Ramon looked around but didn't see anyone moving in the dark. He highly doubted there was someone sitting in that shed. His hand stung, and this whole situation seemed odd.

Was this where they would find the *Dominatus* accountant?

The operative approached the shed, reaching for the handle. A step before he could grab it, he let out a little yelp.

In front of their disbelieving eyes, he fell beneath the ground.

Chapter Sixteen

Ramon army crawled across the grass until he was close enough that he could see over the edge. "What on earth?"

This was a deep hole. The ground was almost frozen solid, and yet somehow, their guy had fallen through a false floor into...

He couldn't see the bottom. Their teammate wasn't making any noise, and Ramon couldn't hear movement.

Bear shouldered up beside him and shone that flashlight of his down the hole.

Ramon sniffed a breath in through his nose. "Dang."

Kenna was rubbing off on him. Helping him clean up his language. He'd put off accepting the rest of what she was offering, unsure a guy like him could ever accept redemption. *Especially* when it was a free gift. He didn't know what to make of it.

What he did know was that falling fifteen feet onto sharp spikes ended a man's life in a gruesome way.

Bear rolled over onto his back and stared up at the sky full of stars. "We need to get him out of the hole." He spoke loudly enough the others could hear it, including the crack in his tone.

Ramon didn't see how they were going to get him out without some serious work. He wanted to get across the hole and into the shed, just in case there really was something to find in there. He pushed up from his supine position and looked around, half wondering if they were about to be picked off by gunfire.

He eased his way around the hole, looking at the edge versus the step in front of the shed. If he breached the door, would it explode in his face?

Only one way to find out.

Ramon saw the others had taken his place on the ground at the edge of the hole. All working as a team to retrieve their man from the place where he died, so they could return him home to his loved ones.

Ramon wanted to be sick.

Another life lost to the fight against *Dominatus.*

It was tempting to believe that one more lost life didn't matter, especially if it was him, provided the end result was that *Dominatus* was destroyed. Taken down. Obliterated. He could agree with these guys on the need for that, as well as understand why Kenna couldn't be the one to take on that fight right now.

Ramon grabbed the door handle for the shed and used it to steady himself on the step. There were a few inches of dirt and grass between him and that murderous hole, but he didn't want to risk stepping on it if he didn't have to.

He slid a lock-pick kit from the thigh pocket of his cargoes and stuck one part in his mouth while he returned the case to his pocket, then he went to town on the lock. A few seconds later, he heard it click. "Flashlight."

Bear looked up at him.

Ramon held out his hand. Bear tossed him the light, and he turned the handle. He ducked his head, eased the door open slowly, and went inside the shed.

Gardening tools were stacked in one corner. Nothing resembled a desk amidst the shelves of yard detritus. Terracotta pots, gardening gloves, stacks of soil. The whole place smelled like musty dirt.

Ramon shone the flashlight around, looking for a computer port in the wall, where the accountant might have plugged a laptop in for a second. Any kind of cabling. There wasn't even a light bulb in the eaves of the small roof.

He crouched and assessed the floor, looking for seams that might indicate a secret area hidden beneath, but he didn't find anything.

He went back to the door where Hollace stood on the far side of the opening, tying off a rope around his waist.

"Nothing in here," Ramon said. "You're going down there?"

Hollace nodded and tossed the rope to his friends, who formed a line to lower him down.

Bear backed up like he was standing guard. "Nothing?"

"Not even power."

The team boss didn't look happy, and Ramon didn't blame him. He stayed where he was and looked around at the terrain. Rolling hills. Old abandoned farmhouses. About a quarter mile away, a building had a light on upstairs. Possibly a house, but he would need to get closer before he could tell for sure.

He continued scanning, looking for movement. Wishing he had Maizie to call for help. How were they supposed to find one guy in this place with nothing but an IP address?

"You guys don't have access to satellites, do you? We

could use some heat signatures to point us in the right direction."

Bear watched Hollace descend into the hole. "I'll call Hazel." He palmed his phone and put it to his ear. "Yeah. We need a pickup for Smythe. He didn't make it." Bear sucked in a breath through his teeth, the hiss audible.

Bear had lost a teammate months ago. Maybe more than a year, actually. Ramon didn't know exactly. After Allie's death, he'd gone off the map. For what, no one knew. Now that he was back, he might be finally dealing with the grief, but more on top would only compound the issue.

From in the hole, Hollace said, "Okay, toss me the rope to secure him."

Ramon grabbed the edge of the doorframe and jumped over to where Bear stood. "Let's go check out that house while these guys are busy." He motioned to the farmhouse next door with the light on.

"Got it." He put the phone away. "Keep working. We'll be back."

The guy at the front of the rope said, "Got it, boss."

Bear set off for the occupied house, walking in stiff movements like he wanted to kick a door in, drag someone out of bed, and punch them until they gave him some answers.

"We don't know who is in there," Ramon said. "They could be innocent."

"I'm wondering if anyone in this town would turn out to be innocent."

"Depends on if there actually *is* anyone in this town."

Bear looked at him, still walking. He slowed a little. "Huh. Let's find out, I guess."

Ramon shrugged. They tromped across the damp grass to the front door, and Bear shoved him out of the way so he could kick it open. That was certainly one way to get out the frustration he was feeling.

Ramon pulled his pistol, holding aim in front of him because he didn't want even a second to pass before pulling the trigger. This wasn't a normal situation—not even close. One of the MSI guys was dead, and whoever was in here knew something.

They cleared the ground floor and headed up the thin staircase with the spindle wood railing. A cat meowed from the top of the stairs, but it only swished its tail as they passed.

The yellow light he'd seen from outside was from the upstairs hall. Each room revealed décor but no people, until the last and biggest.

Side by side, they lay on the bed, holding hands over the covers. Frilly, floral bedspread. Flowers on the wallpaper. A pedestal lamp with a tasseled lampshade. Curtains pulled closed. They both wore pajamas, and their faces showed evidence of a long life. Hopefully, one of love and family, not terror and pain.

"They look like they're asleep." Bear stepped into the room and took a side step, not getting any closer.

Ramon didn't need to check for a pulse. "They've been dead awhile."

The couple looked to be in their seventies or eighties and lay in their bed as if they'd died in their sleep at the same time.

"Maybe everyone in this town is dead."

"I hope not." Ramon headed for the door. "It's hard to interrogate a dead person."

Down the stairs. Back outside.

"Everything about this town is wrong."

Bear emerged from the house, closing the door behind

him. "We might have to go house to house and check everywhere. I don't like going home empty-handed." His phone buzzed. "Yeah, Hazel."

Her voice came from the speaker, so Ramon could hear it as well. "Half a klick to the west, there's a signal that just started broadcasting." She sniffed. "Is Smythe really gone?"

"Tell me about the signal," Bear instructed.

"Someone initiated a connection a few minutes ago that I picked up."

"Sounds like we've got a live one," Ramon said. "Tell us how to get there."

They raced along a single asphalt lane between two short brick walls that were probably built over a hundred years ago. Moss-covered and damp, the whole place would look peaceful and beautiful in the daylight, but right now, he couldn't help thinking it seemed almost deadly.

Hazel directed them to another structure, one that looked a lot like all the other country-style farmhouse buildings. This one had a post office box outside, or what amounted to it in this part of the world.

But when they neared, Ramon heard a high-pitched whir.

He tackled Bear just as gunfire erupted out of the mail slot, aimed right at them. Both of them slammed into the ground, and Ramon kept going so he wasn't on top of the big guy. Bear lifted his shoulders off the ground, raised his gun, and fired.

The shooting stopped.

"Now we're talking." Bear scrambled up and raced at full speed for the door.

It gave under the sheer force of his body. The door fell in, and he landed on it. "Hands up!"

Ramon raced in just as Bear stood.

"I said, hands up!"

Ramon wasn't totally limping, but it was close. Landing on Bear felt like landing on boulders—after falling twenty feet.

He backed up his associate, sweeping the room, while Bear kept aim on the man standing behind the counter.

Older guy, wearing a dark wool sweater that had been knitted. Gray scruff of a beard on his face. Light eyes. Not much hair. He said something in Norwegian—or so Ramon would guess.

"We don't speak your language," Ramon said. "English? Or Spanish?" He didn't lower his gun much.

Bear said, "English," before the guy could answer.

"How can I help you, gentlemen?" He spoke in heavily accented English. Not a computer in sight on the counter. Just an old-style cash register that probably dated back to World War II.

"We're looking for someone." Ramon kept half his attention on the room around him, just in case someone else was lurking. Or this place had a secret room, where the shed hadn't. More booby traps were also an option. "Maybe you can help us."

"I'm the only one here." The old man kept his hands on the counter, in plain view, and didn't move them.

Smart.

Ramon focused on him and got a vibe from the look in the man's eyes, not to mention the way he was standing like there weren't two men in his shop with guns pointed at him.

Bear said, "You can come with us, then. Answer some questions to our satisfaction, and we'll let you go."

"I knew you'd come eventually."

"Did you." Not a question. Bear didn't seem in the mood for a long, drawn-out conversation.

"Let's go." Ramon went behind the counter and took the man's elbow.

He checked around the guy and on the floor. Just in case he was standing on an explosive pressure plate, or some other crazy situation they hadn't thought of.

"We're clear." Ramon motioned with his head. "Boss?"

Bear knew that meant him, but for a second, he looked distracted. "Copy that."

Someone was talking over comms, and Ramon couldn't hear it?

"Anything I should know?"

Bear shook his head. He backed up two steps and stood guard while Ramon walked the man to the door of the post office.

He couldn't help wondering why the guy all of a sudden did something that could be traced back to him. Leading them right to him—with the help of Hazel. A man had died, but nothing else about this seemed like a trap. It almost seemed like Lief Holmberg wanted to be captured.

"Let's go," Bear said. "Time to get out of this crazy town."

Chapter Seventeen

Salt Lake City, Utah

Kenna put her hands on her hips. She was surrounded by rows of trailers, campers, and RVs lined up in the small campsite, but she had her attention on a particular one. More specifically, the RV that belonged to her.

It had been two days since their run-in with that gunman. Since the state police had swooped in and arrested those men. She wanted to kiss the car for protecting them from the attack, but it wasn't the vehicle that saved them—it was the Lord.

She'd thought then that a speeding ticket would be the worst of it, but after the cop was killed, they hadn't been able to simply drive away. The police had dragged them in to make statements while Kenna worried if Maizie and Zeyla were okay.

"This thing needs some serious repairs." She shook her

head at the bullet holes down the side of the RV. The one shattered window in the door. "But I'm glad it isn't you that needs a patch-up." She tugged Maizie over, gave her a hug, and kissed the side of her head.

"Me, too," Maizie said. "It was pretty scary, but when Preston flew over and they obliterated that SUV, I knew we'd be okay."

Kenna loved the mountains surrounding them and the cool temperature of winter. Today was a dry day, but snow that had fallen the week before now sat in dirty clumps on the corners between the rows of campers which had been salted to keep people from slipping or cars from sliding into each other.

She wouldn't mind seeing snow, even if it meant wearing a hat and gloves. "I felt the same when I saw the chopper come to help us. And when that SUV hit the cop who pulled us over, it happened again when the police showed up." Tears sparked in her eyes, and she swiped one from the corner. "Jax was amazing." She glanced over her shoulder where he sat in the front seat of their car. It didn't look much better than the RV right now.

He had his laptop open, probably using a hot spot on his phone, looking up routes to local hospitals just in case she went into labor while they were here.

"He fended off those guys until the police came."

Zeyla strode around the front of the RV like this was any other day. "The neighbor wanted to know if we're here to cause trouble. I wasn't really sure how to answer that since you told me lying is bad."

Kenna held back the smile that wanted to emerge. "I'm not planning to cause trouble. I'm planning to find a family that might be missing, but don't share about the case either."

Zeyla shrugged. "They might know something. You never know."

"True."

Maizie looked at Kenna. "Should I interview people here?"

"You could, if you want to work on your skills. But I'd rather meet up with Ryson and see where he's at with looking for Crystal and the kids, now that we're here."

She'd been reading over the file from that other case on the drive and running through what she might've missed since she'd heard the details of the investigation recounted on the podcast.

"I have a report typed up for us to pass on to the Montana State Police."

Maizie said, "Send it to me, and I'll forward it to them."

"Thanks."

Kenna didn't like that she might've missed an accomplice, but justice would be found, regardless. It wasn't like she had to bring the guy in herself. There were plenty of good cops in the world. The kind who showed up to help a pregnant woman and her husband on the side of the road in Colorado.

Zeyla asked, "What happened to the flash drive and the port?"

Kenna went to the picnic table and sat on the bench. "Maizie copied everything on it."

"Already posted it to the internet." The young woman hopped up on the table and sat with her legs swinging under her. "So now everyone knows what that software company was doing. Even if they were working for *Dominatus*, we put a serious crimp in it by making it public knowledge."

"I enjoy ruining the plans of people who prey on

others." Zeyla folded her arms, looking every bit like the warrior she was. But on occasion, she allowed them to see the softer edges of who she could be.

All of them—Zeyla, Maizie, and Kenna—had been through so much. They'd walked different paths but become people who had hard edges and soft, vulnerable places. Still, Zeyla was one of the most complicated women Kenna had ever met.

"Me, too." Kenna nodded. "If there's something going on with the Feathers family, we're going to find out what it is. It might feel like a small case compared to a lot of what we've been doing lately, but it's important. Maybe even more important than fighting *Dominatus* on a global scale."

Which was, if she was honest, something she couldn't—or shouldn't—be doing right now. Kenna needed to feel like her life meant something. That motherhood didn't mean giving up who she was. It had to be about expanding that person, not contracting her to where she couldn't do what she felt she'd been called to do.

She and God were working out the details, but helping Ellayna meant something to her. Actually, it meant a whole lot right now.

"I need to call Ryson if he hasn't called me back yet."

Maizie looked at her phone. "He's almost here. Unlike Ramon, who has dropped off the map and gone completely dark, Ryson let me add him to our tracking app, so we should all be able to see where he is."

Zeyla shifted her weight from one foot to the other. "You just drop that in there like it's no big deal? Ramon is off the map. We have no idea where he is or what he's doing."

"He knows how to take care of himself." Kenna didn't need to point that out, but sometimes, they all needed the reminder. "I'm praying he's safe and successful. And that he reports in soon." She looked at Maizie, who, surprisingly, hadn't cowered under the intensity of Zeyla's opinion.

Maybe Zeyla had softened a little, but Maizie had definitely grown stronger in the past year or so. She'd adopted some self-confidence and independence. The kind that gave her a backbone.

Kenna nudged her. "You said Ryson is almost here?"

Maizie showed her the screen. The dot that was her friend pulled off the freeway and turned into the lot where the entrance to the campsite was located. This place wasn't big. She could walk a circuit of the campsite in fifteen minutes, and that included going out the entrance and then coming back in, but the place had good showers and laundry facilities. It wasn't the kind of place to have a baby, but that was what hospitals were for.

A silver Toyota slowed to a stop on the single lane at the end of where they stood between the RV and the car—which they'd parked in the space they rented beside it so they could have more room.

Kenna stood as Ryson climbed from the front seat of his car. As she approached, he shook his head. "Never thought I'd see this. But then, I thought that about you in a wedding dress." His mouth stretched into a wide smile; he looked so pleased to see her.

She took in her friend, one of her closest ones for years. They'd met during a hostage situation at a bank back when she'd been an FBI agent and he a police officer. Since then, he'd been promoted and shifted positions. He'd had a family, and she was about to have her first child.

Life moved on, but they were kindred spirits, and what she felt for him never wavered.

"Javier." She spread her arms, and they hugged.

"You're about to have this baby any day, and you come here?"

She found a snooty expression. "There's a hospital here, and it's better than the Podunk medical center where our cabin is." She thumbed over her shoulder at where Jax was but realized he was standing beside her now.

Her husband said, "And if we call the police because we're being shot at, the response time is quicker here."

Kenna pressed her lips together. Jax and Javier Ryson did that man-hug, back-slapping thing and greeted each other like long-lost brothers. They'd known each other as well before she'd met Jax. In fact, Ryson was the one who'd connected them. Through a case, though. Not as a setup.

"Pregnancy is making me nostalgic." She shook her head, unable to believe she was nearly crying again. "This whole thing is ridiculous."

Ryson laughed. "Because you have feelings now?"

She shoved his shoulder. "Quick, talk about work."

Ryson eyed her, an amused expression on his face. "I'd rather discuss why your vehicles look like you've been in a war zone."

"You and everyone else we've met on the way here." Jax shook his head. "But a rental wouldn't have the armor plating Kenna's life requires."

Ryson grinned.

Kenna said, "Let's get out of the cold and have a warm drink. You can fill us in on the search for Ellayna and her family."

She strode to the RV and let Maizie and Zeyla in ahead of her. Or rather, she tried to. The two women wanted to say hi to Ryson first, so she wound up standing there holding the door open.

Their cat, Jolene, ever the intrepid adventurer who

went everywhere with them. Mostly just so she could hide in the corner by the bed—on Jax's side, of course. The cat chose now to emerge from the bedroom and stand by the door.

"No, no, baby. Don't go outside." Kenna shooed her back in and let the door shut behind her. She wasn't able to drink caffeinated coffee right now, but she brewed a pot for the others and made herself instant that was decaf. It tasted good enough and smelled like the java her father had always drunk, so she found solace in nostalgia again. As soon as she could after the baby was born, she was going to have the biggest cup of coffee she could find. And then take an epic nap.

The others came in and settled at the table, but Jax came over and slid his arm around her. "Hey."

She smiled. "Hey."

He dropped a quick kiss on her lips, and she left him to finish the coffee. She took a seat in the passenger's chair, which had been rotated around to face the back.

"Okay," Kenna said. "What's the word on Ellayna?"

Ryson shifted on the seat opposite from Zeyla and Maizie. He shook his head. "We can go to the house. I think you might want to see it, actually. But they haven't been there in days. I went to Crystal's work. She's the receptionist for a tire sales company. They haven't seen her at all this week, and she hasn't called in. The kids haven't been to school or daycare."

"So, no sign of them in days?"

He nodded.

Kenna didn't like the sound of that.

Maizie said, "I can check her bank activity, any credit cards. Can we get into their phones and see if they're being used, or if we can get a location from those?"

Ryson said, "I'm going to see the judge about a warrant this afternoon."

She knew that tone. "While we do what?"

"Crystal's boyfriend works at a T-shirt printing company downtown."

"You haven't talked to him?" Kenna asked.

Ryson said, "He won't talk to the cops. But I know for a fact that he'll talk to you."

Chapter Eighteen

K enna stared at her friend. "You think he knows something?"

"If anyone can find out, it's you." Ryson took the full mug from Jax, who handed over hers at the same time.

"Thanks."

Jax leaned against the closed door and sipped from his mug. "We need a rental car. Maybe two."

Kenna frowned over her drink, the scent making her think of her dad's face with a scruff of beard and the flannel shirts he always wore. She found she missed him at odd times and in strange ways, like the smell of his coffee. If she thought about how he would never get to meet her daughter, she would start to cry, so instead she focused on the family this baby would have and asked, "Why do we need more cars?"

"You and Zeyla can go see the boyfriend."

Ryson said, "His name is Marcus Neerwood."

Jax continued, "I have an appointment at the prison to see Gerald Rickshire."

"They called you back?"

He nodded. "When I was mapping the hospital. I'm not excited to go our separate ways this afternoon, but if you take Zeyla with you and you're within twenty minutes of a hospital..."

"You think I'm going to have the baby this afternoon?"

"I think stress isn't good. But neither is being cooped up in a car for days. When you get out and stretch your legs, things are going to compound, and who knows what will happen."

Kenna folded one arm over her baby bump and held the mug with the other. "Hopefully, no gunmen, murderers, hitmen, assassins, ninjas, explosions, random crimes, fire of any kind..."

"We get it." Jax grinned. "I'm not being paranoid. I'm being prepared."

She loved that he cared about what happened to her. "I'll be safe with Zeyla, and we'll take the tank-car."

Zeyla seemed pleased that Kenna intended to rely on her.

"I'll stay here," Maizie said, looking kind of relieved. "Keep an eye on the RV and work on the financials."

Ryson said, "I'll have the police department tech connect with you. Maybe you can team up?"

Maizie nodded. "All right."

"We should pray before we part ways and get to work on this." Kenna had a fear and desperation in her that drove her to do what it took to find someone. But that had to be tempered with prayer. With trusting that God had the whole situation in His hands. She'd yielded her life to Him, and that meant every part of it was now under the umbrella of His sovereignty.

Jax shifted closer and held her hand. He prayed aloud

for their protection and for success in the investigation, then for Ellayna, Abe, and Crystal, that they would be safe wherever they were. That they wouldn't be harmed but found quickly and rescued.

Ryson picked up at the tail end, and Kenna reveled in the chance to hear him pray aloud. She'd never had that kind of relationship with her friend, but now that she had faith and he had renewed his walk with the Lord, it gave them a whole extra way they could connect. She heard his heart in his words and the wisdom he brought to his roles as husband, father, and police officer.

She carried the warmth of his words and the hope she had from the Holy Spirit with her, holding it close while she and Zeyla headed across the city to the T-shirt printing company where Marcus Neerwood waited.

Zeyla slowed the car for congestion. The freeway that ran through Salt Lake City was just a continual mass of traffic no matter what time of day.

Kenna missed it, but also she didn't. This part of the country was beautiful, and right now, it was freezing. She had liked living here because it was a unique area with a different kind of person who chose to reside here. A mess of religious life and secular culture. Secrets and hidden agendas, rather than overt crime, like in areas with a lot of visible gang activity.

"So, this guy is the dad, or not?" Zeyla fiddled with the radio, adjusting the volume.

Kenna said, "Marcus Neerwood is Bubby's dad. That's Ellayna's little brother, Abe. She called him Bubby before. I don't think Marcus and Crystal have lived together since before Abe was born. If they ever did, or have since, I don't know."

"Two kids, two dads, and no partner helping her at home."

"It's sadly really typical. But people do the best they can, and all our choices have consequences. There are ideals, sure. Ways things *should* be. But it isn't something I've ever experienced. I was raised in a trailer by a single working father."

"I was just asking. Not judging Crystal." Zeyla shrugged, but there was more to it.

"What's up?"

Zeyla glanced over. "It's my deal, not yours."

"Okay, but hit me with it. I want to know where you're at."

Zeyla didn't answer right away, but when she did, it wasn't what Kenna expected. "I just... You're lucky."

"Having a baby in what feels like wartime?" She knew she was blessed, though. How could she not? "I know what you mean. And thanks. I'm glad you get to be a part of it."

"It's all I get."

Kenna waited.

"You're like me. One of their children."

"Am I? Malcom Banbury was your father. You weren't conceived in a lab." Kenna didn't like to think about that, or the woman who had died bringing her into this world. Amara's sister, someone she would never meet.

"It was the only way for her to do it."

Kenna shook her head. "What are you talking about?"

"Mom, when she was pregnant. She went to them and asked them to accept the baby as part of their program. They made me like you, and I'm shocked it didn't go wrong because it could have with them doing that after the fact. But they did more to me than what they did to you."

"I don't really know what you're talking about."

"I can't have children. None of the offspring can except you." Zeyla sucked in a breath. "Mom traded my ability to have children so they could sterilize an entire generation. Every child of *Dominatus* born after you is infertile. None of us can have children."

Kenna stared at her, and her eyes burned with unshed tears. "I've heard that. The general said something about me being the only one. Or it was the president. I can't remember, but I don't want this child to be their chosen one, so I put it out of my mind. At least, the implication of what they were saying and what it meant."

"I didn't want to tell you."

"I'm glad you did." Kenna's heart wanted to break inside her chest. The way it had so many times already. She should be used to it by now, but it still hurt. Every single time. "I'm sorry you can't have children."

"You think I want to bring a baby into this world? No offense. This is a messed-up place on a good day."

"Then why not fill it with good things?" Kenna should have thought that through before she said it. "You could adopt. Change a child's life, or a group of siblings. Give them what none of us had."

"Just me?" Zeyla shot her a look.

Kenna had walked herself into that one. "Or...you know. Whoever."

"I'm not marrying Ramon."

"I mean. Never say never." Kenna had, and now look where she was. "I'd have laughed if you'd have told me I'd marry Jax. Or have a family. Or that any of this would happen."

"We'll see." Zeyla changed lanes and squeezed between

two semis, then jerked the wheel to get them on the off-ramp exit. "Right now, we have people to find and a case to work."

Kenna had to laugh.

"What?"

"You sound like me." The laughter that should be dissipating bubbled up and spilled out. She chuckled while Zeyla looked at her with an annoyed expression. "Sorry."

"You probably don't need to be sorry. Aren't siblings supposed to annoy each other?"

"I guess we'll figure that out."

Zeyla smiled, so that was something at least. "We're here."

Kenna grabbed her phone out of the cup holder and slipped a thin billfold with her IDs in it in her back pocket. "Let's go shake some trees."

"Maybe I should take lead." Zeyla pushed out the door.

They met at the front of the car, and Zeyla beeped the locks. Kenna said, "Because you want to be in charge?" She wanted Zeyla to say it. To admit out loud what she wanted.

"I'm good with being the bodyguard. But you're pregnant. I don't know whether to watch your back or permanently stand in front of you." Zeyla looked at Kenna's baby bump and shook her head. "Preston better get here soon with his team, or I'm going to go crazy trying to figure out how to make it so nothing happens to you."

"There's risk everywhere. You're not in charge of what happens and who lives or dies. None of us are. What we need to do is trust that the God who made the universe is looking out for us."

"Because He's on your side?" Zeyla folded her arms and shuttered her expression.

Kenna said, "Yes, He is."

She knew who she was in the eyes of the Lord. She was His child, and He loved her enough to die to save her. The way He loved every single person in the world, whether they believed it or not. They were guaranteed eternity, not safety in this life. But she still trusted Him.

Zeyla took a step back and angled her body toward the building. "Let's go talk to this guy. You can preach to me later."

Kenna didn't let on that she was disappointed about where the conversation had gone. She had to see it as planting seeds and letting God work in Zeyla's heart. It could take years for her to accept the truth, and Kenna would be in her life, showing her what God had done, whether she decided to trust Him or not.

Zeyla held open the front door of the T-shirt shop, and Kenna went in, her hand close to the weapon at the small of her back. She got a look at the guy behind the counter and almost kept her hand there. "Hey."

The guy lifted his chin. Heavy-metal T-shirt, long hair that needed washing, and sleeves of tattoos. It was cold in here, but he didn't seem to feel it. "How's it going?"

Kenna said, "We're looking for Marcus Neerwood. Is he here?"

The guy lifted his chin again. "He do that to you?"

It took her a second to realize he meant had Marcus impregnated her. "No, it's not his baby."

"That's a relief." His expression didn't change.

"Is Marcus here?"

The guy stared at her. Kenna sensed Zeyla behind her, and the guy's brows rose. Finally, he said, "Marcus didn't show up for work this morning."

"Is that normal, for him to just skip it?" Kenna asked.

The guy shrugged.

"Does he have a locker we can look at?" Kenna dragged out her ID and showed him her investigator license. Thankfully, she had one for Utah. "We're looking for some people who might be missing and in danger."

"You think he had something to do with it?"

Kenna said, "For all we know, he might be missing and in danger along with them." Then again, he could be the reason no one could find Crystal, Ellayna, and Abe.

"Sounds like something for the police to worry about. Not a pregnant chick and her sidekick." The guy tipped his head to the side. "You think I'm gonna let you poke around people's personal stuff?"

"If it could save his life, why not let us look?"

He almost smirked. "Nice try. Now get lost, both of you."

Zeyla shifted, moving around Kenna, who stopped her from going in front of her. "Nope." She tugged her sister back. "Let's go." To the guy, she said, "Thanks for your time."

Zeyla pushed the door open and held it, only speaking when it closed behind them. "You're just gonna give up?"

"No, we just need a new tactic." Kenna led her to the car. "We don't need to argue with that guy and try to convince him to let us see the locker. The police can do the legwork on something like that. We need a lead that is actually going to get us a result."

Zeyla looked over the roof of the car. "So what are we going to do?"

"Let's go to his house to see if he's there. Maybe he's sick." She didn't think that would turn out to be the case, but it got them moving. Shaking trees. Kicking over rocks.

All the analogies that meant she could be distracted from thinking about the men shooting at them in the car.

Even if the police had taken them into custody, or permanently subdued them in retaliation for an officer's death, she didn't know if she could let this one go easily. The memory of it seemed too close to the surface.

"You good?" Zeyla parked in a compact space outside of a two-story building of old, rundown apartments.

"I'm good." Kenna sent Preston a text asking for an update and where they might get the car repaired so it could be back to being an armored vehicle most people would mistake for a regular car instead of a wreck that drew attention everywhere they went.

After stowing her phone, she followed Zeyla to the upper floor. "This is where he lives?"

"According to Maizie. It's apartment three." Zeyla slid out the gun holstered at the small of her back and thumbed off the safety, holding it by her side.

Kenna stood to the side of the door and hammered with the base of her fist. "Marcus Neerwood! Open the door!"

Cars streamed by on the street. Trash had collected on the ground at the end of the balcony where they stood.

Nothing.

She hammered again, but no one answered. Kenna lowered her hand.

"Do you hear that? I'm pretty sure I heard a child or someone in there cry out in distress—" Zeyla lifted her knee and slammed the sole of her boot next to the door handle.

"Yeah, me, too." Kenna bit her lip, trying not to laugh. Zeyla would make a terrible police officer but an exceptional marine—if she could handle all the rules and regulations. She would probably have been kicked out for punching a superior, so it was good that she was a private security specialist. Or whatever she was.

The smell hit Kenna in a noxious wave.

"Oof." Kenna wrinkled her nose. "That's not a good smell."

Zeyla stepped into the house.

"Don't touch anything," Kenna said. "I'll call the police. This is a crime scene."

Chapter Nineteen

Jax stood at one end of the freezing cold room. Colder than outside, even. Each of the round tables, with the attached plastic stools, was empty, and they would stay that way until the guard brought Gerald Rickshire in.

He reached for his phone, but of course, he'd given that to the desk sergeant before coming in here. Same with all his weapons.

A buzzer sounded, and the door opened. Gerald shuffled in, arms and legs shackled with a chain stretching between them. An old man, a shell of who he had been. A piece of garbage, who kidnapped little girls and did horrific things to them. Who tortured and murdered. He didn't even look like the same man whom Jax had talked to in this very prison years ago.

Since then, so much had happened in Jax's life. He'd fought fights he didn't think he'd survive, convinced Kenna to marry him, and now they were about to have a baby. He was going to have a daughter.

Faced with a man who targeted girls, Jax found he

wanted to walk out right now. Just turn and leave. Forget this whole thing.

But another girl, Ellayna Feathers, and her family were in danger.

He had to swallow his disgust and have this conversation, so he walked to the other side of the table where the guard left Rickshire.

The officer said, "I'll be by the door." To Gerald, he said, "No sudden movements."

Gerald practically sneered. A man who thought he was above the law, who let his appetites dictate his actions and did whatever he wanted, destroying lives in the process. That sneer was a flash of a guy who thought he had power over life and death. The guy Gerald had been. But that wasn't the man who sat and looked up at Jax.

Spending the past couple of years in prison had brought him to a low place.

"You remember me?"

The skin around Rickshire's eyes constricted. "Mr. FBI."

"Not anymore. Now I'm just Mr. Jaxton, but my role here hasn't changed."

Rickshire studied him, his thin frame hunched over in the orange jumpsuit. "You think I'm gonna confess to something. Like I seen the light, or what?"

"You can tell me anything you want, as long as it's the truth." Jax wasn't going to be intimidated or baited. "But I have to ask you about Ellayna Feathers."

His eyes flared at hearing her name. "What about her?"

"Have you had any contact with her or anyone in her family? Has anyone else contacted you to talk about her? Has her name come up at all since I saw you last?"

Silence echoed in the room.

"Say her name again." Rickshire closed his eyes.

"No." Jax didn't want to admit she'd been taken by someone. Or that they suspected that's what had happened. But he had to. "She's disappeared. We think someone took her."

Rickshire nearly jumped out of his skin. He flinched so hard the table would've moved if it wasn't bolted to the floor.

"Inmate!" The officer didn't move, but his voice pounded in the air as hard as a punch.

Rickshire stilled. Jax raised his hand, palm out, to the officer.

"Where is she?" Ellayna's kidnapper spoke through clenched teeth. "Who took her?"

"I thought maybe you could tell me." Jax had a hunch, and he played it. "After all, she's yours, isn't she? Ellayna Feathers belonged to you."

He muttered something under his breath.

Jax leaned forward slightly. "What's that?"

He had to get Gerald so angry about how someone else had the audacity to take Ellayna that he started talking.

"I guess someone else gets to play with her now." Jax shrugged. "You lost your shot, thanks to Kenna, but someone else must have had their eye on her. They did what you couldn't."

Jax watched the tendons in his jaw flex as he chewed on the reality of what was happening.

"I guess, one day, you'll get out of here. She'll be older by then, so it won't be the same." Plus, by then, Rickshire would be ancient, if he didn't die in prison. "Makes sense someone else gets a turn."

"You came here to rub it in my face."

Jax held his body steady. "I came to see if you know

who might've taken her. That way, we can get her back." He didn't want to say that they were saving her for this piece of trash, but he would if he had to. Even if saying it made him want to throw up.

"Has anyone come here to ask you about her?"

Rickshire shook his head.

"You don't have many visitors, but people do come to see you. Who are they? Friends and family...or fans?"

"We all have associates."

"The names in the log are fake. We know the IDs are bogus. Tell me where to find James Longstreet. Or Stonewall Jackson."

Rickshire's lips curled up slightly.

"Clearly, they're bogus, unless you have ghosts with Utah driver's licenses coming to see you." Jax flexed his fingers under the table. "One of them knows where Ellayna is. Don't they owe it to you to give her back?"

"Maybe they're doing me a favor."

"Finishing what you started?" Jax shook his head. "I don't think that's how it works. Aren't you the top dog? The one they all look up to. The legend who got away with it for years. Until Kenna Banbury came along and ruined everything."

Now, this man was trying to cause her pain and suffering and hurt Ellayna in the process. Let alone whatever fate Crystal and Abe faced. That had to be why this was happening.

It should connect to *Dominatus*. Maybe it did, but how? All he knew was that it might somehow be linked to their activities. Whatever they had planned for Kenna.

Rickshire shifted in his seat. "Don't say that name to me."

"She has a different name now, but nothing has

changed. She's going to rescue Ellayna because you're going to tell me who took her." Jax paused long enough to pray in his mind. Asking God for impossible things seemed commonplace these days.

Sometimes, those prayers were answered, and other times, they weren't, but God's goodness wasn't predicated on whether or not Jax got what he wanted.

In a place like this, the goodness of God seemed far away. But it was something Jax carried with him everywhere. A small flicker of light in a dark world, chasing away the shadows.

"How should I know?" Rickshire spat out the words. "I've been in here since she caught me. If something happened to that child, it's got nothing to do with me."

That could be absolutely true, but Jax wasn't ready to believe it.

"Who are your friends, Longstreet and Jackson?"

"Find them yourself."

"Ellayna could be dead before that happens."

Rickshire's expression flinched for a second.

"I've got all day, but I don't think you have so much time."

"What are you talking about? I've got years here."

"Are you going to last that long?" Jax asked. "Wouldn't you rather know Ellayna is somewhere safe and that she could still be there if you ever get out of here?"

He clenched his jaw, nausea in his stomach threatening to come up. As an FBI agent, he'd needed that dividing line between good and evil. Between the law and those that enforced it, and whoever sat on Rickshire's side of the table.

Lately good and evil had blurred. Lines were crossed, and they'd wound up in a place he'd never expected. Good and bad side by side in their lives.

Rickshire cleared his throat. "What do I care about one child?"

"Say that again, I might believe it."

"There are a hundred criminals in here. Many of them are far worse than me."

"So prison gave you perspective. Is that it?" Jax studied him. "You're just a small fish in a big pond. A cog in the wheel."

"The world is a big place. There are lots of Ellaynas. Why get hung up on the one that got away?"

"You've been going to therapy, or reading self-help books? Do I have that right?" Or the two men with their fake IDs had talked him through it.

"We all have our part to play."

"What's the grand scheme?" Jax decided then to take the leap. "An evil organization bent on world domination, controlling governments, and using people as pawns in their game let you know you're just a foot soldier. So, you sit here, waiting for orders."

Rickshire's lips curled enough that Jax caught a glimpse of aging teeth in that aging face. "I already got my orders. It's why I'm here."

"This is all some grand plan?"

"You should know that by now, Not-So-Special Agent." Rickshire seemed amused. "'We're all either kings or pawns.'"

"You added Napoleon to your reading list?"

"It passes the time."

"So, you serve the time you were awarded for your crimes." Jax didn't want to write this conversation off as a total loss, but he probably wouldn't get much more out of Rickshire. The guy's defeatist attitude wasn't a surprise. He'd only served a couple of years of his sentence and had many more still to go. The likelihood was that he would die in here and never live life again as a free man.

That was what justice had demanded of him.

"It's what we're bred for," Rickshire said. "To play our role."

Jax stilled. "You're one of them."

"One of who?" Rickshire played innocent, but there was no way Jax was going to swallow that pill. No way.

"Why let yourself get caught? What purpose does that serve?" All he could think was that Kenna was going to flip a lid when she found out that *Dominatus* was connected to that case and the mission she'd been on the night she rescued Ellayna Feathers.

"It serves the will of *Dominatus*."

"Who gives you orders? Do they have Ellayna?" Desperation rolled through Jax. He wanted to grab this guy and throttle him.

"If you want Ellayna, perhaps you should find Gerald Rickshire." He tipped his head back and laughed.

"Explain." Jax clenched his hands into fists on his knees, under the table. Aware he was going to look tense. But why would that be surprising?

"You've met us before. I read all about it in the reports and the newspaper. Saw it on the news, even. The double of Kenna Banbury killed in a bank in Colorado. Is it so astonishing that there would be more of us out there?"

"This is ridiculous. There's no way you're one of their clones, or doubles, or whatever you are. You're Gerald Rickshire, the Seventh Day Killer." Jax refused to believe Kenna had caught the wrong person or that Rickshire—the real one —was somehow out there.

No.

No way.

Rickshire leaned back, swaying on the stool. Looking amused in a way Jax didn't like at all.

Rickshire said, "What if I'm not? What if I'm the guy they had on hand to face the charges and do the time?" He paused. "What if Rickshire is still out there?"

"I think I have ways to find out, and you'll only be wasting people's time." Jax got up and stood behind the stool, facing Rickshire.

In the corner, the officer shifted, ready to take the inmate out of here because the conversation looked like it was about to be over.

"We can find out pretty easily if you're telling the truth or not."

Rickshire shrugged. "Unless my DNA was left at each scene because *I was there.* Not to mention how similar ours is. Maybe you can't even tell the difference?" He laughed at that, as if his own joke was the most amusing one he'd ever heard.

"If she dies because you lied—"

"What will you do?" Rickshire spread his hands, and the chain clinked. "I'm already in prison for life."

Chapter Twenty

"That's insane." Kenna leaned away from Jax, who was sitting beside her at the Rysons' dinner table. "He has to be insane if he thinks we're going to believe that he's a *Dominatus* double."

Also at the table were Zeyla and Maizie, Javier and his wife Valentina, Luci—currently on her booster seat, eating bite-size pieces of dinner with her fingers—and baby Carlos, who was nursing on Valentina's lap under a cover.

Jax gave her a small smile. "How was your day, dear?"

Zeyla snickered, and she and Maizie shared a smile.

Kenna rolled her eyes. "What do you know, there's been a murder?" She didn't want to be callous to a loss of life, but right now, nothing was capable of surprising her. Or so she'd thought, until Jax mentioned that Rickshire insinuated he was a *Dominatus* look-alike.

That the real Gerald Rickshire was still out there, probably being protected by someone powerful within the organization.

She blew out a long breath and reached for another

piece of garlic bread, holding off taking a bite until she said, "Single gunshot to the head, left to bleed out on his kitchen floor."

Valentina reached out to cover Luci's little ears, but it was too late.

"You know, I was raised hearing about murder and learning how to solve it, and I think I turned out okay. It's probably fine."

Valentina's eyes bugged out. Ryson coughed behind his hand.

"Um..." Maizie didn't continue.

Kenna just ate her bread and didn't worry too much about it. There was far too much to worry about with a child of her own, so many ways she could be damaged or put at risk or traumatized. If she started thinking about it, she would wind up spiraling with no way to come up for air.

She should probably be concerned for other children being exposed to evil, but it felt like taking on the weight of the world right now. With how pregnant she was, Kenna wanted to spend a short period of time worrying about her baby. Focusing on her child.

Zeyla said, "The police are going to investigate Neerwood's murder, but it'll take them weeks to come up with a suspect. The detective told me fingerprints and DNA can take that long just to reach the point where it's tested. By then, the guy will be long gone, out of the country, probably."

Maizie lowered her fork, a bit of cheesy lasagna on the tines. "Do we know if it might be connected to what happened to Shawn Terrance? Like, what if it's the same killer?" She put the fork in her mouth.

Kenna wiped her hands on her napkin. "I doubt the deaths are connected to each other, but it's possible the same person was hired to..."—she glanced at Luci, who grinned at her with cheese around her mouth—"do the job."

"So an assassin?" Zeyla perked up.

"Either way, we still need to find Ellayna and her family," Jax said. "If Neerwood was taken out because of it, that means he knew something. Now we'll never know what it was."

"Unless he wrote it down or sent the information to someone." Maizie lifted her brows. "I'll ask the PD techs I've been talking to if we can take a look."

Ryson glanced at the young woman. "Good idea." He nodded, working on his own plate.

Kenna said, "We need to unpack his life. See who he'd have confided in."

Jax nodded, finishing up his bite. "Maybe he has a girlfriend or best friend, or even his mother. He might've shared concerns with them."

Valentina shifted the baby from where he'd been nursing, and her husband accepted the sleepy child. He dropped a kiss on Valentina's forehead. "I'll put him down."

She said something in Spanish, in a soft voice, that Kenna didn't catch.

Ryson took the baby down the hall, while Valentina removed the cover and cut a bite of her lasagna with the side of her fork. "Anything else we can talk about, besides murder?"

Zeyla leaned over the corner and made a little figurine of a horse dance across the table toward Luci, who squealed in delight. "Ma-dur!"

Valentina's eyes flared. "Great. Now I'm being a bad influence."

Kenna sputtered. "I'm not a bad influence."

"I love you, girl." Valentina shot her a look. "But not much of what you do is child-friendly."

Jax sounded like he was trying not to laugh.

"But I guess you'll figure it out soon enough." Valentina motioned to Kenna's baby bump.

"You think I'm going to be terrible at this." The irritation—disappointment?—was going to give her heartburn.

"I didn't say that." Valentina shook her head.

Ryson wandered back in, holding the baby monitor. "Say what?"

His wife glanced at him as he settled back at the table. "That Kenna is going to be a terrible mother."

"You told her about our conversation?"

Kenna glared at him. "Excuse me?"

Ryson looked like his hand had been caught in the proverbial cookie jar. "It's just..." He didn't continue.

Valentina stepped in to save him. "You aren't going to be a terrible mother, Kenna. We just... No one knows what they're doing when they have a child. You learn as you go and hope you don't mess things up too badly."

Beside her, Ryson nodded.

"You're going to choose your own path, and it isn't going to look like what anyone else thinks you *should* be doing."

Kenna pressed her lips together. Jax reached over and held her hand.

Valentina continued, "Because it doesn't need to. You being a mother isn't about what someone else tells you is right. You'll parent just like you live your life. Always looking to do the right thing, to help those who need it. To bring justice."

Zeyla said, "Maybe you should name her Justice."

"No." Jax shook his head. "This child isn't going to represent what we want or what our lives mean. She gets to choose her own path and find her own life, whatever that looks like, without us putting our ideas or expectations on her."

Kenna squeezed his hand.

Valentina said, "I know you'll do the right thing. That you'll do everything you can to keep this child safe. She'll know she's loved and that you're there to keep her safe. That's the most important thing."

Kenna swiped a tear from the corner of her eye.

"We should have dessert before Kenna starts crying into her lemonade." Ryson grinned.

She let go of Jax's hand, grabbed a piece of garlic bread, and tossed it at Ryson's head.

He dodged it, laughing. Luci erupted into laughter along with her father.

Kenna gave herself a second to listen to the sweet sound of a child who felt safe and protected, and knew she was loved, and wondered what her daughter's laughter would sound like. She rubbed a hand down the bump in her midsection, feeling the baby kick against her side. A sign of life she needed often, just to reassure herself that God was protecting them all.

She leaned her head on Jax's shoulder, and he kissed her forehead.

"Take the day off tomorrow," he whispered. "Zeyla and I will get out there and see if we can find Ellayna. You and Maizie can work the computers."

"Yay." She probably sounded tired and like she was being sarcastic. She glanced at Maizie and winked.

The young woman stood with Valentina and helped to clear the table. Ryson took the bread, and Zeyla grabbed the last piece before he headed with the empty plate to the kitchen.

Jax shifted and pulled out his phone, which was vibrating from a call. "It's Preston." He set the phone on the table and tapped the screen. "You're on speaker." He listed off everyone that could overhear.

"Having a party?"

Kenna said, "Family dinner. So where are you?"

Jax let out an amused laugh under his breath. He agreed with her.

Preston said, "Almost to Salt Lake. It's been a long drive, but we should be at the campsite in a couple of hours."

"Sounds good," Jax said, then filled Preston in on the fate of the closest family member that Crystal, Ellayna, and Abe had. He also gave their friend the highlights of his conversation with Rickshire. "We have things to do tomorrow, but we don't have much in the way of leads."

"I'll do what I can to help."

"Thanks," Jax said. "We appreciate it."

"I had a meeting with one of the higher-ups in the Colorado State Patrol before I left. They have those guys from the SUVs in jail or in custody in the hospital. There's no way to know if any of them escaped before they could be caught, or if there are more and we didn't get them all, but they're treating this group—there are seven being charged—as if this is all of the attackers."

Kenna wasn't so quick to assume it was done, but the police wanted someone to answer for the death of one of their officers. Those guys would also be charged with the deaths of Shawn, Gabby, the nurse, the doctor, and the janitor, along with the theft of stolen property. Plus, all the charges that came with chasing her and Jax, firing on them and the RV—putting Maizie and Zeyla's lives in danger. There were a whole lot of things for them to answer for.

Jax asked, "Who are they?" just as Ryson, Valentina,

and Maizie came back in with a tray of brownies, a tub of ice cream, and a stack of bowls.

Preston's voice came through the phone speaker. "They had ID, but near as the police can tell, it's all fake. Their names are all Civil War generals, and if that isn't interesting enough, they tried to take fingerprints for these guys, and all of them have had the tips of their fingers burned until they have no discernable prints."

"Civil War generals?" Jax shifted on the chair.

Doing so dislodged her head, but that was fine. She sat up and turned a little in her seat so she could face him. "What is it?"

Jax glanced at her. "The names of Rickshire's visitors."

"So, it's connected." She didn't want Rickshire to be right about what he'd implied. By all rights, he shouldn't have anything to do with *Dominatus*. If he did...

It wouldn't change the need to find a family in danger.

Jax said, "At least it gives us somewhere to start."

Ryson paused, cutting into the brownies. "Civil War generals?"

"Yep," Jax said.

Even Maizie looked interested. Zeyla had her attention on the brownies, like she wanted to grab a handful and shove them in her mouth. Kenna didn't blame her because they had a caramel drizzle on top and smelled amazing.

Preston said, "So, we look for crimes with the same MO, right? Civil War general aliases, and burned off fingerprints?"

"It's somewhere to start," Kenna said. "First thing tomorrow."

"Sounds good. I'll be there soon." Preston ended the call.

She smiled. "Preston is turning into an honest-to-good-ness investigator."

"Just don't ask him to hack a computer system," Maizie said. "He has no clue about technology."

Zeyla glanced aside to look at her. "It isn't something anyone can do. Your skills are pretty amazing."

Maizie looked like she wanted to hug the other woman. Kenna kind of wanted to see her try.

"Brownie time." Valentina seemed determined to get them to clock off for the day and was giving it a valiant effort.

"Good idea." Kenna nodded.

Zeyla said, "I think anytime might be brownie time."

Jax chuckled. "Too much of a good thing makes it not a good thing."

"Maybe when it comes to brownies," Ryson said. "But not everything."

Luci flung her toy, and it landed on the floor, which was unexpected enough it caused her to start crying. Jax shoved his seat back. "Hey, girl." He rounded the table and held his hands out for a second so she could see he wanted to pick her up.

She lifted her arms, and he drew her out of the booster and into his arms.

"You wanna get your toy?" Jax tipped her so she could reach for it, then drew her back up dramatically. She squealed with delight.

Kenna watched the whole thing, soaking it in.

"Want me to throw this at your head?" Ryson held a spoon with a bite of brownie like he was going to use it as a catapult.

"That would be a waste of brownie."

Valentina laughed, passing bowls. "Someone talk about

something other than murder, or I'm going to get a deck of cards and teach you all how to play something."

Kenna glanced around at these people, her heart full of love for her family. Those she spent all her time with, and others she missed dearly. They would all be a part of her daughter's life.

Lord willing.

Chapter Twenty-One

Washington, DC, Federal Courthouse
Present Day

"That's what happens when an evil group of people terrorize others because they believe they can do whatever they want," Kenna said. "As if the simple fact of how long they've been in existence *means* they can do whatever they want."

"And it's your job to fight them?" Hasworth wandered toward the jury, which everyone knew was posturing. But no one in a courtroom ever believed it wasn't at least partly a show.

Kenna and the US attorney, a federal prosecutor, were on the same side. Kenna wasn't the one on trial. But that didn't stop her from feeling as if the spotlight was on her.

Someone coughed at the far end of the room.

Hot lights for the cameras caused sweat to bead at the

small of her back. She could hear the scurry of pen across paper, and it felt like an ocean of eyes were on her.

Hasworth continued, "You're just an average PI, right?"

"I'm not sure I'd ever say that," Kenna responded. "After all, nothing about this journey has been average."

"I'd say that's accurate, given that you took on a dangerous cult with only a seventeen-year-old and a retired FBI agent."

"You forgot my friend Dixie. She's a realtor."

Someone in the room snickered.

Kenna tried her best not to react to that. They wanted her to recount the entire story? Fine. Everyone was going to be here for hours. But they really did need all the context of *Dominatus* and the threat they posed to the world.

And why, in the end, she had chosen to make a stand against them in her own way.

She sniffed back the tickle of tears.

"I take cases," Kenna said. "It might not be average, but it isn't complicated. I had no idea any of this would happen. How could I have known?" She barely paused before continuing, "I would never have guessed that after saving a group of illegal immigrants from captivity in Colorado, the sheriff responsible for that crime would come after me and my family and ship us down to Mexico as captives subject to torture."

She hadn't thought much about that time recently, but the thankful prayer rose again in her heart, and she had to stop for a moment and say the words in her mind. *Thank You.* They had survived, and Maizie hadn't been hurt when she'd come down to rescue them.

"But in the outcome, I got to right a wrong. I got to expose a corrupt FBI agent and exonerate a man whose reputation had been ruined by her."

Hasworth went back to her table and flipped over a paper. "You're referring, of course, to Ramon Santiago?"

Kenna nodded. "That's his name."

"And you deemed him trustworthy? Someone you could rely on to keep classified secrets and protect innocent people in your care?"

You never saw him with Maizie. "Turns out I'm a good judge of character."

"It also seems you believe yourself to be judge, jury, and executioner." Hasworth spread her hands. "Isn't that what some might believe? That you pick and choose who to save and whose life to end."

"Not always." She'd rather have challenged the prosecutor on who she had killed, exactly. Because Kenna hadn't pulled the trigger on the dirty FBI agent who had ruined Ramon's career. She hadn't done anything with that creepy child in the secret room in that house—couldn't have done anything.

The child might have had sociopathic traits, but she'd been cared for in their own way.

The Rosenburg family had been determined to steer US policy. For years, they'd succeeded.

Now they were no more.

Leaving a power vacuum for *Dominatus* to fill in the US, the way they did in other parts of the world.

"You honestly expect this court to believe the past few years of your life have somehow been part of a 'master plan' that the defendant was part of?"

"Doesn't matter what the court believes. What matters is what can be proven." Kenna shrugged, even if she didn't feel that easy about any of this. "And the master plan isn't on trial. Neither are the people behind it."

"You're right. We're here to ascertain if the woman

behind that desk"—Hasworth pointed at the defendant—"is guilty of the deaths of twenty-three people in Chicago."

Kenna didn't look at the defense table. She couldn't meet the eyes of the woman on trial. After all, they were alike in so many ways. One tiny shift in how things had gone, and Kenna would be the one on trial, not her.

"Then we have to talk about New Orleans," Kenna said. "Or you can't hope to understand what she's been through. What any of us have been through. You can't know because you didn't live it. That's why I have to tell my story."

Chapter Twenty-Two

Of course, Jax told her to wait where she was while he came around. Not that she couldn't get out of the car by herself, but if he wanted to help her, she could accept the assistance.

Jax pulled the door open, and Kenna turned in the seat, putting her feet on the ground. He held out his hand. "You're still a crime fighter who kicks butt on a regular basis."

She grabbed his hand, and he hauled her up out of the car. "I just happen to be a very pregnant crime fighter." Plus, her feet hurt because they'd walked two miles this morning for exercise, talking through the case details and working out what they were going to do next.

"This is her place?" Kenna scanned the squat structure —a trailer in the center of the park. One of fifteen or twenty with dirty snow packed between, and icy roads that no one had salted. Kenna had her boots with thick tread on, but she still walked carefully.

Jax glanced at her, looking unhappy.

"It's just a conversation." She wasn't going to sit around all day wishing Ellayna was found. That wasn't what would get her back. Sure, she could pray all day, but it felt so much better to do something, even just a quick trip out to interview someone who might be able to shed some light on these events.

The family's disappearance.

Yet another murder.

"Her son was killed. She might not want to talk to us." Jax knocked on the front door, then hit the button for the doorbell.

"People used to expect guests to show up without warning. People went visiting their neighbors to spend time with them. So many people these days don't even answer their front door. Especially not if they look at the camera and see it's someone they figure is selling something."

Jax shook his head, looking amused. "If she doesn't answer, we both get what we want. Is that it? I keep you from being exposed to potential danger, and you get to leave the RV for a bit."

She was about to respond when the door opened an inch. An older woman in a pink T-shirt with a unicorn on it and gray leggings answered, wearing fuzzy slippers on her feet. She had dull blonde hair and some makeup, but not much. "Who are you guys?"

"Ma'am, my name is Oliver Jaxton. This is my wife, Kenna Banbury. We're working with the police on a case and wanted to ask you some questions."

The woman looked at Kenna's midsection, emphasized

by the fact that she couldn't zip up her puffy army-print jacket over the baby bump. Hopefully, it made her look more harmless than a crime fighter who kicked butt. Which, of course, she was still very capable of doing.

Mostly.

After she'd taken a nap.

"We were so sorry to hear of your son's death."

The woman's expression hardened. "That's the case you're working? I didn't figure the police would waste much time on Marcus. I didn't."

"Is it okay if we come in?" Kenna didn't want to ask to use the restroom too early, but she would if it got them inside.

The woman backed up, holding the door.

Jax stepped in first. "You're Denise Neerwood?"

"That's right." She waved. "Sit wherever you want." Then she shut the door behind them.

Kenna went to the couch and perched on the edge. Denise had a plate and mug on the table, along with a couple of worn paperback romance novels, but otherwise, this place seemed neat and tidy. "Again, we're really sorry for your loss. No matter what kind of man he was, a life lost in violence is always a sad thing."

Denise leaned against the back of a recliner. "He and I parted ways a long time ago. I wasn't surprised to hear he'd been shot."

Jax stood to the right, over by a lamp, like he was standing guard over the room. A sentry. The man who had chosen to be the one who always looked out for her. "Any idea what he might've been into that got him killed, or if someone in his life might want to harm him?"

Denise shrugged. "I don't know the answer to that."

"It could be a long-standing feud, for all we know. You might be able to help us find whoever did this."

She didn't seem super convinced by Jax's inference that she could break the case.

Kenna had nudged Ryson earlier about getting a rush on the forensics from the murder scene in Marcus's apartment. Hopefully, ballistics from the weapon used or some other DNA evidence would be discovered that matched a suspect.

"You think he had some kind of vendetta? More likely, he ripped someone off, and they killed him."

Kenna said, "He's the father of Crystal's son, Abe, isn't he?"

Denise's expression softened. "My grandbaby. Light of my life."

"You get to spend time with him often?" She didn't know if Denise was aware that the family was missing. Kenna might need to break this to her gently.

"Crystal calls if she needs help with the kids, like picking up Abe if she's gonna be late from work."

Kenna asked, "What about Ellayna?"

"That child has always been older than her years," Denise said. "I'm sure you're aware of what happened to her."

Jax looked at Kenna, but she just nodded.

Denise continued, "Doesn't want a babysitter. Thinks she can watch her brother, no problem, as if she's a little adult trapped in a child's body."

"I remember being twelve. Thinking I was so grown up." Kenna smiled. "Were you aware that no one has seen Crystal, Ellayna, or Abe, in a couple of days?" She paused to give Denise a second to absorb that and watched the older woman's eyes flare. "I'm worried about them. I think someone might have taken them."

She'd asked Zeyla to go to their house and have a look around, given that the police were barely beginning these missing person cases. And there was currently no reason to believe they'd been kidnapped, even.

Denise shook her head, as if she couldn't believe what she was hearing. "What do you mean *taken?*"

Jax said, "They haven't shown up at any of their usual places in a few days. This morning, we discovered their phones are switched off, and none of Crystal's debit or credit cards have been used."

"What about the car?" Denise glanced between her and Jax. "Crystal could have taken them on a trip."

"Any idea where they might have gone?" Kenna asked. "A favorite place, or someone they might've gone to visit?"

Denise looked at the ceiling and shook her head slowly. "It's not like Crystal has a vacation cabin somewhere. She doesn't even take trips. She has two jobs and two kids, and Lord knows Marcus never helped her with any of it."

Kenna needed to figure out if his death was connected to their disappearance or not. Otherwise, it might be two completely unrelated cases.

"How much did he see Abe?" Jax asked.

Denise shrugged. "He'd show up once in a while. I think Crystal didn't really like to tell me because she probably thought I'd get upset. But he'd come over late, after Abe was in bed, and expect her to wake him up so he could see his son. He'd ask her for money."

Kenna didn't want to think ill of the dead, let alone speak it, but this guy could've been a better human, and father, in a lot of ways—or so it seemed.

"If he was killed because someone took them, then I

hate to say it, but he was probably involved." A look of disgust crossed Denise's face. "Who knows what he got himself into. I don't even want to think that a son of mine would put his family in danger, but he turned out far too much like his father for my taste. He never would listen to reason. Always had to do things his way."

She drew in a shuddering breath and continued, "I hope you're able to find them, whatever happened."

"We hope so, too." But hope was something that seemed flimsy until the concrete answer made itself known.

Hope seemed almost like something that might not pay off. The push and pull between taking action herself and waiting on God—trusting Him for the outcome—was probably something it would take her whole life to figure out.

Right now, the stakes of not finding them were far too great. Three lives snuffed out. Three reasons to doubt the goodness of God, even though she *knew* in her soul that the two didn't cancel each other out.

Kenna curled her hands into fists on her knees, wanting to do something that would get her a step closer. But how? It seemed impossible when there were no answers at hand.

Kenna had one final question to ask. "Denise, have you ever heard of a group called *Dominatus?*"

Denise flinched a little. "What is that?"

"People who do bad things, like kidnap families. I don't mean to worry you, but there's nothing about this situation that reassures me." Kenna stood. "I believe they're in very real danger, and I intend to find them."

Denise didn't quite meet her gaze. "How would I know about people like that?" She shifted her weight from one foot to the other. "I hope you do find them. They've been through so much. They don't deserve this."

Kenna stuck her hands in her coat pockets. "Denise, is

Ellayna the kind of kid who would take it upon herself to do an interview with a true crime podcaster to talk about her experience with the Seventh Day Killer? Would she have told her mother about it?"

Denise sighed. "I don't want to say she's that kind of child, but I wouldn't be surprised. Did she really do it?"

Kenna nodded. "We have the audio. He interviewed her."

And if they didn't find out who he was, they might never solve this case.

Denise said, "I have no idea if she told her mother about it. None of them said anything to me last time I saw them."

"And when was that?" Jax asked.

"A couple of weeks ago. Abe had a head cold, and Crystal asked me to go to the store and pick up her grocery order. Other than the baby being sick, they seemed fine."

"Thank you for your time," Kenna said.

She walked first to the front door, and Jax protected her back. Then he went first outside, trusting that Denise wasn't a threat—at least not any more than someone out front might be.

But there was no one on the street, just the same chilly scene of old snow and dampness everywhere. The blue sky didn't seem to fit, but the lack of clouds just made everything colder, and the temperature hadn't warmed enough to melt the remainder of the snow.

The rental he'd picked up might not have the same armor plating as their vehicle, but it was a whole lot less conspicuous to drive while the other one was being fixed.

Kenna got in the front seat and checked her phone. She had a missed call. Zeyla had followed that up with a text. "Zeyla is at the house. She said she found Ellayna's phone."

"Good. We need to find them."

"Problem is what we might find when we do." She didn't want to lose hope that the young family would still be alive, but no one had received a ransom demand. Unless that was what Marcus had been doing that got him killed. "We have more questions than answers right now."

Jax put the car in drive and pulled out. "Let's go see what the phone can tell us."

Chapter Twenty-Three

As soon as Jax pulled the car into the RV park, she spotted Preston sitting at the picnic bench with his laptop open. He had a jacket under him on the seat, a hot cup beside him, and he wore a beanie and a pair of fingerless gloves. Thick sweater and jeans. He looked like a model from an L.L. Bean catalog.

Jax had just parked when Maizie opened the door to the RV like she knew they'd arrived. Kenna gave her a wave and got out. "You connected to the phone?"

Maizie said, "Yeah. How did it go with Abe's grandma?"

"No idea who might've taken them. No idea who killed Marcus."

Maizie's expression saddened. "They must be so scared."

Jax hopped up to the stepstool in front of the door and gave the young woman a side hug. "We're going to find them. And we need to keep praying that they know God is with them, as much as we're praying for a lead."

Kenna didn't want to say aloud that she was starting to wonder if the family was still alive. Gerald Rickshire had implied he was connected to *Dominatus*, something that could link the disappearances to that group.

The only play she had to find out if it was true would be to call the president.

Kenna went over to the picnic bench and sat opposite Preston on the cold seat. "What are you working on?" She was assuming it was family business, but it could just as easily be personal.

"I just got a call. Your car repairs will be finished tomorrow morning."

Kenna's brows rose. "That fast?"

He shrugged.

"I don't want to know how much this is costing you." But she did want her car back, and if he was willing to pay for it...she was going to pad his Christmas gift.

"You think I care about how much it costs?"

She leaned her elbows on the table. "Fine. I guess I'll just owe you one forever."

"Don't worry, I'll cash in at some point." Preston gave her a soft smile.

Jax settled by Kenna, and Maizie came out of the RV with her laptop and a blanket. Kenna glanced at the young woman. "Did Zeyla get you a connection into Ellayna's phone?"

Maizie nodded. "She was heading back here, but I told her the police need the phone." The young woman made a face. "She wasn't happy, but she's meeting with Ryson."

"The techs missed it at the house," Kenna said. "If they even searched it all that thoroughly."

Jax said, "They probably looked to see if Crystal and the kids packed a bag, so they could decide the family just left town, and that's the most they'll do unless there are signs of foul play."

Kenna leaned against him. "Maizie, did Zeyla tell you where the phone was?"

"Under Ellayna's bed, like it slid there."

Kenna glanced between Jax and Maizie. "That could indicate there was a struggle. She might've been grabbed and dropped it, or she knew there was danger and shoved it under the bed, hoping no one would find it."

Maizie looked at her computer screen and typed on the keyboard. "The phone has everything you'd expect your average teen would have. Social media accounts, streaming entertainment apps, all the things you'd think a twelve-year-old might not be ready for. Also, there are no family restrictions or time limits on her device, so maybe we want to talk to Crystal about adding those when we find them."

"Good idea," Jax said. "Kids shouldn't have unlimited access to media until they know how to regulate themselves. The dopamine hit is too addictive, and there's far too much risk of seeing or hearing something they're not ready for."

Maizie looked at him. "I actually added it to my phone because I never had access to social media or entertainment before now. I don't know how to use it in a healthy way either, even though I'm an adult. Stairns set time limits, and if I need more time at night to watch something, I have to send a request." She grinned. "He's pretty funny about it. He said I should do the same for him."

Kenna loved that the two of them related to each other like family. "Even old dogs need to learn new tricks. Like how to use different apps on their phone."

Maizie grinned. "I taught him how to send me a video of Cabot. Now he does it every day."

She smiled. "I'd love to see them."

"No problem. As far as Ellayna goes, I've got texts in

her messages and in the apps she uses. No emails with anyone, just spam, but that's not surprising for a kid."

Kenna smirked and heard Jax chuckle quietly beside her.

"Huh." Maizie stilled. "She was talking to someone, making a plan for when to meet. Or connect. I think it was a phone call."

"The podcaster?"

Maizie said, "Maybe. She has his name saved in her contacts as Rich Waters."

"The name of the guy on the podcast is Steven, right?" Preston asked. "At least, the name he uses for it."

Kenna nodded. "So far, all we've been able to ascertain is that it's an alias he uses for it. There's no other way to trace him. Except for this name. But maybe that is fake as well. Ellayna might have made it up."

Aside from the federal government opening a case, which would be difficult to justify when he didn't seem to have committed a crime, all they could prove was that he was just a horrible person who interviewed children for ratings.

She'd decided that no matter how gentle he was with Ellayna during the interview, he still shouldn't have done it.

Without probable cause, no one could get a warrant to compel whoever was behind any of the podcasting apps to give up his personal information.

It might not even lead anywhere.

"Now we have the number he was using to communicate with her," Maizie said.

Kenna touched her hands together in front of her. "Please tell me it's not a burner phone. Please, please, please."

Jax squeezed her knee. "Yes, Lord," he prayed aloud.

"Hang on, I'll run the number through some searches." Maizie had access to legal and not-so-legal avenues for finding out all kinds of information.

Now that the president had told the world they worked for her, Kenna figured she could pitch in if Maizie got into trouble with the law and they found themselves needing to get her a good defense attorney.

"Bingo."

Preston leaned over and looked at her screen. "I like bingo. Bingo is good."

Maizie almost smiled. The young woman's lips were starting to turn blue, despite the blanket. She needed to go back inside, and if she was honest, Kenna did as well. She needed a whole lot of things that she didn't have, but contentment had to exist in the gap between what she thought she should have, or know, and what she possessed.

"His name is Wallace Lofton. According to this, that's who the phone is registered to."

Kenna silently thanked God for even this much of a lead. The prayer spilled out onto her lips. "Thank You, Lord. We need to find this guy."

"There can't be that many Wallace Lofton's out there, but how do we narrow down which one is the podcaster?" Preston asked.

Jax said, "I can give the name to an FBI contact and have them run every Wallace Lofton that exists. Ryson can do the same."

"There's one Wallace Lofton in this area. He's thirty-nine and moved here from Seattle three years ago. He is a card-carrying member of the Salt Lake City Private Investigator Cohort and the president of another group who looks at cold-case murders that are as yet unsolved." Maizie scanned the screen of her laptop. "That's all I can see from his Facebook without hacking his account to get a look from the inside."

She paused long enough that Kenna nearly asked her what she'd discovered, but Maizie continued before she could. "There's a conversation here on a post he shared." Her nose wrinkled.

"What is it?" Kenna bounced her knee up and down.

Maizie said, "What is *murderabilia*?"

"Ah." Kenna nodded. "Think memorabilia, but for murder."

Preston's head jerked. "That's a real thing? Gross."

Jax said, "Sadly, yes. And it is awful. But some people collect memorabilia from murders like they're items worth putting on display. It's pretty despicable. Like collecting Nazi stuff. They want tokens from true crimes so they can show them off like collectibles."

"There's a black market for everything, I guess." Preston leaned back on the bench seat, as if he needed to absorb the blow of how awful people could be.

"We need to know if he bought or sold anything," Kenna said. "This sounds like the right guy."

"I'll call my buddy at the bureau here in town. See what he can dig up on this guy."

"Tell your friend not to take too long," Kenna said. "I'd rather just go knock on his front door."

Jax hesitated but said it anyway. "Preston and I can go. You and Maizie can stay here and dig up this guy's entire life."

Kenna pressed her lips together because that actually sounded like a decent division of labor. "Call Zeyla also. She needs an assignment."

"You don't want to go?"

Because she hadn't argued with his suggestion to stay

here? Kenna said, "I already found one dead body. I filled my quota. If there's a door to knock on, you go right ahead."

Jax leaned over and kissed her cheek. "Good deal."

Kenna leaned on his shoulder and not so gracefully climbed free of the picnic bench seat. "Let's go, Maze. We've got a case to work."

Maizie gathered her things, and they went inside, where Kenna immediately set about making hot chocolate. She peeled her coat off and switched the sweater she was wearing for a longer, more insulated knit one with a single button that fastened over her baby bump.

The process of getting her arms in it sent an odd cramp through her middle. Kenna bent forward slightly and braced her hands on the edge of the kitchen counter, blowing out a long breath through the sensation.

"Kenna, you okay?"

She could see Maizie out of the corner of her eye, sitting at the table with her laptop facing where Kenna stood. All she could do was nod. Give the sensation a second to pass. "I'm okay."

The kettle clicked off.

"I'll make your drink," Maizie said. "You get some rest."

"Thanks." Kenna took her phone, and wandered to the bedroom, where she crawled onto the bed and slumped down with her head on the pillow, lying on her left side. A moment later she could see Jax and Maizie having a whispered conversation.

There were still at least ten days for this baby to stay right where she was and keep growing, and be safe. *Nothing to worry about.*

She leaned the edge of her phone on the bed so she could see the screen and realized she had missed a call.

Kenna dialed her voicemail and put in the code. "Probably spam." She didn't have the number saved.

Jax appeared at the entrance to their bedroom, holding a steaming mug. "What's that?"

"Kenna? Why didn't you answer the phone?" A child. A young girl. *"I don't know where I am. Kenna, help me."*

Everything in her chilled. "Ellayna."

Chapter Twenty-Four

Across town, on a residential street, Jax strode down the sidewalk toward Lieutenant Ryson. Surrounded by a group of cops in tactical gear, mostly SWAT officers, he was currently on the phone.

Ryson spotted him, and the shift in his body language drew the attention of the other officers. He said something into his phone, then hung up. "We have it. Let's go."

One of the officers in SWAT gear held up a hand to stay Jax's approach. He put a hand on a rifle that was currently clipped to his vest. "Sir—"

"He's with us, Simmons." Ryson motioned for Jax to go with him. "Everyone, move into position."

Ryson didn't give Jax much chance to catch up, so Jax picked up his pace and jogged the last few paces on the salted sidewalk. The grit crunched under his boots. He'd double-layered his shirt with base-layer thermals and stuck with a thinner long-sleeve outer layer, with a protective vest over it.

Part of him would still rather be wearing a badge, but Jax loved this life.

Ryson fast walked to the few cops who'd hunkered down where they could see the front door of the house.

"You got the warrant squared away?" Jax asked him.

Ryson nodded. "Soon as the judge found out Ellayna called your wife, he signed it. This guy had her into something she never should have been into. I mean, *interviewing* a twelve-year-old for his podcast? Talk about sick."

Jax said, "We don't even know for sure if this is the guy, but it's looking pretty good. Wallace Lofton has an online account at this site that's like a dark web eBay. He buys and sells mementos from crime scenes. The more gruesome, the better."

Ryson looked like he wanted to hurl. "And he might have the whole family, including a toddler, in there?"

Jax nodded with his lips pressed together.

"Kenna okay? I figured she'd be here."

"She's fine." Jax prayed that the girl would answer the phone, even if Maizie said it wasn't pinging off any cell towers. "Probably trying to track Ellayna."

"How's that work if Zeyla found the kid's phone under the bed?" Ryson scanned the house, not once looking at Jax.

For the operation to succeed, neither of them could afford to miss something if it happened. "She was calling from a different phone. A burner."

Ryson said, "All right." He lifted a radio to his mouth. "All positions, move in."

Jax drew his weapon.

Ryson glanced at it. "Don't discharge that unless you have to. Even if I have a chief who told me to give you carte blanche access to anything you want."

He might regret letting Jax know that. After all, if he wanted to, he could leverage Ryson's position and force his hand to get something the lieutenant didn't want to give him.

Cops streamed across the front yard, and a small team of officers—one of whom had a battering ram—approached the door. They were inside in less than a minute, storming the house.

"Hey."

Jax glanced over his shoulder and spotted Zeyla approaching, wearing her usual black jeans and sweater, but with a jacket over it and no hat or gloves. Her nose was red.

Jax said, "Hang back until they clear it."

She nodded but still followed behind him to the front door. "Is it weird that I want them to be in there as much as I don't want them to be in there?"

"I'd rather they'd never been taken in the first place." Jax stepped up onto the front stoop, beside which someone had taped a now-faded *No Soliciting* sign. "But that's not real life."

Inside, he could hear the police yelling, clearing rooms as they went.

Jax heard enough that he stepped inside. "Where have you been?"

She shrugged. "Around."

He hadn't seen her much since the family dinner at the Rysons'. "Have you heard from Ramon at all?"

She shook her head, looking like she was trying to convince him it wasn't a big deal. There was no indication she cared that Ramon was currently AWOL, doing whatever with Bear and his team.

Besides, they all had more important things to do here.

A younger officer circled back to the front entry. Blond hair shaved tight on the sides, slightly longer on top. Light blue eyes. "The lieutenant said to join him. Down the hall."

The guy caught sight of Zeyla and blinked, standing there dumbstruck.

Jax heard her snort under her breath. He didn't blame the guy, though. She had that warrior-princess thing going on, a little edgier than Kenna. An air of danger that some guys liked. This guy didn't know who she was or why she was at an active scene. All of it made her that much more interesting.

Jax headed down the hall toward the gathering of cops at a doorway. "Ryson!"

"In here," he called back.

Ryson was on the other side of the hall, opposite the gathering of cops, alone in the room with the suspect's things.

Jax asked, "What's going on?"

"Artwork." Ryson shook his head. "Clear it out, guys!"

Then he went back to the dresser drawers, while a bunch of "Yes, Lieutenant!" calls echoed across the hall.

Jax realized the officer had come with Zeyla into the room. She stood by the door with her arms folded.

"I'm Officer Bridget, what's your name?"

Jax turned away from him. "This is the bedroom?" Bit of an obvious observation, given the bed. "What's across the hall?"

"Another bedroom, but it belongs to someone older. Or it used to. The bed is empty, but there's a depression and enough pill bottles and stuff you'd find in a hospital room that I figure the guy had an older family member he was taking care of."

"So this is Wallace's room." Jax walked to the closet and slid the door open. "Whoa." He stepped back and took in the row of rifles leaning against the wall. Handguns on the shelf. Boxes of ammo. "Was this guy looking to start a war?"

Zeyla came over and stared at the guns, muttering to herself. He caught the word "Russian," so he said, "You recognize some of these?"

"Cheap, Eastern European knockoffs. Half of them probably misfire the first time you squeeze the trigger. Some collectors think they're interesting enough to buy and sell, as if they're collectibles." She shrugged. "They just aren't the usual American-made stuff. It's more novelty."

"Or because they're so different, they look scary." Officer Bridget peered between Zeyla and Jax.

They both turned to look at him.

Bridget nearly flinched but stood his ground. "I mean, when you're waving it around, that is."

Jax left them to it, glancing at the interesting artwork in the hospital room—a mannequin dressed like a showgirl in the corner. Except someone had stabbed her in the heart.

He kept going, looking for... He wasn't sure what, but it beat standing around or going through drawers. Maybe he had a computer. Recording equipment for his podcast.

Or did Wallace Lofton rent another location to do the recordings?

Did he have a basement or a storage unit?

That could be where they might find Crystal, Ellayna, and Abe.

Living room. Kitchen. Even the detached garage on the side of the yard, and the shed out back. Jax walked through all of it, moving fast. Clearing it in his own way. And, if he wanted to admit it, bleeding off some of the tension of not knowing what would happen next with Kenna.

Worrying that the baby, and his wife, might not be fine. Anything could go wrong during a pregnancy, and the chance went up during labor astronomically. Not that he'd done an internet search on statistics or anything.

Still, the point was to not let her know that he was terrified of what could happen. The point was to create a calm, relaxing environment so that their daughter stayed put for as long as she needed. With the best chance to be born healthy.

He strode out of the shed and looked at the house, breathing hard. Hands on his hips.

Trying to figure out how he was going to be calm and supportive when there were so many things he had no control over that might go wrong. Jax could do everything in his power to make sure it all turned out okay, but anything could happen.

He could lose it all.

Zeyla stepped out of the back door. Ryson followed her, and they met him in the middle of the yard. Grass crunched under his feet. "Did we find anything?" Otherwise, this trip had been for nothing. "Anything at all?"

Zeyla folded her arms. "The guy is probably dead because he was a loose end, and whoever took them is going to get away with it. If they're even still alive."

Jax and Ryson both turned to her.

"You asked." She shrugged, which hunched her shoulders. "I thought we were free to give our opinions."

Ryson said, "We have no idea where he is or if he knew about them being taken. He isn't here, and neither are they. That's the bottom line."

"So you keep searching. All-points bulletin." Kind of like Kenna trying that phone number over and over again. A futile exercise, but at least it made her feel better. A little, anyway.

Ryson nodded. "And we loop in the FBI. Get all the available people we can looking for Lofton and that family."

Jax nodded. "No phone or computer?"

"Correct," Ryson said.

"No secret rooms, or hidey-holes?" Zeyla asked.

"Not that we found." The corner of Ryson's lip twitched, but he didn't smile.

Jax was glad, given that there was nothing funny about this situation. "But we have the number Ellayna called Kenna from, and we can track Lofton's credit cards, online activity, and his phone."

Ryson nodded. "Correct again."

"Assuming it wasn't a prerecorded message on the phone." Jax hated the implication as soon as he said it. "All we have is one body and now four missing people."

"Lofton will turn up. No way a guy like this is smart enough to disappear a family with no trace." Zeyla shook her head. "He's low-level. A nuisance. The goal was for him to draw attention to Ellayna. Probably so that Kenna would come here. Meanwhile, they take Ellayna, her mother, and her brother, and no one has a clue how or when or where they are."

"They?" Ryson asked.

Zeyla stared at Jax, as if willing him to argue with her. "You know this has *Dominatus* written all over it."

He didn't want to say that aloud. Not to civilians or people he cared about that could get caught in the cross fire. But life didn't often go as he planned.

"The group that you guys took down?" Ryson asked. "The task force with the president. You caught the guy, right? That General...whoever."

"Schnell." Jax muttered the word.

"They aren't gone," Zeyla told him. "They did this, and you know it."

She turned and walked away, and when she reached the patio, she kicked a metal watering can across the lawn.

"There's more than just one general?" Ryson asked. When Jax nodded, he asked, "What's your next move if you are hunting for more of those sickos?"

He knew what he wanted to do, and it wasn't what he had to do.

"I need to make a phone call."

Chapter Twenty-Five

Somewhere over Alberta, Canada

It was way past time for Ramon to check in with Kenna. To update her on what Bear's team was up to and decide between them whether to thwart their efforts or help. It all depended on how far Bear planned to go.

Turned out it was pretty far.

The problem was, they'd taken his phone when he got on the plane in California, before they'd left to go to Norway.

Ramon scrubbed his hands down his face and looked out the small airplane window over his left shoulder, but all he could see outside was the whiteness of thick clouds.

"You should try and get some sleep." Bear slid into the seat next to him.

"I need a phone more than I need sleep."

Opposite them, in a seat that faced them on the other side of a table, Lief Holmberg stared at them. He hadn't said anything since the post office, but the guys didn't miss a chance to toss a comment his way about the death of their teammate.

Bear said, "So you can call your friends and tell them what we're doing?"

Ramon wasn't going to lie, because he didn't need to. "Checking in with Maizie for information is a reflex."

He watched Holmberg to see if there was any reaction to her name but saw nothing. Then again, the guy had been stoic since they found him. The only one in the town—or so it seemed. Waiting for them.

A town with a unique genetic profile, probably the result of a *Dominatus* experiment undertaken generations ago—the first of its kind. Ramon didn't even want to know how all that went down. It made him want to shudder just thinking about it, which made him wonder if not knowing might actually be worse. That just allowed his mind to come up with all kinds of terrible ideas.

Ways humans had tortured each other for centuries. Because they could, or just wanted to, or for profit—or in the name of medical research.

Think about something else.

There was only one other thing uppermost in his mind. The fiery explosions he'd seen around the town as they drove away. Fireballs in the distance. He'd thought about it in the two or so days it had taken them to covertly traverse the country, cross the national border out of Norway, and get to the airstrip where this plane had been waiting for them.

"When were you going to tell me that destroying Vinterdal on the way out of town was the plan the whole time?" Ramon looked at Bear, thinking about that comms communication right before they left the post office.

"Who says it was?" Bear shrugged, most of his attention on Holmberg. "I could have razed the whole place, but I didn't. What I did was strategic. Despite the fact that they cost me a brother." He slapped his chest.

Grief had rung in his tone like a bell, calling those around him to come and participate in his sorrow.

"Americans. So sentimental."

Ramon looked at Holmberg, their prisoner. He didn't seem worried about what they might do to him, more than simply binding his wrists on top of each other so he couldn't do anything with his hands.

He hadn't said anything else or asked for anything.

Bear looked about to burst out of his chair. Ramon held his hand in front of the guy for a second to keep him where he was, a kind of check that a friend would give. Touching him was probably a bad idea.

"I'm sure you've lost people before," Ramon said. "Or did your time as a soldier make you calloused to the loss of life?"

Lief said, "People come, and people go."

The question was, did he have no family and care about no one, or did he just want them to believe it? If the goal was to not show any weakness in any way, Ramon would also argue he cared about nothing. That way, it couldn't be used as leverage in a...negotiation.

Did he think he was going to be tortured?

Ramon looked down at the man's hands and saw the tips of his fingers resembled those of the janitor. Fingerprints burned off for security, leaving only scars and one less way for an investigator to discern his identity. But they'd found him perfectly easily using his DNA. Not even any other indicator. The people who lived in Vinterdal were just entirely too exposed to the world, given that a simple test told them where the janitor had come from.

A simple trip—simple give or take—yielded them this guy. The accountant.

"It was too easy."

Bear looked at Ramon, incredulity in his expression. "You wanted us to lose more than just one guy? Maybe get into a deadly firefight? It was a snatch and grab. We got what we came for." Bear motioned at Holmberg with a flick of his fingers.

"That's the problem," Ramon said. "I think *Dominatus* also got what they wanted."

The skin around Holmberg's eyes contracted slightly.

Bear shifted in his chair. "Maybe you're the kind of guy who's never satisfied. You've been through a lot, and you got your life back. But maybe you don't think you deserve it."

Ramon nearly laughed. "You think an overblown sense of guilt is causing me to self-sabotage every mission I go on?"

"You thought you had Schnell," Bear said. "Turns out it was one of their clones." Another flick of the hand toward Holmberg. As if this guy was the representative for the whole of *Dominatus*. And maybe he was, at least right now. "You're scrambling for a win. Trying to get on my team because you can't settle enough to accept that you have good things in your life. That it's okay to accept the blessing, even though you don't deserve it."

"Are you going to preach at me? Because I get enough of it from Kenna." And the truth was that Ramon had been starting to seriously consider spiritual things. Not just because their enemy seemed so powerful they might need some divine intervention to win against *Dominatus*. But also because his life had been blessed.

All of them had shown him what grace meant by

bringing him into their family. Accepting him as one of them. A brother. Treating him as if he wasn't the man he had been for so long.

If that wasn't an example of redemption, he didn't know what was.

But Bear shoving it at him this way? No. Ramon wasn't going to be converted because Bear argued him into believing.

Ramon had to make his own way.

"This is all quite fascinating."

Ramon looked at Holmberg. "So *Dominatus* just wanted a closer look at what they're up against. Is that it? You volunteered to be taken so you could see who we are and learn what you can before they get you back." Ramon leaned forward in his seat.

"Not happening," Bear said. "You're going to tell us everything you know about *Dominatus* and give us access to all their financials."

"That will take a while," Holmberg said, his expression placid. "Telling you everything I know."

"I have a better idea." Bear reached across the aisle. One of his guys slapped a phone into his hand, then a newspaper.

Bear set the paper on Holmberg's lap with the headline —and the date—visible, along with the fact that his hands were tied together. He took a photo of the guy. "Time to see if they care about you at all."

Their captive snorted under his breath.

While Bear typed on the phone, Ramon said, "You don't think they care? That's a shame. Being expendable." He paused. "I've been in a lot of situations where I feared for my life, and knowing someone was coming to rescue me made it a whole lot more manageable."

"As I said"—Holmberg sneered now, but it looked brittle—"Americans are so sentimental."

"This isn't just about you being Norwegian. It's about right and wrong. Maybe you lived with this your whole life. You grew up knowing *Dominatus* as your lord and master, and there was nothing you could do to escape. You had to toe the line, do what you were told, or else. Right?"

Ramon tried to gauge Holmberg's response to that before he continued. "You don't know any other way."

He'd suspected for a long time that it functioned like a cult.

The leaders, charismatic and unflinching in requiring loyalty or death. The subjects, cult members who lived or died by their loyalty to *Dominatus*. Some were criminals, who got to indulge their evil appetites. Guys like Dr. Buzard, who used their research to create monstrous things that Kenna and her team had barely managed to stop—or survive.

Within the group, there were factions, but someone at the top had to know what everyone was doing. Or, as Bear had concluded, the person who controlled the money had access to it all. They knew what each part of the organization was doing.

Did this man have that kind of position?

If he did, it was highly unlikely he'd have allowed himself to be captured. And now that he had, it was equally unlikely he was going to tell them anything. Or offer anything in exchange for better treatment.

"And you're going to save me?" Holmberg asked.

Ramon stared at him for a long time. "Everyone deserves redemption." That had to be said, but also "If I thought it might work, that would be my plan. But saving one person in *Dominatus* at a time, stripping them of every foot soldier they have, and dismantling the entire operation from the bottom up isn't going to work."

The whole thing was too big. The backlash would be swift and decisive; they'd be cut off before they could finish.

Bear leaned toward him a little. "That would be why my plan is better."

"Care to share?" Ramon asked.

Bear showed him the phone screen, and the photo that had been uploaded to...something. Looked like a message board, probably on the dark web.

Along with the photo of Holmberg with the newspaper was a note:

Open for negotiations. Send your representative.

Ramon said, "You want one of them to meet us?"

"I'm kind of hoping they send the president, but maybe she's busy." Bear got up and walked down the aisle to the back of the plane.

Ramon looked back at Holmberg. "I guess you're not the one they wanted to talk to."

"We all have our part to play."

How many times had he heard that recently? Ramon was starting to feel like this was a theme from these guys. It reminded him of that quote that was supposed to have been said by Napoleon Bonaparte, "'We are all either kings or pawns, emperors or fools.'"

Ramon didn't like the sound of it. He'd rather be a king or emperor than a pawn or a fool. But how was a guy like him supposed to elevate his own life? Seemed more like you were either born at the top or at the bottom.

Could a guy at the bottom live life as a pawn but wind up on top in the end? Could he come up with a plan that subverted what they all thought was the natural order? That was the question.

Ramon had to figure out the answer.

He stared out the window again, thinking through it all. Wondering what kind of plan would net him that result. And whether he should pray, asking God for one. Seemed like He could drop that info into Ramon's brain like a download—He was God, after all.

But Ramon was still himself.

A black dot appeared in the distance. He leaned toward the window, and the dot got bigger. "Are we expecting company?" he asked in a loud voice to the plane in general.

Bear raced down the aisle to the cockpit.

A second later, he reappeared. "Everyone, buckle up! Things are about to get hairy."

Chapter Twenty-Six

Ramon kept watching out the window. One dot became two, and then the dots came close enough that he could make out fighter jets. "Did we catch an escort coming into US airspace?"

"I don't think they're here to escort us." Bear sat across the aisle, directly in line with Holmberg, where Ramon could see the nerves on Bear's face. The Norwegian might have missed that, but his expression had also changed.

The *Dominatus* accountant was nervous.

"Is this a response to the request for negotiations?" Ramon shook his head. "Don't tell me *Dominatus* has some kind of policy of not negotiating with terrorists, or people who disagree with them."

"This certainly won't be a negotiation." Holmberg looked out the window.

"They're here to kill you and all of us along with you? Because you're just a small part of their operation. You played your role, and it's over?"

"As opposed to what exactly?"

Ramon leaned forward. "Tell me what I need to know

about them. Tell me how to destroy *Dominatus* now, once and for all. I'll transmit that information to people who will do it. They'll see this through to the end, and you'll die knowing you did something good for once."

"You know nothing about me."

"I know you don't want to die. That you'd choose instead to live and go back to your life. That you like things the way they are." Ramon didn't know where that came from, but he decided to just go with it. "It isn't your choice to be traded like this and murdered along with the rest of us. How about, just this once, you defy everything you were taught and step out of line? Take a stand against them."

"How noble."

Ramon said, "When death is staring you in the face, maybe nobility is all you have to cling to. Knowing your life meant something, and that you stood for something good. That you saved lives instead of destroying them."

Holmberg stared at him. Then he looked out the window.

"Think fast. Time is running out."

At least, that was the impression he was getting.

Ramon glanced at Bear. "How far are we from where we're going?"

"Not far. Twenty minutes, maybe."

"Can we outrun these guys?" Dumb question, but it was out of his mouth now. In the space of a few breaths, he'd been wise and stupid.

Maybe he should take his own advice and get his life on the right footing before it ended. Stand for good, and admit that everything Kenna had said about God, sin, and salvation was true.

The airplane shuddered.

Ramon asked Bear, "Turbulence?"

"Only a matter of time before they shoot us down."

Ramon leaned over and peered out the window. "Those planes are closer now." Too close for his liking, actually. Would they bump this plane and force it down? "Do we know what they want?"

Bear looked at his phone. "The reply came in. *Send a picture of Holmberg dead, and we'll leave you alone.*"

The Norwegian whipped around in his seat. "You lie."

"See for yourself." Bear handed over the phone. Holmberg took it awkwardly between his bound hands, and Ramon ended up holding it for him. Which gave him a look at the screen.

Bear had been truthful about the reply.

"They want you dead." Ramon let Holmberg see the screen for a few moments longer, then tossed the phone back to Bear. "Care to stick it to them in your final moments?"

Let the guy think they planned to agree in order to save themselves.

"You're going to do it." Holmberg looked around, his expression pleading. "You're going to kill me?"

Bear shrugged. "Decide quickly, but I'm not letting *Dominatus* take any more of my men from me."

Holmberg glanced across the aisle, at the other guys that Ramon couldn't see unless he twisted all the way around. His jaw set. His eyes went dark with the knowledge that this was it—decision time. He was facing the end.

But did he go down like a lamb being slaughtered, or did he fight to the end?

"Tell us what we need to know," Ramon said. "Before we're all killed." Sure, it was self-serving, but it was also real life. "We can work something out. Get us all out of this."

Holmberg stared at him. "Get me a computer."

Bear unclipped his seat belt and took a laptop handed to him by Hollace, who sat directly behind Ramon. He opened it on the table in front of their captive and sat beside him, probably so he could see what Holmberg was doing the whole time.

"Make it fast, before someone out there in our escort gets an itchy finger."

Bear had only just finished saying that when the whole plane shuddered again. Turbulence lifted the plane in the air for a second. If Ramon had been holding a drink, it would have spilled in his lap. Instead, all he could do was wait while Holmberg typed on the keyboard.

"There." Holmberg sat back, defeat in his body language. "That's the server where I keep all their financial information. It's all there. Everything."

All the secrets of *Dominatus*. Ramon wanted to snatch the laptop and get Maizie access to the whole cache of information in one go. Instead, he sat where he was, trying not to look like they had just gained a win. Given the squadron of fighter jets surrounding them with their missiles locked on, it wasn't time to celebrate.

They weren't out of danger yet.

"You think they'll stand down?" Ramon asked Bear. "We can't destroy the organization quickly enough to get these guys to back off in response." He looked around, a plan coalescing in his mind. "With some supplies, we could make it look like Holmberg is dead."

"They'll still fire on you." Holmberg lifted his chin. "They'll just do it to ensure that I'm gone."

"I'll message them back. Attempt to negotiate." Bear looked at Holmberg. "With this information, we can finally destroy them."

"Congratulations." Holmberg bit out the word.

Bear got up, taking the laptop with him. He passed it across the aisle to one of his guys. Hazel, their tech, was probably already looking at the information. Copying everything from the server, just in case there was some kind of signal embedded in the log-in that Holmberg had used, which might initiate a program that would start destroying everything stored on the server before they could see it.

Ramon wanted to shake his head. At himself. He'd been hanging out with Maizie too much if he was thinking like this. There was no reason for Holmberg to do something like that, unless he planned to martyr himself, and either way, he figured MSI would be pulling the trigger. He'd given up hope, so what did it matter?

He looked at the other man. "You did the right thing."

At least, he hoped Holmberg had actually given them what they needed.

"I'll die with pride." Holmberg lifted his chin. "Is that it?"

"Something like that." Ramon looked at the planes out the window, again so tempted to pray that it seemed like the words settled on the tip of his tongue.

As he watched, the aircraft banked away from them and flew off.

"They left." He looked at the other guys. "The ones on this side just flew away. How about that side?"

One of the men over there said, "The planes on this side did as well. They're gone."

He didn't seem surprised.

Ramon frowned, which Bear caught when he exited the cockpit.

"It's taken care of."

Ramon stared at him.

"What?"

Holmberg said nothing. He just stared out the window. Did he know he'd been played?

Ramon had been played as well. "You needed me to act natural, so you didn't let me know you had pilots on speed dial?" That, or this man would never see Ramon as one of them.

"Don't take it personal." Bear settled into his seat across the aisle. "We have what we came for."

He didn't mean Holmberg. He meant the information. "And the message board?"

"Hazel does good work."

Ramon swallowed. All of it was a play. A pretty elaborate scheme to get Holmberg to believe they were going to kill him—that he'd die either way. By Bear's hand, or in a fiery plane crash courtesy of *Dominatus*.

And it had worked. He'd given up the information.

Holmberg started to chuckle under his breath, and it bubbled up into laughter that spilled out of his mouth.

Ramon's ears popped. The plane dropped out of the clouds, and he spotted a mountain range topped with plenty of snow. On the wing, the moisture from the clouds started to harden into ice but didn't stick around and wound up running off in streams.

It took less than fifteen minutes to descend, and then the flaps lifted on the wings. He heard the landing gear deploy and tried to guess their location from the terrain. Somewhere in the Rocky Mountains, so past the Midwest. Maybe Montana, or Wyoming more likely, given how long they had been going south.

The plane bumped onto an asphalt airstrip with only a handful of buildings in the surrounding valley. All around the plane was a wall of mountain peaks, making him feel like they had landed in a bowl that occurred naturally in this part of the country. Wide enough at the base for a facility. Or a military installation.

"Where are we?" Ramon looked at Bear. "What is this place?"

"One of Schnell's installations. We relieved him of it and dispatched his men right after he was arrested. But before he dropped off the radar." Bear tipped his head. "You don't happen to know what the president did with him, do you?"

"Why? You need a pen pal?"

Bear chuckled. "Just curious. I know they've got black sites where they hold dangerous enemies of the state. I figure he's in one of those, and we'll never see him again."

"So along you come to scoop up his assets. Just like at the platform."

"You make that sound like it's a bad thing." Bear shrugged.

"You have a cell around here for this guy?" Ramon motioned at Holmberg.

Bear just lifted his brows.

Ramon shook his head and looked out the window. Three military-style Humvees headed across the grass toward the runway.

When they were able to open the door, cool air rushed in from outside.

Definitely high altitude. High in the Rocky Mountains, at a secret base formerly occupied by the military.

He definitely needed his phone back. The rest of the Banbury Investigations team was going to be interested in this.

Bear's phone rang, and Ramon descended the stairs, listening to the guy behind him say, "Uh-huh," and "Nuh-uh," over and over. Then, "Got it."

When they stepped off the bottom step, facing off with the private security guys who had approached in their vehicles, Ramon finally got a look at the whole place. This was a massive military training facility, no doubt about it. They'd scored huge in getting their hands on it.

But how had they even known it was here?

Bear dragged Holmberg forward and said to one of the men, "Get a secure video connection set up. The president wants to talk to this guy."

Ramon turned to him. "That's who was on the phone?"

Bear ignored him.

Ramon dragged his shoulder around, making everyone around them—except their captive—reach for their weapon. Ramon lifted his hands. "We're cool. But I want an answer to my question." This was unbelievable. "You guys are taking orders from the president?"

Bear said, "Welcome to MSI."

Chapter Twenty-Seven

Salt Lake City, Utah

Kenna paced up and down the center aisle of the RV, doing a poor job of waiting. Reciting random verses from various psalms to herself, working on what she had memorized so that she would always be able to recall it. "I'm driving you crazy."

"Are you sure?" Maizie didn't pause typing on the keyboard. "Because it seems to me like you care about this girl."

"But right now, I'm compromised. It's a case I should give to someone else to work on because I'm too close to it. I have only emotional judgment and no ability to be rational."

"It's good exercise," Maizie said. "It's cold outside, and you could slip on the ice."

Kenna glanced at her young friend, but Maizie wasn't looking at her. She was worried Kenna would slip, Kenna was worried about Maizie's privacy, and Jax was worried about all of them.

Kenna leaned over the table and swiped on her phone, looking up Bible verses about worry. Turned out there were a few. Too many to choose from right now. No wonder people tended to worry. Did saying "just don't" really work? Maybe. It seemed simple. God had a logical idea for how to deal with it.

Think about good things.

Prayer. So her mind could dwell on Him and the fact that, with her life yielded to Him, it meant He was in control of what happened. He was sovereign over her life. *Lord, help them.*

"Jax should be back soon."

Kenna shot Maizie a smile. "I don't need him. I'm a strong, independent woman. I'm not sitting at home, waiting for him to show up just so that I can feel better. Thank you very—"

The door swung open.

She watched him enter. "Hey."

"Hey, yourself."

Maizie tipped her head back and started laughing.

Jax frowned. "What?"

"I have no idea." Kenna slid her arms over his shoulders and linked her fingers behind his neck. "How was your day?"

He kissed her, a smile tugging at his lips. "I wish it had been more fruitful, but there's still time." He kissed her again, then unzipped his jacket one handed and pulled off his beanie. Both were tossed on the bed before he came back down the hall putting his sling back on. "Anything from Ellayna?"

Kenna shook her head. "Not since that first message."

Her stomach clenched just thinking about it, giving her a sinking feeling in her chest that she didn't like. They could be dead. She might never find them.

Because she had missed the call.

Not to mention the questions of where on earth Ellayna and her mother and brother were and how the girl had managed to call Kenna from someone else's phone.

"They're clearly in trouble, though." Kenna bit her lip. Jax touched her shoulder, and she leaned into his strength for a moment, then said, "Maizie is going to tell me as soon as the phone is turned back on."

"If she's purposely saving the battery, that's a good thing. Wherever she is, she knows to call you because you'll help her." Jax pulled out his phone, which was ringing. "It's Ryson."

He slid a finger across the screen, then put it on speaker. "Hey, it's me. You've got Kenna and Maizie, too."

"Good," Ryson said. "A couple of patrol officers found Wallace Lofton's car. They're sitting on the street, waiting for us."

"I'm on my way. Just text me where."

Kenna leaned over. "I'm coming, too."

Jax didn't argue, thankfully. "We'll be there." He hung up the phone. "You sure? Or are you just stir crazy?"

"I want to find this guy. I can wait in the car if I need to."

He nodded. "I picked up the car on my way back. Preston is returning the replacement."

"Great." Kenna figured they didn't need to talk more if it was settled. At least, not until she got in the car.

As Jax pulled out, she asked, "Where's Zeyla at? Someone really should be with Maizie."

"You think she needs protection?" Jax stopped the car,

even though the front end was now sticking out onto the lane between rows of recreational vehicles.

"Only in the general sense. Not that she's specifically in danger." Kenna called Zeyla, who picked up before the first ring.

"What's wrong? Are you in labor?"

Kenna chuckled. "Not as far as I know, but the day is still young. Who knows, I might have this baby right in front of you, and you'll have to help me through the whole thing. As the stalwart auntie available for anything we need."

Silence was Zeyla's response.

"Or you could go to the RV and hang with Maizie."

"I can do that." Zeyla sounded relieved, which only made Kenna laugh more.

"Thanks." She hung up, then let the full volume of her amusement out. "That was funny."

"I think you like freaking her out."

"Not my fault she has a problem with bodily fluids. We all read the same pregnancy book."

"She's the only one who looked white as a sheet when she got to the birthing part."

Kenna let out an audible sigh, releasing the last of the amusement. "Can't wait to see her with diapers."

"I'm glad you're amused."

"It beats being terrified."

"Yes, it does."

"I'm still terrified."

He reached over and held her hand, driving with the other. "Me, too."

It didn't take long to get across town to where the police were waiting, sitting on a street corner near an older-looking strip mall. The car had been left parked alongside a dumpster off to the side that was overflowing with trash. The chain-link enclosure where it lived was propped open with a concrete block.

The nose of the car nearly touched the left side of the enclosure.

Kenna glanced around, getting a look at the scene, while Jax parked. The uniformed cops and Ryson were now over by the car. One officer had a flashlight, even though it was daytime, and was shining it in the driver's window. Probably to try and see in the dark corners of the car.

"Want to stretch your legs?" Jax turned off the engine.

"Yes, thanks." She shoved the door open and he was around the car in a second, holding out his hand. They met Ryson over by the vehicle. "Any sign something happened to him?"

Ryson gave her a side hug but addressed his officer. "What have we got?"

The guy stepped back, which didn't give him much room between the door and the fence the dumpster backed up to. "His wallet is on the floor. Passenger's side."

Jax peered in that window. "Keys are still in the ignition."

The officer looked down the lane, along the fence, behind the car, his gaze assessing. A breeze ruffled his hair and the collar of his police department uniform coat.

Kenna said, "You think he ran?"

The cop nodded to her and Ryson. "Yes, ma'am. I think something happened to him." He looked at the ground and crouched. A second later, he said, "There's a single shoe under the car."

Ryson said, "Get some gloves and search the vehicle."

The cop's partner said, "Yes, Lieutenant," but the words were eclipsed by a semitruck driving past on the street beside them.

Kenna wandered to the back of the car and looked at the trunk but didn't see any signs the lock had been picked. "Can one of you pop the trunk?"

The cop by the driver's door opened it and reached in. A second later, the rear hatch popped up.

Jax strode over as if something was going to jump out at her. Right. Something very well could have, but it didn't. She waited and let him open it, his gun drawn. The other officers covering him.

"No Wallace." She stuck her hands on her hips. "Are those zip ties?"

Jax leaned over the open trunk. "Looks like he broke out of them. Possible, but also really painful."

Kenna winced. "Question is, did he run?"

She surveyed the ground around the trunk of the car and spotted what might be a drop of blood on the ground. "Someone who can crouch, maybe take a look at this, please?" She made sure they saw it and kept going.

Jax came with her, tracking her while she followed the trail of blood. The lane behind the storefronts was empty of people, but not trash. It looked like a homeless person might have camped back here at some point. There was no sign of them now.

Maybe scared off by the sight of a man, bleeding and stumbling past.

She kept going. The lane spilled out onto a street. Kenna looked for blood on the ground and spotted some in the road. "He crossed here."

Jax held her hand, and they walked through a gap between cars across the street. Ryson stayed behind them.

"There."

She looked to where Jax pointed and nodded. "I see him."

She picked up her pace, but he let go of her and jogged over a berm of grass in front of an office building to where a man lay against a tree. She looked around. "How did nobody see him?"

"Looks like that office is for rent. Maybe no one uses it right now." Ryson had his radio out. "Jax! Ambulance or coroner?"

Kenna moved close enough to see for herself and saw the rise and fall of his chest just as Jax yelled, "Ambulance!"

She looked at the street, trying to find someone who should've seen this man. Looking for a window…a storefront. Someone watching from their house. A crowd gathered on the street. But there was nothing.

If the cops hadn't discovered the car, and she hadn't followed the blood trail here, this guy could have bled to death or succumbed to exposure and died out here.

Kenna would have failed.

Jax crouched in front of Wallace Lofton and shook his shoulder. "Wallace? Mr. Lofton, I need you to wake up!"

The guy had blood drips coming from his mouth. He'd been beaten, but there were no lethal wounds, or he wouldn't be alive now. Who knew how long he'd been sitting here, unnoticed. "He's got to be hypothermic by now." She shook her head. "I can't believe no one saw him."

"Maybe it hasn't been that long." Jax touched the side of Lofton's neck with the back of his fingers. "He's hanging on, but he needs to see a doctor now."

She needed *answers* now. This guy might look like a victim, but he could have information that could help find Ellayna. Kenna lowered in a crouch, far enough that she could put one knee on the cold, hard ground beside the podcaster's body.

"Wallace." She patted his cheek. "Tell us where they are."

The guy groaned. He lifted his head, but it rolled around and flopped on the other side.

Jax said, "Hang in there, Wallace. Help is on the way." Jax pulled off his jacket and laid it on the injured man, insulating him some from the cold temperature in the air.

Kenna wasn't feeling quite so charitable. "Where are they, Wallace?"

Jax didn't react to her question, thankfully. She wanted an answer, and there was enough frustration and powerlessness built up in her after hearing Ellayna's cry for help to demand information. After all, this guy coerced a twelve-year-old into being a guest on his podcast. Even someone only interested in ratings would think twice about doing that.

"Wallace." She patted his cheek again, and he finally opened his eyes. "Where are they?"

Air puffed from between his lips. "My..." He started to lose consciousness. "Office." His head drooped again, and his chin touched his chest.

"He's out." Jax shifted. "Back up because the ambulance is here."

"We need the whole story as soon as he wakes up, but right now, we need to find his office."

"I have a better idea." Jax stood. "You and I follow the ambulance to the hospital. Zeyla can go to the office with Ryson."

Chapter Twenty-Eight

Of course, they'd had to find the office first. Ryson and a contingent of cops had gone, with Zeyla in tow. Even though there was a chance Ellayna, her mother, and her brother were there, Kenna had done what Jax asked and went to the hospital instead. So the pregnant woman could wait close to doctors and emergency medical care.

She tapped her heel on the floor, bouncing her knee up and down. Even the waiting room smelled like despair. Did she really want to have her baby in a place like this?

Jax sat beside her, texting Maizie about everything. Getting live updates from the police and Zeyla as to what they'd found at Wallace Lofton's office. "Okay." He glanced at her. "They aren't there. What *is* there is a collection of recordings, tapes he used to get the interview with Ellayna and some others on record."

"Tapes?" She didn't quit bouncing her knee even though it was probably annoying everyone around her.

The hospital intercom buzzed, and a Doctor Young was asked to report to surgery.

"Literal tapes. The tiny ones you put in a handheld

voice recorder." Jax scanned her, head to toe but didn't say anything about what he discerned. "Guess he thought himself some kind of investigative reporter."

"Pretty sure they use apps for those now."

"But an analog tape stuffed in a drawer is a lot harder to hack than an electronic file." Jax's expression softened. "Which is irritating Maizie to no end. She thinks he did all the production on a computer, and the only thing he did online was upload the file to the podcasting site so it released. She used the desktop computer, which Zeyla said was ancient, to get into his online accounts, and apparently, there are several weeks' worth of episodes already cued up, ready to release."

"Did they shut it down?"

He nodded.

"Where is Ellayna?"

A tendon in his jaw flexed. "I'm sorry, but we don't know."

An elderly woman came down the aisle and took a seat in front of them, pulling knitting from her purse. The needles started to clack together. "How are you folks?"

Jax said, "Good, thank you. You?"

"Oh, I'm hanging in there. Waiting for the hubs to get done with his dialysis." She glanced between them. "You know, if you want that baby to come, you should pace up and down the halls. You see the pregnant women doing that all the time."

"She can stay where she is for now." Kenna patted her baby bump. "As long as she needs to be there."

The woman frowned, rather than agreeing that was a good idea. Kenna didn't really need to get into her personal life with this woman.

She shifted on the seat and put her bent knee on Jax's

thigh. She whispered to him, "I asked where they are, and he said his office. Why were they not there?"

"Maybe he thought you were asking about the tapes?"

"He'd better wake up soon."

Jax hesitated but caught himself. "I nearly asked if you wanted coffee."

"So mean."

He put his arm around her. "You love hot chocolate and apple cider. Some tea."

"Very few kinds of tea. Basically, just black with milk."

She felt him chuckle, and he kissed the side of her head. His phone buzzed, and he looked at it, immediately tensing. "Maizie says Ellayna's phone just came back on. It's giving us a GPS location, but she could be within half a mile of there, or it could be spoofed." The phone buzzed again. "The signal is bouncing around. It's in a completely different place now."

While he told her all that, Kenna fumbled with her coat on the seat beside her, tugging it out from under the shoes of the kid curled up asleep on the seat beyond it. She pulled out her phone and dialed Ellayna's number.

She bit her lip with the phone against her ear, listening to it ring. *Come on, come on.* It wasn't quite a prayer, more her trying to will Ellayna to answer the phone. Which, of course, wasn't more than just wishful thinking.

Lord.

She didn't get the chance to say more to God because the call connected.

"Kenna?"

She sucked in a deep breath. "Ellayna, tell me where you are."

"I...I don't know."

Beside her, Jax made a call of his own. He put the

phone to his ear, and she heard him tell Maizie to trace the call, to get a triangulated location.

Kenna shut her eyes. "Where's your mom?"

"She won't wake up."

"What about your brother?"

"He keeps crying." The connection faltered. It sounded like she said something else, but Kenna didn't catch it.

"Ellayna?"

"I'm here."

"Describe what's around you. What kind of place are you in?" She opened her eyes. "Tell me what you see."

"Okay. The walls are metal. There aren't any windows, but they gave us a lamp and three phones. But they don't have much battery. I turned them off to save it, so they don't run out too fast."

"I'm glad you turned one back on. That was a good idea. We're trying to find you."

Ellayna started to cry. "I don't know where we are."

"Are any of you hurt?"

"No, but mom is sleepy. And I can't get the door open." She sniffled. "I tried, but it's locked."

"Have you seen anyone else?" She didn't want to use the word "captor" but might have to. "Like whoever took you."

"Not since I woke up. I think it was yesterday, but it's been dark all this time. I don't know what time it is."

But they were unhurt, and no one was coming in the place where they were being held. "You're doing great. Ellayna, listen to me. You're one of the strongest people I know. You are going to be okay."

Silence greeted her.

"Ellayna?"

The call dropped.

She twisted to face Jax, far too tense for being this pregnant. "Please tell me you got that?"

He shook his head, his jaw set in frustration. "The signal is bouncing around over multiple states. She can't pin it down."

Kenna squeezed her eyes shut, willing away the burning sensation. She didn't want to break down in tears in a hospital waiting room.

"I see the doctor." He pointed toward the nurses' station. "Let's go find out if Wallace is awake."

"If he is, I'm going to pummel him."

Jax set his hand on the small of her back as they crossed the room. "Someone already did, remember."

"Sorry, you just discovered your wife has a violent streak."

"In defense of a child who needs saving." He looked at her as they stopped in front of the counter. "You think I'd have a problem with that?"

He probably figured it would be a hundred times worse with their child—which was good for them both, because their daughter would be as safe as she could be with two parents who would move heaven and earth to protect her.

Or it was only fine because she would be exhausted and busy with a baby for the foreseeable future, and he thought it would keep her out of trouble.

She wasn't going to worry about which it was right now, even if that was a good way to disassociate from reality and her fears for Ellayna. "We need to know if Wallace Lofton is awake. There should be a police officer at his door."

The cops had told the staff here who they were and that they got full access to the patient as investigators. So, the staff had told them to wait in the waiting area.

The nurse glanced aside, causing the light to reveal

shadows on her face. She was exhausted. The doctor lifted a tablet from the counter behind the desk. "Lofton?"

"Yes," Jax said.

"He's awake. You can talk to the officer at the door, but I'll speak with the patient before you can go in."

Kenna nodded. "We appreciate the chance to speak with him. It's very important. There's a family missing. A mother and two children."

The doctor's mouth opened for a second as he hesitated at hearing that, then he said, "Come with me."

He buzzed them through a set of doors into a long hallway. She didn't see the officer at the door until they turned a corner at the end and came to a shorter hall.

The doctor glanced at her obvious condition but didn't make small talk.

"Only one contraction so far," Kenna said. "But if something starts up, at least I'm in the right place."

He flushed. "That's right. Though, you'll want to be up on the eighth floor of the tower."

"Good to know."

Jax squeezed her hip, and when she looked at him, he winked. Whatever that meant.

The doctor went into the room, and she could see Wallace Lofton in his hospital bed. Hooked up to machines monitoring him but awake and sitting up.

She stood at the door where he could see her—and recognize her. Whether he remembered her from when they found him or not, he should know who she...

Yep. His eyes flared with recognition.

She'd tuned out whatever Jax and the officer were saying to each other.

"You can come in," Lofton called from his spot.

Kenna waited until the doctor left, then rushed to his

bedside, wanting to strangle him. "You have some nerve. You're a piece of garbage, scum—"

Jax slid an arm around her, easing her back from the bed. "Okay, Mama Bear. Give me a sec, okay?"

She didn't want to but nodded. Her teeth gritted so hard they hurt.

Kenna stepped back.

Jax grabbed the rail and leaned into the guy's space. Majorly in his space. "If there wasn't a cop watching us, my hands would be around your neck right now."

Lofton's eyes widened.

Kenna had a hundred questions about how he'd come to interview Ellayna or why on earth he'd thought it was okay to do that in the first place. "Where are they?"

He flinched. "What are you talking about?" His gaze shifted between her and Jax, probably wondering which one of them would hurt him if he didn't give them the right answer. That was the problem with torture, apart from it being illegal, the person—the *victim*—just told their interrogator whatever they wanted to hear to make the pain stop.

"Ellayna, her mother, and her *two-year-old brother* are somewhere, we have no idea where, locked in a metal room in the dark." Kenna's blood pressure was probably through the roof right now.

She had to calm down, or she wouldn't be of any use to this case.

She set a hand over the baby, centering herself. Not just the case, but her family.

"You think I took them?" His voice rose in volume and pitch.

Meanwhile, Kenna drew in a long, cleansing breath. She held it at the top and then pushed the air out slowly. *Lord, be with them. Be with us. Help us find them.* She prayed Crystal wasn't injured and that Ellayna would be able to comfort her brother.

"This is happening because of you." Jax straightened, folding his arms across his chest. "Your interview put them in danger, so you're going to tell us everything you know about the family and who might want to target them. Or I'll make sure you're charged with all the same crimes as whoever took them."

"You can't..." He looked over at the cop at the door.

"You think I'll argue?" The officer shook his head. "I heard that podcast. The lady is right; you are a piece of trash."

Wallace looked at Kenna. "It really is you."

"Get over it. This is all your fault." She wasn't going to back down. "I want to know everything you know. *Now*."

Chapter Twenty-Nine

"I know who you are."

Kenna turned away and found the seat in the corner, which was, of course, as uncomfortable as it looked. She settled on the chair and looked at Wallace as if that didn't bother her one bit. "Good for you."

She'd spent years trying to live an anonymous life. Doing her thing as under the radar as she could. People like Wallace Lofton didn't seem to care that she would rather live a quiet life.

A few weeks ago, she'd found a Bible verse that even said she should aspire to exactly that—a humble, quiet life. But no. People like him. Like the president. They didn't leave her alone long enough to actually figure out what she wanted. Instead, it was about what *they* thought she should be.

She gave him her most disdainful expression. "You've spent weeks recounting everything I've done for the past few years. Of course you think you know who I am. But the fact is, we just met a few minutes ago, and I can honestly say that you know nothing about me except a bunch of facts. Or what you read in a report."

"Yeah?" Wallace Lofton dug up some bravado from somewhere. "Don't think I read about Maizie in a report. And I can tell you this, she isn't some Canadian homeless girl like everyone thinks."

Whether or not Kenna would've believed the story that Zeyla, Ramon, and Maizie had come up with as a cover for her background didn't matter.

"Fine. You know everything," Kenna said. "Tell us all of it."

Wallace blew out a breath. His left eye had a shadowed appearance that would probably be a dark bruise by tomorrow. "I don't even know where to start."

Jax asked, "Do you know where Ellayna is?"

Wallace shook his head. "I didn't even know they were missing until you told me. I had no idea."

"Then start at the beginning," he suggested.

The cop at the door said, "How about you start with what happened to you? I need a statement, and I need to know whether to expect someone to show up here and try to kill you."

Kenna watched his body language and his mannerisms, as Jax was also likely doing. It wasn't a foolproof way to tell if someone was lying or being truthful, but a trained observer could get pretty close.

Wallace said, "I thought I was getting mugged."

"Did you see the guy?" The cop had a notebook out now, a pencil in one hand.

"It was a woman."

Kenna's mind immediately went to the *Dominatus* assets she'd faced, most of whom had been women. Was that who had targeted him? He had to be a threat to something they were doing, or at cross-purposes in some other fashion, for them to think he was a chess piece worth taking off the board.

"Okay," the cop said. "Did you see her face? Did she say anything?"

Wallace shook his head. "I know who it was. She jumped me outside my office. Kicked and punched me." He swallowed, probably not pleased to have to admit he'd been overpowered by a female.

Most men had greater upper body strength. But training could overcome the imbalance between opponents that existed in genetics. And catching him by surprise?

"She knew what she was doing, Wallace. She's a trained asset. She might as well be a full-blown CIA agent." Kenna figured that might make him feel better.

"And I was the chump on the receiving end." Wallace shot her a look. "Is that it? The guy who didn't know any better?"

Jax said, "We've all been there. Did she say anything to you?"

He shook his head. "She knocked me down, made me stay down. Then she tied me up and had me stand up. She shoved me into the trunk at gunpoint."

"And you have no idea why?" the cop asked.

Wallace didn't answer right away.

Kenna said, "Wallace, why did she target you? It was a warning. What was the message you were supposed to receive loud and clear?"

"She tried to kill me. I think the message is that she wanted me dead."

Kenna shook her head. "If she wanted you dead, she'd have actually killed you. This was a warning." Maybe, this time, he would accept it.

What was it Jax had just said? *We've all been there.*

"Who is she?" Jax shifted his weight from one foot to the other, towering over the end of the bed.

"Her name is Sylvia Caughton. She's an investigative reporter."

When he paused for a few seconds, Kenna said, "Okay, so tell us how you know her. How is she connected to your life, or your podcasting?"

"That was all her idea." Wallace sniffed. "She didn't like that I wanted out. You're right. It was a warning." And given his expression, he didn't like that one bit.

Whether he didn't like that she was right or that it really had been a warning, Kenna didn't know.

Wallace continued, "I wanted out, like I said. The podcast...it wasn't right having that girl on. I mean, it was interesting and all. But a child?" He shook his head. "It didn't feel right."

"Did you talk to her mother at any point?" Kenna asked.

Wallace looked remorseful. "No."

"If it didn't feel right," Kenna said. "Then you shouldn't have done it. That's the bottom line."

"They were going to kill me."

"Didn't sound like you were under duress on the recording." She shrugged. "Sounded like you were enjoying yourself."

"They told me to make it look good, okay?"

"And you collect evidence from murder scenes, so it's like a hobby for you. Guess you were excited." Kenna sat back in the chair, irritation bubbling up in her. This guy had taken her life and made it entertainment. "Now a family is in danger because of it."

Jax asked, "When did you first meet this Sylvia Caughton?"

"A few months ago. We met on an app, started talking, and went on a date. She told me she's part of this secret society, if you can believe it." Wallace shook his head. "They paid off my debts. All of them."

"Student loans?" Jax asked.

"That, and my townhouse and the online betting stuff. Football, basketball, and whatever. You know?"

Jax acted like he did know. "And you were so grateful you agreed to...what? Interview Ellayna Feathers against your better judgment?"

"The whole podcast was their idea." He shrugged. "I'm a crime buff, but I've never done anything like that before. They set it all up. I just had to record the episodes, and they made sure it got a lot of downloads."

Kenna said, "And you never once wondered why they were using you as a pawn?"

"I knew that's what was happening." He sniffed again. "It got the Ukrainians off my back. They were about to kill me if I didn't come up with the fifteen thousand I owed them."

Definitely a pawn.

They'd found a guy stuck between a rock and a hard place, owing dangerous people money he didn't have. In came a beautiful woman with a proposition that got him out of his mess, no big deal—he didn't have to do that much. Just talk about something he loved, true crimes.

Kenna could imagine the entire conversation. Sat across the table from a trained asset who used her looks and her powers of persuasion, Wallace had fallen for it all. Never once realizing that he was getting into a worse situation than he was previously in. At least, not until it was too late.

Kenna needed him on the defensive so he would say more than he intended, so she pressed him. "And you didn't ask too many questions because it was a pretty sweet gig. Right? She was gorgeous and interested in you. She persuaded you that you'd been thinking about doing a podcast for a while."

Wallace glanced to the side. "After I interviewed Ellayna, I didn't want to do it anymore."

"But the episodes were released anyway," Jax said. "You didn't stop it from going live."

"I didn't put those together. They did." Wallace looked down at the blanket over his lap. "I came into the office one morning, and someone had been in there."

"Did you report a break-in to the police?" the officer asked.

Wallace said, "No, but I knew it was her. The episodes had been loaded onto the portal that publishes them, and I couldn't delete them. I couldn't even access it because they changed the password. They locked me out of it completely, and then yesterday, she jumps me."

After a few seconds of quiet, the officer said, "You mentioned a secret society?" He didn't seem to believe it was a real thing.

Too bad he was wrong. That part, at least, had been the truth. Which made it interesting that the asset had chosen to share it with him. Using the secret as part of her persuasion.

Wallace said, "That's what she told me. At first, I thought she was crazy, right? But she had powerful people behind her, because I knew my computer had been hacked. They obviously know how to spoof a person's voice since they added the intro and the outro to my podcast interview with Ellayna. There was a whole spiel in there that I never said."

"Like software that mimics your voice?" Jax asked.

Both of them had seen *Dominatus* computer software that could make it look like someone was on a video call, or some other kind of media, when they weren't. As long as there was someone to say the words, the program superimposed an avatar of the person over the top. They'd fooled plenty of people that way.

Wallace shrugged. "They were watching me. I found bugs in my house, and there were weird deposits and withdrawals in my bank account. Stuff like that. When I told her I wanted out, she said the job had to be finished. But I wasn't going to do more."

"Do you know why they wanted the podcast to happen?" Since it was about her, Kenna figured she was at least partly connected to the reason why this had been their plan. Even if it was only a distraction.

Wallace said, "They wanted your attention. They wanted the story out."

Maybe. Was that the truth, or simply what Wallace believed?

"They wanted me distracted," Kenna countered. "That's why they had you interview Ellayna. It was about throwing me off my game and making it harder for me to realize what was really going on."

Problem with that was she still didn't exactly know what was really going on.

At least, not more than the fact that a family had been kidnapped. "She didn't say anything about Ellayna, Crystal, and Abe being taken and kept somewhere?"

"Of course not! I'd tell you." Wallace flushed. "They're really missing?"

Jax said, "Abe's father, Crystal's ex, was shot in his home. People are dying, and you're in the middle of this."

After a moment's pause, he asked, "Did you kill Marcus Neerwood?"

"What? Of course not!"

It seemed to Kenna like the conversation was going around in circles.

"If anyone did, it's Sylvia. She's the one who tried to kill me. Of course she killed that guy. She's the one that's crazy, not me."

Of course he blamed the woman at the middle of all this. She couldn't really fault him for that, but it would wind up getting him in serious trouble. She should probably recommend that he get a good lawyer.

Kenna stood. "I hope that's true, because if anything happens to them? We already told you that you'll be tried for the same crimes. That's what happens when you're an accessory to anything. Kidnapping. Multiple counts of murder."

He stared at her. "I didn't do anything to them!"

"Shame that's not how the justice system sees your responsibility for what happened. And too bad for what might happen to you if you don't tell us where to find Sylvia Caughton."

Chapter Thirty

"It's downloading now." Maizie sat facing her at the table in the RV.

Kenna had headphones on, and she could hear Maizie through those, rather than from the passenger's seat that she'd rotated around so she could sit up. She couldn't easily get between the table and the back of the seat, not if she was going to sit there for a while. She even had a footrest set up.

"Whoa."

Thank You. Kenna had been about to lose her mind if they didn't actually get a lead they could move on. "What is it, Maze?"

Zeyla had turned down the request to wear a camera, but she was on comms. She'd picked the lock on Sylvia Caughton's high-rise apartment and searched the whole place until she found an external hard drive in the wall safe. Instead of leaving, she'd connected it to the tablet she had in her backpack and gave Maizie access to the drive while she finished walking around.

"We've got some serious problems." Maizie shook her head. "She has a ton of research on here, everything there is to know about Kenna and the rest of us. Ramon's FBI personnel file. All of it."

Kenna looked at her own computer. She had Sylvia Caughton's social media and her profile at the newspaper she worked for open in her browser. "Maybe Jax could pass on to the FBI that they've had a security breach while he's there talking to them."

The investigation into the disappearances of Crystal and her two children had become a federal case, and Ryson had gone with Jax to confer with the feds on everything they knew about it. Hopefully, the feds could find some use for their tech to find the family. Kenna was running out of ideas.

She wanted to find Sylvia Caughton herself and interrogate her about where they were, but the woman hadn't shown up recently.

Zeyla said, "This place is a wash otherwise. There's nothing here that's personal. It looks like it's been staged. I wouldn't be surprised if all the furniture has the retail tags tucked out of sight."

"You're going to get out of there?" Kenna said into the headset mic.

"On my way out."

"Copy that." To Maizie, she said, "Anything else?"

"I'm not sure you want to know."

"Just tell me." Kenna might need to lie down, but she could handle the hard news. This woman was a *Dominatus* operative, according to Wallace. He had nothing to do with this; he was only a victim. If she believed what he'd said, this woman had to be the key they'd been looking for.

"Newspaper articles all written and ready to be sent."

"So she really is a reporter?" Kenna hadn't expected that. "I thought it was just a cover."

"Maybe this is *Dominatus* weekly news or something," Maizie said. "Do they do that, Zeyla? Put out updates to the whole organization?"

"Huh."

Maizie looked at Kenna, probably thinking the same thing. Was that really all Zeyla was going to tell them? The woman was downtown, at a fancy high-rise. It might be a cover or the address that had been secured to keep her cover intact or some kind of bolt-hole. A place to do business under the guise of it being her home.

"Zeyla?"

The other woman was quiet, then finally, Kenna heard her respond through the headphones. "I have that CD. Maybe it's a thing, being raised as we were. This might actually be something personal."

"Or the cover needed a taste in music, and she just picked what she knew."

"Maybe. It's telling, though." Zeyla stopped abruptly. "Please hold."

The connection crackled.

"There's no one to back her up."

Maizie asked, "Does she need it?"

"I don't love the situation." She tapped her foot in the air in a rhythm, her feet stacked on a small drinks cooler they usually kept in the car. "Part of me wants to call around. See who can come here and help us out. We need more coverage."

"Like Amara and Bruce?"

Kenna nodded. "Maybe even Stairns."

"I don't need a babysitter." Maizie shot her a look.

"Zeyla needs backup. So does Jax. Who knows what Preston is up to right now." Not to mention the two of them were the only ones in the RV. Just a pregnant woman and a young adult with limited skills in protecting herself. "I'm getting my gun."

Kenna set the laptop on the other front seat and slid off her headphones. She wandered to the bedroom closet and pulled out the small lockbox where she kept a loaded 9mm. She checked it but put the safety on before she wandered back to her seat.

"Are you serious?" Maizie said into her headphones.

Kenna passed her, glancing at her face so she could get a read on what was being said from her expression. It didn't provide much insight. She grabbed the laptop, slid the headphones on, and tucked the gun by her leg on the seat. "What's going on?"

Maizie reacted. Not quite a flinch, but it was close.

"Zeyla?"

"Fine," the other woman said over the comms channel. "I'm in the stairwell now, by the way. I just mentioned Mom since you brought her up."

"Last time I talked to her she was going to tell me something important. We never got to finish our conversation." Kenna had called her back a couple of times since but had gotten no answer. "Do you know what she was going to tell me?"

"It's not that Mom thinks you'll hate her for it. It's just that it's bad. Maybe she regrets what she did, but I think she did the world a favor."

"We have to find a family. Do I need to know this in order to do that?" Kenna figured she'd get what was being said. They had priorities and, right now, those leaned more toward finding this *Dominatus* asset and figuring out what she'd been up to.

"Maybe it's connected, and maybe it isn't. How do we know?"

"It's definitely connected," Maizie said.

Kenna glanced over at her, frowning.

"I'm sending it to you," Maizie said to Kenna. "Zeyla, tell her what you told me."

Silence on the line echoed while Kenna opened the message Maizie had just sent. The attached document, a PDF, was an article...about Kenna.

Expert PI Unable to Locate Missing Child

"She wrote an article about how I'm failing to find Ellayna? And she hasn't posted it yet?" If the reporter wanted to rub it in her face, she was running out of time to do that. As soon as they located Sylvia Caughton, they would find Ellayna. "Maybe it's still part of the cover. Just for fun. Or it's a code."

"It's significant," Zeyla said. "Because you're the only *Dominatus* offspring in this generation who is able to have a child."

She had only found that out because *Dominatus* wanted her to know why they thought she was special. Kenna didn't care. The life she and Jax had created was theirs and didn't belong to this dark group.

"Any information is information they'll use as leverage. They don't know how to do anything other than manipulate everyone around them."

"So tell me how it was done?" Kenna wasn't sure she wanted to know, but she had to ask.

"She's the one who did it," Zeyla said. "She introduced an anomaly in the gene sequence that sterilized every child conceived in our generation. Except her sister's child."

"Why didn't she skip you, too?" Kenna swallowed against the lump in her throat.

"Part of the reason why it worked was because she allowed them to give her child the anomaly," Zeyla said. "If she was going to do this to the children, she wasn't going to save herself. She was going to hold herself and her child to the same standard."

"I'm sorry." Kenna swiped a tear from her cheek.

Zeyla cleared her throat. "We should talk about this when I get back. I'll be there soon."

The comms channel went dead.

Kenna peeled off her headphones. "Is she okay?"

Maizie looked at her computer, a sheen of tears in her eyes. She sniffed. "She's on the sidewalk now, heading to where she parked the car."

Kenna laid her head back on the seat. "We need to find Sylvia. She knows where Ellayna is."

Maizie said, "I know. She hasn't used her credit cards or her phone. Same for Marcus and Wallace and Crystal. She's not using theirs either."

"Hopefully, Marcus is the only one of them who is dead." Kenna looked at the article. "She was really raking me over the coals. According to this article, I'm basically inept." Kenna kept scanning, skimming what Sylvia had written. "But then it mentions my skills and my aptitude? It's more like a report on my performance than journalism, but it certainly has a flavor of that."

Maizie said, "There's an article about the president battling health issues that might be affecting her job performance. It has the same part at the end that yours does, her aptitude and ability to function long-term while under stress."

"Do you know if she actually has health issues?"

Maizie shrugged. "There's nothing on a basic web

search, but maybe they're privy to information the general public doesn't get access to."

"That I believe. *If* this is a *Dominatus* news report." Kenna sighed. "The more I learn about them, the more I'm disturbed and the less I'm surprised."

"But if you told some regular person on the street, they'd think you're some crazy conspiracy theorist."

Kenna grinned. "Isn't that the truth. To us, it doesn't sound like such a crazy thing that they took Wallace Lofton's voice and created additional podcasts after he said he wanted to quit. That they just...pretend to be someone."

Huh.

She frowned.

Maizie asked, "What is it?"

Kenna shut the lid of her laptop and looked at the young woman. "You had access to that program at one point, right?"

"Yeah, when you were held captive and they were using Jax's face on calls to shut down the former president. The president was trying to build a team to fight *Dominatus* in the US."

But they'd killed him.

Kenna pushed the fear away as if she could hold it back by sheer force of will. "Is there a way to tell that a voice was produced by the program?"

"You want me to run the podcasts through it, see what was real and what wasn't?"

"Maybe, but I was thinking something else." Kenna jogged her knee up and down, wondering if she was right or if she was actually losing her mind and doubting everything she believed. "I want you to run the voicemail I got from Ellayna through it. I want to know if it was really her."

Maizie flinched. "What makes you think it might not be

real? We know they're capable of capturing and hurting people. Why would they need to fake it?"

"Call it instinct, because I'm not sure I can put my finger on it exactly." It was more like a culmination of a few things, like the way the articles were written and how this whole thing had gone down. And why Marcus Neerwood needed to die.

The reason why a software company in Pueblo killed a man about to expose them.

"Find out if it's really Ellayna."

Maizie said, "And if it isn't?"

"They're still missing, and we need to find them," Kenna said. "But they might not be the victims we think they are."

Her phone and Maizie's phone started to chime simultaneously, but Maizie was quicker to look at hers and react. She tapped the screen, and Kenna heard it ring through the speaker.

"What's up, Maze?"

Maizie had called Jax. Kenna looked at her phone and saw the alert just as Maizie said, "Zeyla's phone pinged a Mayday. She's in trouble."

Chapter Thirty-One

WASHINGTON, DC, FEDERAL COURTHOUSE
PRESENT DAY

"You honestly expect us to believe the Rosenburgs were hiding a child in a secret room?" The lead defense attorney stared at her from behind his table.

Kenna still remembered being in the back hallway of that house in Arizona. Looking through the glass at the child, who was playing with her dolls.

So creepy. That was the only thing she could think right now. How utterly creepy it had been, and how she'd wanted to do something for the child. But who wanted to take on someone else's responsibility in the middle of a major case?

Back then, she hadn't believed that a child was in her future.

Now, she was glad that she got to devote all her effort to raising her daughter.

"I saw her, but it wasn't my job to intervene in her care.

They weren't mistreating her." In fact, given the child's... temperament, having on hand care with all the money in the world behind it might have been the best situation possible.

"And where is the child now?" As if that was the point.

Then again, was there a point to all these questions? She'd been trying to give context but they'd gone on several tangents.

"I don't know where Lydia Rosenburg is." Kenna was determined not to get ruffled by his attempt to put her off-balance. "We did look. My associates and I made a concerted effort to discover where the child might have ended up and if she is receiving psychological care. We found nothing. It was as if the child never even existed."

"But you saw her. You expect us to believe that the FBI agent you're speaking of, Cecelia Warren, was her mother, and a criminal was her father. And you just happened to see this mysterious child that may or may not even exist."

Kenna said, "The child's father wanted her back. He kidnapped a friend of mine and asked that I kidnap the child so we could exchange the two."

"Yes." The defense attorney slid on a pair of reading glasses and surveyed papers in an open file on the dark wood table. "Mr. Ramon Santiago. It's a shame he isn't here. I had some questions for him as well."

I'm sure you do. "I'm the one on the stand, aren't I?" She glanced at the judge, then at the gallery of people. "Ramon isn't here."

She fought the well of emotion that rushed up in her.

Walk with me, Lord. She'd drawn from Him so much through this season. Looking for comfort. For peace, even though there was no peace to be had in this situation.

"All this court needs to know is that my associates and I

took care of one national conspiracy before. Is it so astounding that we did it again?"

The lawyer stared at her. "The FBI arrested the Rosenburgs and rounded up the family. You weren't there, as far as I recall. Isn't that correct?"

"Aren't I here to testify about something that happened when I wasn't there?" Kenna let that question settle in the air between them. "Over the years, people I care about died. I have to live with that. I have to live with all of it. But you can't say I didn't do everything I could to stop *Dominatus*. Never mind that, over and over, I tried to get out. I tried to live my life and have nothing to do with them. Over and over, they kept dragging me back into it. Kidnapping me. Hurting people I love. When I found an opportunity to end them, I took it."

"We'll be talking about that, Mrs. Jaxton. Don't worry. But first, I'd like you to tell me about this man." The lawyer held up a photo of Preston.

"It's not like I left him out of the story. I met him in Arizona at the same time I was trying to take down the Rosenburgs."

"That's when you discovered *Dominatus*, isn't it?"

"It took me some time to figure out how far-reaching they were." And she'd believed a former president was the head of that particular snake. *Little did I know.*

"And you never once suspected that Preston Lightwood was one of them at any point?"

She wanted to roll her eyes. "Life is never that cut-and-dry. This isn't about good and evil. It's about what the court can prove. Preston isn't the one on trial here."

"His involvement—"

Hasworth shot out of her chair. "Objection."

The judge said, "Sustained. Mrs. Jaxton is right that Preston Lightwood isn't the one on trial."

The defense attorney said, "And yet, he's also conveniently absent. Almost as if everyone in Mrs. Jaxton's life has left her to face this court alone. Interesting that she refers to her associates often. Actively protects them. Hides their real identities. Is almost brought up on charges of interfering in a police investigation and aiding and abetting a fugitive. *And* puts her life on the line for people who don't even have the decency to show up when she's testifying in the biggest case of all."

Kenna bit the inside of her lip. She didn't want to cry. Mostly because this guy would think he'd upset her.

She didn't want to think about watching that coffin lowered into the ground.

Rain streaming from the sky like tears. Her black shoes sinking into the grass while she held her daughter tight to her chest, wrapped under her coat. Jax beside her, holding an umbrella.

All of them huddled around her. Locked together in their grief. Supporting each other.

Preston had been *there*. Why did he need to be here?

Kenna bit out the words, "No charges were filed."

She wasn't the one on trial.

"Do you want to know about *Dominatus* or not? Because those people are responsible for the death of the former president and the head of the CIA. I think that would be more significant than talking about my friends."

The defense attorney asked, "Did you ever meet the president? That's another crime you weren't present for, correct? Seems to be a pattern."

"Yes, I did meet him," Kenna said. "In London."

Chapter Thirty-Two

"There!" Maizie pointed out the front windshield.

Kenna jerked the wheel to the side of the street where Preston stood on the sidewalk, waiting for them. As soon as she'd put the car in park to disengage the door locks, he climbed in the back seat.

"Are you my rideshare?"

Maizie giggled.

"Buckle up." Kenna threw it in drive and hit the gas. "We're already late."

"Funny how that works." Preston sounded amused.

"You want us to get there and not be able to help?" She gripped the wheel and focused on following the car's directions to where Jax was currently pinging on the map.

Maizie turned in the seat and looked back at him.

Preston said, "No offense, but Jax is already there. Zeyla

knows what she's doing. What are a pregnant woman and a nineteen-year-old tech genius going to do in a firefight?"

"I'm not offended." Maizie straightened in her seat. "But Zeyla is going to take me to the range when we get the chance. She's going to teach me about weapons and keep working with me on self-defense."

"I could hit them with the car." This thing was indestructible. Kenna, unfortunately, was not. But right now, that wasn't the point.

Preston gasped. "It was only just fixed!"

Kenna got distracted from being amused and nearly missed her turn. She took the corner sharply and spotted two black SUVs blocking the entry to a shopping mall parking lot. Beyond them, in the dark, she saw flashes of light.

Gunfire.

The parking lot seemed mostly empty, with just a few cars over at the far end by a restaurant. Everything else looked closed, or just derelict at this time of night.

Maizie dialed, and they all listened to it ring. "Come on, Zeyla. Pick up."

"Call Jax."

She dialed again. While it rang, Preston said, "Why do those SUVs look familiar?"

Maizie said, "Those guys from Pueblo found us here! The ones who killed Gabby."

"Now they're trying to get Zeyla? Oh, no way." Kenna let the car nearly pass the blocked entrance, then swung the wheel hard. She bumped the car up onto the curb and drove along the sidewalk around the SUV where men were hunkered down firing at her family! She wanted to ram their vehicle, but what would that accomplish?

The call connected. "I can't talk right now."

"We're here to help!" Kenna yelled over in the direction of the phone, both hands tight on the wheel.

Gunshots pinged off the side by Maizie.

Preston whimpered. "The car was just fixed."

Kenna sped up a bit, avoided the dark streetlight that must've been shot out and bumped off the curb at the end. She couldn't see much in the dark, but swinging the car to the right got her headlights in the right direction.

She lit up Zeyla and Jax hunkered down on the far side of Zeyla's car. Unfortunately, that gave the bad guys a better view of them.

Kenna kept going and stopped with the hood of the armored car in line with the back right side of Zeyla's car. She rolled her window down. "I'm your rideshare!"

Jax lifted up. "Go!"

Zeyla ran around the back of the car as Kenna rolled the window up. Jax covered her. Bullets pinged off the right side of Kenna's car. Within moments, the two of them were in the back. She spotted a guy almost at the door right when Jax slammed it.

She shoved the car in reverse and hit the gas.

Whoever she bumped over wasn't going to be having a good day.

Kenna winced. "Sorry. But you chose this life, bud."

She shifted into drive and hit the gas again, speeding away as fast as she could while Zeyla and Jax breathed heavily in the back seat. It sounded like both of them had been running a marathon and were now out of breath.

"Where to?" Kenna asked.

Jax said, "How about you drive around the corner, and we'll switch seats."

"I'm fine. Police station? Hospital? Home? They'll find out where we live pretty fast if we just leave them loose and don't make sure they're arrested," Kenna said. "If we call Ryson and they're following us, the police could set up a roadblock trap. Right?"

"I have some scratches, but I don't need to see a doctor," Zeyla said.

"Jax?"

He didn't answer right away. "I'm good. We had it handled, and the FBI or cops were on their way to the scene. Now all they'll find is shell casings."

"Because I rescued you?"

"We had it handled."

Maizie glanced in the back. Preston was silent. Kenna didn't really know what to say. Jax could be irritated that she'd entered a dangerous situation with unknown risk. Or he could be irritated that she'd left the RV at all. She didn't know which it was.

"We need to find Sylvia Caughton."

Maizie said, "I still need to run that analysis of Ellayna's voice."

"I need to go talk to the feds *again*," Jax said.

Maybe that was why he was mad. "I can go with you, if you want? I'll explain that you had no choice but to leave the scene."

Preston patted the shoulder of the seat. "Take a left here."

Kenna complied. "Where are we going?"

"Tell Ryson to meet us at Bashevis diner on Sixteenth."

"I'll text him," Jax said.

Zeyla said, "I am hungry." When Maizie looked back at her, she said, "Adrenaline."

Kenna saw the sign for the diner rotating above a squat building and pulled into the parking lot. The ground dipped under the car wheels, and she drove through a couple of potholes before she found a good space out of the light of streetlamps. In a dark corner, where their car might go unnoticed by black SUVs full of gunmen looking for her and her family.

The idea of that made her want to stay in the car, because she knew she was safe in here.

It gave her a small hint of what Jax was probably feeling right about now. Plus the adrenaline. Plus frustration. Plus wondering when the baby would come.

"Do we know what those guys wanted, apart from revenge?" She shut off the engine.

Zeyla said, "They didn't ask. They trailed me when I left Sylvia's building and followed me after I got in my car. Tried to run me off the road." There was a short pause, and she said, "Thanks for showing up."

Kenna waited.

Jax said, "No problem." Then he said louder, "I was happy to help until the cavalry arrived."

Kenna really wasn't going to sit at home when her family was in danger—and she had a million-dollar armored car. "I need a milkshake."

Jax said, "Stay put a second."

The rest of them got out. He opened her door for her and helped her out of the front seat. She groaned as she straightened.

"Did you hurt yourself?"

She shook her head. "I forgot how uncomfortable it is doing defensive driving. I feel like I bruised my tailbone going up that curb."

He shook his head, an incredulous look on his face. At least, from what she could see in the dim light.

"I love you."

He chuckled, sliding his arms around her. "We should

get inside. Not that it's safer than being exposed out here." But he didn't let go of her, he leaned in and slid his nose along hers, giving her a distracting kiss that made her wish maybe she *had* stayed at home. "I love you, too. Hopefully, I live long enough to enjoy raising our baby with you and having you drive me crazy for years rather than expiring on the street because you gave me a heart attack."

"I hope so, too." She kissed him back, trying to be equally distracting to him as he was to her. "I love this car, too. We should keep it."

He laughed, walking her over to the front door of the diner with his arm around her waist. His head close to hers. Muttering about how she liked to change the subject so she wasn't under scrutiny.

Kenna wanted to point out that she wasn't the one who'd been shot at, but now probably wasn't the time.

Jax opened the door, and she went in first. The diner had a couple of customers and two waitresses. Kenna found Preston and Maizie at a booth in the far corner. As she crossed the room, Zeyla emerged from the back hall where the sign indicated the restrooms were. Kenna said, "This is where you come to eat?"

She liked the place just fine. It had a hometown feel, like a lot of the spots she'd eaten at with her dad growing up on the road while he solved cases—and hiding from *Dominatus* so thoroughly that she hadn't even known they existed.

Preston was a billionaire. This wasn't his usual scene. "You'll see." He looked pretty pleased with himself.

Kenna pulled a chair over from a neighboring table and sat with her back to the wall between the booth and the neighboring table. "Don't ask me to slide in there. I'll never get out."

Jax sat at the table to her left, between her and the window. Or the door. Her protector. She reached out, and he held her hand.

Maizie got all dreamy-eyed.

"What are we doing here?" Kenna squeezed his hand.

Jax said, "Ryson and his cops will be here in a few."

The waitress, in a salmon-colored uniform, pushed through a door with a circular window and came over on white sneakers. Her eyes lit, and her entire expression beamed with happiness. "Kenna!"

She managed to stand up before the younger woman got to her. "Nora Thibodeaux." She opened her arms, and Nora gave her a hug. Kenna laughed. "It's really you."

"It's been a while." She shoved her hair back behind her ear; the rest of it was gathered behind her head.

"Since New Orleans, when you had your baby." Kenna laid a hand on her abdomen. "How did you get here from Seattle?"

"I wanted to strike out on my own." Nora lifted her chin in Preston's direction. "He convinced me Salt Lake City was a good place to raise a child. Now it's your turn." She grinned. This young woman, whose life had been torn apart thanks to criminals in the south, had given birth under the worst kind of circumstances and then accepted Preston's offer of a place to live.

"It's a girl." Kenna grinned back. "How is Elvira Makenna Sanders?"

Nora laughed, tugging out her phone to show Kenna the lock screen—an image of Nora and a chubby little girl with two bottom teeth and an infectious smile. "She's so big. And so happy. There's an older lady who lives next door to me, and while I work, she stays with Ellie."

"I told her she doesn't have to work." Preston didn't look up from his phone.

Nora rolled her eyes. "And I keep telling you I'm not the kept woman of an older billionaire. What will people think?"

Preston didn't seem to care. "I'm still putting you and Ellie in my will."

"And I'm still working. I'm taking care of my daughter and building a life for myself." She shook her head. "Even if it's cold as all get out up here."

"You miss the bayou?"

Nora shook her head. "Not one bit."

Kenna gave her another hug. "I'm so happy for you."

"Thank you."

A tear escaped from the corner of Kenna's eye, and she swiped it away. She shifted her chair closer to Jax's and sat where he could put his arm around her, leaning into his side. Nora took their orders, and Kenna decided she wanted fries and a milkshake.

"You need some protein."

Kenna nudged his side. "That's why I'm going to eat one of your chicken fingers."

His phone buzzed. "Ryson said there's an officer down callout at the other end of the precinct, so he has to go there first. He'll be here afterward."

Zeyla said, "And if those guys find us here? They're clearly still after what they wanted—the drive we copied and couriered back to that company." She paused for a second. "Or they want revenge for what we cost them."

"They probably think we forced them to kill Gabby." Meanwhile, Kenna figured they might have been the ones who'd killed Gabby's brother, too. "All for the software. Which they didn't get."

"What are you thinking?" Jax asked.

"Just that if it was *Dominatus*, they sent the wrong people. Or they didn't realize they'd be going up against us."

"I thought they waited for us to find the drive, and then they showed up." Maizie glanced over from her computer.

"Maybe." She had a point. "Then they used Gabby to try and get it from us. Now they're mad."

Jax said, "That makes the most sense."

But why did she feel as if there was more going on? *Dominatus* was involved, but what did they want with that software? Whoever wanted it should've just done a business deal with the software company—or a hostile takeover. Why hire mercenary-type guys to get it? The visibility on a murder case was far too great. They could've gotten what they wanted without anyone knowing.

It almost felt as if they were a distraction. A way to keep Kenna and her family busy. A way to test what they would do—or what resources they had now.

Was that why it seemed off?

Nora set the tray in front of them on the table and came back with another for the booth. Zeyla grabbed her cheeseburger and took a huge bite.

Kenna leaned her head toward Jax, and he said grace for them both in a quiet voice. She squeezed his knee and opened her eyes.

Sylvia Caughton stood just inside the front door, wearing dark jeans and a black sweater with a dark gray coat over it. She looked exactly like the photo on the news outlet website. Like a redheaded actress who probably disliked how many freckles she had and worked extra hard not to have any extra pounds on her body. She was highly trained and dangerous.

Zeyla whipped out of her seat and turned, raising her

gun to point at the woman in the doorway. Jax stood as well, his gun drawn.

One of the men at the bar slid off his stool and rushed into the kitchen. She heard a "Hey!" and then a door slammed.

Sylvia lifted her hands. "You haven't been getting my messages, have you?"

"You want to talk?" Jax asked her, his voice ringing with authority.

"I came here unarmed."

He crossed the room halfway. "Hands against the wall. If you are unarmed and you just want to talk, you get patted down."

Chapter Thirty-Three

Sylvia sat across the table from Kenna, who was going to eat in front of the woman even if it was rude. Kenna grabbed a napkin and wiped some grease from the fries off her fingers. "Did you send the police on a wild goose chase so you could come here?"

The woman had a placid expression. Kenna wasn't sure why she seemed to be able to tell that someone was a *Dominatus* operative. It wasn't anything mystical or in her genetic code. More like the way they walked or held their heads. Like they weren't quite comfortable being out in polite society.

Kenna was just mad this woman was interrupting their meal. Jax had his arms folded across his chest. Maizie had stopped working on her computer, and Preston had put his phone down. Even Nora was listening from the counter.

Kenna grabbed another fry and dipped it in her milkshake like this was a normal meal with friends. "Are you gonna answer the question?"

"We hardly need to be concerned with local law

enforcement." Sylvia had the edge of an accent that sounded European.

"Because you're above the law, is that it?" Definitely a *Dominatus* way of thinking.

Sylvia glanced over at the booth where Maizie and Preston sat. "Do they have to be here?" Her attention settled mostly on Zeyla, who returned it with a death stare so cold it could have frozen water in a glass.

"Yes, they have to be here." Kenna wasn't changing any of her habits or negotiating with this woman. She could ask what this woman wanted and let her talk, or they could get right to the point. "Where is Ellayna?"

Sylvia held her hands clasped between her knees, and her legs were crossed one over the other. It gave her an elongated appearance—and made it look like she was cold. Probably because of the ice in her veins.

"That's for you to figure out, isn't it?"

Kenna tipped her head to the side. "So you aren't going to help or give me a tip? Point me in the right direction, at least." Or reveal that she had no idea.

But *Dominatus* prided itself on being in control of everything, or at least, knowing everything. So like the identity of the kidnapper. Or the place where they were being held...

Was that so hard?

"The rules of engagement prohibit me from giving you assistance."

Kenna stared at her. Then she looked at Zeyla. "Any idea what she's talking about?"

Zeyla didn't look at her, she kept all her attention on Sylvia. Looking for any reason whatsoever to get out of her seat and intervene in the situation again. End the conversation. Possibly end Sylvia herself—with lethal force.

"Wartime contingencies, or some kind of grand operation going on?"

"If I ask, is she going to tell me what's going on?"

Zeyla asked, "Do they ever?"

"I am still here, and I can hear your conversation," Sylvia said with a snooty tone. "It's rude to talk about someone as if they're not there."

Kenna looked at her. "You know where Ellayna and her mother and brother are being held." She crossed her arms. "Seems like I just had a conversation with someone else about them being an accessory to murder. Right. It was the guy you beat up, shoved in his trunk, and dumped on the side of the road where he wouldn't be found for a while."

Sylvia's expression didn't change. The woman gave her nothing. "There are people in the world whose lives are important, and others are expendable."

"I don't believe that."

Sylvia's eyes flared at that. "You can't possibly believe that others are as important to the world as you are." She looked incredulous.

"What if I do?"

"Then you, at least, must believe that your child—"

"She's not part of this. She isn't part of *Dominatus*. You don't get to use her. Not even simply to make a point."

Jax's body tensed, but he didn't move.

Kenna said, "So tell me. Where do I find them?"

"You're supposed to be the one that finds them," Sylvia said. "Isn't that what I said? Maybe you should listen."

"Or what?" Kenna shrugged. "Seems like I'm doing fine not taking advice from *Dominatus*. Maybe you could all continue to leave me alone and let me live my life."

"Is that a joke?" Sylvia looked like she wanted to laugh but wasn't sure she should. "None of us are free."

"Disagree."

"Freedom is an illusion. People cling to their rights and their *freedom* and for what? So they can believe the lie and pretend they're not beholden to the law or paying their taxes?"

"I thought you were above the law."

Sylvia said, "We all swear allegiance to something."

"And none of us is free?"

"Of course not. Every action has a consequence, for good or ill. One day, even our thoughts will be regulated, cataloged, and controlled. Society can't possibly be left to govern itself. Our leaders have to take more decisive action and make sure that insurrection is squashed before it erupts. It's the only way there can be peace and prosperity in the world."

Kenna stared at her for a second, trying to absorb the implication of that without it turning out in her mind like a dystopian future where a select few at the top controlled all humans against their will. Peace and perfection—on the surface. Below that, it was manipulation and subjugation.

She glanced at Zeyla.

"I wish I was surprised to hear that's the plan." Zeyla looked like she wanted to be sick.

Kenna turned back to Sylvia. "You think I'm going to allow my family to live in that world?" She would fight with everything she had to keep it from happening.

The battles she'd faced would be nothing in comparison.

"There's no way the world will allow *Dominatus* to put a tracker in everyone's mind." She shook her head. "Good luck even trying to convince people it's a good idea."

If they needed her input, she planned to be in

Wyoming at her cabin. Living a quiet life and raising her daughter with Jax.

Sylvia just stared at her. Probably confident that the slow creep of *Dominatus* taking over every facet of society would ensure their victory in the end. An insidious plan that spoke of great patience.

Kenna said, "That's why you needed one of your assets in the president's chair."

She planned to vote for the not-evil candidate for the next election. Although, it wasn't always so easy to tell. Life didn't usually come with black-and-white decisions. Sometimes, it was about choosing the least bad option.

Sylvia shrugged very slightly, only barely moving.

Kenna figured if she could keep the woman talking, eventually the police would arrive, and they could arrest Wallace Lofton's kidnapper. But if they didn't make it soon, Jax and Zeyla would have to detain her. "So in the long term, it's about total control over the human race? It's good to have goals. I have plenty of my own."

She prayed for wisdom as she spoke, asking God to give her the words to speak. That was better than allowing her anger and frustration to bubble up, borne of powerlessness, which would just give her an attitude.

Sylvia softened her gaze. "I'm sure you won't be surprised to know that there are some of us who would fully support your participation. Your advice."

"You think I'm going to what...join the board of directors or something?"

"It's one option," Sylvia said. "General Schnell was a key part of the group, as was Dr. Buzard, the senator that you murdered, and the director of the FBI." She looked up and to the side, as if trying to think of more people in *Dominatus* that Kenna had killed.

Kenna said, "There was an asset in England. That was a tough fight. She was good." And then Bruce had shown up to help her. "The president is the one who took down Schnell, by the way. Schnell isn't dead; he was simply shipped off to some military black site where he's been buried. His identity scraped from all existence."

"A little dramatic, isn't it?"

Kenna asked, "Why doesn't *Dominatus* do that with all their enemies?"

"We aren't in control of the apparatus of justice, crime, and punishment. If we need to eliminate a dissenter, there are more decisive methods."

"And yet, I'm still alive." She refused to believe that everyone in her family was alive simply because they weren't a threat.

"You carry one of the only children of—"

"Yeah," Kenna cut her off. "I've already heard the whole thing. I'm so special. I'm practically the chosen one." She laid a hand on her baby bump. "Or she is."

"Did you pick out a name yet?" Sylvia asked.

"If I had, it wouldn't be your business."

Zeyla said, "You can refer to her as *your worst nightmare*. Because that's what I'm going to train her to be."

Maizie snickered. Jax's tension cracked, and she knew he was about to say something.

"Our child isn't going to be a part of this fight," Kenna told Sylvia.

"And yet, she already is."

"If you didn't come here to tell me where to find Ellayna, you should just go. I don't want to hear anything else you have to say." Kenna sat back in her chair.

"This is a test you have to pass on your own merit. I can't help you."

A test?

Sylvia stood. "Someone threw your name in the hat. I guess all that's left is for you to prove what the rest of us already know. That deep down you're one of *us*."

"You need to explain that."

"You aren't part of *Dominatus* yet, so why would I have to explain anything to you?" Sylvia left her chair pushed out and walked to the back hall, where she disappeared out the rear exit.

"Please tell me I can chase her down." Zeyla shifted from the seat, grabbed the edge of the table, and planted one foot on the floor. Ready to move fast.

"And do what?" Jax sounded like he wanted to be sick. He touched two fingers to his forehead. "That was fun."

She looked at him. "She gave us nothing."

"I wouldn't say that."

"What do you mean? She could have handed us a lead."

"I think she wants you to get one yourself," Jax said. "Because it's *a test*."

Kenna shook her head. "You think that means something?"

"She also mentioned the rules of engagement." Jax looked at Zeyla. "Any idea what's going on?"

"You aren't going to like it."

Kenna asked, "Do we ever?"

Zeyla almost smiled. "If it's a test, it's because *Dominatus* wants to know what you can do. You're supposed to prove yourself to them."

Of course, she'd volunteered to do that. She'd *asked* them to test her.

Kenna wanted to lean forward and plant her forehead on the table and groan a lot, but bending that way wasn't an option right now. Instead, she opted to do it to the side and land with her forehead on Jax's shoulder.

"Of course, they can't leave me alone. Of *course*."

He shifted and put his arm around her, drawing her closer into his side. "Who cares what they want, or what they're doing. We're still going to find Ellayna, right?"

"Yes." She just needed to know where to look.

Maizie was back on her laptop. "Remember those articles about you on Sylvia's hard drive?"

Kenna looked over. "I remember."

"There were others about the president. So if this is a test, and she's reporting back to the rest of them on your progress—"

Zeyla cut in, "Like a journalist, more interested in sensationalism than facts."

Maizie nodded. "What if the president is also being tested? Hers is about health problems. Maybe she has to prove herself in her job."

"I guess I could be grateful I'm not the only one in the spotlight. But what is it for? Just to see what we're made of?" She already knew they were disturbed enough to do that. So, it wasn't super surprising that they would get their kicks from putting people under pressure and watching what happened.

"Makes me want to go back to Wyoming and hide in the cabin."

Jax said, "You wouldn't rest knowing Ellayna is still out there."

Kenna closed her eyes. *God, help us.*

Chapter Thirty-Four

"She said that?" Ryson glanced over, his face shadowed. Jax stomped his boots on the sidewalk, trying to get warm when it was freezing out here. He had his hands tucked in the pockets of his wool overcoat. Insulated pants on. Extra layers on top, a beanie, and gloves. "Yep. All this is some kind of test."

"Do you need to tell the FBI?" Ryson motioned to the house with a black-gloved hand, where the FBI's tactical team was breaching the house of one Rich Eastbury.

"They seem to be on it, looking for Ellayna. After all, they found this guy in her DMs on social media." Jax's stomach turned at the thought of a twelve-year-old being harassed like that. Groomed, so that Rich would get her out of her routine in a way she was unprotected. Then he would have her. "Let's see what he says."

The FBI had confirmed that Rich was in the house. He'd been chatting online to who knew what kind of other perverts or victims for a couple of hours. Until his door exploded in and his entire world erupted into a flash of light.

Jax could just about hear shouts from inside the house. "Kenna called the president as soon as she got back in the car."

Ryson shook his head. "It's still crazy to me that they have each other's number. Actually, it's crazy that she outed all of you in that press conference and told everyone you guys work for her."

"Thankfully, she's been pretty hands off. It might even be over. Kenna said she sounded really irritated, told her she didn't have time to hear about it, and hung up on her."

"I didn't vote for her."

"No one did, but we're the only ones that seem to disagree with how she's running things. Then again, all those people she's got who think she walks on water don't know that she's actually an asset for *Dominatus*. If we explained, we would only sound like we're trying to incite something seditious."

Jax was determined to continue their tactic of keeping their heads down. It didn't keep Kenna out of danger. He'd been trying to get her to lay low in the RV more, not that it was a foolproof way to keep her safe. But then she had come to his and Zeyla's rescue at that shopping mall. Driving right into the middle of an active shooter situation.

"She terrifies me."

"The president?"

Jax chuckled, shaking his head. "My wife."

Ryson barked a laugh and clapped him on the shoulder. "You married her."

"How do you do it? The world is terrifying, and yet you leave your house. You go to work and trust that nothing will happen to them while you're on shift."

"It's why I do the work. I want the world they live in to be safe."

"But you aren't there to protect them."

Ryson said, "You want to be her twenty-four seven bodyguard?"

"For her and the baby."

"Eventually, you have to let them out of your sight, bro."

Jax nodded. "I know that. I'm here, aren't I? I'm living with it. But it still feels like the fear is eating me up from the inside."

"That's because you're trying to carry it. You're trying to turn the fear into something else or make it less. The fact that you have it in you in the first place is..." Ryson blew out a breath. "Do you know how many fathers I meet on this job who don't give two hoots about their kids? Who couldn't possibly care any less that something might happen to their children? That they might ever be unsafe, unprotected, and get hurt?"

"I'm not like them, I get it."

"And that—just that—is an *amazing* thing. It's not rare. It's a miracle. Humans are selfish. We don't do the right thing. We fail. You're over here tearing yourself apart trying to figure out how to allow nothing to happen to them."

"But I'm gonna fail. I'm gonna choose wrong, and they'll get hurt."

Ryson said, "Yeah, you will at some point. They will get hurt. You can't stop it, though you can maybe mitigate some of the fallout. Or the worst could happen, and you might not survive. The point is whether you're going to waste the time you have worrying about keeping them safe or whether you are going to *live*. That's why the Bible says to choose life."

Jax had chosen worry and fear a whole lot lately. Probably too much.

Ryson clapped him on the shoulder again. "You've got

to let it go and trust God has it all in His hands, or you'll wake up in twenty years and realize you wasted your life instead of enjoying what you have now."

Ryson's radio crackled. "All clear, Lieutenant. You and Mr. Jaxton can come in."

"Time to go live in the moment." Jax set off. They headed along the sidewalk, past the stump of a tree that had been cut down but not dug up. The roots ran under the sidewalk, pushing it up so that the surface was uneven.

The front door was open. An FBI agent stood there on guard with his weapon angled down at a forty-five. He nodded as they passed.

Inside the house, it seemed as if every light had been turned on. The yellow glow cast a weird filter over everything, and with the warmth indoors, it created a kind of haze in the air.

Ryson led him through the house, going first because he was the cop here. Jax was only a civilian. They didn't have to include him, but out of courtesy for the guy who used to work in the FBI office here—and what they knew of Kenna's story—they'd allowed him access. The bottom line was that these special agents knew him personally, not just what the news had said about him in the past few years.

The lead agent here was Dires, an ex-NFL football player who'd gone straight to Quantico from a Super Bowl loss a few years ago. He was arguably a better agent than quarterback, but not by much. The guy towered over everyone in height and was wider than most in his shoulders. He turned to see them come in. "Gentlemen, Rich has some things he'd like to say."

The guy had been allowed to sit in a wooden chair pulled over from his dining table—a folded card table that didn't match anything else. Even the two chairs were mismatched. Jax looked around and spotted a laptop on the recliner in the living room.

He had thinning brown hair, nothing on top but a few greasy strands. A T-shirt that was too big for his frame, and stained tan pants.

Jax said, "Go ahead."

Rich blinked, opening his mouth and smacking his lips together like he had a bad taste in his mouth. To the FBI's credit, he didn't look like he'd been roughed up. Just surprised. "What do you want to know?"

Dires said, "We already know you were trying to groom Ellayna Feathers."

His eyes flared. "Who?"

Jax shook his head. "Don't play dumb. You were trying to connect with her online, and now she's missing."

The FBI would've searched the whole house. If they'd found the family, this would be an entirely different conversation.

"You think…" Rich glanced between them. "I didn't do anything!"

"That's debatable, I think," Ryson said. "Depending on your definition. Seems like you do plenty."

"What matters is what we can prove beyond a reasonable doubt." Dires folded his arms, which made him look even bigger.

The terrified-dad part of Jax wanted to ask if he was interested in leaving the FBI and coming on staff with Banbury Investigations as a bodyguard. But that would ruin a good career that made a real difference in the world.

"I didn't take them!" Rich fought against the cuffs securing his hands behind the chair. "I didn't do it!"

"Can you prove that?" Jax shrugged. "Because we've got enough evidence that you might be the kidnapper that a judge granted these feds a warrant based on it. We can now tear apart your *entire* life. We'll know everything you've been doing and everyone you've been talking to."

Rich let out a shout of frustration. He fought harder against the bonds, sweating through his T-shirt now.

"Start talking," Dires said. His tone made Jax want to start talking.

They hadn't worked together here, as Dires hadn't been an agent for that long. But the guy's history meant he quickly rose to a prominent position in the office. He was the poster boy for the FBI, a star turned career cop—though he could never do undercover work with such a recognizable face. He was a guy who had turned down millions because he wanted to seek out justice.

During his final season, he'd suffered a couple of injuries. No doubt he'd seen the writing on the wall and quit while he was ahead. Exactly the kind of guy the FBI would invest in, hoping he'd have a long career.

"I didn't take them. They aren't here, are they?" It was more of a statement than a question.

Jax was inclined to believe him.

Rich continued, "I don't go anywhere but work and here. So, I don't have them stashed anywhere else."

"No?" Dires asked. "No side trips on your way home, driving past the park on Tenth? Slowing down to watch the kids play."

Rich's jaw flexed. His eyes darted to the side.

"Now isn't the time for games," Jax reminded him.

"Tell me this." Dires flicked up his chin. "The day she went missing, you stopped messaging her. Before then, you'd been sending messages regularly. Seemed like you might be making some progress. Why'd you suddenly stop if you didn't have a reason to believe she wouldn't be reading them anyway?"

Jax caught where this was going. When Rich didn't say anything, he picked up where Dires had left off. Driving the point in a little further. "You knew there was no point sending the messages. Seems to me that you knew they were gone, so you quit. How's that, Rich? How did you know they were gone?"

Rich muttered under his breath.

"What's that?" Jax wanted to lean in because it would be patronizing, but the guy would probably try to headbutt or bite him. But he had to know he'd been caught. "You know what happened."

"I saw them."

Jax's stomach clenched.

Dires asked, "What did you see?"

"I like to..." Rich swallowed. "Drive past her house. When I know she gets off the bus and walks to her house. I sit across the street."

"Nice view?" Dires's insinuation was clear.

"I just watch! I didn't touch her. I swear."

That might make him at least responsible, or an accessory. He hadn't stopped it from happening. They were still missing. "What did you see, Rich?"

"An SUV; it was black. It parked in the driveway, and these men knocked on the door. When it was opened, they shoved inside and dragged out all three of them." He hesitated. "The baby was crying."

Jax had seen far too many of those vehicles lately. He got the precise date and time from Rich, then said, "And no one on the street called 911 after hearing and seeing this commotion?"

Jax wanted him to realize that he should've been the

one to call the police. But also, if there had been so much noise that he heard it in his car, someone else must have noticed. Right? It couldn't have been that everyone on the street was gone or busy or unable to notice their neighbors were being kidnapped.

"No one is around at that time. That's why I do it then." Rich swallowed. "She gets off the bus by herself and walks alone."

Jax clenched his teeth. "And these guys took them out of the house?"

"They rushed the mom down the steps with the baby in her arms. Ellayna was behind them. Hands over their mouths, so they couldn't make noise. One of them picked up Ellayna and tossed her over his shoulder, then I think he threw her in the vehicle. But I couldn't see exactly."

They had been taken against their will. *Hands over their mouths.* Might have been nothing, but it might have been chloroform. "Did you see the license plate of the vehicle?"

"The back didn't have one. I didn't see the front. It sped away."

"And the men?" Dires asked. "Assuming the kidnappers were men."

Rich nodded. "One of them looked over at my car. I saw his face. Got a good look. I knew I should remember it, just in case the police came knocking, asking about it."

Jax didn't like where this was going.

"If you drop all the charges against me, I'll give you the sketch of his face that I came up with." Rich's expression turned smug. "I used an online program where you can do like a police sketch. It's a good one, if you ask me, anyway. You can find the kidnappers."

He'd come up with a serious piece of leverage. Jax was

almost impressed. "The warrant covers his computer, right?"

Dires nodded.

Rich screamed. "I want a deal!"

Jax turned back at the doorway to the living room. "Tell them you provided key evidence in their investigation. Maybe even saved lives. You'll get your deal."

Of course, he couldn't promise that, but he didn't care about anything but getting these people back.

A black SUV sounded a whole lot like those guys from Pueblo. Had they come here to take the Feathers family?

Jax sat on the couch and dragged over the computer. He looked at the files on Rich's hard drive. It didn't take long to find the right file type.

The image Rich had come up with was a decent representation, but it would never hold up in court. These things had to be done officially. The hair was dark and curled on the man's head. High cheekbones and a pronounced jaw. Definitely the hard-edged look of a mercenary. The kind of person who would kidnap a family, probably for money. There had been no ransom. The phone calls didn't fit a revenge plan—they would have been killed already.

Unless Kenna was right, and the calls from Ellayna had been done using the *Dominatus* software. In that case, they might not still be alive.

Ryson appeared at the door. "Got it?"

Jax looked over at his friend. "I know who took them."

Chapter Thirty-Five

Undisclosed Location

Ramon paced back and forth in the small entryway where they'd left him. The smell of burned coffee came from somewhere. The double doors to a hall—he could see through a small window in each side—were locked, and no one had passed through there that he'd seen.

He turned and paced again, surveying the empty space.

Stagnant air. A glass door to outside—also locked.

An empty corner with no chairs. A reception counter. No computer, nothing in the drawers, and no electronics.

All that was left to do was punch a hole in the walls and see what he could find. Ramon paced back to the reception desk and climbed up. He reached with both hands and shoved a ceiling tile out of the way, expecting... No idea. And the only thing he could do was look up there.

Unless he figured out a way to climb into the ceiling and get out of this desolate entryway so he could start exploring this building. One in a row of early twentieth-century military structures. Maintained well but not updated much. Purposed and repurposed.

"Care to explain what you're doing?" Hollace stood at the open front doorway, holding the door with his body. Letting cool, fresh air in from outside. Wearing a suit and tie and shined shoes.

Ramon looked at him, still standing on the reception counter. "None of your business."

They'd taken him on that mission to Norway and brought him here, creating the ruse that they were all going to be killed, but only so the accountant would give them access to his books.

Ramon jumped down, seeing this man he'd have called...well, not a friend. Maybe a colleague. He'd have said he trusted the guy. But now he knew that MSI—Bear and his team—were working for the president.

No way was he going to trust them.

They were doing the bidding of *Dominatus*. Following someone who was an asset of theirs, reporting to her and taking orders.

There was no excuse for this.

"Care for the tour?" Hollace motioned with his head at the outside, with its blue sky and frosty green grass. The backdrop of mountains.

Ramon didn't want to stay here, so he said, "Sure."

He was trying to act nonchalant. He needed a phone or a computer, and then he was going to stock up. Take his chances on those mountains surrounding this secret military base and get back to his life. These weren't people he was prepared to help.

Hollace backed up as Ramon approached, still holding the door.

Ramon strode outside like he hadn't just been locked in that lobby for four hours. "So, you guys live here now? What happened to the deep-sea platform?"

They hadn't heard from MSI in weeks. No surprise, given that none of these guys would have been quick to confess to Kenna that they'd made a deal with the devil.

"Too far out. We still control it, but we needed to be in a more central location." Hollace led him along the street in the center of the base. "There's a contingent there, but not many. We have too much to do."

"This is one of General Schnell's compounds? His secret bases?" Ramon wasn't going to explain about Spokane and the run-in he'd had with a look-alike there—some of the most gruesome displays of murder he'd ever seen. All for clientele who wanted to rub elbows while death was on display.

"Places we can fly under the radar are few and far between." Hollace walked a steady pace, his dress shoes getting dirty.

"Probably helps when you have protection from on high." Ramon threw it out, just to see what the guy did.

"The enemy of my enemy is my friend?"

"Try again." Ramon frowned, pushing his body to keep up with the pace. He hadn't eaten or had water since they landed. The dehydration from flying was making his head swim.

"I didn't have time to think of a story you're going to accept. I was busy burying my friend."

Ramon stopped outside a Quonset hut. Hollace turned to face him.

Ramon said, "If you're taking orders from *Dominatus*, you'd have to think twice after they murdered your friend.

You went into their territory, but you didn't have protection?"

Hollace stared at him, not even grief in his expression. "Do you want the tour or not?"

Ramon waved with his hand, and they set off again, into a building with multiple satellite dishes on the roof. It had been modernized, but the decorator hadn't figured out how to hide all the wires that now ran along the top of the wall, through a hole in a vent above the door, and into a room filled with computer equipment.

One entire wall was nothing but screens. The only person in the room was Hazel, the MSI computer tech—their version of Maizie. She typed on a Bluetooth keyboard she had on a strap around her neck so that it sat in front of her. While she entered keystrokes, she also wandered around, looking at different displays.

Over to a metal table, probably not meant to hold beverages. Ramon didn't know what science had been done on these tables over the century since this place had been consigned. She lifted a tall cup and drank from the straw in big gulps.

Ramon swallowed against the thick dryness in his throat. "What do you guys have?"

Hazel turned and smiled. "Ramon!" She came over, set a hand on his arm, and lifted up to her tiptoes to kiss his cheek. "It was a beautiful ceremony, wasn't it?" Her expression faltered. "Maybe you weren't there. I don't remember seeing you actually, now that I think about it." She wrinkled her nose. "You might need a shower, bro."

Ramon shrugged. "Among other things. You have the information that accountant gave us?"

Hazel glanced at Hollace, who nodded slightly. "It's been a puzzle, that's for sure. Don't get me wrong, he gave us so much." She waved a hand at the screens, as if the rest of them knew what they were looking at. "But it's all in code. It'll take time to crack it."

"Maybe you should reach out to Maizie," Ramon suggested as casually as he could. "Collaborate and see if you can figure it out."

Hollace shifted his weight. "Let's go, Ramon. We can continue our tour."

Hazel looked almost sad.

"Nice to see you." Ramon was surprised Hollace didn't grab his arm and drag him out.

In the hall, he forgot to temper his frustration.

"What is your problem?" Ramon didn't bother holding back his irritation. "You could get all this done faster if you ask for help, but you've got Hazel in there carrying the weight of all this on her shoulders. If you reached out to Banbury Investigations and let them help you, I wouldn't have had to dig up your team and force myself in."

"You think you found us?"

Ramon frowned. "You can't expect me to believe you let me in."

Hollace said, "I don't have to prove it to you."

"You should tell Kenna what you're doing." Ramon wasn't going to back down from that.

"You might think she can do anything, and she might be your boss, but she doesn't need to be a part of this."

"Why?"

"Because the whole point of it is to keep her out!" Hollace's face reddened with anger. "I just buried a guy I've known for decades. You think I'm going to bring in a pregnant woman and put her life in danger? Watch her get cut down? No one here is going to bring her into *anything*."

"And that prohibits you from passing on information.

Or status updates? You're working with the enemy!" And Ramon had just ruled out any shot he had at sneaking around to find a phone or computer. They knew the second he had access to either, he would contact Kenna as fast as he could.

Let her know they were working with the president.

"Things are happening," Hollace said. "You have no idea what is going on."

"Then I guess I'm the one who needs a status update." Ramon folded his arms. "Because you obviously have something going on."

"You think we need help? Or you wanna keep criticizing what we do here?" Hollace clearly didn't like that.

Ramon wasn't used to people criticizing his behavior. Usually, they just labeled him a murderer and went on with their lives. Why did he even care what these guys thought? "You were supposed to be good guys. Now you made a deal with the wrong side. I just want to understand why."

"Things are far more complicated than you know. Kenna has work to do, and no one wants to see her hurt." Hollace sighed. "The *goal* is to fix this situation once and for all. To get the right person in charge of *Dominatus*. We all thought that Kenna could take them down, but who's going to ask a pregnant woman to fight that battle?"

"What right person?" He'd been under the impression, from Kenna herself, that a woman couldn't be in charge of *Dominatus*. So that ruled out the president, thanks to evil organization misogyny. Who was left? "The accountant?"

That whole situation had been beyond weird.

They hadn't fought anyone. They'd been caught in a couple of traps and lost a man. But in the end, their target had effectively turned himself over to them.

"I don't have to explain anything to you." Hollace's expression had hardened. "Now keep walking."

Ramon shook his head. He didn't need to win this guy over, and he probably couldn't convince him to say more than he should. It wasn't like he could torture the guy, persuade him, or hand over a bribe.

His thoughts spun, and he slammed against the wall.

"Careful." Hollace grabbed his arm and dragged Ramon outside. Across gravel to another door on the far side. "Let's get you somewhere you can lie down. Get a drink of water. All that. Sound good."

"I'm not an invalid." His head hadn't cleared, though. He felt like he was swimming in his own mind. Trying to surface.

Dehydration. Exhaustion. Hopefully, nothing worse than that.

The hallway tunneled in front of him, as if it was a hundred feet long. Hollace led him past rooms. Doorways with tiny windows. Beside one was a TV screen that made Ramon stop.

He had to...

Thoughts wouldn't come together in his mind.

The screen showed a living room, a mother holding a toddler. Bouncing him on her lap. A young teen girl lay on the other couch. Stretched out watching TV.

Hollace tugged on his arm again, and Ramon stumbled forward. "Come on." He touched a button on a key panel, and a buzzer sounded.

Hollace pulled the door open and shoved Ramon inside, the air stuffy like that lobby he'd been shut in. He stumbled and almost went down, but he managed to catch himself and straightened. The room swam around him, everything rotating.

Expecting a prison cell, or something like it, he was surprised to find the room furnished like a hotel suite with a kitchenette to his right. A brown-haired older woman sat at the table, dealing out a deck of cards. An older man got up from the couch, setting aside his book and standing. "Ramon?"

The door clanged shut behind him, the sound echoing through his head and birthing a dull ache in his skull.

Ramon reached up and touched his forehead, trying to focus and push the headache away. "What?"

His mouth couldn't form the words. Exhaustion reached up and swallowed him into the oblivion.

They rushed over, and Ramon stared up at Amara and Bruce. Why was he on the floor?

He didn't have a chance to ask before everything went black.

Chapter Thirty-Six

Ramon came back to awareness slowly, like pushing up through deep water to breach the surface. He scrubbed both hands down his face, realizing quickly that he wasn't in a hotel bed. It wasn't like he had an actual home, per se. So, waking up in an odd location wasn't unusual. Normally, it wasn't on a couch. Or in a small room that had been decorated to look like a bland hotel room that should have been renovated ten years ago.

Ramon pushed up onto one elbow, blinking while his eyes adjusted. The door was dark green and looked like a heavy fire door but with a small window in it, crisscrossed with wire. Like the door to a holding cell.

"He's awake." Bruce pushed his chair back from the table and left his plate and mug behind, ambling over. "How are you feeling, bud?"

Amara sat opposite Bruce, making Ramon think of someone playing a card game. But she was eating now.

"What's going on?"

"Take it slow. You were pretty exhausted."

Ramon pushed himself all the way up and leaned back

against the couch. Someone had removed his shoes, and there was a sharp prick on the inside of his elbow. Looked like he'd been stuck with a needle. "What did—"

"Right." Bruce settled in the armchair to his right. "That was us, I'm afraid. You were pretty dehydrated from whatever you've been up to. It was the easiest way to make sure you got enough fluids."

"You have medical supplies in here?"

Bruce said, "We asked for them when you didn't wake up. Hollace got us what we needed."

"But he didn't let you leave." Because they were being held captive here.

"That's the deal, bud."

Ramon shook his head.

"What's going on outside this base?" Bruce asked.

It wasn't a good sign if Bruce didn't know. Amara was usually pretty in charge, or at least the one in the know. Right now, she seemed almost...sad. Subdued. Nothing like her usual self.

Ramon explained about the janitor, the town in Norway, and the guy they'd brought back.

Amara said, "So he's here."

Bruce didn't respond to that.

Ramon had to find a way to get out of this room. He needed to steal a satellite phone from someone on the base and call Kenna. Let her know... What? He barely understood what was happening, and none of it was good.

He managed to get up.

"There's a bathroom through there." Bruce pointed to the corner on the left side, farthest from the door. "And coffee in the pot."

"What time is it?" Ramon reached up and stretched,

trying to work the kinks out of his back. How long had he been asleep?

"Just after eight in the morning."

Ramon shook his head. He took care of pressing business first but went to the front door after, when he really wanted coffee. He wanted to get out of here more than that.

There was no handle on this side, just a metal plate that had been screwed into the door frame.

He pushed on the door, then checked all the drawers in the little kitchenette for something he could use as a screwdriver. "Where are the knives?" He needed the flat edge of a butter knife, at least.

"No knives."

When he turned to Bruce, the guy was casually taking a sip of his coffee. Ramon said, "So you've resigned yourself to sitting here doing nothing?"

"Tried to get out." Another sip. "I got all the way to an office while Amara created an elaborate distraction. The phone had no dial tone, and the computer wasn't connected to the internet. They took great pains to explain to us what a "closed system" means and how there's no way to contact the outside world."

"Bear had a sat phone." Ramon poured himself some java.

"You won't see him. Just a couple of the others." Amara wore slacks and flat shoes with a plain knit sweater. No makeup.

Maybe that was the difference in her. She seemed more...natural. Like the woman she was underneath, when the bravado had been stripped away.

"We need to contact Kenna and let her know what's happening." He leaned back against the kitchenette counter. "I'm not sitting here doing nothing."

Bruce glanced at Amara, his jaw hard. "There's nothing you can do—"

"If you call me 'bud' one more time, I'm going to throw this mug at you," Ramon warned. "I don't think you just turned yourselves over to them. Maybe you should tell me how the two of *you* got here."

Then, he was going to persuade them that if all three of them worked together, they would have a greater chance of getting out of here.

Or two of them could create enough distraction for the third to escape.

He'd still rather take his chances on the mountain, battling the temperature and the terrain, than sit here feeling as if he was useless.

Amara glanced at Bruce, then set her fork down. "There's more food keeping warm in the oven. I just made an easy breakfast casserole."

"Right, because that's such a normal thing to do in captivity."

"We all have to eat. A hearty meal will give you better energy." Amara leaned back on her seat. "Do you want to sit?"

Ramon found he couldn't argue, but it still felt like he was being led into a trap.

Amara gathered Bruce's dirty dishes and put them in the sink, then she brought down a plate from the cupboard above the coffeepot. She lifted the small dish out of the oven.

"That smells good."

Amara handed him a spatula. "It isn't a trick."

She sat back down, while he served himself a portion and poured more coffee. He sat across from her. "How did you get here?" He paused, his fork almost to his mouth. "Wait. How long have the two of you been here?"

Bruce shook his head. "At least a month, maybe a little longer."

"And no one noticed? Surely Kenna, or any of them, would have realized you weren't answering your phones. I didn't hear anything about you being in trouble." Kenna would be here herself, mounting a rescue. Maybe. If she wasn't pregnant, anyway. "Zeyla doesn't know you're in trouble?"

Amara said, "It's better if they don't come. They'd be interfering and tying up everyone here in dealing with them, when there's important work to be done."

"Go back to the beginning and explain." Ramon shoved a full fork into his mouth.

"We were tracking down a package being moved through *Dominatus* transport routes," Amara said. "They use their own system for shipping. Smuggling, really. We had no idea what it was, but we knew it was big based on the personnel they had guarding the routes and the vehicle they were using. Important and sizeable, at least. When we caught up to the truck and started to pursue it, we were able to stick a tracker on the vehicle.

"Of course, they quickly found that. But we got a general direction and worked out that it was coming this way."

Ramon said, "I barely have a clue where here is."

"Middle of nowhere, Wyoming," Bruce interjected.

Amara continued, "When we got close, the roads were single-lane. The truck slowed, and it became harder to follow them without being spotted. We hung back, scoured the area, and realized it was all a top secret US government facility. But the guys in Humvees following the truck were people we knew."

"MSI team members."

Amara nodded. "We realized they must have come on board with *Dominatus*, but we figured it was against their will. Our mission switched to attempting to liberate them from the people forcing them to do what they were told."

"But it turned out, they weren't being coerced. They were here voluntarily." Ramon shook his head. "That's what I can't wrap my head around."

"You don't need to," Bruce said. "All you need to know is that they have a plan, and it's a decent one."

Ramon turned to him. "You can't be serious. You bought in?"

"Not much we can do about it from in here. They're going to do what they're going to do." Bruce shrugged, sitting forward on the chair and planting his elbows on his knees. "This is bigger than what we want."

"We need to get word out."

Amara said, "For what purpose? There's nothing we can do to stop it, and Kenna should be kept safe from having to deal with it."

"You think she's doing nothing, resting in the RV? She sent me to find out what they're doing *because* she's been worried that they're out of contact. Now I find out that MSI is working for *Dominatus*? This is unbelievable."

"Is it?"

"We're supposed to fight all of them." He tossed his fork on the plate, and it clattered against the stoneware. "They've made the wrong choice signing up to *help*. You can't possibly think this isn't a huge problem."

"We're in a fight, but not against MSI," Amara said. "This is a fight for the soul of *Dominatus*."

Bruce picked up the thread of the conversation. "One that Kenna doesn't need to be involved in."

Ramon glanced between them. He pushed his chair back and got up to pace. "You have to know I respect the two of you. The way you've been fighting this for years, trying to do the right thing. I understand the need to atone for what you've done in the past and make things right. You *know* I get that. Probably more than anyone. But you made the wrong choice. This isn't how we stop them, and that's the only way this is going to end." He shook his head. "Please tell me this is a plan to tear them apart from the inside. *Something.*"

Amara said, "They need a new leader. We're going to make sure it's someone we can at least control, even if it isn't someone we trust. A person that is going to take the whole organization in a new direction."

"If you can't beat 'em, join 'em? That's your whole plan?"

"I don't need to join them," Amara said. "I've been part of *Dominatus* this whole time."

"Fighting against them from the inside!"

She didn't speak right away. "You weren't far off the mark in talking about redemption. We do all have things we wish we could wash away or at least make up for."

"So you sit around here as punishment. Letting someone else take care of the problem?"

"There's only so much we can do if they won't let us out. Clearly, we can't put up much of a fight as captives."

If he'd been in here for weeks, Ramon might actually feel the same way. But right now, he wanted to start a fight with someone that would end in him escaping.

"We're biding our time," Bruce said.

"Until you get an opportunity? That means one of them

has to slip up and give you a window to strike. A breach of security." These guys were better than that. As far as Ramon had seen, anyway. "You have no idea what's going on out there. Do you even know what their plan is?"

"They're waiting as well. At least, now that you brought back the accountant."

Ramon turned to face Amara. "You know who Lief Holmberg is?"

She nodded. "I used to be married to him, so, yes." After a second, she added, "It didn't last long."

Bruce waved a hand, dismissing her comment.

"The point is that he's a moderate. That's why they kept him as their financial officer for so long. He's unflinchingly honest."

"Okay, so?" Ramon let a little of his frustration bleed through in his tone.

Amara sighed. "He's going to be the new head of *Dominatus*. It's the best-case scenario. Once the wedding is completed, he'll be installed as the leader."

"Wedding?" Ramon shook his head. "Who is he marrying?"

Chapter Thirty-Seven

Kenna woke slowly, aware of the weight of her husband's arm over her hip. Protecting her and the baby, even in his sleep. There was no way to extricate herself without him waking up, so she rolled toward him instead and found him blinking awake.

"Don't get up. You came in late." She kissed his forehead.

"Text."

"I'll look." She kissed his nose, then his lips, and left him in bed. She sat up and found her slippers on the floor by the bed where she'd left them. After grabbing her phone off the charger, she took a sweater from the hook in her thin closet and slipped it over her shoulders.

She slid open the dividing door between their bedroom and the rest of the RV and saw Zeyla asleep in the recliner chair between the dinette table and the driver's seat. A blanket over her legs, her shoes still on and sticking out the end.

Above the front seats, she could see Maizie's loft bed, the size of a double mattress. Not even enough room for her to sit up with clearance over her head. The cat was up there with her, lazily sleeping. Maizie lay on her front with her elbows over a pillow, working on her computer.

She looked at Kenna, who gave her a small wave. Maizie smiled back.

Kenna pressed the button on the electric kettle, so she could make a warm drink, and checked her messages. The most recent was from Jax just after two thirty in the morning.

> The suspect ID'd a kidnapper as one of the
> MSI guys. Can't believe it, but I think
> they're also our shooters in the black SUVs.
> First thing: we need to get Bear on the
> phone and get answers.

She'd gone to sleep not able to rest, knowing he was out with Ryson and the FBI rounding up a suspect they believed was the person who took Ellayna and her family. Then, she'd woken up. So, apparently, she had been able to rest. Or, at least, her body decided she was done for the day, and she fell asleep instead of waiting up for him to get home.

She hadn't even woken up when he got in.

The guy needed to sleep in this morning. Thankfully, making some calls didn't put her life in danger.

Kenna called Ramon first since she'd sent him to infiltrate Bear's team. When he didn't answer, she hung up without leaving a voicemail. If he'd been captured by someone, she didn't need to be in his messages giving away information. He had to be able to sell whatever story would keep him alive.

That thought made her stop and say a prayer for him. After that, she poured her drink and took her seat in the front passenger's chair, still in its rotated-around position. Her feet ended up not that far from Zeyla's. She read her Bible before she kicked the other woman's shoe and got her to start waking up.

After all, Kenna intended to grill Bear.

With her morning started right, and Ramon covered in prayer, she said another and dialed Bear's number.

"Kenna?"

"Yeah, it's me." She tried to keep her voice down a little and noticed Zeyla had her eyes open now. "I'm actually surprised you answered. I have a question."

"Is it about Ramon?"

He could tell her anything he wanted to say, but Kenna wasn't going to take it at face value at this point. "Any idea if he's all right?"

"You mean was his mission to infiltrate my team successful? You could say that. He's been pretty helpful."

"Great." Kenna tried not to sound sarcastic. "If you don't need him, you could always cut him loose."

"Did you have that baby yet?"

She ignored his question. "That isn't what I want to talk to you about. Listen, you know I respect you guys. I'm usually all in on whatever you're doing, even if it isn't how I'd go about solving a problem. But this time, I think you guys might have gone too far."

"What are you talking about?"

"We have an eyewitness who identified one of your guys as a kidnapper. A twelve-year-old, her mother, and her two-year-old brother. Want to tell me what that's about?"

Bear said, "Someone saw them?"

"Yeah, I'd be pretty unhappy as well if someone on my team was so sloppy." Never mind that they'd committed a crime. They'd also given Ellayna access to a phone so she could call Kenna that one time, keeping her on the search, but not in the past few days. What was going on?

"That's not what I meant."

"I'd love to hear an explanation, Bear. A family is missing, and you're the only lead we have to the perpetrators."

"Stress isn't good for the baby."

"And working a case is?"

Zeyla got up, shoving aside the blanket and going to the coffeepot. She checked under the lid, then hit the button.

"Where are they?" Kenna gripped the phone when she'd rather throw it across the RV. But that would wake up Jax.

Zeyla downed a tall glass of water, ducked her head into the fridge, and came out with a banana.

Bear said, "I think it's your job to find them, isn't it?"

"You sent your people to shoot at my family, and you think you can just distract me? I know you're behind this. Tell me where you are, and we can meet up. Hash this out." She knew Bear well enough to be certain that something else was going on.

She just had no idea what it was.

"I'm nowhere near you and too busy to make the trip."

"Whoever is here, tell them I want a face-to-face. I expect answers and cooperation." Otherwise, she was well within her rights to tell law enforcement who they were and how to find them. The MSI operatives here in Salt Lake City would be the subject of a manhunt by police and FBI agents looking for kidnapped victims. There was nowhere they could hide without some serious help.

It made her think of the president and the disastrous call that had been. So what if she was busy? Yeah, she was the president. Why would she *not* be busy? But this was life or death for that family, and some things were more important than politics.

Actually, there were plenty of things that were more important than politics.

It's too early for this.

"Tell your people here that I want to talk."

Bear said, "Just follow the leads you have and find that family, Kenna." He hung up.

Kenna rolled her eyes and dropped the phone in her lap. "Well, that was pointless."

Zeyla looked over, in the middle of pouring her coffee. "You thought he'd just admit they're behind the kidnapping?"

"I don't understand any of this."

"Me either," Maizie called out softly from above Kenna. "But I have something you probably want to see."

Kenna shifted to the edge of the chair. Zeyla came over with her hand out. Kenna clasped her forearm, and Zeyla helped her stand. "Thanks."

Zeyla saluted her with coffee. "I'll put the oven on and start the bacon."

"Don't smoke out the RV like last time."

Zeyla grinned. "I'm happy to make breakfast, but you have to accept the consequences."

Kenna turned away and reached up to grab the ledge by Maizie. There was a ladder, but she tucked it up there with her overnight so it wasn't in the way.

Maizie leaned over and looked down at her. "Just don't start doing chin-ups. Everyone already thinks you're a superhero. You have nothing to prove."

"I could if I wanted to."

Zeyla said, "I highly doubt that."

Kenna frowned at her. "Shh."

Zeyla snorted, hitting the button to ignite the oven. Kenna heard the gas whoosh to life. "Crack the window, at least." When she turned back to Maizie, she said, "What did you find?"

"I couldn't sleep because I was thinking about what you said. You know, about the *Dominatus* software that lets them fake a voice call. It's probably a whole lot easier on the phone than it is with a video because you don't have to worry about lag. You just type in the response, and the computer sends it in the person's voice."

Kenna bit her lip. "I really didn't want to believe the phone call was faked and I wasn't really talking to Ellayna. I don't know if it would be better or worse for me to be right. They'd still be gone."

"And they would likely be with people we would've said we trusted," Zeyla pointed out.

"I still don't have enough information to let it go." She asked Maizie, "Do you have a strong reason to believe the call was faked?"

Just the question left an odd taste in her mouth.

It certainly did sound like this was some kind of test. If MSI really was working with *Dominatus*? She didn't even know what she was going to do. Ramon had been fed to the wolves. Ellayna and her family were caught in the cross fire.

Maizie shifted her laptop far enough to the edge that Kenna could see it and bent the screen forward. "Look at the audio."

On the black screen were two thin horizontal white lines. Between them was a red scribble of waveforms.

Maizie said, "This is her talking, leaving you that voice-mail. I stripped out only her voice, and there's nothing else."

"Like the mic just picked up her voice really well with no outside background noise."

"That's basically impossible. At the least, it would pick up the air moving when she breathed. But she said her brother was there, right? How was he totally silent while she was leaving this frantic message?"

Zeyla said, "Maybe he was asleep."

Kenna frowned. "It's hard to believe it was literally silent wherever she was."

"Seems more like the recording was made in a sound-proof booth of some kind. That's the only explanation for why there are no background sounds. No noise. Nothing ambient."

"Or someone worked on the recording after and stripped it out."

"I'd have to record a call live to be able to analyze that, but it's possible they recorded the message and then sent it to your voicemail." Maizie scrunched up her nose. "But how did they do the phone call? That was live. You'd have noticed an odd delay."

"There wasn't one." Kenna lowered her arms before her hands went numb. "Maybe they used the voicemail to create a baseline to then fake the call. But why do any of this? They were taken, and we know it's MSI who is behind it. They're the ones harassing us." She flinched. "Are they the ones who killed Gabby? Because that's insane."

"Same SUVs, right? That's what Jax said." Zeyla lifted the butter knife she was holding and stuck it in her mouth to lick off whatever was on it. Looked like sauce she'd been spreading on white bread.

"The same kind. There are a lot of SUVs in the world."

Zeyla frowned. "Would they really give us the runaround like that? For all we know, they killed Shawn Terrance and wanted that information so badly they killed Gabby, too. Are they so far gone and so desperate for the tech from that software company that they went to this extent?"

"They either wanted it badly for themselves, or they knew they had to get it off the market so no one had access to it," Maizie said. "Either way, it doesn't look good."

Kenna blew out a breath. "They've got a whole lot to answer for. I say we press the issue. Force them to confront us with what's really going on."

There had to be a way to call them out that they couldn't deny.

"That could backfire." Zeyla set a hand on her hip. "Unless we have a good plan."

Kenna said, "Then I guess we need to come up with one."

"Good thing I'm making bacon."

Chapter Thirty-Eight

Kenna leaned her hips back against the kitchen counter. Jax sat at the dinette, halfway through his sandwich stacked with thick-cut bacon. Zeyla had gone for a run to burn off some of the tension of sleeping upright in a chair. Kenna figured she just wasn't a big fan of close quarters and needed her own space on occasion.

Or she was hoping those guys in the black SUVs would make another move.

Maybe both.

"I don't like any of this," she said.

Maizie had come down from her loft bed and taken a shower. Now she sat in the driver's seat with her laptop on her knees. Wearing wide-leg jeans and a loose-fit T-shirt. Her wet blonde hair was tied up in a messy bun on the top of her head. "He really told you to find the family?"

Kenna nodded. "He probably knows where they are, and he wants me to work the case. Like solving a puzzle. It's a distraction at best; that's the only explanation."

Ellayna and her mother and her brother were gone. Supposedly kidnapped and being held somewhere.

But if MSI was behind it, then why was Crystal's ex dead?

Even if they'd taken the family, someone had taken Marcus Neerwood's life. She had a few theories as to why he was dead but no evidence to prove one was more likely than the others.

"I don't like the idea that MSI put a bomb in Gabby and pushed her off that bridge." Jax shook his head. "I'd never have said they were capable of doing something like that."

"I knew they were capable," Kenna countered. "But I thought they had more integrity than to kill an innocent person."

Maizie said, "Unless she wasn't all that innocent. But that's too much collateral damage."

It was certainly *an* explanation. And it fit, but Kenna still didn't like it. "I don't like the idea we're being played. That we've been played on multiple occasions for the past few weeks."

Ramon might be the only person who could tell her what was going on, and he was out of contact. Same with Bruce and Amara. Even Zeyla had tried reaching them, but it was as if all their phones were off.

Kenna jogged her heel up and down, using the movement to try and jog an idea loose from her brain. But she was being purposely kept in the dark. So how could she possibly figure out the answers.

"If it wasn't for MSI being in the middle of this, I'd think it was *Dominatus* giving me the runaround. Distracting me because they have something big going on— probably something to do with the president."

Jax turned and leaned against the window, one leg on the seat and his foot in the aisle. "What if we assume that's true? It could mean they're using the guys from MSI because we're more likely to believe them. We trust them, right? So, if they say it's all good, then we're more inclined to go along with it. To not try and uncover whatever sinister thing is going on underneath."

Maizie said, "That, and if MSI is the one shooting at us, then it makes sense why none of us has been hurt."

Kenna looked at Maizie. "They missed on purpose."

"It fits," Jax said. "If we assume MSI doesn't want something bad to happen to any of us. Perhaps they're the ones who took the job with *Dominatus* because they can then actively ensure none of us gets hurt."

"But Gabby was fair game," Kenna pointed out.

Jax tipped his head to the side. "Maybe those guys in Pueblo weren't MSI, but someone else. The guys here in the black SUVs are supposed to be the bad guys who wanted the tech from that software company, but they're just pretending? But Bear wouldn't stand for losing his men."

Kenna said, "All he said was find the family. Sounded more like he's bought in all the way. We haven't heard from the software company."

"They got their tech back." Maizie gave her a pointed look. "If they don't know we have a copy of all the files, maybe they think the damage from the leak will blow over. Those other guys believed they'd failed after they realized what we gave them wasn't real."

"Any break-ins, or incidents at the company office?"

Maizie said, "I've been keeping an eye on police reports, social media, and the company website, but there haven't been any reported incidents. I was wondering if those guys from the bridge were going to try again."

"The company might purposely keep it hush-hush." Unless someone suddenly died under suspicious circumstances or was murdered. That was a lot harder to bury. "Question is whether what's going on here in Salt Lake is connected to what we were working in Pueblo, or if they are two separate incidents with different perpetrators."

All of it was just a distraction from worrying about Ramon. Kenna grunted. "We have a whole list of things we don't like about what's going on, but no concrete proof of anything, and the bottom line is that Gabby was killed because we took the case. Not to mention that Ramon might be in serious danger. Wherever he is."

Jax's expression softened. "What happened to Gabby wasn't our fault."

"She might not have been kidnapped if we hadn't taken the case." Sometimes, things were just that simple. "She would still be alive."

Jax said, "Gabby wanted answers about what happened to her brother. None of us knew that would be the result."

Kenna didn't know what was going to allow her to let it go. She probably just needed to grieve. Visit the woman's grave and apologize. But none of it would change what had happened; it would just alleviate some of the guilt.

"So, they tell you to focus on finding Ellayna and her family now," Maizie said. "Like you need something to do. Like they're doing you a favor or something."

Kenna pushed out a long breath.

Her phone rang. She looked at the screen, then lifted it from the counter. "It's Ryson." She answered it and put it to her ear. "Hey, what's up?"

"I'm going to ask you a question, and you're going to be very careful about your answer."

She thought about the audio recording from her voicemail because it didn't sound like there was any other noise on the line. This could be fake like her conversation with Ellayna. "Ryson—"

She heard a heavy door click shut and then the sound of traffic passing by wherever he was.

"I need you to tell me if you or Zeyla went into Marcus Neerwood's house. I need to know what you touched. Specifically."

Kenna's mind conjured that smell. The realization Marcus Neerwood was dead and had been that way for several days by the time they found him. "Why do you need to know what we touched at the scene?"

"Just answer the question."

Kenna didn't like the sound of this either—add that to the long list of things that were "not okay" right now. "If you find a boot print on the front door, it belongs to Zeyla. I didn't go inside. She walked around, but I told her not to touch anything. I don't even think she touched the body. He was clearly already dead."

"You have two problems."

"Okay." Kenna bit her lip.

"The first is that forensics found Zeyla's print on the frame of the door, like she touched it going out."

"I watched her step out. She didn't touch the door frame."

"The other problem is that the ballistics on the weapon used matches the death of another man shot in his home."

She already knew the name he was about to give her.

"Shawn Terrance."

Kenna closed her eyes. "The same person who killed Shawn Terrance also killed Marcus Neerwood."

Jax shifted in his seat, straightening at that news.

"And the Salt Lake City Police Department believes the killer is Zeyla?"

"You didn't hear it from me." Ryson hung up.

Kenna lowered the phone. "Maizie, where is Zeyla now?"

Maizie's fingers flew over the laptop keyboard. "Coming back into the RV park. She'll be here in a couple of minutes."

"Okay." Kenna needed another nap or to be able to drink coffee, if she was going to figure this out.

Jax said, "She's being framed for two murders."

Kenna clenched her fingers on the edge of the counter, holding on as if it would keep her stable. "If they were able to point at her as one of those people on the bridge, I think they'd be doing that as well. Ballistics between the two murders matches, and they think Zeyla did it."

"So they have the murder weapon with her prints on it?"

"If they do, Ryson didn't tell me. Maybe he wasn't allowed to say that much, and he just told me what he could."

The RV door opened, and she stepped in, kicking off her tennis shoes outside on the rug in front of the door.

Jax shook his head. "Risky move, giving us a heads-up. We could put Zeyla on a bus and ensure she disappears."

Zeyla looked around, her brow lined with sweat from her run. Still wearing her leggings and a thin running jacket and gloves. "Why am I disappearing?"

Kenna explained about the prints found at the scene.

Zeyla muttered under her breath, shaking her head. "You know, you try to go straight, and they always get you in the end." She stomped to the dinette and slid in across from Jax, her frustration evident in every movement.

Maizie asked, "Could this be another distraction?"

"More likely, it's a way to get Zeyla out of play, because

they know she's a threat." Kenna had to admit... "At least, she's more of a threat than me right now."

"So, I'm going to be arrested, is that it?" Zeyla asked.

Jax shook his head. "That's why it was risky for Ryson to tell us. You're the kind of person I would consider a flight risk."

"So sweet." Zeyla smirked.

She thought that was a nice thing for someone to say about her? Never mind, of course she did. "We can get you the best lawyer. Prove this is a setup."

"If *Dominatus* is behind it, there isn't going to be a paper trail," Zeyla said. "I'm as good as convicted."

"You don't know that," Kenna told her.

"They'll have paid off everyone they need to. No evidence left of what really happened or who killed Marcus and Shawn."

"There has to be because it wasn't you." Kenna wanted to fight this with every breath she had. But the fact that it could be yet another distraction made her want to do what Jax had suggested—put Zeyla on a bus. Or a plane to some South American country with no extradition agreement. Get her out of play because they refused to be manipulated.

"You aren't even going to ask me if I did it or not?"

Kenna rolled her eyes. "You think I need to?"

Zeyla shrugged. "I might have. I could secretly be an assassin, and you'd never know."

"I want to find that funny," Maizie said. "But right now, it really isn't. And besides, we know where you were during the times of death. Because you were with us. So we know you didn't do it. Even if you *could* have."

Zeyla glanced at Maizie, a sisterly smile on her face. "Don't forget it."

Maizie didn't seem to find that so funny either.

Jax said, "Preston probably has some high-priced lawyer on retainer who can fight for your freedom. Convince the police you didn't do this because the evidence was faked and you have alibis."

Zeyla said, "Preston? The guy who was wrongfully convicted of murder and served the whole sentence."

Kenna winced. "That doesn't mean the same thing is going to happen to you."

"I'm not just going to roll over and let them put me in prison. This isn't a fight we need to take on because I don't want to and you'll be busy having that baby." Zeyla shrugged like it was a done deal. "So, they can arrest me...if they can find me."

Maizie's expression saddened.

Kenna said, "None of us wants to lose you."

"I know," Zeyla said. "That's why I'm still here, even though with anyone else I'd have taken off to do my own thing a long time ago."

As far as working with Zeyla, and her being part of their family, that was as close to a declaration of love and affection as they were going to get from the woman. Probably ever.

"If you want to stay," Kenna said, "no one is going to take this. We'll fight with everything we've got."

Zeyla said, "Sometimes, everything you've got isn't enough."

Kenna refused to believe that. "It has to be enough."

Chapter Thirty-Nine

"Whoa." Maizie shifted to the edge of her chair, all her attention on her computer.

"What is it?" Kenna went over to the passenger's seat and sat so her feet could get a break.

Zeyla got up from the dinette. "I'm going to shower and pack. Hopefully, the police don't come here with an arrest warrant before I'm done with that."

Jax watched her go, his expression like he wanted to say something to her but didn't know how to convince her to stay. The truth was, Zeyla might be right. It would be far better to avoid the fight entirely than risk life in prison. Even if it meant living the rest of her life on the run, a fugitive from the US government.

It wasn't much different from the life she'd lived so far. If anyone could make that situation work, it was Zeyla. But it also meant they would never see each other again. Zeyla would never get to be an auntie to Kenna's baby.

"Take a look at this." Maizie stood and placed her laptop on the dinette table. Jax shifted so he could see.

Kenna said, "Someone tell me what it is." She closed

her eyes, praying for Zeyla, since asking for a slowdown in the work of a police department didn't sit quite right. She respected too many cops in this city to be comfortable asking for them to meet roadblocks in bringing Zeyla in for questioning. Or arresting her.

Still, she took a moment and told God how she felt. He knew, but it was part of the process that she let her thoughts have airtime. So she could articulate her fears and ask for wisdom.

"MSI sent you this?"

Jax's question brought her attention around to the others in the RV. Maizie and Jax, the two people she was closest to in the world right now.

Kenna laid a hand over the baby, who was currently playing soccer with her insides. She shifted in the seat. "This kid is trying to bust out."

Jax looked at her with a kind of wonder. "I don't want to work this case. I want to drive to the cabin and forget all of it."

She said nothing because she agreed, but they both knew they wouldn't do it. At least not without knowing for sure that Ellayna and her family were safe...and Zeyla. "What did MSI send?"

The shower switched on in the bathroom.

Maizie slid across from Jax. "It looks like a contract, right?"

Jax nodded. "This is an invoice paying for the contract. Which is interesting in itself, since this isn't what happened." He scrolled down the page. "It had to have been a dark web transaction, and this is the paper trail. Maybe they found it and intervened." He looked at Kenna. "Someone was hired to capture Ellayna Feathers from her home, and the orders include a note to dispatch anyone else in the house."

"What does that mean?" Maizie asked.

"It means Abe and Crystal were going to be killed." Jax looked at the screen again. "If MSI came across this, maybe it's the reason why they sent their people to take the whole family. They knew there was a threat in play, and they stopped two murders, plus whatever was supposed to happen to Ellayna after she was taken."

"Any way to know who hired whoever they hired?" Kenna didn't bother explaining. They would know what she meant.

"We should be able to track the contract killer from this bank account number, right, Maizie?"

She nodded in answer to Jax's question. "I'll track it down."

"Did MSI say why they sent it?" Kenna asked.

"The email just says that we probably want to see this." Maizie tapped the screen of her laptop and showed Jax something.

He said, "They have to be letting us know why they did what they did."

"Because we're interested in digging into it, or because they want us to ignore the fact that *they* are the ones who did the kidnapping?" Kenna breathed through a couple more kicks. "They can just tell us where to find the family, and we can call it even."

"I would like to know who hired the contract killer. Then we'll know where the threat is actually coming from."

Kenna made a face.

Jax smiled at her. "I'll see if I can set up a meet, get the guy to tell me who hired him."

"Assuming it was a man." Kenna shrugged. "I suppose

I'm sitting at home during this operation? Probably waiting for the police to show up with a warrant for Zeyla's arrest."

Maybe she was just grumpy. It wasn't that she was feeling sorry for herself, necessarily. More like she felt kind of blah, and it was self-soothing to be annoyed at everything.

Lord, there are things that could be resolved before this baby comes. I'm not trying to tell You when she should be born, but there's probably a sweet spot here somewhere.

It wasn't out of the question for a woman to go over her due date, even by two weeks, but Kenna didn't really want to be pregnant for another month.

Jax came over and leaned down, kissing her in way that successfully distracted her from being grumpy. "Maizie can be in charge while I'm gone."

Kenna gasped, shoving at his shoulder playfully.

Maizie giggled.

"Don't get distracted," Kenna told her. "We need to find a contract killer, I guess."

Jax smiled at her. "It'll take some finesse to get a face-to-face meeting. Maizie and I can work on a dialogue with the person who was paid to take Ellayna and then work on the plan."

Kenna realized the shower was still on, which wasn't like Zeyla. The woman took the fastest showers Kenna had ever known—and she shut the water off halfway through. Even Zeyla couldn't pretend nothing bothered her. She was likely in there figuring out what she was going to do about the police issuing a warrant for her arrest.

While Jax and Maizie talked over their plan and navigated the dark web message boards they knew, Kenna read through another short section of Scripture. It wasn't about what to do when your close family member was going to be wrongfully accused of murder, but it gave her a sense of peace anyway.

Was this email from MSI a lead on the real case here or just another way to keep Kenna busy while they did...whatever they were going to do?

Jax said to Maizie, "We can say we want a job done."

"Do we say we're...us? Or do we pretend to be someone else?"

"Do you have alt accounts you can use?"

"I'd set a new one up now, but it'll be too suspicious that it has no history."

Jax asked, "Do you have history on this message board?"

"I interact on occasion, just to keep the username active. Mostly just asking questions about companies we're investigating."

"Like the software company in Pueblo?"

Maizie leaned back in her chair. "You think that's how someone knew we were working it?"

"Not necessarily," Jax said. "I doubt you blew our cover. But it's possible that at least MSI is monitoring what you're doing online. Even on the dark web."

"You think Hazel has my usernames?"

Jax shrugged. "She might even have put a worm in your computer last time you guys were together."

Maizie went quiet.

"We don't need to rehash anything. We're good."

"Okay." Maizie nodded.

Kenna didn't love how soft her tone was, and it was clear she still felt guilty for withholding information she knew about Kenna's captivity from Jax when he could have used the lead. But at the same time, it hadn't given anyone a lead about where she was being held. It was all meant to be leverage to force Maizie to do what the bad guys wanted. Purely so that she would be torn up inside about it.

Yet more insidious tactics. The kind MSI seemed happy to have employed to get what they wanted.

Kenna's phone alarm sounded at the same time that Jax and Maizie had alerts go off on their phones. "The perimeter?" Kenna asked.

Jax swiped through his phone. "Yes."

Maizie said, "It's a lot of cops. A *lot*."

"Stay where you are." Kenna held out a hand. She knew why they were there, and unfortunately, Zeyla hadn't managed to get away. She was still in the shower with no idea the police were currently surrounding the RV.

Kenna lifted her foot and stretched it far enough that she could nudge down the latch on the door, and then she pushed it open two inches. The startled face of a police officer stared back at her through the gap between the door and the frame.

She lifted her chin. Lifted her hands and showed him her empty palms. Her leg didn't want to be up that high for much longer. "Get the door."

Thankfully, he grabbed the door and caught it before it shut.

"Kenna Banbury?"

She said, "You already know that, or you wouldn't be here."

"So, you know who I'm looking for."

Jax got up and came to the door, and she knew he would have rather been between her and the armed cops, but there wasn't room for that. "Do you have a search warrant?"

"No, sir. Only an arrest warrant for Zeyla..." The cop frowned. "What's her name?"

"The paperwork says Zeyla Adams."

Kenna said, "Better than Smith, I guess."

The cop was still frowning. "Excuse me?"

One of the other cops, currently out of sight, said, "This also says she might be known as Zeyla Smith or Zeyla Clarke. So who knows? There's a photo, and we can confirm her ID when we have her prints."

And then she'd be nailed for two murders. Arrested officially and, down the road, sentenced to decades in prison, if not the rest of her life.

Kenna blinked away the burn of tears.

"I'll go see if she's going to be done in the shower anytime soon." She shifted to the edge of the seat. Jax held out his hand, and she clasped his elbow. "Thanks."

She squeezed his side with her other hand as she passed and nodded her head to Maizie to go with her.

"What are we going to do?" Maizie asked as they moved down the aisle in the RV to the bedroom. The bathroom was between, but she wanted Maizie out of sight of any eager cops.

"I don't know. But I'm guessing by now Zeyla has a plan." Kenna knocked on the door. "Zeyla!"

She did it loud enough that the cops heard, giving Zeyla a second to think—or prepare—once she realized what Kenna's tone meant.

Jax said, "This is my residence, and you do not have permission to enter."

Kenna bit her lip. She knocked again on the door while Maizie stood by her, worry in her features.

No answer.

Kenna tried the door latch, and it swung open toward her. Steam billowed out of the bathroom, revealing an empty shower. No Zeyla. Just a cell phone on the edge of the sink.

She's gone.

Chapter Forty

"I can't believe she just left."

Kenna bit her lip at Maizie's words and looked out the windshield at the dark night sky, heavy with clouds that probably meant snow would be falling tonight. They'd talked to the cops for hours and eventually let them look through the RV. It wasn't like there was anywhere inside that Zeyla might've been hiding, but it at least assuaged their curiosity to look.

Over the comms channel they had open, Jax said, "We should probably get out of town as well. It's going to look suspicious, but I don't want to be around when the cops start pointing fingers."

Kenna wanted to finish this, to see for herself that Ellayna and her family really were safe. Then she'd feel all right about leaving town. "If this guy never shows, we can talk about packing up. I'll call Preston, and he can give up the fight to get that software company to admit what they were doing."

Given that her team had MSI messing with them, and someone who wasn't Zeyla had murdered two people, it would be safer to leave. Preston was going to be another story.

She'd managed to reach him earlier but hadn't had the chance to talk for long. He'd been in a meeting with people he refused to identify, even though he told her they could put pressure on the company to admit Shawn had been right.

As if appealing to someone's sense of decency was going to work in the world of cutthroat business? She had told him good luck, even though she didn't believe in luck. She could've prayed for him to get a result, but even that would've been halfhearted.

Preston wanted it all to go public, which meant whoever was doing wrong had to admit the truth. She was mostly worried he'd come across Shawn and Marcus's real killer and get himself in trouble, but the guy didn't listen to her.

"If the feds or the police here have questions, we can give them Bear's number," Kenna said.

"Or the president's." Jax stood over at the far end of a parking lot under a streetlamp, so she could see his outline from here. The killer who'd been contracted to take Ellayna and kill her family was on his way.

Actually, he was hitting the point where he was late.

After hours of conversation with the police, Maizie and Jax realized they had a reply from the guy. In the end, they convinced him that Jax was a wealthy socialite with money to burn and a serious grudge against his business partner. He wanted the guy gone with no witnesses and no trace— no body left to be found.

Maybe the guy needed cash, because he'd agreed to meet when Jax insisted their agreement be made in person.

It wasn't ideal, and they didn't even know who this

guy was. There hadn't been time or a way to dig into his background. Even the bank account on the invoice MSI had sent them had been nothing but a dummy account where money landed and was transferred somewhere else within seconds. Wired to another country, somewhere with more lax financial laws, where records weren't a necessity.

"Maze, did you make any progress tracing more of those accounts?"

In the back seat of their car, Maizie sighed aloud. "I have another fifteen, at least. It goes around and around in circles, is split up, transferred again, divided, and then it lands in an account in one large amount. Then it's divided again and moved to multiple accounts."

Jax said, "What about that forensic accountant you were working with a while back?"

"I sent what I have. I'm waiting for her to get back to me."

Kenna watched her husband, noting he didn't display any impatience. She would be pacing up and down. But when playing the character of a guy with way too much money, he'd opted to be cool as a cucumber.

She, on the other hand, wanted to yell at Zeyla. The woman had given them all the slip. Out the bathroom window. Or no one had noticed her slip into the bedroom, where she could have used the hatch in the floor that went through to the storage area underneath. It was supposed to be for security purposes.

The only thing she'd left behind was the phone—and on the screen, Kenna had found a message to her that hadn't been sent.

I'll miss you.

As if that made up for the fact that all of them would worry for the rest of their lives where she was. If she was okay.

Kenna scrubbed the tears off her cheeks and felt Maizie's hand on her shoulder. She squeezed the young woman's hand, not wanting Jax to be distracted by their emotions right now.

"I see someone." Jax's voice crackled over the open comms line.

Thank You. Hopefully, they would discover who had hired the man for the job MSI had intercepted. Even if he hadn't completed it, they had surmised that the first payment was sent. The second would've been made after the job was completed, but that didn't happen. Had he tried to contact the buyer to explain?

Car headlights split the darkness on the far left side of this parking lot. No one else would be out here tonight in this derelict spot with cracked asphalt and rundown buildings. Businesses that had closed years ago when the economy leaned away from manufacturing and toward more white-collar jobs in downtown high-rise buildings.

"How will we know if it's him?" Maizie asked.

"We'll see if he goes near Jax," Kenna said. "And then we'll know from what he does next."

Which was why she'd insisted her husband wear a bulletproof vest, while she and Maizie sat in the armored car.

With Zeyla gone and Preston busy, she needed to call Stairns and see how he felt about coming here to lend a hand with protection.

The team was far too scattered, and she didn't like it.

Across the lot, the car turned in a half circle and parked where she could see the headlights. Too far away from her for the occupant to know she and Maizie were sitting over here, but their vehicle would be visible. Thankfully, the tinted windows would disguise their presence.

Kenna worried her lip between her teeth. She wanted to distract herself with a drink of her water, but then she would only need to pee, and she would be the one derailing this operation. She needed to continually give her worries to the Lord. Trust that they were doing the right thing.

A single occupant got out of the driver's side of the car. Male. Not quite as tall as Jax, he had stocky shoulders and short legs but a longer upper body, which gave him a squat appearance.

He approached Jax, his stride not so much slow but definitely measured. Hands in sight. Probably a gun on his person somewhere—maybe more than one. A guy who lived with caution, not knowing if a bullet would be around the next corner.

"You're the one?" Jax asked.

"If you have the money."

Jax motioned to the duffel by his foot. For the sake of the ruse, they'd filled it with stacks of junk mail they'd retrieved from a recycling center before it could be processed. Bundled pieces of paper that would look enough like money the guy would be convinced they'd brought the cash. Until he unzipped the bag and saw the truth.

He would know this wasn't about purchasing his services by then.

"If I'm gonna hire you, I'll need to know you are who you say you are." Jax still looked relaxed.

She took a moment to admire how good her husband was at undercover work. And all the other things that made him so innately *Jax*. He would pass a whole lot of great qualities to their child.

"You wanna see my resume?" The guy had a low voice with a gravelly edge to it. At least, it sounded like that through the comms channel.

Kenna had asked Maizie about analyzing his voice and putting it through a program that might be able to find a match from the internet and social media. But without a better recording of his voice, they wouldn't be able to get a definitive answer.

"You say you're legit." Jax shrugged. "How do I know you aren't just some guy on the dark web taking money and screwing people over?"

"Fine, you want proof I've done this before?" The guy dragged a cell phone out of his pocket and tapped the screen before holding it out. "That enough for you?"

Jax didn't move.

"Swipe the screen."

Jax pushed off the light pole and moved closer. The guy was fast, but Jax had been expecting something to happen. As he reached out his hand, the contract killer grabbed his forearm and punched Jax in the side with the cell phone hand.

He probably hadn't expected the thickness of the vest to meet his fist. But then, Jax had injured ribs.

Kenna's stomach clenched, even though she knew what Jax was going to allow to happen. She watched her husband twist his hips and land a punch of his own. The two grappled, hitting at each other in close quarters.

Jax got his leg hooked around the other guy's, but the contract killer forced it and got control as they tumbled to the ground. Using barely a second to get the upper hand, the killer ended up on top.

Kenna winced, trying to keep her thoughts to herself.

That looked like it hurt. He was already injured from the explosion at the hospital. She gasped.

The guy had Jax pinned now. Not exactly the plan, but then none of them had anticipated the speed with which he'd gained control.

Come on.

The killer leaned over him. "I've killed people for less than that disrespect."

But he would hardly get contracts if he treated people like that. Why take the meet if it wasn't his norm?

Jax said, "So I shouldn't check that you're for real before I hand over a hundred thousand dollars? I could've hired someone off the street for ten grand, and they could've put a bullet in a guy's brain no problem. I came to you because you were recommended."

The guy shoved off Jax but didn't get far. Jax moved as well. The guy straightened, kicking off Jax's grip on him before striding over to the duffel. He unzipped it and looked inside, swearing loudly.

Jax had already rolled over on the ground, raised a gun, and pointed it at the guy.

The contract killer reached for the back of his belt.

"Got your gun."

The guy swore.

"Fine, I lied. But I can pay you. It's just for answering some questions and not for killing anyone."

The guy froze where he stood, on the wrong end of a gun—his own gun.

Jax shifted and got up, first on his knees, and then he rocked and stood in one move. "You still get a hundred thousand. I'll have it sent to whatever account you want. But I want answers."

The killer would know he was never going to be able to

run faster than a bullet. Even if he tried, there was too much of a chance Jax wouldn't miss. He had to agree, or he was going to lose his life—or a leg.

The guy's body language radiated anger and frustration. "What do you want to know?"

"Who hired you to kidnap Ellayna Feathers and kill her mother and brother?"

"I didn't do that job."

"I know," Jax said. "Because they're still alive. I want to know who paid you the first half for the job."

"Why? They weren't there; they were already gone!"

Jax asked, "Did you tell whoever hired you that or try to give their money back?"

The killer laughed. "Not my fault I couldn't do the job. Someone else got there first."

"How did they contact you?"

"Why do you care?" The guy shifted, his movements jerky.

Jax said, "Not your concern. I just want everything you know about these people. So *I* can find them."

The guy shook his head. "How do you think they found me? Same way you did."

"I meant what I said about paying you. And I don't want to shoot you, but I will if I have to. All I want is their information."

Kenna watched the guy look at his boots for a second. Assessing his options.

He finally looked up. "You know what happens to people who talk? Won't matter if you paid me or not. Fact is, you might as well put a bullet in my brain. I'm done anyway."

"I'd love to talk you into quitting," Jax said. "I'll know I made the world a better place tonight."

"A do-gooder?" The guy laughed. "This gets better and better."

Kenna spotted a flash of movement in her rearview. But it happened so quickly she wondered if she saw it. Nothing else happened. Jax faced off against the guy, and she was fine here with Maizie in the car.

Jax said, "I'll give you an email address. Or a phone number. You send everything about these people you have to the place I give you. When I can confirm it checks out, I'll deposit money into your account."

"So, I send a text, and you let me walk away? I don't get paid until later?"

"I'm keeping this gun."

Kenna would have as well. Better than getting shot in the back when the guy left. It was probably going to turn out to be the weapon in some unsolved crimes, so she figured they'd be turning it over to the police.

It might even be the gun used to kill Marcus Neerwood and Shawn Terrance.

Kenna caught a quiet whirring outside the car and only just recognized she was hearing it when her door opened. Someone pulled Maizie's door open at the same time.

The dome light above her went on.

Maizie yelped as she was dragged out of the car.

Kenna said, "Hey, what—"

Across the parking lot, Jax yelled, "KENNA!"

A stinky cloth was shoved in her mouth before she could finish what she was saying. The smell of it rushed up into her nostrils, and she tried to pull it out. Her fingers glanced over a hand on her face, and she scratched at it.

But the chemical did its job, and everything went black.

Chapter Forty-One

Kenna stared at the room full of people, half of whom should have gone home hours ago. They'd all stuck around, as if what she had to say was of vital importance. That she might have changed the fate of the world.

This farce of a court case needed to be done already.

"You've been through a lot, haven't you?" Hasworth was back on her feet. The prosecutor was supposed to be here to prove the defendant was responsible for the deaths of all those people in Chicago, while the defense attorneys proved she was acting under duress. Not in control of her actions. Or that she believed she was acting in a kind of self-defense.

"Plenty of people face trauma in their lives. Mine might be different, but it's not the worst a human has endured. I've made it through a lot, survived, and built a family." Kenna grabbed a tissue from the box the judge had given her and dabbed the corners of her eyes.

"That's a gracious way to look at it."

Kenna said, "I've met a lot of people who've gone through worse than me. Working cases. Finding victims. Children. Vulnerable adults. I was able to fight back in a lot of the situations I found myself in. And I was never alone."

Even when she'd thought she was by herself. Without hope, the way Bradley had believed he was when he took his own life.

Kenna had always had God with her, even in the darkness when she hadn't known He was there. *Emmanuel.*

"What a heartwarming story." The lead defense attorney stood, a distinctly mocking tone in his voice. "Defeating the big, bad evil in the world. The power of love and family. Meanwhile, my client had no one to stand with her. She was completely alone. Isn't that true, Mrs. Jaxton?"

She wasn't supposed to answer a question like that. But Kenna wasn't an FBI agent who had to follow the rules anymore.

"We all make our own choices," Kenna said. "And we have to face the consequences of those choices. That's what integrity is."

"Your Honor—" Hasworth began.

The defense interrupted. "It's unorthodox, I know. But this has been an unorthodox trial from start to finish."

The judge asked, "Would the defense like to cross-examine the witness?"

Kenna wasn't sure which of them thought she was going to make their point for them. Hasworth wanted her to provide testimony on how this was all probably inevitable. How the defendant had been raised as an asset for *Domi-*

natus. How she had been taught to take life and insinuate herself into situations like a spy.

The defense wanted her to talk about how there was no way she could ever have escaped her fate. It would always have been tied up with *Dominatus*. That, in a way, they'd done this to themselves in pushing her to the point that she'd effectively snapped and killed them all.

"Yes, Your Honor." The defense attorney looked at her.

She didn't look at the defendant. Kenna couldn't even meet her gaze. She didn't know what she would see there.

He asked, "Is it true that your parents were both a part of this group, *Dominatus*?"

"Yes, they tried to escape it. My mother—at least, I think of her as my mother—faked her death to keep my father safe. She went back to *Dominatus* and later raised her other daughter as part of the group. She felt she had no choice but to keep my father and me safe by allowing us to believe she was dead."

"And my client?"

"She likely never knew any other life than theirs. Children are born to the women *Dominatus* claims as mothers, raised by parents who are part of the group in a kind of adoption. Those children are then raised to be assets who infiltrate every facet of society in a grand plan to steer a country, or the whole world, the way *Dominatus* has planned for it to go."

Kenna had seen it with her own eyes. She'd been manipulated by them, duped by them, nearly torn to pieces by them. She'd lost family members to the fight. In the end, it could have cost her everything, but God had His hand on them through it all.

She continued, "Her future would likely have been to become one of their mothers. They consider that their highest honor. But the woman isn't given a choice. They're selected as nothing more than an incubator for the next generation."

"It's my understanding that there's a generation of women in *Dominatus* who will never have children. That it was, in fact, your mother who sterilized everyone except you."

Kenna nodded. "That's correct. They've managed to get around the problem by artificial insemination, but the women of *Dominatus* won't have children that are their own."

Her mother had tried to deal a blow to the group, but once again, they'd adapted. There were factions within the group who would never give it up. Kenna and her family had taken on the task of finding and dismantling every part of *Dominatus* until she had put a stop to all of it.

But she'd had to make the worst kind of choice in order to put herself in the position to do that.

A choice she just knew the defense was about to bring up.

"The goal is to dismantle them," Kenna said. She had to say that. People needed to know—especially *Dominatus*—that the group was on borrowed time.

One mass casualty event, as tragic as that was, hadn't dealt a death blow to the group. There was still work to be done. But Kenna and the rest of Banbury Investigations were in this fight until the very end.

She'd made that promise, and she intended to keep it.

The defense attorney almost looked smug. "My client, acting under the worst kind of duress, attempted to do just that. Because after a lifetime of subjugation and terror, she found the power to fight back. To act in self-defense."

"As I stated when I began, I wasn't present to witness

the event." She wanted to call it a massacre, because that's what it had been. But that was a term the media was using, trying to sensationalize the biggest trial in decades.

He continued, "It's my understanding that you are now the head of this group, *Dominatus*. You're their leader, are you not?"

Kenna stared at him, unwilling to lie under oath. "Yes, I am."

Chapter Forty-Two

Jax didn't hang around to see if the guy was actually out cold. He just left him to slump on the ground and ran across the parking lot faster than he'd ever run in his entire life, ignoring how much his ribs hurt.

Two black SUVs pulled out of the parking lot, leaving Kenna in the front seat. Taking Maizie. *MSI took Maizie.* Jax wanted to run after her, but they were too far away by the time he reached his wife.

He stumbled and nearly went down, scrambling to round the open door and crouch there beside Kenna. "Please, please." He touched two fingers to her neck and found her heart pounding.

She was out cold.

Jax smelled an odd scent and leaned in to smell the area around her mouth. That wasn't chloroform—thankfully.

But whatever they'd shoved in her face had knocked her out.

"Kenna." He shook her shoulder, then realized he'd rather have his hand over the baby. *You're going to be okay, baby.* Their daughter would be born healthy to a healthy mother and raised in a loving family with two parents. *Lord, I believe.*

Jax was trusting God with everything he had right now.

Determined not to lose either of them.

But he'd already lost a daughter. He looked in the direction those SUVs had gone and found only an empty street full of shadows. Maizie was gone. He wanted to call Bear and tear the guy apart for this.

Whatever kind of plan MSI had, they were done. Jax was never going to trust them again.

Kenna stirred. He patted her cheek. "Wake up for me, babe."

Jax dug out his phone, fully intending to call 911. But Ryson had called him earlier. He hit redial and called the lieutenant back.

"Ryson."

"It's Jax. I need an ambulance and police presence at this location. Maizie was taken by whoever shot at Zeyla and me the other day, and Kenna was knocked out by something. She needs to see a doctor." He relayed the cross streets and explained where they were.

"I'll get units on the way now, and I'm coming, too." Ryson's voice sounded strained. "Is she okay?"

Jax knew he meant Kenna. He didn't want to threaten murder to a cop, implicating himself if anything happened to MSI and their people later. But he was also barely hanging on. "Just get here."

Kenna groaned, her eyes fluttering.

"There you are." He patted her cheek, then ran his hand down her arm. Reassuring himself that she was here. That she was waking up, and their baby was going to be fine. "I'm going to fix this."

He glanced out the windshield at the spot where he'd left the contract killer and saw the guy's arm move when he reached up and touched his face.

Jax looked back at Kenna and saw her eyes fluttering. "I'll be back." He squeezed her hand, then pushed up and raced back to the guy. He dragged the man up by his shirt, pulled an arm behind his back, and walked him over to the hood of the car.

He shoved the guy against the hood and secured his hands behind his back, patting him down thoroughly just to ensure the guy didn't have weapons hidden on his person.

Then he turned the guy and had him sit.

"Do you have a name?" Jax stood over him.

The guy looked defeated, but Jax wasn't going to assume he didn't have fight left in him. He could hear sirens in the distance and knew help would be here soon enough.

"What does it matter?"

Jax said, "It matters to me."

"Whatever just happened, I didn't have anything to do with it."

"I know that," Jax said. "But my daughter was just kidnapped, and my other daughter's life is in danger. She hasn't even been born yet. So you're going to help me resolve this situation so that she can be born into a world that's a safe place."

"Jax!" Kenna's yell cut right through him.

He stepped to the side, keeping one eye on this guy. "I know!" he yelled back. "Stay there for a second."

Police cars streamed into the parking lot, lights and sirens going.

"I can hand you over to them, along with a full rundown of who you are and what you do. I'm sure they'll be thorough in compiling a case against you. Or I can tell them you were instrumental in me figuring this out."

"Because I should believe you hold sway with the police?"

"I'm part of a task force." That was the official story, at least. "I could call the president right now, and you could ask her if I hold sway. If my wife is the kind of person who makes the feds sit up and listen."

The guy just stared at him while the sirens cut off.

Jax heard cars park and doors slam. "Who hired you?"

One of the cops ran over to Kenna and crouched to speak to her. The other approached Jax's side. "You're the one who called the lieutenant?"

"That's right," Jax said. "My daughter, she's nineteen. She was just kidnapped from the back seat of the car by men driving black SUVs. My wife is pregnant and needs medical attention."

"No, I don't." She held on to the cop's arm, standing up out of the car.

Jax's stomach clenched, but he didn't order her to sit back down.

"And this guy?" the cop beside him asked.

"He's about to tell me who hired him for a contract kill." Jax folded his arms across his chest.

The killer lifted his chin. "I didn't kill anyone. I don't have anything to do with what just happened here. And you can't prove either of those things to be untrue because they aren't."

Kenna leaned against the car, like she was shaking off a

daze. "We know you didn't finish the job, but you accepted payment for it."

"Who paid you?" Jax asked.

"All I have is a username. *Grand Master.*"

Another car bumped the curb and sped into the parking lot. Ryson's brakes squealed, and he shoved the door open to race over. "You guys all right?"

Jax moved to Kenna, gathering her into his arms. "We're all right. Maizie was taken."

She leaned her head on his shoulder. Jax threaded his fingers through her hair so he could feel her heartbeat in her throat again. To reassure himself that she really was okay. The baby needed to be checked out, but she hadn't been harmed. Just knocked out by whatever they'd used.

"I'll put this guy in the car." The officer took the killer's arm and led him to the black-and-white patrol car.

Ryson stood in front of them, his attention on Kenna. "Why take Maizie?"

Jax swallowed hard. He didn't have an answer. "What about her laptop?"

Kenna didn't move out of his arms. Ryson went to the back seat and looked. "It isn't here."

Jax shook his head, but he didn't know what to say. Maizie had been through so much. MSI knew that, and they still did this? They'd destroyed any goodwill they had with him, and probably also with Kenna, by doing this.

Ryson asked, "Is it possible they needed her for something?"

"They could have asked." Jax clenched his jaw. He was probably holding Kenna too tightly, but she didn't seem to mind. She was doing the same.

"They're still in town. We'll put a BOLO out for the

vehicles, but it would be better if we had license plate numbers." Ryson scratched his jaw.

The other uniformed officer wandered back over with his partner—though they'd arrived in separate vehicles. "Your guy in there is talking now. Says he'll give you what you want to know about this Grand Master person. You guys know what he's talking about?"

Jax nodded. Kenna slid her arms from around him.

Then an ambulance pulled into the parking lot.

Kenna stiffened. "I don't need to see a doctor."

"You might not, but the baby does, and that is nonnegotiable."

Thankfully, she didn't argue. Ryson held out his hand, and she took it. He walked her over to the ambulance, where the EMTs climbed out.

Jax went with the officers. "What did he say?"

One of the cops said, "I think he saw you and your wife. Maybe he's got a soft spot." He opened the front passenger's door, and Jax slid in, facing the back.

Through the grate, Jax could make out the killer's features in the dim light. "I need all the help I can get right now. Which is good for you because it means I can put in a good word. You can make a deal."

He'd already mentioned the Grand Master.

"Do you know who it is? This Grand Master who hired you. Do you have his name?"

The guy looked out the window, toward Jax's car. "I have his IP address. I do my homework on who I'm working for."

Jax wrote down the series of numbers the guy had memorized. "Did you know who I really was when you came here?"

"Have to admit, I was curious about Banbury Investigations. But mostly, I didn't want to get jammed up in something I didn't do. Guess I miscalculated that one."

"I'll make it clear with the district attorney what your role was—and wasn't. You didn't hurt anyone as far as I'm aware." His history was another matter. "You and I aren't enemies."

"You have plenty of those. You don't need me to be one."

Jax said, "You served, didn't you?"

The guy nodded.

"Ever meet a Major General Schnell?"

He nodded. "I know what you guys did. I know about the military bases he had and that he was doing research. There was only one on the news, but we all know the problem was a lot more widespread than that."

"Can you tell me where all the bases he controlled were located?"

The guy thought for a second. "Spokane, the one you guys found. Nevada. Texas. Pretty sure there's one in Wyoming, but I don't know where."

MSI had a base of operations somewhere, and it wasn't a research platform off the coast of Alaska.

What he needed was for Maizie to contact him somehow when she got to where she was going. That way, he'd know where she was being held, and he'd be able to come and rescue her.

"There's a lieutenant." Jax motioned to Ryson. "Javier Ryson. Tell him everything you know about *Dominatus*."

Jax got out of the car because he'd rather be with Kenna, and he had the IP address. They'd have to figure out how to find the guy with their computers and no Maizie to help them with all their tech needs.

But she was so much more to them than just support staff. She was family—the daughter they'd adopted.

Two steps from the car, a shot rang out across the parking lot. Glass shattered.

"Gun!"

At the cop's cry, Jax dropped to the gravel. He winced, covering his head with his arms. No more shots sounded in the air.

"He's dead!"

Jax rolled over and saw the back window of the cop car had blown out. The contract killer had been murdered.

One of the two officers said, "Lieutenant!"

Ryson yelled back, "Go!"

Both officers ran off in the direction the shot must have come from. Jax got up and ran in a crouch to the back of the ambulance. He got in and shut one half of the door. Kenna sat up on the bed, an exasperated looking EMT on the bench beside her.

"Ma'am?"

She lowered the oxygen mask from her face. "I'm fine. The baby's heart rate is fine."

She was arguing with the EMT, but still, Jax nodded because he'd needed to hear that.

"And I got a voicemail," she said.

The EMT said, "I'm still recommending you be seen by a doctor, even if that's just your obstetrician."

"Sure. I'll do that." She handed him the oxygen mask and scooted to the end of the bed.

Jax said, "We're not exiting this ambulance until the shooter is in custody."

Ryson lifted his radio from his belt and held it to his mouth. "Copy that." To them, he said, "They're entering the building."

"If I had to guess? I'd say they're looking for Sylvia Caughton."

"That makes sense, given that witnesses stated a woman visited Wallace Lofton at the hospital."

Jax shook his head. "What are you talking about?"

"Right. Zeyla's stuff superseded that," Ryson said. "Wallace Lofton died in his hospital room. It looks like a result of his injuries, like a blood clot got loose and ended up in his brain, but I'm not convinced she didn't usher him along. The woman who visited him."

Kenna frowned. "She left him alive long enough to talk to us, then she came back and killed him?"

"So he could tell us they were using their deep fake voice technology for the podcast," Jax said. "So that we would realize you didn't speak to Ellayna?"

"That means *Dominatus* wanted us to believe MSI was right in the middle of this."

Jax nodded. "I think you're right about that."

Not that it completely made sense. Though, if *Dominatus* was at work and didn't like MSI's involvement, their aim might simply have been to drive a wedge between Banbury Investigations and Bear's team.

That was the only thing he'd learned so far that might make him inclined to give Bear and his team the benefit of the doubt that they might be on the right side in all this.

Ryson's radio crackled. Someone spoke through it, but Jax couldn't make out what they were saying. "Copy that." To them, he said, "The shooter is gone."

"Great, let's get out of here." Kenna shifted all the way over to where Jax stood so she was sitting on the end of the bed. She waited.

If he pushed it, she would probably go to the hospital because he asked her to.

He looked at the EMT. "You heard the baby's heartbeat?"

The guy nodded. "It was strong, and she was moving around."

"And her blood pressure?" He motioned to Kenna.

"No higher than I'd expect it to be."

Jax looked at her. "You can stay here while I bring the car over."

Kenna nodded. "I'll play you the voicemail in the car. Ellayna says her captors will trade her and her family for Shawn Terrance's drive and the port it goes into. We have two days to get to Evanston, Wyoming."

The EMT shook his head. "Who are you people?"

Chapter Forty-Three

Kenna held the phone to her ear so she could listen to it again, even though she'd already done that a hundred times on the drive over here. Even though they knew it was likely a fake that MSI had created using *Dominatus* tech.

She still wanted to hear Ellayna's voice.

"Kenna? It's me, Ellayna." They even made her sound nervous. *"The people keeping us here want to make an exchange. They want you to bring the tech that you retrieved from that company in Pueblo. The drive and the...port."* It sounded like she was making sure to say it right. As if this twelve-year-old really was under duress. *"And they'll let us go if you hand it over. They want to meet at your cabin in Wyoming in two days' time. Noon."*

Kenna lowered the phone and let the rocking chair

move back and forth. She stared out at the snow-covered land in front of her. The neighbor's place, a tiny red barn that dwarfed the house beside it, was almost too far away to see. Mountains in the distance.

They'd forced her to come home to make the exchange.

Now her RV was parked in the shop Jax had constructed months ago. Preston's helicopter had a weather cover over it but still looked totally conspicuous in the yard, and his dogs were leaving paw prints all over the snow around the house. He was staying in her RV, and he had security guys camped out over the property in little tents. They were here to work patrols but also sort of looked like they were having a blast camping out in the snow.

A small SUV had made its way from the highway to the west, down the single-lane road to her front gate. She already knew who it belonged to.

Kenna called out over her shoulder. "They're here!"

Jax pushed open the screen door, then shut the front door to the cabin behind him. He needed a blanket as well if he was going to be out here without a coat. He glanced at her and saw the phone. "Listening to it again?"

"It's the only thing I can do. Maizie is gone, and I can't get her back. Ramon isn't here. Amara and Bruce aren't answering. Zeyla is...keeping herself safe." She sniffed back tears. "At least we can do this. But I have no idea what to think. Our friends are the ones who created this whole situation."

She just couldn't let go of the betrayal. It stung that MSI had chosen to work with *Dominatus* and not even trusted her. They just took it upon themselves to do...whatever this was that they were doing.

The small SUV pulled into the drive Jax had plowed

between the road and the shop, parking off to the side. Elizabeth and Craig Stairns climbed out.

Kenna shifted to the edge of the rocking chair and swung the blanket around her shoulders.

Elizabeth waved her back. "You don't have to get up."

"It's good to stretch my legs," Kenna said. "I've been sitting for a while."

Elizabeth came up the porch steps and held her arms open. Kenna gave her a hug, difficult because of the person between them. Elizabeth's breath caught in her chest. "I can't believe they took her."

"I know."

The other woman leaned back, and Kenna saw Jax and Craig shake hands. Craig Stairns, once a marine. An FBI agent for years. A tough, weathered lawman who'd seen it all and lived with the scars to prove it. He looked wrecked. All because a young woman had nestled her way into his heart, and now she was in danger.

"Right now, we need to save Ellayna and her family." Jax swallowed. "And Maizie."

"Tell me what to do." Stairns lifted his chin. "We need these guys to answer for what they've done. Putting innocents in danger. Taking Maizie from us." He shook his head, his jaw set. "I brought weapons."

Jax motioned with his chin toward Stairns's car. "Let's take a look."

Kenna took Elizabeth inside so she could use the bathroom after so many hours in the car. She poured the older woman a glass of water and handed it to her when Elizabeth came into the kitchen.

"Thanks." Elizabeth smiled, settling onto a barstool at the counter. "This is an adorable little cabin."

Kenna smiled. "It's not just cute. It's got some upgrades, and it's fully satellite connected."

"Doesn't that put you *on the grid*." She sounded awkward saying the words. "Rather than staying off it so you're safe."

"It makes more sense for us to be connected if we need to call for help or if someone on the team needs to get information to us." Kenna hit the button on the kettle so she could make tea, then realized there wasn't much time before the exchange. She clicked it off.

She just needed something to do while she waited. It felt like she'd done everything possible to distract herself since MSI had taken Maizie and she'd discovered the voicemail in her inbox. No call in her call history. Someone had simply dropped the message in her voice mailbox remotely.

She should assume this was a setup, but these people were supposed to be her friends. They wanted tech she had turned back over to the software company who owned it—but apparently, they knew she'd made a copy of everything before she posted it all online.

"What's the plan for when they show up?" Elizabeth looked at her over the rim of the glass. "You aren't going to face down these gunmen, are you?"

"I just want Maizie, Ellayna, and her family safe. But Jax came up with a good plan, and there's a whole team here to keep me safe." Kenna had her gun on her. She wasn't going to put herself in danger, but Bear and his team, hopefully, didn't intend her harm.

Lord, protect us.

This would be a delicate balance.

"And when you go into labor?" Elizabeth asked, not beating around the bush.

Kenna laid a hand on her baby bump. "Hopefully, she won't decide to arrive in the middle of everything."

"You should be resting, not working. But a lot of women don't have that luxury. We don't all get to ignore our responsibilities and put our feet up for days while we wait for a baby to come. Especially not with jobs, other children in the house, and husbands who claim not to know how to boil water."

"But I cook a mean chicken fried steak." Stairns strode in and came over to his wife, tugging her against his side and kissing her.

"Chicken fried steak sounds good." Kenna smiled at Jax, who came over and stood by her.

The buzzer by the door sounded, then a voice came through the small speaker there—the property intercom. "Movement on the perimeter. Two black SUVs and a gray sedan between them on approach. ETA five minutes."

Jax went over to the panel by the door and pressed the button. "Copy that. Move into positions."

"Understood."

"What's the plan?" Elizabeth asked. "Assuming I'm staying in here, and if this baby comes, I'll be elbow deep in placenta."

Kenna tipped her head back and laughed. "I'm hoping that doesn't happen before we get this situation sorted."

Elizabeth shook her head. "In my experience, babies come when they want. Not on your timetable." She eyed Kenna. "I want to know the minute you start having contractions."

"That's fair." Kenna nodded.

Jax put his arm around her shoulder. "Let's pray real quick before they get here."

She closed her eyes, leaning her head on his shoulder

and listened to him ask for a special blessing on this operation. For safety for those who were vulnerable, and protection for Kenna and the baby. He prayed they would get answers and that Maizie, Ellayna, and her family would be free.

"Amen."

Jax kissed her. "Love you."

"Love you, too." She touched his cheeks and kissed him, then grabbed the shotgun from on top of the refrigerator and cocked it. "Let's do this."

Kenna ignored Elizabeth's sputtering and went to the porch, where she sat with her blanket on her lap. She hid the shotgun down the side of her leg, in the folds of the blanket where it would be out of sight. Plus, it was really cold out here, and the blanket was going to help keep her warm beyond the layers she was wearing.

The trio of vehicles pulled to a stop on the road at the end of the drive. They didn't turn in.

Doors opened on the front and rear SUVs, and MSI operatives she knew climbed out. She spotted Bear and Hollace, men she would have said she trusted just a few months ago. Men whose lives she'd worked to save.

Jax walked down the porch steps, while Craig came to stand at the rail in front of her. Kenna could have pointed out the spots across the property around them where Preston and his team were hiding. They'd chosen the positions carefully so no one would be aiming at MSI agents with Kenna in their line of fire.

The majority of them were on either side of the cabin, looking in the same direction she was.

Bear met Jax halfway down the drive. She couldn't hear the conversation as he'd opted to not have comms in. Jax said something to Bear, who reacted. Taking a step back and shaking his head.

He strode past Jax who yelled after him, "Hey!"

Bear jogged over to the porch. Craig had a weapon up and aimed before he got near Kenna. Jax followed him up the steps and grabbed his arm, spinning him back. "You don't go near her!"

More men climbed out of the vehicles, moving in formation across the front yard. Their boots sank into the snow as they rushed over to protect their boss.

Preston's security force emerged on either side of the house, yelling as they strode forward with weapons of their own aimed at the MSI team. "Weapons down! Hands up!"

Someone yelled, "Freeze!"

They didn't stop until Bear held up a hand, creating a standoff.

Jax was almost nose to nose with him now. "Tell your men to *back off*."

"We came here for an exchange."

"Hand over the family you kidnapped and tell your men to stand down."

Bear swallowed, thinking for a moment. He reached up to his lapel and grasped it for a second. "Pull back to the car while I sort this out."

Jax said, "Let the family go."

"Give me the tech you have, and I will." Bear lifted his chin. "That's why we're all here."

"Not the only reason, but one of them."

"So you just wanted to accuse me of kidnapping Maizie as well? I haven't touched her." Bear seemed offended. "I can't believe you'd even think that."

Kenna said, "Is it so crazy? You have Ramon. He isn't answering his phone. Where are Amara and Bruce, Bear?

Have you seen them?" Right now, she wasn't even sure she had spoken with Amara a few days ago—or however long that had been. Felt like forever. "Someone knocked me out with a chemical and took Maizie. The same people who shot at Jax and Zeyla. Your people."

Bear shook his head. "That wasn't us."

"You really expect us to believe that?" Jax asked. "You must think we're stupid. You're behind basically everything that's happened to us in a week. You probably planted Zeyla's prints at those two crime scenes so that she'd get arrested. Picking apart our team. And for what? Because you work for *Dominatus* now?"

Bear backed off from Jax, turning slightly so she had a decent shot at his center mass if she lifted the shotgun.

She left it where it was, for now. "Why did you take Maizie?"

Chapter Forty-Four

B ear looked at her, a haggard expression on his face. "We didn't take Maizie."

"Your people took Ellayna. Why would I believe you didn't take Maizie?" Kenna looked out at the view off her front porch. What a nightmare this had turned into. Cold air blew across the snowy fields and rattled the screen door. Kenna spotted the dogs running across a field and heard a whistle.

She looked back at Bear. "Let them go, and we'll talk about this, because you guys have some explaining to do."

"We don't work for you, Kenna."

She didn't think they worked for her, but she had thought they were friends. Colleagues. People who kept each other in the loop and shared information. She was about to argue but didn't get the chance.

He said, "We work *with* the president."

"Is that supposed to put us on the same side, then? The president exposed my team to the world and put us all under the spotlight. And for what? So she could make herself look better. Now it seems like you're the reason behind everything going on with us." She leaned back in the rocking chair. "What am I supposed to believe? Except that you kidnapped a family and are holding them against their will."

Bear said, "They're good in the car. We need to talk first." He grabbed his radio and held the button. "All positions hold at the vehicles."

The MSI operatives started to back up to the vehicles, creating a perimeter around them. No one relaxed. If anyone with MSI made a wrong move, Preston's security team would open fire.

Bear said, "There's a faction of MSI that broke off from us when our boss, Earl Jonas, was killed. They went their way, and we went ours."

Jax had told her about that because it happened right around the time he rescued her from *Dominatus*. Yet another time when Maizie had been in danger, and Kenna hadn't been able to help.

She wouldn't let Maizie suffer now.

Bear continued, "They split from us, and we haven't been able to figure out what they were up to."

"You were busy," Jax said. "Taking over old military bases that Schnell controlled. Scooping up assets after he was arrested. Building up your team with our people."

None of this convinced her that they didn't have Maizie. But if it was some rogue division of MSI, then they'd knocked her out with something that wouldn't hurt the baby. Not that she was going to thank them, but with the *Dominatus* people she'd met being so adamant that they didn't want to hurt her baby, that might be the only part that fit.

"And working for the president," Jax finished.

"Which is funny," Kenna said. "Because I thought we were the ones under her thumb."

A tendon in Bear's jaw flexed. "A few weeks ago, we intercepted a transmission between the interim Grand Master and the rest of *Dominatus*. It said that they intended to choose a new leader and that it would involve testing each of the candidates to see who came out on top. That person would be the new leader, along with their spouse. A single person with authority, or a power couple who could push the group into the future.

"One of the names on the list was yours. One was the president. There are a few others on it, such as Petyr Blazevic and a guy we found in Norway—the *Dominatus* accountant, Lief Holmberg. Each one was to face a test that would stretch them to their limits."

Bear shifted his weight from one boot to the other. Resigning himself to telling the whole story. "Also on the list were your mother, Amara, and Bruce."

"A power couple."

"We had to take several players off the board. We knew if we could control the outcome of the tests, we could ensure the person we wanted was sworn in as the new leader. We went to the president with a plan to make sure it was her that ended up in charge. I mean, she's a public figure. She has a solid reputation and is gaining popularity. If we paired her with one of the men on the list, she could land in the top spot."

"And you believed she would be a good fit as their leader?"

Bear looked at her. "We told her that if she became dangerous, we would take her out."

"You threatened to end the life of the president of the United States?" Jax asked him, a dark look on his face.

Bear said, "We're at war with these people. This is how we end the war."

"What about Jax and me?" Kenna asked. They'd certainly thought through the plan. She wanted to know to what extent they'd done that.

Bear sniffed. "We knew what the test was going to be."

"The killer was hired to take out the baby and Crystal and kidnap Ellayna so I'd have to find her."

Bear nodded. "That's why we sent you the contract, so you'd understand."

"You intercepted and saved their lives."

"We've been keeping them safe. But we need that tech to finish the job. We have to make sure the president gets the vote. That's why she's getting married tomorrow to the Norwegian accountant. The software will manipulate the polling and ensure a win."

"You're going to rig the election," Stairns said.

Bear nodded. "Then we control *Dominatus*."

"What about Shawn Terrance, Marcus Neerwood, and Wallace Lofton. Three men dead because of this." She shifted her weight on the chair, and it started to rock, which meant she had to keep hold of the shotgun.

"There's a *Dominatus* asset onto us. She's trying to find information about my team so she can stop us," Bear said. "I'm hoping she finds the faction first. They're the ones who shot at you and Zeyla."

Kenna wasn't going to admit she'd met the asset. "Who planted Zeyla's prints at the murder scenes?"

"The *Dominatus* test had to strip you of your team. That's why Zeyla was taken out of play. And likely Maizie, too." Bear looked like he was about to lose his cool.

"Your people? Working for *Dominatus*? That's who is doing all this, putting me through my test?" The asset had to be Sylvia Caughton. Kenna had been played on more than one front through this whole thing. "They should've told me so I could let them know where they could shove their test."

Bear said, "I'll send a team, and they'll get Maizie back. These are my people who went rogue. It's my responsibility to clean up the mess."

He had to know they'd spoken to the killer. After all, the team who took Maizie knew where to find them. "We have an IP address for the person who hired the contract killer to take out Ellayna's family."

"Chicago?"

She frowned. "How did you know where the IP address would lead?"

"The person behind all this is the interim Grand Master. The governor of Illinois," Bear said.

She couldn't picture the man's face in her mind, but she could imagine what kind of person he was. "Of course, it's a governor."

"The president is getting married in Chicago tomorrow. The governor will be officiating. They're going to force the vote right after the ceremony and get the GM to swear them in as the couple in charge of all *Dominatus*."

"Honestly," Kenna said. "I don't care what they're doing. I don't want anything to do with this. You should have told me they were going to be testing me. I'd have made it real clear where I stand on being considered as the new leader of *Dominatus*. The answer is no."

The only thing she cared about was Maizie.

"You don't get to object. That's just how it works, and you were on the list." Bear lifted a hand and shrugged. "None of us can stop it."

"So they'd have killed me if I refused?"

"No, that would have harmed the baby," Bear said. "They'd have killed Jax."

Kenna stared at him, her lips pressed tight together.

"None of us asked to be a part of this. That's why my team left you out of it. We didn't want you anywhere near them or any of their operatives. We were trying to keep you safe, Kenna. To let you live your life."

By giving her a constructed "test" to keep her occupied? Of course, they'd think that would satisfy her.

She had more questions. "Where are Bruce and Amara?"

Bear said, "They're supposed to be witnesses at the wedding. That way, they can put their collective vote toward the president and Lief."

"This entire situation is insane." She wanted to shake some sense into him and all of them.

"Give me the tech you got from the software company. I'll let the family out of their car, and we'll leave. You don't need to have anything to do with it."

Jax folded his arms. "We're supposed to sit here and wait for you to get Maizie back from the people who were your team? There's no way we're going to do nothing."

"As soon as I'm able, I'll find them. I'll get her back for you."

Stairns shook his head. "Not good enough. Not after what she's been through. We're not waiting for you to make this deal with the president and get yourselves in a position of power so you can think you're controlling *Dominatus*. You're all cracked if you think they're going to listen to you. That having your pick in power will change anything."

Bear said, "I get that you care about Maizie. I care about Maizie. We all do. But this is about the whole world. We can't let them choose their leader. We *have* to make sure the choice is the right one."

"You can have the tech. You give us Ellayna and her family, and I suppose we owe you for saving their lives. But you're going to send Ramon, Amara, and Bruce home. You're going to give us what we need to find Maizie, and then you're never going to contact us again."

Jax glanced at her.

Kenna wasn't going to back down. "You and I"—she motioned between herself and Bear—"we're done."

"Bruce and Amara—"

"I don't care what you have planned or who you've forced to be involved." Kenna lifted her chin, wanting them back with her but knowing they could take care of themselves. "I only want my family back, and you're going to make that happen. Maizie. Ramon. Amara and Bruce. Send them all home, Bear."

Bear turned his head and stared at the line of vehicles. Chewing over what she'd said? It wasn't that complicated. And she was *so* done with this. He'd made the wrong choice, and now Maizie was caught in the middle.

Kenna was *not* going to allow her to become collateral damage.

"People are getting killed. Lives are being destroyed because of these people. Because of their *tests*. Because they think they can do whatever they want." She took a breath. "Now you have my people in danger, right in the middle of this insane plan. Maizie is in danger. Amara and Bruce have to stand up in front of people who've been trying to kill them for years. Ramon is a guy trying to do the right thing, and what do you have him doing?"

"He would have stopped us."

"What does that tell you about what you're doing?

Ramon is a guy who chose integrity instead of descending into the depths of what life could have turned him into. He chose to protect people and work every day to bring justice and make the world a better place," she said. "The fact that what you're doing put you on opposite sides of this war should be a huge red flag that what you're doing is *not* the right thing."

Chapter Forty-Five

Ramon sat in the middle row of the vehicle but knew for a fact that he couldn't get out. The doors were locked, and he'd only be exiting this vehicle when it stopped, and someone opened the door for him. The rest of the seats were filled with Bear's men, including Hollace, who sat on the seat beside him.

Another identical vehicle behind had Amara and Bruce in it. The one in front held more men.

The convoy turned down State Street, driving between the towering high-rise buildings that blocked out any view of stars he might have had.

Hollace shifted and pulled out his phone, answering it with a snapped, "Hollace." His attention shifted toward Ramon just a fraction. "Is that a good idea?" Whatever the answer to his question, he responded, "Understood."

Hollace held out the phone to him. "It's Kenna."

Given what Amara and Bruce had explained that these people could do with voices, he said, "Am I supposed to take your word for it?"

"Unless you want to miss your chance to speak with her."

Ramon grabbed the phone. "Hello?"

"Is it really you?" The soft alto of her voice drifted over him. Sounding so much like Zeyla that, for a second, he didn't know which woman was speaking.

"I could say the same thing." He swallowed against the lump in his throat. "Things didn't go exactly as planned." Now *he* was a part of the plan, but he didn't think these guys would let him explain it to her.

He'd questioned Hollace about how wise it was to bring him on their big operation—the wedding and whatever else was going on. Hollace had told him that Ramon's presence meant that Kenna herself was advocating for the president and Lief Holmberg to be the new *Dominatus* leaders.

As if she could vote by proxy, using Ramon as her spokesperson.

No way was he going to just go along with whatever they told him to do. Not if he didn't agree.

"Same here," Kenna said. "We've been talking with Bear about everything. Some of it was a surprise, given that we thought he was the one who had Maizie removed from the back of my car. But he says it wasn't his people. It was a faction of their group who broke away after Earl Jonas was killed."

"We're supposed to believe that?" Ramon's gut clenched. "Where is she?"

"Jax got a message from an online message board, and we think it's from her. She just landed in Chicago."

"Guess where I am," Ramon said, aware that everyone in the vehicle was listening to what he said.

"Preston and Stairns are on their way with Bear and his people, headed to the same place. Jax is staying with me, but I get the impression he's torn. He wants to be there to get her back."

"We'll get her back." That was a promise Ramon would always make.

"You'll have help. You won't be doing this on your own," she said. "Even Bear is livid that they took her, though he thinks he knows why."

"Do I want to know?"

"It isn't about *her*. Though, that might be part of the reason. Bear thinks it's also about how she had all the files from the software company on her computer. They took that as well as her."

Ramon clenched down on his back teeth. "They want the tech?"

"So did Bear. He's in for a battle if he wants to sway the vote by every means he can manage. But your only focus is Maizie. They can do whatever they want, destroy each other, I don't care. I told Bear that."

"Understood."

"They want you to throw in with them?"

"On your behalf. But if I know where you stand on it, I can take that route. I'll get her back for you."

"I know you will."

"Are you safe where you are?"

Kenna said, "I have Jax, and Preston's security team—including protection dogs. Elizabeth will be here for the delivery."

"You could go into town to the medical center." Ramon shook his head, a smile tugging at his lips. A little normalcy in the middle of an intense operation to manipulate *Dominatus* and all the worry about Maizie. At least, as much normalcy as Kenna was capable of having.

The woman was turning downright domestic.

Ramon couldn't wait to see the big, bad investigator melt when she was holding her baby.

"We'll see." Kenna chuckled.

Hollace motioned for the phone.

Ramon said, "I'll get Maizie and bring her home."

"I know you will. Whatever happens, Ramon...I love you."

"I know you do, *Hermana*. Stay safe."

Hollace took the phone out of his hand.

Ramon asked, "How long until Bear and the rest of your people get here?"

The driver pulled over to the curb at a swanky hotel, and the other cars did the same. Apparently, this was where it was all going down.

"A couple of minutes. They're right behind us." Hollace climbed out his side.

Ramon tried his door handle, and it was locked. One of the guys in the back seat snickered about child locks. Ramon kept his mouth shut, and when the door opened, he hopped out, striding to the vehicle behind, where Amara and Bruce got out, wearing their wedding finery. Amara had a black evening gown on, and Bruce wore a suit. Ramon's suit made him look like an FBI agent—go figure.

All he needed was a weapon.

"There's a rogue faction of Bear's people, and they've taken Maizie. We think she's going to be here."

Amara's expression flashed with anger. Bruce moved closer to her. "What can we do?"

"My only priority is Maizie. Preston and Stairns will be

here also." Ramon lowered his voice. "If you want to delay the proceedings while I find her, that's up to you."

Bruce nodded sharply.

"I'll do more than delay it." Amara gathered up the folds of her dress and headed for the revolving door entrance.

A bellboy lifted his arm and spoke into a comms receiver in his sleeve.

US government agent?

Ramon wasn't going to assume that anyone in this hotel was who they seemed to be. But he couldn't search room by room until he found her. He needed a plan of action, and attending the wedding might be a good first step. Whoever had taken Maizie might have brought her to witness it like the rest of them.

"Everyone into the lobby, please!" Hollace motioned to them all, waving his arms like a vacation tour guide.

Ramon and Bruce followed Amara and found her looking around the people in the lobby. She kept moving, searching every corner. Looking at the people sitting in alcoves, and even at the bar.

"Where is the wedding taking place?"

Bruce said, "In a ballroom off the first floor, so we have to go up the escalator."

"I'm hoping she'll be there, and we'll know for ourselves if she's all right." Ramon didn't have much else he could do.

Bruce said, "None of us is going to let anything happen to her, as much as we can do to prevent it."

"I'm more worried about what we can't prevent."

"Let's keep moving, people." Hollace ushered them to the escalator.

Halfway between the ground floor and the next, he spotted more of the MSI operatives coming in the front.

Preston and Stairns were with them, and both caught Ramon's wave.

Good. He almost had the makings of a team of his own.

A group who would all do whatever it took to get Maizie back.

Upstairs, the doors to the ballroom were open. Ramon stepped off the escalator at the top and waited for Hollace. "I didn't come here to attend a wedding."

"Yes, you did. We all did."

Ramon was surprised the guy didn't grab him and try to force him into the ballroom. "You know they have Maizie?"

Hollace nodded. "None of us are happy about that, but if we want to resolve this situation, we have to keep playing this out. It'll work."

"You think I care about your plan."

"Someone has to vote on Kenna's behalf. You're the one here that's closest to her."

"That's not true, is it?" Ramon pointed out. "If they have Maizie, then they have Kenna and Jax's daughter. You think they're going to measure my vote against hers and argue it holds more weight?"

Hollace swore under his breath. "I'll tell Bear."

More people streamed up the escalator, stepping off and moving past them like they were excited to attend the wedding. Then again, it wasn't every day that the president of the United States got married. Sitting presidents were usually already married, and since this was the first single and female president, it should be a big deal.

But the whole thing was being kept hush-hush.

When Bear stepped off, he asked, "What is it, Hollace?"

Ramon gave the guy a second to tell his boss what they'd come up with and held out his hand for Preston.

"Hey. Thanks for coming." He sounded like an usher or groomsman.

Preston nodded. "We'll get her back to Kenna."

Stairns said, "Ramon."

To his surprise, the other older man opened his arms and gave Ramon a hug. "Good to see you."

Ramon cleared his throat. "I appreciate you coming."

Preston's attention shifted over Ramon's shoulder. "Amara is headed this way."

Ramon turned and saw both her and Bruce rushing out of the ballroom. When they got close enough, Amara said, "She's in there. They've got her standing up in the wedding party."

Ramon wound between all of them and skirted people going into the ballroom, about to elbow a guy out of the way if he didn't walk faster. He stepped into the room full of cream-colored fabric chairs. Hanging chandeliers brightly lit with a soft yellow glow, and cream walls that looked like they'd been wallpapered with fabric.

She stood at the far end of the room.

Stairns almost collided with him, coming in so fast to see her.

Maizie's hair was loose and long, curled over her shoulders. She wore a white dress no better than a nightgown and stood on the stage at the front beside another woman Ramon didn't know. Both of them held small bouquets of flowers.

What on earth?

He clipped a woman's shoulder but didn't stop, moving fast down the aisle. Aware of men moving in from both sides like bodyguards going to intercept. The groom and another guy to the right, watching him.

Maizie's eyes widened at the sight of him tearing down

the aisle to get to her. She shook her head, and he saw her mouth the word *Don't.*

Ramon heard a muffled pop, and two barbs hit his chest.

White-hot lightning whipped through his entire body like a flash. His legs crumpled under him, and he heard Maizie scream his name.

Face to the carpet, his body twitched through the effects of the stun gun until every last bit of electricity dissipated.

Someone rolled him to his back. "What are we going to do with this one?"

"Sit him in a seat with everyone else." The governor of Illinois stepped over Ramon.

He wanted to grab the guy's foot but couldn't move.

Two men lifted him by his armpits and dumped him in a chair. He couldn't even lift his head. Stairns and Preston sat either side of him, Stairns on the aisle.

"I guess someone had to test what they were going to do to anyone who didn't play along with this ridiculous farce," Preston muttered.

Stairns said, "At least they didn't just kill him."

Ramon couldn't even grunt. He managed to lift his head and look at Maizie, just in time to see a tear roll down her cheek.

Chapter Forty-Six

"Dearly beloved...isn't that how it goes?" The governor of Illinois stood at the front of the room. The president and Lief Holmberg were on the step below him so everyone could see him over the top of their heads. He seemed to be enjoying himself. "The leadership of our people takes strength. It takes collaboration and a firm hand."

Ramon tuned out what he was saying and looked at Maizie. She didn't appear hurt, just upset. If Stairns made a run for it, could he get to her before someone hit him with the same kind of stun gun they'd fired at Ramon?

"We need a distraction," he said quietly to the men on either side of him.

Preston lifted his chin in a nod.

"Then we can—"

The wrinkly lady in front of them turned around and shushed them. She had on pearls and huge earrings and a pair of silk gloves. Was Ramon supposed to apologize? She was the enemy as far as he was concerned, a woman who knew about *Dominatus* and probably used her position within the group to continue living this lavish lifestyle she obviously enjoyed.

What a charade.

He wanted to stand up and start yelling. Maybe right around when the governor, officiating the wedding, asked if anyone had any objections. Ramon was going to jump up like this was a courtroom and he was a lawyer. *I object!*

The whole idea they could get *Dominatus* to have the leadership Bear wanted was ridiculous. They'd still be in operation. What they should be doing was destroying them, but aside from killing everyone in this room that wasn't his friend or part of Bear's team, he didn't know how they could do that.

Probably Bear had thought all this through, decided he wasn't a mass murderer, and opted for the nonlethal way to fight them.

The governor asked, "Do you, Lief Holmberg, pledge to lead our people with strength and keen insight into the future?"

The accountant they'd brought back from Norway said, "I do."

He'd walked into this, probably knowing exactly why Bear and his team were there. Maybe they'd even told him ahead of time, and so he'd had all the operatives who likely lived in that town back off. But they hadn't backed off with their traps.

The operation had cost Bear the life of one of his men.

All to make a point that they controlled life and death?

Ramon gritted his teeth.

"And do you," the governor continued, "Madam President, pledge to lead this country under the authority of your husband and all of *Dominatus?*"

The president didn't respond right away. "That's not what I was told you were going to say."

"Do you agree, or not?" the governor asked her.

She just stood there.

"You didn't think you were going to be an equal, did you? You're well aware of how this works. You've been a part of our group since birth. This position is an honor we bestow on you. Do you accept, or not?"

She looked at Lief, who said nothing. He didn't seem to be surprised.

She asked, "What about the changing landscape of the future?"

The governor said, "It won't change so much that a woman is in charge." He laughed, coughing slightly. Blood coated his lips, and he used a handkerchief from his pocket to wipe it away.

"He's dying," Preston whispered. "That's why he's not lobbying to be in charge. He's trying to leave them in good hands."

The governor lifted his arms. "Strength and power!"

Most of the congregants in the room responded back to him, "Strength and power!"

The governor lowered his arms. "Agree or leave, Madam President. There are more wives to be sworn in."

Ramon's focus whipped over to Maizie and the woman beside her. Both dressed in white.

The president gasped. "I'm not going to be one of many!"

Lief turned to her. "You're going to be what I tell you to be, dear."

She shoved him away and screamed, then went for the governor. She grabbed him with her hands around his neck and started to choke the life out of him. "I'll kill you! I'll kill all of you!"

Men rushed over to drag her off.

"Go!" Ramon shoved at Stairns.

Even if the guy didn't run for Maizie, Ramon would. But Stairns caught on fast and raced down the aisle. Ramon followed, sprinting over to Maizie.

A man dived at him, but Ramon was ready.

Stairns reached her at the same moment Ramon twisted around to punch the guy away. Another man jumped on his back and then a swarm of them were there.

"You dare interrupt these proceedings!" the governor screamed.

Someone punched Ramon in the stomach, and a second later, he was on his face on the carpet again. This time, with a knee in his back.

Across from him, on the other side of Lief Holmberg, they'd done the same to the president.

"I'll marry him!" The other bridesmaid hopped over Ramon and went to stand where the president had been a second ago.

Maizie hid behind Stairns, who had his hand close to the gun on his hip.

"It's never going to stop." It would never be over. Ramon knew that.

The governor hissed, "Shut your mouth."

Ramon stared at the president, her tears leaking onto the carpet. These people would continue to do whatever they wanted, refusing to back down or bow to anyone. They would use others for their own gain, or pleasure, anytime they wanted. It wasn't just about keeping Kenna safe or protecting Maizie. It wasn't about Kenna and Jax's baby growing up in a safe world. This was about everyone, everywhere.

It was about the world.

A messy, tragic, beautiful place where a lot of people tried to live good lives and enjoy peace while they could. Where there would always be a need for the brand of justice that saved innocents and didn't leave people lost and forgotten but fought always for a better world.

The president shoved off one of the men holding her. "Let me up!"

Ramon couldn't move with this knee painfully pressed into his back. He started to demand the same, but the president yelled over him.

"Let me up! I've changed my mind." She straightened, brushing down her dress. "I'll agree. I just want to be what I can be to *Dominatus*, even if it's not what I thought."

One of the men by her, suited guys who had put their Secret Service badges out of sight for this. *Dominatus* operatives whose job it was to protect their asset—the one they'd installed in the White House.

She smoothed down her hair. "Get out of my place." She lifted a finger and flicked it to the side, indicating the other bridesmaid should move back to her spot. "I'm going first, and you can get used to it."

"Very well." The governor seemed less enthused than before but willing to continue.

If they tried to marry Maizie to this Lief Holmberg guy, Ramon was going to—

The president moved fast, yanking a pistol from inside the agent's jacket. She spun around and squeezed the trigger before she even aimed. The first shot went wide, while shots two and three landed squarely in the governor's chest.

She spun again and fired at the man she was supposed to marry. Lief Holmberg fell to the floor, half on Ramon. The weight on his back lifted off.

Agents over to the right pulled their guns, but this was the president. No one fired at her.

She turned and shot three people in the front row, then pointed her gun at the bridesmaid who'd been happy to take her spot.

Ramon shoved Lief off his leg and scrambled up. "Ma'am—"

She fired, a glassy kind of fury on her face.

"Madam President!" Bear raced down the aisle. "We will shoot if you don't put that gun—"

She pointed the weapon at Maizie. At Stairns, in front of Maizie.

Ramon raced at her, slamming into her shoulder and taking her down to the floor. But the gun had fired. He wrestled the weapon from her and rolled her to her front, pulling her arms behind her back while she screamed.

"I've got her." Bear looped plastic ties over the president's wrists.

Ramon shoved off her and scrambled across the slumped bodies to where Maizie was on her knees with Stairns across her lap.

"Ramon!" Her features twisted, and tears rolled down her face.

Stairns had blood on his chest, soaking into the material, expanding outward while he struggled for breath. He lifted his hand and touched Maizie's arm.

Ramon squeezed her shoulder, kneeling on the other side of Stairns.

Bruce and Amara raced over with Preston, who said, "I

can get an air ambulance, have them land on the roof. We'll get him to the hospital."

Ramon watched the life start to flicker from Craig Stairns's eyes. He leaned down to the older man and whispered in his ear. "You saved her. No one is ever going to forget that."

When he moved back, Craig's features had slackened, and his head lolled to the side. Ramon touched two fingers to his neck and felt for a pulse.

Maizie whimpered. "Don't do this to me. Don't leave me."

Amara crouched beside her and put her arm around the young woman. Maizie shoved her off. "No! He isn't gone!" She clutched Craig's body, pulling him up to her and bending over him. Holding on tight. Trying to hang on to him. "Don't leave!" She shook with the force of the sobs.

The room had descended into chaos around them.

Someone fired a gun across the room, and the bullet slammed into the glass behind the stage. Preston and Bruce ducked down. Ramon looked at Bear, who handed the president off to people that Ramon figured were Secret Service agents.

He pulled his gun and said, "Copy that," to whoever had spoken to him. Bear jumped a dead body and raced for men who were fleeing the room. His rogue teammates. "You're dead, Cullers! This is your doing!"

"What a mess," Preston said.

"The police will probably be here soon." Bruce looked around, scanning for danger. "They won't have a clue what to make of this."

Ramon looked over at the agents standing around the president. She sat at the far end of the front row, her back straight. Chin high. Not looking at any of them. He looked back at his friends. "I don't want Maizie here when the police arrive."

He touched her shoulder. "We need to go."

"I'm not leaving him."

Ramon's heart squeezed in his chest at the look on her face. Her world had been torn apart. But he would do what he'd promised Kenna he would do.

Bring her home.

"Come on." He gathered her into his arms and stood, forcing her to go with him. She didn't need to be here with a dead body any longer, and he didn't want her to have to give the police a statement.

Bruce said quietly, "We'll make sure Craig isn't alone. We'll take care of everything and bring him home."

Maizie looked like she didn't want to go.

Preston said, "Go."

Ramon lifted Maizie into his arms. "You're freezing."

She curled her hands into the lapels of his blazer and tucked her face in his neck.

"Time to go home." She said nothing. He kicked open a side door and found a hallway. "Maybe you'll have a new baby sister by the time we get there."

Ramon headed for the nearest exit door, aware he was going to have to find her some more clothing because it was freezing outside, and she only wore a thin dress. He set her on her feet just inside the door.

Gunshots rang from down the halls at the other end of the hotel.

Maizie flinched.

Ramon slid off his jacket and wrapped it around her. "It doesn't seem like it now, but I promise it's going to be okay."

"He just stood there and let her shoot him so she wouldn't shoot me."

Ramon pulled her into his arms. "Any of us would have done the same. That's what family is. We lay down our lives for each other."

She blinked back tears. "'Greater love.'"

"What's that?" They needed to go, not spend too long in this hallway.

"Something Kenna said. 'Greater love has no man than this. That he lay down his life for his friends.' But she said it was about Jesus."

"I guess we need to start listening." Ramon shifted to put his arm around her and lead her toward the door. "Come on, kiddo. Let's get you home."

Chapter Forty-Seven

Kenna bent to give Cabot a rubdown, then told the old mutt to go lie on her bed. It was far too cold for the dog to lie outside. She pushed open the front door of the cabin and found Ramon standing with Jax on the porch.

Her husband turned to her. "How are they?"

"Helping each other as best they can. But both of them are a mess." She stepped into Jax's arms. "Having Craig here so they can bury him will be good. They can say goodbye."

She wiped her damp cheek on his sweater while he rubbed her back and held her and the baby inside her close. "This baby needs to be born already."

Jax chuckled. "Have you heard from Ellayna?"

Kenna nodded against his chest. "She said they're all

settled back at home and to tell Preston thanks for letting them ride there in the helicopter."

Ramon just stared out at the land, saying nothing.

"You okay, bro?"

He shook his head.

"Maybe having a funeral will be good for all of us." Kenna knew she needed to be present for the grieving process.

Jax said, "Elizabeth will probably want him buried in Colorado, so he can be close to her."

"I want to ask Maizie to bring the Airstream here, but she might want to be near to Elizabeth for a while."

Jax nodded.

Ramon cut in abruptly. "Is it really in the Bible that friends give their lives for each other?"

Kenna knew he'd been wrestling with something since he'd brought Maizie here and they'd told Elizabeth what happened to her husband. She hadn't expected it to be this.

Jax said, "It was talking about Jesus, because that's what He did. He gave his life for all of us. His friends."

"I don't think I'm his friend." Ramon shook his head. "I'd know if I was, right?"

Kenna remembered feeling like that, as if she could never be good enough to be accepted by God. But that was the significance of grace. That God had freely given Himself to be their sacrifice so that each person who believed in what Jesus had done could be accepted into His family.

Just like they'd accepted each other into this family.

She hated that they'd lost Craig. That Elizabeth would have to live without her husband, and their children without a father. That Maizie would never have him there to support and protect her.

But any of them would've done exactly what he had. In the moment, they'd have stepped in front of a bullet for any of them, and things would have turned out the same.

Because that's what family did.

"You can be," Jax said. "All you have to do is say a prayer. Believe that what Jesus did was powerful enough to wipe away every bad thing you've done and replace it with His goodness. It's an exchange. Death for life."

Ramon nodded. "Okay, how do I do that?"

Kenna swiped tears from the corners of her eyes. She eased into her rocking chair and listened, praying her thanks while Jax led Ramon in the sinner's prayer. Asking for Ramon to find the peace he'd been searching for.

She ran a hand over the baby...who needed to figure out how to move this thing along. Now that their lives had calmed down, at least for now, she was ready to have this child. *Anytime now.*

The last she'd heard, the president had been arrested for multiple counts of murder. Bear had been in the throes of a firefight with rogue operatives when the police arrived. Hollace had been killed, and Bear had caught a bullet in the arm. The rest of them had been arrested.

Bruce and Amara had given the police a statement and gone to find a place in Salt Lake City, so they wouldn't be too far away when the baby came.

Preston had bought several of the surrounding properties, so Kenna and Jax didn't need to worry about neighbors, and she occasionally spotted his dogs roaming in the snow.

Ramon lifted his head. "Thanks, Jax."

"Of course." Jax held out his hand, and they shook, a lingering clasp of brotherhood and mutual respect. When they let go, Jax asked, "Does that sound like a helicopter to you guys?"

"Maybe Preston is coming back from somewhere."

Ramon moved to the edge of the porch. "Whoever it is, they're headed this way."

Jax went with him, and they both stepped down onto the front walk, guns drawn and in their hands. Watching the helicopter land on the space Preston had his men clear off.

The side door opened, and a woman climbed out, wearing skinny jeans and a heavy jacket. Red hair.

"Sylvia Caughton." Kenna stayed where she was because she didn't feel like standing. Whatever this woman had to say, the guys could relay it.

The *Dominatus* asset came along the cleared path, holding a small box in her hands. As she neared Jax and Ramon, she said, "I'm not here to harm anyone."

"Why are you here at all?" Ramon asked her.

"I need to speak with Kenna."

Jax glanced over his shoulder at her, and Kenna shrugged one shoulder.

After Jax frisked her, Sylvia came up the porch steps. "I'd have thought you would've had that baby by now."

"Is that why you came?" Maybe the small box she held was a baby shower gift.

Sylvia shook her head. "I'm sure you're aware by now of what happened in Chicago."

"*Dominatus* is done. That's all I need to know."

"The candidates who perished..." Sylvia seemed sad about that, so maybe she did have a heart. She cleared her throat. "Of those who remain, each has been given a vote of whether they wish to lead us or suggest another on the list be given the position. You can probably guess what Bruce and Amara have chosen. They believe you should be the leader of *Dominatus*."

And it had nothing to do with *Dominatus* believing they would never really be able to control Amara.

What did that say about how they felt about her?

Kenna lifted the water glass she'd set on the floor beside the chair earlier and forgotten to take back inside and pitched it at the woman. Water hit her front, and the glass fell to the porch and shattered. "Get off my property."

Inside the cabin, her dog barked.

"We need a leader."

"You're done," Kenna said. "There's nothing left. Give it up."

"If you would—"

Ramon pulled her back by her arm. "You heard the lady. Get off her property."

Sylvia stumbled back. "You are the leader. It's already been decided." She set the box on the rail of the porch. "There's nothing you can do about it."

"I want Zeyla's name cleared," Kenna said. "Prove that she was set up, and get the charges dropped, and I'll consider it."

Jax lifted one brow, but Kenna would have to explain later that she had zero intention of going through with it.

"It's already done. There's nothing to consider."

"If any of you comes onto my land, I'll have security take care of you." Kenna lifted her chin. "Consider that your only warning. No one comes near me or my family. Not ever."

"There's no need to make things difficult. Just accept the fact that—"

"No. Go away."

Ramon shoved her off the steps. She stumbled but didn't go down. "Get lost."

"I don't need to repeat it, but I'll escort you to your

chopper, and you can go." Jax followed her, keeping a distance. Making sure she went without a fuss.

Ramon lifted the box from the rail. "What do you want me to do with this?"

Kenna shook her head. "What is it?"

"Probably some kind of orb of power, or whatever they give their leader." He tore the lid off the box. "Huh." He pulled out a pair of pink baby-sized socks. "She knows you're having a girl, I guess." He frowned. "There's a flash drive in here, too."

She watched Jax stand with his arms crossed, his pistol still in his hand, while the helicopter took off. His hair ruffled with the whipped-up air, snow swirling around him.

Ramon went inside.

She said, "Don't let the dog out with this glass."

Jax came back over, ambling up the steps with his gaze on her. A look of contentment on his face that she loved. An expression she'd helped put there. "I can't believe you actually threw a glass at her."

"I guess I should sweep the glass off the porch."

"I got it." He grabbed the arms of the chair and leaned down, kissing her gently. "I love you."

"I know."

"Is she going to hurry up and get here?"

Kenna laughed. "I was thinking the same thing when you were praying with Ramon. You did good, by the way."

"Thanks." He kissed her again.

She sat back in the chair, and the baby decided to dance around, kicking the top of her belly since she'd turned.

Jax came back out with a dustpan and brush. He swept the porch, then let Cabot come and sit by her, wearing a doggy overcoat.

"Hi, puppy." Kenna reached down and scratched her

nose, and the dog wagged her tail on the wood planks. "You're a good doggy, yes, you are."

She'd been through a lot in her life, just like the rest of them. But she accepted every change with a kind of peace that said a lot about her contentment. With the people she knew around her, it didn't matter where she was. There was safety and happiness there.

Ramon came out with Jax, carrying a laptop. "She gave us all of it."

Kenna said, "All of what?"

"*Dominatus*," Ramon said. "We have the member list, all their information, and every major operation they had going for the past few decades. There's more still that I haven't looked at. That woman, their operative, she handed the entire group over to us."

"That isn't a fight I'm going to take on," Kenna said.

Jax leaned against the porch rail, the tips of his ears red with cold. "Maybe we don't need to take them on. Maybe we do what Kenna Banbury does. Hand the evidence and the suspect to the police and let justice happen. Let the feds and the police take the whole group apart."

"I like that idea." Kenna nodded.

She held out her hand, and Jax helped her out of the chair. Kenna felt an odd sensation and looked down to find wet between her feet. "Uh..."

"Your water just broke?"

"Don't ask me. I've never done this before!"

Ramon chuckled. "Now she freaks out. Guess you're not as cool as you think you are."

She looked at Jax. "Get me a glass. I'm going to throw it at him."

"Maybe later." Jax kissed her. "Right now, I think we're

going to the medical center in town so you can have this baby."

Kenna looked around flustered. "We need to..."

Jax touched her cheeks. "I've got this. Okay? Don't worry."

She nodded, and he kissed her again. Then he handed her the car keys. "You go get in the car. I'll tell Maizie and Elizabeth what's happening."

"Okay."

Ramon set the laptop on her chair and held out his hand. "Come on, I'll walk you to the car."

"Thanks." She stepped carefully down the porch steps, hearing Jax in the cabin calling out to the women. They were going to want to come to the medical center. "Are you coming?" She looked over at Ramon as they walked the path to the garage.

"Wouldn't miss it." He patted her arm, linked through his. "I'll sit with Maizie and Elizabeth. Make sure they're okay."

Chapter Forty-Eight

"Thanks to the tireless work of the men and women of the Federal Bureau of Investigation, the organization known as *Dominatus* is no more." Kenna felt a surge of satisfaction in knowing Jax had called it "the Kenna Banbury way." Knowing the task was complete now allowed her to sleep soundly, to live in peace, and to continue to have a good relationship with law enforcement.

Just in case she needed it in the future.

The courtroom door opened, and Jax stepped in, holding their baby in his arms. He sat back down on the row he'd claimed for their family, tucking the empty bottle back in the diaper bag. Maizie leaned over beside him and touched the baby's forehead.

Beyond Maizie, Amara sat beside Bruce, and beside Amara were Zeyla and Ramon, their heads close. Whispering together. Since the charges had been dropped and the real murderer located, the right person—an MSI rogue operative—was in prison, Zeyla was a free woman. She seemed content to spend her freedom with family, and Ramon.

Kenna tore her gaze away from them and looked at the president, Miriam Tetherton, where she sat behind the defense table. On trial for multiple counts of murder.

Kenna said, "I have no doubt in my mind that after a lifetime of mindless service to them, years of training that most of us would consider torture and committing horrible crimes in their name...the president would resemble a member of a cult. A woman whose identity had been chosen for her, who realized in that moment that she had no rights. No future other than what they decided to give her."

Kenna swallowed past the lump in her throat. "But she also murdered one of my dearest friends in cold blood and nearly tore more of my family from me."

They had buried Stairns not far from his home in Colorado, and no one in the family had been the same since. Her biggest source of grief was that he hadn't lived long enough to meet her daughter.

"You, yourself, testified that you weren't there, Mrs. Jaxton," the defense attorney pointed out. "How can you possibly understand the duress my client was under in that moment or at any other time in her life?"

Kenna said, "You asked for my statement, and that's what I've given this court. Whether I understand her or not isn't relevant to my testimony, but the fact is that I *do* know what it's like to have your freedom taken from you. To believe you'll be killed. I know what it's like to be captured, to have a life growing inside me and not know if my captors mean my child harm—or if they intend to torture me to learn the extent of our strength.

"I survived *Dominatus* like so many other people connected to them. I didn't let them win. I didn't let them take my choices from me or turn me into someone other than the person I am. And I don't blame them for being who they are. They didn't know any different, all they knew were their own selfish desires.

"That's what put me and my family in danger. Maybe the president knew there was nothing she could do to change what they decided. There was no way to find the power to fight them alone, and so she took the fight into her own hands and destroyed lives."

According to what Ramon had told her, in that moment, the president seemed not to care who she was shooting at. But Miriam Tetherton had taken out the top leadership in a strategic manner and then attempted to kill the other "wives" that Lief Holmberg was supposed to have had. Maizie had been caught in the middle, made a pawn—because of Kenna.

The defense attorney said, "Maybe the president believed she had no other choice, as you've said. She took back the power because they forced her to defend herself. Couldn't that be true?"

Kenna shook her head. "That's the thing about 'taking back your power.' Often, the vulnerable and broken person finds the strength to stand up for themselves. And sometimes, they take it too far, and they become the abuser."

It was something she'd been talking to Maizie about recently. Now that the young woman had opened up a little about how she'd felt being a captive, almost being forced to marry a much older man once again. She didn't want Maizie to use the strength she'd found against others like a weapon, purely so she wasn't the vulnerable person anymore.

Kenna turned to the judge. "I don't have anything more to say."

"Prosecutor Hasworth?"

She rose slightly out of her chair and said, "No further questions, Your Honor," then she sat.

He slammed his gavel down. "This court is in recess until tomorrow."

Chapter Forty-Nine

CENTRAL MEDICAL CENTER
EVANSTON, WYOMING

"Ready?" Jax stood beside the bed, holding their baby. The little bundle of her daughter was wrapped in a pink blanket.

Kenna brushed back damp hair from her forehead and held out her arms like this was the first time she'd held her baby. Again. "Yes, definitely."

He laid the baby in her arms. "Eliana, this is your mommy." He settled on the edge of the bed, while the nurse and doctor bustled around on the other side of the room, giving them a moment of privacy, just the three of them.

"Eliana?"

"It means God has answered." He touched the baby's fuzz of hair. "Eliana Hope Banbury."

"I think you mean Eliana Hope Jaxton."

"She's your daughter. Look at her. She's already causing trouble."

Kenna shook her head. "It almost sounds like you think that's a bad thing." She lifted her chin, trying to seem perturbed. She wanted a daughter who took after her and for people to consider them like two peas in a pod. But if this little one grew up to be wise and strong like her father, Kenna would have no complaints.

"Eliana Hope Banbury Jaxton."

He smiled. "It's a long one, but I like it."

Kenna ran a finger down her cheek. "She's perfect."

"You both are." He leaned down and kissed her, then laid a gentle touch on Eliana's forehead. "You did good, Kenna. Actually, you were amazing."

"Thanks."

"And I've decided she's never investigating a crime in her life. She's never going near a bad guy or a case or any of that. She can do something nice. Like sell cotton candy, or work in a library."

Kenna chuckled. "You've decided."

"Yes." He grinned.

"I guess we'll see what the future holds. What path she takes, and where God leads all of us."

"As long as it's together, that sounds good to me."

Kenna leaned her cheek against the baby's head and closed her eyes.

"I'll let you two get some rest and go give everyone the good news." Jax went to the door and opened it. On the other side, a delivery guy held a huge bouquet of flowers.

"Oliver Jaxton?"

"That's right."

The guy handed over the flowers. "Have a good day. And congrats!"

Jax brought the flowers to the bedside table and pulled out the card. He slid the thick paper from the envelope and read, "*I bet she's gorgeous.* It's signed, Z."

Kenna smiled. "Zeyla."

"I talked to my buddy at the FBI. I have a feeling you'll be seeing her soon enough."

"Thanks."

Jax leaned down and kissed her. "Get some rest. We've got all the time in the world."

He eased the door shut behind him, and Kenna looked down at her daughter again. Eliana Hope. Their baby.

Living proof of what God had done and how far He'd brought both of them.

Thank You.

Keep Reading For...

- Where to find more great Lisa Phillips books.

- How to sign up for Lisa's newsletter and get a FREE book.

- Where to find Lisa on social media.

About the Author

Find out more about Lisa Phillips at her website, where you'll discover more romantic suspense fan-favorite series and heart-pounding thriller novels.
https://authorlisaphillips.com/

If you loved this book, please consider sharing about it on social media. Or leave a review at your book retailer website, on Goodreads, or on Bookbub. Your review will help others find great books to entertain and encourage them!

Signup for Lisa's newsletter by scanning the QR code below to stay updated on sales, new releases, and recommendations for your TBR pile. New Subscribers even get a FREE book!

Find Lisa on Social Media!

facebook.com/authorlisaphillips

instagram.com/lisaphillipsbks

bookbub.com/authors/lisa-phillips

Also by Lisa Phillips

Find out more about Brand of Justice at my website:

https://authorlisaphillips.com/product-tag/brand-of-justice/

Book 1: Cold Dead Night

Book 2: Burn the Dawn

Book 3: Quick and Dead

Book 4: Over the Limit

Book 5: Skin and Bone

Book 6: Dust and Ashes

Book 7: Long Road Home

Book 8 : Dead to Rights

Book 9: Fear No Evil

Book 10: Out of Time

Book 11: Every Which Way

Book 12: One More Chance

Book 13: Storm and Tempest

Book 14: Now or Never

Book 15: Every Last Step

———

Other series by Lisa:

Last Chance Downrange

Chevalier Protection Specialists

Last Chance County

Northwest Counter-Terrorism Taskforce

Double Down

WITSEC Town (Sanctuary)

Numerous other titles including several with *Love Inspired Suspense*, find the complete list here (or scan the QR code):

https://authorlisaphillips.com/all-books/

9 789888 552300